THE FIRST TASTE OF ECSTASY . . .

Christina slipped her hands around his neck, her fingers entwining in his soft, curly hair.

Lyon would have spoken to her, but he was certain his voice would betray him. Her touch was driving him to distraction.

He placed a kiss on her forehead. Christina closed her eyes and sighed, encouraging him. He kissed her on the bridge of her nose next, and finally reached her soft lips. The hunger inside him seemed to ignite.

She wasn't resisting. No, her soft moans told him she didn't want him to stop. He knew her action was instinctive, yet the way she slowly arched against him made him just as wild.

Lyon dragged his mouth away from hers with a harsh groan. "I want to make love to you, Christina," he whispered. "If we're going to stop, it has to be now."

Christina's head fell back as he rained kisses along her throat. Her hands, still entwined in his hair, clenched, pulled, begged. "I don't want to stop, Lyon."

She knew he'd heard her. She looked into his eyes, saw the desire there.

"Do you know what you're saying to me?"

Christina answered him the only way she knew how. . . .

Books by Julie Garwood

Honor's Splendour
The Lion's Lady

Published by POCKET BOOKS

Julie Garwood

The Lion's Lady

POCKET BOOKS

New York   London   Toronto   Sydney   Tokyo

For Gerry

This book is a work of historical fiction. Names, characters, places and incidents relating to non-historical figures are either the product of the author's imagination or are used fictitiously. Any resemblance of such non-historical incidents, places or figures to actual events or locales or persons, living or dead, is entirely coincidental.

An *Original* Publication of POCKET BOOKS

POCKET BOOKS, a division of Simon & Schuster Inc.
1230 Avenue of the Americas, New York, NY 10020

ISBN: 0-671-70505-9

First Pocket Books printing December 1988

10 9 8 7 6 5 4 3 2

POCKET and colophon are registered trademarks of
Simon & Schuster Inc.

Printed in the U.S.A.

The Lion's Lady

Prologue

❧

The Black Hills, America, 1797

It was time to seek the vision.

The shaman waited for the Great Spirit to send him a sign. One month passed, then another, and still the gods ignored him. But the shaman was a patient man. He continued his daily prayers without complaint and waited for his humble petition to be heard.

When the moon was covered by a thick mist for four consecutive nights, the holy man knew the time had arrived. The Great Spirit had heard him.

He immediately began his preparations. After gathering his sacred powders, rattle, and drum, he made the slow climb to the top of the mountain. It was an arduous journey, made more difficult by his advanced years and the dense fog the evil spirits had surely sent to test his determination.

As soon as the old man reached the summit, he built a small fire in the center of the ledge overlooking the valley of the bitterroot. He sat down beside the flames with his face turned toward the sun. Then he reached for his powders.

First he sprinkled sage over the fire. The shaman knew all evil spirits hated the bitter smell. The scent would make them stop their mischief and leave the mountain.

The mist left the mountaintop the following morning, a signal to the holy one that the mischief makers had been chased away. He put the remaining sage powder away and began to feed incense to the flames. The scent was made sweet by the addition of sacred buffalo prairie grass. Incense would purify the air and was known to attract benevolent gods.

For three days and nights the shaman stayed close to the fire. He fasted and prayed, and on the fourth morning he reached for his rattle and drum. He then began the chant that would bring the Great Spirit closer.

During the black hours of the fourth night, the shaman's sacrifice was rewarded. The Great Spirit gave him his dream.

While the holy man slept, his mind was suddenly awakened to the vision. The sun appeared in the night sky. He saw a speck of black that grew and took shape, until it was magically transformed into a vast herd of buffalo. The magnificent animals thundered above the clouds towards him. An eagle, gray with white-tipped wings, flew overhead, leading them on.

As the buffalo drew closer, some of their faces became those of the holy man's ancestors who had traveled to the Afterlife. He saw his father and his mother, his brothers, too. The herd parted then, and in the middle stood a proud mountain lion. The animal's coat was as white as lightning, the spirit Thunderbolt's work no doubt, and the Great Spirit had given the lion's eyes the color of the sky.

The herd of buffalo again enclosed the lion before the dream abruptly ended.

The holy man returned to his village the following morning. His sister prepared a meal for him. Once he'd taken his fill, he went to the leader of the Dakota, a mighty warrior named Gray Eagle. He told his leader only that he must continue to guide his people. The holy man kept the rest of his vision to himself, for the full meaning had yet to be revealed to him. And then he returned to his tipi to remember his vision with his dyes. On a soft deerskin hide he painted a circle of buffalo. In the center he drew the mountain lion, making certain the color of the animal's coat was just as white as he could recall, the color of the eyes just as blue as a sky in summer. When the rendering was completed he waited for the dye to dry, then carefully folded the skin and put it away.

The dream continued to haunt the shaman. He'd hoped to be given some comforting message for his leader. Gray Eagle was grieving. The shaman knew his friend wanted to pass leadership on to a younger, more fit warrior. Since his daughter and grandson had been taken from him, the leader's heart hadn't belonged to his people. He was filled with bitterness and anger.

The holy man could offer his friend little comfort. And no matter how he tried, he couldn't ease his anguish.

From anguish came the legend.

Gray Eagle's daughter Merry and her son were returning from the dead. The Dakota woman knew her family believed both she and White Eagle had been killed. Gray Cloud, bastard leader of the tribe's outcasts, had deliberately provoked the battle near the river's edge. He'd left bits of Merry's clothing on the riverbank, too, in hopes Merry's husband would believe his wife and son had been swept away with the others by the swift current.

The tribe would still be in mourning. Though it seemed an eternity to Merry, it had actually only been eleven months since the attack. She'd kept careful count on her reed stick. There were eleven notches now. Two more were needed to complete a full year by the Dakota reckoning.

It was going to be a difficult homecoming. The tribe would welcome White Eagle back into the family. Merry wasn't worried about her son. He was, after all, first grandson of their chief, Gray Eagle. Yes, there'd be much rejoicing with his return to the fold.

The fear, of course, was for Christina.

Merry instinctively tightened her hold on her new daughter. "Soon, Christina," she crooned softly to the baby. "We'll be home soon."

3

Christina didn't appear to be paying any attention to her mother's promise. The fidgety two-year-old was trying to wiggle out of her mother's lap and off the speckled mount, determined to walk beside her older brother. Merry's six-year-old son was leading the mare down the slope into the valley.

"Be patient, Christina," Merry whispered. She gave her daughter another gentle squeeze to emphasize her order.

"Eagle." The baby wailed her brother's name.

White Eagle turned when his sister cried out to him. He smiled up at her, then slowly shook his head. "Do as our mother orders," he instructed.

Christina ignored her brother's command. She immediately tried to hurl herself out of her mother's lap again. The little one was simply too young to understand caution. Though it was a considerable distance from the top of the horse to the hard ground, Christina didn't appear to be the least intimidated.

"My Eagle," Christina shouted.

"Your brother must lead us down into the village, Christina," Merry said. She kept her voice soft, hoping to calm the fretful child.

Christina suddenly turned and looked up at her mother. The little girl's blue eyes were filled with mischief. Merry couldn't contain her smile when she saw the disgruntled expression on her daughter's face. "My Eagle," the child bellowed.

Merry slowly nodded. "My Eagle," Christina shouted again, frowning up at her mother.

"Your Eagle," Merry acknowledged with a sigh. Oh, how she wished Christina would learn to imitate her soft voice. Thus far, that lesson had failed. Such a little one she was, yet gifted with a voice that could shake the leaves off their branches.

"My mama," Christina bellowed then, jabbing Merry's chest with her chubby fingers.

"Your mama," Merry answered. She kissed her daughter, then brushed her hand across the mop of white-blond curls framing the baby's face. "Your mama," Merry repeated, giving the child a fierce hug.

Comforted by the caress, Christina settled back against her mother's chest and reached for one of Merry's braids. When she'd captured the tip of one braid, she put her thumb in her mouth and closed her eyes, using her other hand to rub Merry's hair across the bridge of her freckled nose. In a matter of minutes, she was sound asleep.

Merry pulled the buffalo hide up over the baby so that her delicate skin would be shielded from the summer's midday sun. Christina was clearly exhausted from their long journey. And she'd been through so much distress in the past three months. It was a wonder to Merry that the child could sleep at all.

Christina had taken to trailing behind White Eagle. She mimicked his every action, though Merry noticed the baby always kept her in sight as well. One mother had left her, and Merry knew Christina was worried she and White Eagle would also disappear. The little girl had become extremely possessive, a trait Merry hoped would lessen in time.

"They watch us from the trees," White Eagle told his mother. The boy stopped, waiting for his mother's reaction.

Merry nodded. "Keep going, son. And remember, stop only when you've reached the tallest tipi."

White Eagle smiled. "I still remember where my grandfather's tipi is," he said. "We've only been away eleven months," he added, pointing to the reed stick.

"I'm pleased you remember," Merry said. "Do you also remember how much you love your father and your grandfather?"

The boy nodded. His expression turned solemn. "It will be difficult for my father, won't it?"

"He's an honorable man," Merry announced. "Yes, it will be difficult for him, but in time he'll see the rightness in it."

White Eagle straightened his shoulders, turned, and continued on down the hill.

He walked like a warrior. The boy's arrogant swagger was almost identical to his father's. Merry's heart ached with pride for her son. White Eagle would become chief of his people when his training was completed. It was his destiny to rule the warriors, just as it had now become her destiny to raise the white-skinned baby girl sleeping so innocently in her arms.

Merry tried to clear her mind of everything but the coming confrontation. She kept her gaze directed on her son's shoulders as he led the mare into the center of the village. Merry silently chanted the prayer her shaman had taught her to chase away her fears.

More than a hundred Dakota stared at Merry and White Eagle. No one said a word. White Eagle walked straight ahead and came to a halt when he'd reached the tipi of his chief.

The older women edged closer until they surrounded Merry's horse. Their faces mirrored their astonishment. Several women reached out to touch Merry's leg, as if the feel of her skin beneath their hands would confirm that what they saw was real.

They petted and sighed. Merry smiled over their show of affection. She glanced up and saw Sunflower, her husband's younger sister. Her good friend was openly weeping.

Thunder suddenly broke the silence. The ground trembled from the pounding of horses being ridden back down into the valley. The warriors had obviously been informed of Merry's return. Black Wolf, Merry's husband, would be leading them.

The flap of the chief's tipi opened just as the braves dismounted. Merry watched her father. Gray Eagle stood at the entrance and stared at her a long while. His leathered face showed his stunned reaction, but his eyes, so warm and kind, soon misted with emotion.

Everyone turned to watch their leader now. They waited for him to give the signal. It was Gray Eagle's duty to be the first to welcome Merry and her son back into his family.

Gray Eagle turned just as Merry's husband walked over to stand by his side. Merry immediately lowered her head in submission. Her hands started trembling, and she thought her heart was pounding loud enough to wake Christina. Merry knew her control would vanish if she looked at her husband now. She would certainly start to cry. That wouldn't be dignified, of course, for such a show of emotion would shame her proud husband.

It wouldn't be honorable either. Merry loved Black Wolf, but the circumstances had drastically changed since she'd last seen him. Her husband would have to make an important decision before he welcomed her back into his arms.

The chief suddenly raised his hands to the Great Spirit above. His palms faced the sun.

The signal was given. A resounding cheer echoed throughout the valley. Chaos erupted as Merry's son was embraced first by his grandfather and then by his father.

Christina stirred in Merry's arms. Though the buffalo skin concealed the baby, there were several startled gasps when the movement was noticed by some of the women.

Black Wolf held his son, but his gaze was directed at his wife. Merry dared a timid look up at him, caught his pleased smile, and tried to smile back.

Gray Eagle nodded several times, showing her his joy and his approval, then slowly made his way over to her side.

The holy man stood outside the purifying tipi, watching the reunion. He understood now why he hadn't seen Merry's face or White Eagle's in his vision. The rest of the dream's meaning continued to elude him. "I am a patient man," he whispered to the spirits. "I will accept one gift at a time."

While the shaman watched, a path was made for the chief. The braves ignored Merry and gathered around Black Wolf and his son. The women swelled forward again, for they wished to hear what their leader would say to his daughter.

Some of the more enthusiastic braves began to shriek with joy. The shrill noise jarred Christina awake.

The baby had little liking for her dark confinement. She pushed the buffalo hide away from her face just as Gray Eagle reached Merry's side.

Merry couldn't decide who looked more surprised. Christina seemed to be quite fascinated by the huge man watching her so intently. She was a bit uncertain, too, for she put her thumb back into her mouth and scooted up against her mother's chest.

Gray Eagle didn't even try to mask his astonishment. He stared at the child a long moment, then turned to look up at his daughter. "There is much for you to tell us, daughter," he announced.

Merry smiled. "There is much I would explain, Father."

Christina caught her mother's smile. She immediately pulled her thumb out of her mouth and looked around her with curiosity. When she found her brother in the crowd of strangers, she reached out with both hands for him. "Eagle," she shouted.

Gray Eagle took a step back, then turned to look at his grandson.

Christina fully expected her brother to come and fetch her. When he didn't immediately obey her order, she tried to squirm out of her mother's lap. "My Eagle, Mama," she bellowed.

Merry ignored her daughter now. She stared at her husband. Black Wolf's expression was hard, impassive. He stood with his legs braced apart and his arms folded across his chest. She knew he'd heard Christina call her mama. The baby spoke the Siouan language as well as any Dakota child and had shouted her claim loud enough for the entire village to hear.

Sunflower rushed over to help her friend dismount. Merry handed Christina to her, thought to caution her friend to keep a firm hold, but it was already too late. Christina easily slipped to the ground, landing on her padded backside. Before Sunflower or Merry could reach for her, the little one grabbed hold of Gray Eagle's legs, pulled herself up, and ran to her brother. The baby's laughter trailed behind her.

No one quite knew what to make of the beautiful white-skinned baby. A few older squaws reached out to touch Christina's golden curls, for their curiosity was too great to contain. The little girl allowed their pawing. She stood beside her brother, barely reaching his knees, mimicking his stance, and clung to his hand.

While Christina didn't mind being touched, she made it quite clear she didn't want anyone near her brother. When the chief tried to embrace his grandson again, Christina tried to push his hands away. "My Eagle," she shouted up at him.

Merry was horrified by her daughter's behavior. She grabbed Christina, managed a weak smile for her father, then whispered to her son, "Go with your father." Merry's husband had abruptly turned and disappeared inside Gray Eagle's tipi.

The moment she was separated from her brother, Christina started crying. Merry lifted the baby into her arms and tried without success to soothe her. Christina hid her face in the crook of her mother's neck and wailed her distress.

Merry's friends surrounded her. No one dared ask about the child until a full accounting had been given to her husband and her chief, but they smiled at the baby and patted her soft skin. Some even crooned the sleeping chant to the little one.

The shaman caught Merry's attention then. She immediately hurried over to stand in front of the holy man, then affected a rather awkward bow.

"Welcome home, my child," the holy man said in greeting.

Merry could barely hear the old man over the screams of her daughter. "I have missed you, Wakan," she said. Christina's wails became ear-piercing, and Merry gently shook her. "Hush, baby," she said. She turned back to the shaman and said, "My daughter roars like a lioness. Perhaps, in time, she will learn. . . ."

The incredulous look on the shaman's face stopped Merry's explanation. "You are ill, Wakan?" she asked, worry sounding in her voice.

The holy man shook his head. Merry noticed that his hands trembled when he reached out to touch Christina. "Her hair is the color of white lightning," he whispered.

Christina suddenly turned to stare at the shaman. She soon forgot her distress and actually smiled at the strange-looking man whose ceremonial feathers seemed to grow out of the top of his head.

Merry heard the shaman gasp. He did seem ill to her. "My new daughter is known by the name Christina, holy one," she said. "If we are allowed to stay, she will need a Dakota name, and your blessing, too."

"She is the lioness," the shaman announced. His face broke into a wide smile. "She will stay, Merry. Do not worry about your child. The buffalo will protect her. The spirits will counsel your father, and your husband as well. Be patient, child. Be patient."

Merry wished she could question the shaman further, but his order to wait couldn't be ignored. His reaction to Christina puzzled her. She wasn't given more time to worry about it, however, for Sunflower took hold of her hand and pulled her toward her home.

"You look exhausted, Merry, and must certainly be hungry. Come into my tipi and we will share our midday meal together."

Merry nodded. She followed her friend across the clearing. Once they were settled on the soft blankets inside Sunflower's home, Merry fed her daughter and then let her explore the tipi.

"I've been away such a long time," Merry whispered. "Yet when I returned, my husband didn't come to me."

"Black Wolf still loves you," Sunflower answered. "My brother has mourned you, Merry."

When Merry didn't comment, Sunflower continued, "It is as though you have returned to us from the dead. After the attack, when no one could find you or White Eagle, some believed you'd been swept away by the river. Black Wolf wouldn't believe that. No, he led the attack against the outcasts, thinking he would find you in their summer village. When he returned without you, he was filled with grief. Now you've come home to us, Merry, yet you bring another man's child with you."

Sunflower turned to look at Christina. "You know how much your husband hates the white man, Merry. I think that is the reason he didn't come to your side. Why have you taken this baby for your own? What happened to her mother?"

"Her mother is dead," Merry answered. "It's a long story, my friend, and you know I must first explain to my husband and my father. I will tell you this much," she added in a firm voice. "If the tribe decides against accepting Christina, then I must leave. She is now my daughter."

"But she has white skin," Sunflower protested, clearly appalled by Merry's fierce announcement.

"I've noticed the color of her skin," Merry answered with a smile.

Sunflower saw the humor in her friend's comment and laughed. The sound was immediately imitated by Christina. "She's such a beautiful child," Sunflower remarked.

"She'll have a pure heart, like her mother," Merry said.

Sunflower turned to reclaim a clay jar Christina had just overturned. Merry helped her scoop up the healing herbs the baby had sprinkled on the ground. "She's a very curious child," Merry commented, apologizing for her daughter.

Sunflower laughed again. The tipi looked as though a strong wind had just passed through. The baby echoed the sound again.

"It isn't possible to dislike such a joyful child," Sunflower remarked. The smile soon faded when she added, "But your husband, Merry. You know he'll never accept her."

Merry didn't argue with her friend. She prayed Sunflower was wrong, though. It was imperative that Black Wolf claim Christina as his daughter. The promise she'd given Christina's mother couldn't truly be fulfilled without her husband's help.

Sunflower couldn't resist the urge to take the baby into her arms. She reached out for Christina, but the little one scooted around her and sat down in Merry's lap.

"I would like to rest for just a few minutes, if you'll watch Christina for me. I warn you," Merry hastily added when

Sunflower nodded eagerly, "My daughter gets into constant mischief. She's too curious to be fearful."

Sunflower left the tipi to gain permission from her husband for Merry and Christina to stay with them. When she returned, she found Merry sound asleep. Christina was curled up against her mother's stomach. Merry's arm was draped over the baby. The little one was also sleeping. Her thumb was in her mouth, and one of Merry's braids rested on her face.

Merry and her daughter slept for several hours. The sun was just setting when Merry carried Christina down to the river to bathe. Sunflower trailed behind with fresh clothing in her arms.

The baby loved the water. The day had been hot and sticky, and the child seemed to delight in splashing in the cool water. She even allowed Merry to wash her hair without making too much fuss.

Merry had just emerged from the water with her daughter when Black Wolf suddenly appeared. He stood on the bank with his hands resting on his hips—a challenging stance, yet Merry could see the tender expression in his eyes.

He confused her, giving her this show of affection now. Merry turned away from her husband to dress herself and Christina.

Black Wolf waited until Merry had finished her task, then motioned for his sister to take the child away. Sunflower had to pry Christina's hands away from her mother. The little girl screamed in distress, but Merry didn't argue with the command. She knew Sunflower would look after her child.

As soon as they were alone, Merry turned to face her husband. Her voice trembled as she told him everything that had happened to her since being taken captive.

"At first I thought their leader, Gray Cloud, wanted to keep us so that he could barter with you. I knew your hatred for each other was fierce, but I didn't think he meant to kill us. We rode for several days—nights, too, when the moon was bright enough—and finally made camp above the brown valley of the white trails. Gray Cloud was the only one who touched us. He boasted to the others that he was going to kill your son and your wife. He blamed you, husband, for his dishonor."

Black Wolf nodded when Merry paused in her recitation, yet didn't offer any comment. Merry took a deep breath before continuing. "He beat our son until he thought he'd killed him. Then he turned on me."

Merry's voice broke. She turned to look at the river. "He used me the way a man uses an unwilling woman," she whispered.

She started to weep then, for her shame was suddenly overwhelming. The memories tore at her heart. Black Wolf reached out to take her into his arms. His touch immediately calmed her. Merry sagged against his chest. She wished she could turn around and cling to her husband, but she knew she needed to tell the rest of her story before she sought his solace.

"An argument broke out among them, for they'd seen the wagons below. Though Gray Cloud was against it, in the end it was agreed by the others that they would attack the whites and take their horses. Gray Cloud stayed behind. He was furious because they went against his decision."

Merry didn't have enough strength to continue. She wept softly. Black Wolf waited several minutes for his wife to go on with her story, then gently forced her to turn around to face him. Her eyes were tightly closed. He wiped the tears away from her cheeks. "Tell me the rest of this," he commanded, his voice as soft as a gentle wind.

Merry nodded. She tried to take a step back, but Black Wolf increased his hold. "Your son awakened and began to moan. He was in terrible pain, husband. Gray Cloud rushed over to our son. He pulled his knife and was about to kill White Eagle. I screamed and edged closer, as close as the rope binding my hands and legs would allow. I cursed Gray Cloud, trying to goad him into turning his anger on me. My plan distracted him. He used his fist to silence me, so fiercely I fell backwards. The blow made me sleep, and when I next opened my eyes I saw a white woman kneeling beside me.

She held White Eagle in her arms. Christina, her baby, was sleeping on the ground next to the woman. Black Wolf, I thought my mind was playing tricks on me until my son opened his eyes and looked at me. He was alive. It was the white woman who saved him, husband. Her knife was in Gray Cloud's back.

"I didn't know where she'd come from until I remembered the wagons trailing below the ridge. I trusted her, too, from the very beginning, because of the way she held our son. I begged her to take White Eagle away before Gray Cloud's followers returned from their raid. The woman wouldn't leave me, no matter how much I protested. She helped me onto her horse, lifted my son into my arms, then led us into the forest, carrying her own child in her arms. The woman didn't speak again until we stopped to rest many hours later."

"The gods favored us that day, for the renegades didn't chase after us. Jessica, the white woman, thought they might have been killed by the people they attacked. We found a cabin high in the hills and wintered there. Jessica took care of us. She spoke the missionary's English, yet all the words sounded very different to me. When I remarked upon this, Jessica explained that she had come from a distant land called England."

"What happened to this woman?" Black Wolf asked, frowning intently.

"When spring arrived, White Eagle was well enough to travel again. Jessica was going to take Christina back down into the valley, and I was going to bring your son home to you. The day before we planned to leave, Jessica went out to collect the traps she'd set the day before. She didn't return. I went searching for her. She was dead," Merry whispered. "A mountain bear had caught her unawares. It was a terrible death. Her body was mangled, barely recognizable. She shouldn't have died in such a way, Black Wolf."

"And this is why you have the white child with you?" Black Wolf asked, though he was already nodding over his own conclusions.

"Jessica and I became sisters in our hearts. She told me all about her past, and I shared my own with her. We made a promise to each other. She gave me her word that if anything happened to me, she'd find a way to bring White Eagle back to you. I also gave her a promise."

"You wish to take the child back to the whites?" Black Wolf asked.

"I must raise Christina first," Merry announced.

Black Wolf looked stunned by his wife's statement. Merry waited a moment before continuing. "Jessica didn't want Christina to go home to this place called England until she was fully grown. We must make Christina strong, husband, so that when she does return to her people, she'll be able to survive."

"I don't understand this promise," Black Wolf confessed, shaking his head.

"I learned all about Jessica's family. She was running away from her mate. She told me this evil man tried to kill her."

"All white men are evil," Black Wolf stated.

Merry nodded. She didn't agree with her husband, yet she wanted to placate him. "Every day Jessica would open a book she called her journal and write inside it. I promised to keep this book for Christina and give it to her when she's ready to go home."

"Why did this man try to kill his wife?"

"I don't know," Merry confessed. "Jessica believed she was a weak woman, though. She spoke of this flaw often, and she begged me to make Christina as strong as a warrior. I told her all about you, but she told me little about her mate. Jessica had the sight, husband. She knew all along she would never see her daughter raised."

"And if I'm against this plan?" Black Wolf asked.

"Then I must leave," Merry answered. "I know you hate the whites, yet it was a white woman who saved your son. My daughter will prove to be just as courageous in spirit."

"Her daughter," Black Wolf corrected, his voice harsh.

Merry shook her head. Black Wolf walked past her to

stand next to the river. He stared out into the night a long while, and when he finally turned back to Merry, his expression was hard. "We will honor this promise," he announced.

Before Merry could show her gratitude, Black Wolf raised his hand. "Sunflower has been wife for three summers now and still hasn't given her husband a child. She will take care of this white-skinned baby. If my sister isn't willing, another will be found."

"No, we must raise her," Merry insisted. "She's my daughter now. And you must also take a hand in this, Black Wolf. I promised to make Christina as strong as a warrior. Without your guidance—"

"I want you back, Merry," Black Wolf said. "But I won't allow this child into my home. No, you ask too much of me."

"So be it," Merry whispered. Her shoulders sagged with defeat.

Black Wolf had lived with Merry long enough to recognize that her stubborn determination was now asserting itself. "What difference will it make if she is raised by you or by another?"

"Jessica died believing you and I would raise her daughter. The child must be taught the skills needed to survive in the white man's world. I bragged to Jessica about your strength, husband, and I—"

"Then we'll never send her back," Black Wolf interjected.

Merry shook her head. "I would never ask you to break your word. How can you ask me to dishonor my pledge now?"

Black Wolf looked furious. Merry started to cry again. "How can you still want me for your wife? I have been used by your enemy. I would have killed myself if I hadn't had White Eagle with me. And now I'm responsible for another child. I can't let anyone else raise her. In your heart, you know I'm right. I think it would be better if I took Christina away. We'll leave tomorrow."

"No." Black Wolf shouted the denial. "I have never

stopped loving you, Merry," he told her. "You will return to me this night."

"And Christina?" Merry asked.

"You'll raise her," he conceded. "You may even call her daughter, but she belongs only to you. I have only one child. White Eagle. I will allow Christina into my tipi because her mother saved my son's life. But this child will have no meaning in my heart, Merry. I will ignore her completely."

Merry didn't know what to make of her husband's decision. She did return to him that night, however, and carried her daughter with her.

Black Wolf was a stubborn man. He proved to be as good as his word, too. He did set out to ignore Christina thoroughly.

It was, however, a task that grew more challenging with each passing day.

Christina always fell asleep next to her brother. Yet each morning, when Black Wolf opened his eyes, he found the baby girl snuggled up between him and his wife. She was always awake before he was, and always staring up at him.

The child simply didn't understand he was ignoring her. Black Wolf would frown when he found her watching him so trustingly. Christina would immediately imitate his expression. If she'd been older, he would have thought she dared to mock him. But she was only a baby. And if she hadn't been white-skinned, he knew he'd find amusement in the way she trailed after his son. Why, he might even have been pleased by the baby's arrogant swagger.

Then Black Wolf would remember Christina didn't exist inside his mind. He'd turn his back on the child and leave his tipi, his mood as black as rain clouds.

The days blended into full weeks as the tribe waited for their chief to call Merry before the council. But Gray Eagle watched his son-in-law, waiting to see if he could accept Christina.

When Black Wolf separated his son from Christina, Merry knew something had to be settled. The baby didn't understand what was happening, of course, and spent most of her waking hours crying. She became extremely fretful and finally quit eating altogether.

Desperate, Merry went to her father and put the problem in his lap. She explained that until he, as chief, openly acknowledged Christina, the women and children would continue to follow Black Wolf's lead and ignore the child.

Gray Eagle saw the wisdom in this argument. He promised to call the council that evening. He then went to the shaman to seek his advice.

The holy man seemed to be just as concerned about Christina's welfare as Merry was. The chief was surprised by this attitude, for the shaman was known to be as hostile towards the whites as Black Wolf was.

"Yes, it is time to call the warriors together. Black Wolf must change his heart towards this child. It would be best if he made the decision alone," he added, "but if he refuses to bend in his attitude, I will tell the council the fullness of my vision."

The shaman shook his head when he saw his leader was about to question him. He walked over to a folded animal skin and handed it to Gray Eagle.

"Do not untie this rope, do not look upon this drawing until the time is right."

"What is this drawing, Wakan?" Gray Eagle asked. His voice had turned to a whisper.

"The vision I was given by the Great Spirit."

"Why have I not seen this before?"

"Because I didn't understand the meaning of all that was revealed to me. I told you only that I'd seen the eagle flying above the herd of buffalo. Do you remember?"

Gray Eagle nodded. "I remember," he said.

"What I didn't tell you is that some of the buffalo were changed into the faces of those who had gone to the Afterlife. Merry and White Eagle weren't among the dead, Gray Eagle. I didn't understand at the time, and didn't want to counsel you until I could solve the riddle in my mind."

"Now we both understand," Gray Eagle announced. "They were not dead."

"But there is more to the vision, my friend. At first I thought the sight of the buffalo meant that hunting would be plentiful. Yes, that is what I thought."

"And now, Wakan?"

The holy man shook his head again. "Do not open the skin until Black Wolf has again stated his position. If he refuses to claim the child, the drawing will sway him. We cannot allow him to go against the spirits."

"And if he decides to call the child his? Will the drawing remain a mystery?"

"No, one and all must see the drawing, but not until Black Wolf has chosen the right path. The recounting will then reaffirm his wisdom."

Gray Eagle nodded. "You must sit beside me this evening, my friend," he announced.

The two men embraced each other. Gray Eagle then returned to his tipi with the animal skin. His curiosity was great, but he forced himself to be patient. There was much to be done before this evening's council. The preparations would take his mind off the skin and what the drawing would reveal.

Merry paced the confines of her tipi until all the warriors had gathered into a circle around their leader's fire. Christina had fallen into a fitful sleep on the pallet she no longer shared with her brother.

When one of the younger braves came to take Merry to the meeting, she left Christina alone, certain the baby was too exhausted to wake before morning.

The men were seated on the ground, with their leader at one end of the long oval. The shaman sat on Gray Eagle's left side, Black Wolf on his right.

Merry slowly walked around the circle, then knelt down in front of her father. She quickly recounted all that had happened to her during the past year, putting great emphasis on the fact that Jessica had saved White Eagle's life.

Gray Eagle showed no outward reaction to this tale. When his daughter finished her recitation, he gave her the formal signal to leave.

Merry was on her way back to Christina when Sunflower intercepted her. The two women stood in the shadows of the clearing, waiting to hear what their leader would decide.

Merry's son was next called to give his version of what had happened. When the boy finished, he went to stand directly behind his father.

All of a sudden, Christina appeared at her brother's side. Merry saw her daughter take hold of White Eagle's hand. She started to go after the child, but Sunflower restrained her. "Wait and see what happens," Sunflower advised. "The warriors will be angry if you interrupt them now. Your son will look after Christina."

Merry saw the wisdom in her friend's advice. She kept her gaze on her son, hoping he'd look her way so that she could motion for him to take Christina back to their tipi.

White Eagle was listening to the fierce argument being given by the majority of the warriors. They all wished to show their loyalty to Black Wolf by supporting his decision to ignore the child.

The chief nodded, then deliberately suggested that an old woman called Laughing Brook take on the duty of raising the child. Black Wolf immediately shook his head, denying the idea.

"Merry's child would suffer at her hand," Black Wolf announced to the warriors. "I could not let this happen. The child is innocent."

Gray Eagle hid his smile. Black Wolf was opposed to giving the child to the crazed old squaw, proving he did in fact care.

The problem would be to make Black Wolf realize the full truth—a difficult challenge, the chief realized, for his son-in-law was a proud, stubborn man.

The chief reached for the animal skin, thinking to put an end to the dispute now, but the shaman stayed the action with a shake of his head.

Gray Eagle let the holy man have his way. He rested his hands on the folded skin and continued to mull over the problem while the warriors argued with one another.

And in the end, it was Christina, with her brother's gentle prodding, who solved the problem for everyone.

Black Wolf's son listened to the harsh debate over Christina's future. Though the boy was only six summers, he'd already shown streaks of his father's arrogant nature. Uncaring what the retributions would be, he suddenly pulled Christina along with him as he edged around to face his father.

Christina hid behind her brother now, though she peeked out at the angry-looking man staring at her brother so ferociously.

The chief was the only one who saw the baby mimick Black Wolf's scowl before she pressed her face against White Eagle's knees.

"Father," White Eagle announced, "a white woman saved my life so that I could return to my people."

The boy's fervent words gained an immediate silence. "Christina is now my sister. I would protect her as well as any brother would protect his sister."

Black Wolf couldn't contain his surprise over the arrogant way his son dared to speak to him. Before he could form a reply, White Eagle turned to where his mother stood. He pointed to her, looked down at Christina, and said, "My mother."

He knew full well what was going to happen. Christina had proved to be quite consistent in her possessiveness. What belonged to White Eagle belonged to her as well. White Eagle only had to repeat the words once before the little girl scooted out to her brother's side. She pulled her thumb out of her mouth long enough to shout, "My mama." Then she smiled up at her brother, waiting for him to continue this new game.

White Eagle nodded. He squeezed her hand to let her know he was pleased with her answer, then turned until he was staring at his father again. He slowly raised his hand

and pointed at Black Wolf. "My father," he announced in a firm voice.

Christina sucked on her thumb while she stared at Black Wolf.

"My papa," White Eagle stated, giving Christina's hand another squeeze.

Christina suddenly pulled her thumb out of her mouth. "My papa," she bellowed, pointing her finger at Black Wolf. She then looked up at her brother to gain his approval.

White Eagle glanced over to look at his grandfather. When the leader nodded, Christina's brother nodded to her.

It was all the approval the little girl needed. She let go of White Eagle's hand, turned, and scooted backwards. Without showing the least bit of fear, she fell into Black Wolf's lap.

Everyone watched the baby settle herself. Black Wolf visibly stiffened when Christina reached up and caught hold of one of his braids. He didn't push her hand away, though, but turned to look at his chief.

Gray Eagle was smiling with satisfaction.

Merry rushed over to kneel down in front of her husband, keeping her head bowed. Black Wolf could see how his wife trembled. He let out a long, controlled sigh of acceptance.

"My children have no place at this council. Take them to our tipi."

Merry immediately reached out to take Christina into her arms. She was prying her daughter's hand away from her husband's braid when the full impact of what he'd just said settled in her mind.

His children.

Merry really did try not to smile, but when she glanced up at her husband, she knew he could see her joy. And certainly her love.

Black Wolf acknowledged both with an arrogant nod.

Gray Eagle waited until Merry had taken the children away. "Do I now have a granddaughter?" he asked Black Wolf, demanding confirmation.

"You do," Black Wolf answered.

"I am pleased," Gray Eagle announced. He turned to the shaman then and asked him to tell the council about his vision.

The holy man stood and recounted his dream to the warriors. He slowly unwound the rope binding the deerskin and held it up for all to see.

There were many startled murmurs. The shaman silenced the group with a dramatic sweep of his hand. "We are the buffalo," he said, pressing his hand to his chest. "The lion does not belong with the buffalo. On this earth, they are enemies, just as the white man is enemy of the Dakota. Yet the gods test us now. They've given us a blue-eyed lioness. We must protect her until the time comes for her to leave us."

Black Wolf was clearly astonished by the shaman's words. He shook his head. "Why didn't you tell me this sooner, Wakan?" he asked.

"Because your heart needed to learn the truth first," the holy man answered. "Your daughter is the lioness, Black Wolf. There can be no mistake. Her hair is the color of white lightning, and her eyes are as blue as the Great Spirit's home in the sky."

Christina's bellow of anger suddenly echoed throughout the village. The shaman paused to smile. "She has the voice of a lioness, too," he remarked.

Black Wolf smiled with the others and nodded.

The holy man raised the skin into the air. "Merry's promise will be fulfilled. The spirits have decreed it."

Christina was formally accepted into the tribe the following evening.

They were a gentle people, the Dakota. Everyone opened their hearts to the blue-eyed lioness and gave her treasures beyond value.

They were intangible gifts that molded her character.

From her grandfather, Christina was given the gift of awareness. The old warrior showed her the beauty, the wonder of her magnificent surroundings. The two became inseparable. Gray Eagle gave Christina his love without restraint, his time without limitation, and his wisdom when she demanded immediate answers to continual little-girl questions of why and why and why. Christina gained patience from her grandfather, but the greatest treasure of all was the ability to laugh at what couldn't be changed, to weep over what had been lost, and to find joy in the precious gift of life.

From her father, Christina was given courage, and determination to finish any task, to conquer any difficulty. She learned to wield a knife and ride a horse as well as any brave—better, in fact, than most. She was Black Wolf's daughter and learned by observation to strive for perfection in every undertaking. Christina lived to please her father, to receive his nod of approval, to make him proud of her.

From her gentle mother, Christina was given the gift of compassion, understanding, and a sense of justice towards friends and enemies alike. She mimicked her mother's ways until they became a true part of her personality. Merry was openly affectionate with her children and her husband. Though Black Wolf never showed his own feelings in front of others, Christina quickly learned that he'd chosen Merry because of her loving nature. His gruffness with his wife in front of the other warriors was all part of his arrogant manner. Yet in the privacy of their tipi, Black Wolf more than allowed Merry's petting and soft words. He demanded them. His gaze would take on a warm expression, and when he thought his daughter was sound asleep, he'd reach for his wife and give her back all the gentle words of love she'd taught him.

Christina vowed to find a man like Black Wolf when the time came for her to choose a mate. He would be a warrior as proud and arrogant as her father, as demanding and protective of what belonged to him, and with the same fierce capacity to love.

She told her brother she'd never settle for less.

White Eagle was her confidant. He didn't wish to break his sister's innocent determination, but he worried for her. He argued in favor of caution, for he knew, as well as everyone else in their isolated village, that Christina would one day return to the world of the whites.

And in his heart, the truth tormented him. He knew, with a certainty he couldn't deny, that there were no warriors like his father in this place called England.

None at all.

Chapter One

Lettie's screams were getting weaker.

Baron Winters, the physician in attendance to the Marchioness of Lyonwood, leaned over his patient and frantically tried to grab hold of her hands. The beautiful woman was writhing in agony. She was clearly out of her head now and seemed determined to tear the skin off her distended abdomen.

"There, there, Lettie," the physician whispered in what he hoped was a soothing tone. "It's going to be all right, my dear. Just a bit longer and you'll have a fine babe to give your husband."

The baron wasn't at all certain Lettie even understood what he was saying to her. Her emerald-green eyes were glazed with pain. She seemed to be staring right through him. "I helped bring your husband into this world. Did you know that, Lettie?"

Another piercing scream interrupted his attempt to calm his patient. Winters closed his eyes and prayed for guidance. His forehead was beaded with perspiration, and his hands were actually shaking. In all his years, he'd never seen such a difficult laboring. It had gone on much too long already. The Marchioness was growing too weak to help.

The door to the bedroom slammed open then, drawing the baron's attention. Alexander Michael Phillips, the Marquess of Lyonwood, filled the doorway. Winters sighed with relief. "Thank God you're home," he called out. "We were worried you wouldn't return in time."

Lyon rushed over to the bed. His face showed his concern. "For God's sake, Winters, it's too early for this to happen yet."

"The baby has decided otherwise," Winters replied.

"Can't you see she's in terrible pain?" he shouted. "Do something!"

"I'm doing everything I can," Winters yelled back before he could control his anger. Another spasm caught Lettie, and her scream turned Winter's attention back to her. The physician's shoulders heaved forward with his effort of restraining her. The Marchioness wasn't a small woman by any means. She was extremely tall and well rounded. She fought the physician's hold on her shoulders with a vengeance.

"She's out of her mind, Lyon. Help me tie her hands to the posts," Winters ordered.

"No," Lyon shouted, clearly appalled by such a command. "I'll hold her still. Just be done with it, Winters. She can't take much more. God, how long has she been this way?"

"Over twelve hours now," Winters confessed. "The midwife sent for me a few hours ago. She ran off in a panic when she realized the baby isn't in the proper position for birthing," he added in a whisper. "We're going to have to wait it out and pray the baby turns for us."

Lyon nodded as he took hold of his wife's hands. "I'm home now, Lettie. Just a little longer, my love. It will be over soon."

Lettie turned toward the familiar voice. Her eyes were dull, lifeless. Lyon continued to whisper encouragement to his wife. When she closed her eyes and he believed she was asleep, he spoke to Winters again. "Is it because the baby is almost two months early that Lettie is having so much difficulty?"

The physician didn't answer him. He turned his back on the Marquess to lift another cloth from the water basin. His motions were controlled, angry, but his touch was gentle when he finally placed the cool cloth on his patient's brow. "God help us if she gets the fever," he muttered to himself.

Lettie's eyes suddenly opened. She stared up at Baron Winters. "James? Is that you, James? Help me, please help me. Your baby is tearing me apart. It's God's punishment for our sins, isn't it, James? Kill the bastard if you have to, but rid me of it. Lyon will never know. Please, James, please."

The damning confession ended with a hysterical whimper.

"She doesn't know what she's saying," Winters blurted once he'd recovered his composure. He wiped the blood away from Lettie's lips before adding, "Your wife is delirious, Lyon. The pain rules her mind. Pay no heed to her rantings."

Baron Winters glanced over to look at the Marquess. When he saw the expression on Lyon's face, he knew his speech hadn't swayed the man. The truth had won out after all.

Winters cleared his throat and said, "Lyon, quit this room. I've work to do here. Go and wait in your study. I'll come for you when it's over."

The Marquess continued to stare at his wife. When he finally lifted his gaze and nodded to the physician, his eyes showed his torment. He shook his head then, a silent denial, perhaps, of what he'd just heard, and abruptly left the room.

His wife's screams for her lover followed him out the door.

It was finished three hours later. Winters found Lyon in the library. "I did everything I could, Lyon. God help me, I lost both of them."

The baron waited several minutes before speaking again. "Did you hear what I said, Lyon?"

"Was the baby two months early?" Lyon asked.

Winters didn't immediately answer. He was slow to recover from the flat, emotionless tone in Lyon's voice. "No, the baby wasn't early," he finally said. "You've been lied to enough, son. I'll not add to their sins."

The baron collapsed in the nearest chair. He watched Lyon calmly pour him a drink, then reached forward to accept the glass. "You've been like a son to me, Lyon. If there is anything I can do to help you through this tragedy, only tell me and I'll do it."

"You've given me the truth, old friend," Lyon answered. "That is enough."

Winters watched Lyon lift his goblet and down the contents in one long swallow.

"Take care of yourself, Lyon. I know how much you loved Lettie."

Lyon shook his head. "I'll recover," he said. "I always do, don't I, Winters?"

"Yes," Winters answered with a weary sigh. "The lessons of brotherhood have no doubt prepared you for any eventuality."

"There is one task I would give you," Lyon said. He reached for the inkwell and pen.

Long minutes passed while Lyon wrote on a sheet of paper. "I'll do anything," Winters said when he couldn't stand the silence any longer.

Lyon finished his note, folded the sheet, and handed it to the physician.

"Take the news to James, Winters. Tell my brother his mistress is dead."

Chapter Two

Your father was such a handsome man, Christina. He could have chosen any woman in England. Yet he wanted me. Me! I couldn't believe my good fortune. I was only pretty enough to be passable by the ton's measure, terribly shy and naive, the complete opposite of your father. He was so sophisticated, so very polished, kind and loving, too. Everyone thought he was the most wonderful man.

But it was all a terrible lie.

*Journal entry
August 1, 1795*

London, England, 1814

It was going to be a long night.

The Marquess of Lyonwood let out a controlled sigh and leaned against the mantel of Lord Carlson's receiving room. It wasn't a casual stance but one employed for necessity's sake. By shifting his considerable weight, Lyon was able to ease the throbbing in his leg. The injury was still a constant irritant, and the sharp pain radiating up through his kneecap did absolutely nothing to lighten his somber mood.

Lyon was attending the party under duress, having been successfully nagged into doing his duty by escorting his younger sister, Diana, to the event. Needless to say, he wasn't at all happy about his circumstances. He thought he should try to affect a pleasant expression on his face, yet couldn't quite manage that feat. Lyon was simply in too much pain to care if others noticed his sour disposition or not. He settled on a scowl instead, his usual expression these days, then folded his arms across his massive chest in a gesture of true resignation.

The Earl of Rhone, Lyon's good friend since Oxford pranks, stood beside him. Both were considered handsome men. Rhone was dark-haired, fair-skinned, and stood six feet in height. He was built on the lean side, always impeccable in dress and taste, and gifted with a lopsided smile that made the young ladies forget all about his crooked nose. They were simply too mesmerized by his enviable green eyes to notice.

Rhone was definitely a lady's man. Mothers fretted over his reputation, fathers worried about his intentions, while unseasoned daughters ignored their parents' cautions altogether, competing quite brazenly for his attention. Rhone drew women to his side in much the same way honey drew a hungry bear. He was a rascal, true, yet too irresistible to deny.

Lyon, on the other hand, had the dubious distinction of being able to send these same sweetly determined ladies screaming for cover. It was an undisputed fact that the Marquess of Lyonwood could clear a room with just one glacial stare.

Lyon was taller than Rhone by a good three inches. Because he was so muscular in chest, shoulders, and thighs, he gave the appearance of being even larger. His size alone wasn't enough to thoroughly intimidate the stronger-hearted ladies hoping to snatch a title, however. Neither were his features, if you could take them just one at a time. Lyon's hair was a dark golden color, given to curl. The length was left unfashionably longer than society liked. His profile mimicked the statues of Roman soldiers lining

Carlton House. His cheekbones were just as patrician, his nose just as classical, and his mouth just as perfectly sculptured.

The warm color of his hair was Lyon's only soft feature, however. His brown eyes mirrored cold cynicism. Disillusionment had molded his expression into a firm scowl. The scar didn't help matters much, either. A thin, jagged line slashed across his forehead, ending abruptly in the arch of his right eyebrow. The mark gave Lyon a piratical expression.

And so the gossip makers called Rhone a rake and Lyon a pirate, but never, of course, to either gentleman's face. These foolish women didn't realize how their insults would have pleased both men.

A servant approached the Marquess and said, "My lord? Here is the brandy you requested." The elderly man made the announcement with a formal bow as he balanced two large goblets on a silver tray.

Lyon grabbed both glasses, handed one to Rhone, and then surprised the servant by offering his gratitude. The servant bowed again before turning and leaving the gentlemen alone.

Lyon emptied his glass in one long swallow.

Rhone caught the action. "Is your leg bothering you?" he asked, frowning with concern. "Or is it your intention to get sotted?"

"I never get sotted," Lyon remarked. "The leg is healing," he added with a shrug, giving his friend a roundabout answer.

"You came away lucky this time, Lyon," Rhone said. "You're going to be out of commission for a good six months, maybe more. Thank God for that," he added. "Richards would have you back in jeopardy tomorrow if he could have his way. I do believe it was a blessing your ship was destroyed. You can't very well go anywhere until you build another."

"I knew the risks," Lyon answered. "You don't like Richards, do you, Rhone?"

"He never should have sent you on that last little errand, my friend."

"Richards places government business above personal concerns."

"Above *our* personal concerns, you mean to say," Rhone corrected. "You really should have gotten out when I did. If you weren't so vital to—"

"I've quit, Rhone."

His friend couldn't contain his astonishment. Lyon knew he should have waited to give him the news, for there was a real concern Rhone would let out a shout. "Don't look so stunned, Rhone. You've been after me to retire for a good while now."

Rhone shook his head. "I've been after you because I'm your friend and very likely the only one who cares what happens to you," he said. "Your special talents have kept you doing your duty longer than a normal man could stand. God's truth, I wouldn't have had the stomach for it. Do you really mean it? You've actually retired? Have you told Richards?"

Rhone was speaking in a furious whisper. He watched Lyon intently.

"Yes, Richards knows. He isn't too pleased."

"He'll have to get used to it," Rhone muttered. He raised his glass in salutation. "A toast, my friend, to a long life. May you find happiness and peace. You deserve a bit of both, Lyon."

Since Lyon's glass was empty, he didn't share in the toast. He doubted Rhone's fervent wish would come true anyway. Happiness—in sporadic doses, of course—was a true possibility. But peace . . . no, the past would never allow Lyon to find peace. Why, it was as impossible a goal as love. Lyon accepted his lot in life. He had done what he believed was necessary, and part of his mind harbored no guilt. It was only in the dark hours of the night, when he was alone and vulnerable, that the faces from the past came back to haunt him. No, he'd never find peace. The nightmares wouldn't let him.

"You're doing it again," Rhone announced, nudging Lyon's arm to gain his attention.

"Doing what?"

"Frowning all the ladies out of the room."

"It's good to know I've still got the ability," Lyon drawled.

Rhone shook his head. "Well, are you going to frown all night?"

"Probably."

"Your lack of enthusiasm is appalling. I'm in a wonderful mood. The new season always stirs my blood. Your sister must also be eager for all the adventures," he added. "Lord, it's difficult to believe the little brat has finally grown up."

"Diana is excited," Lyon admitted. "She's old enough to start looking for a husband."

"Is she still . . . spontaneous? It's been over a year now since I last saw her."

Lyon smiled over Rhone's inept description of his sister's conduct. "If you mean to ask me if she still charges into situations without showing the least amount of restraint, then yes, she's still spontaneous."

Rhone nodded. He looked around the room, then let out a sigh. "Just think of it. A fresh crop of beautiful ladies waiting to be sampled. In truth, I thought their mamas would have made them stay home, what with Jack and his band of robbers still on the prowl."

"I heard the thieves visited Wellingham last week," Lyon commented.

"Caused quite a stir," Rhone interjected with a true grin. "Lady Wellingham took to her bed after making the vow she wasn't going to get up until her emeralds were recovered. An odd reaction, to my way of thinking, when you consider how much thieving her husband does at the gambling tables. The man's a flagrant cheat."

"I understand Jack only robbed the Wellinghams. Is it true he left the guests alone?"

Rhone nodded. "Yes. The man obviously was in a hurry."

"Seems to me he's aching to get caught," Lyon said.

"I don't agree," Rhone answered. "Thus far, he's only

stolen from those who I think needed a good set down. I actually admire the man."

When Lyon gave him a puzzling look, Rhone hastened to change the topic. "The ladies would approach us if you'd smile. Then you might begin to enjoy yourself."

"I think you've finally lost your mind. How can you pretend to enjoy this farce?"

"There are those who think you've lost *your* mind, Lyon. It's a fact you've been secluded from the ton too long."

"And it's a fact you've endured one too many seasons," Lyon answered. "Your mind has turned to mush."

"Nonsense. My mind turned to mush years ago when we drank sour gin in school together. I really do enjoy myself, though. You would, too, if you'd only remember this is all just a game."

"I don't play games," Lyon said. "And war is a better description for this scene."

Rhone laughed, loud enough to draw curious stares. "Tell me this, friend. Are we pitted against the ladies, then?"

"We are."

"And what is their quest? What do they hope to gain if they conquer us?"

"Marriage, of course."

"Ah," Rhone replied, dragging out the sound. "I suppose they use their bodies as their weapons. Is it their battle plan to make us so glazed with lust we'll offer anything?"

"It's all they have to offer," Lyon answered.

"Good Lord, you are as jaded as everyone says. I worry that your attitude will rub off on me."

Rhone shuddered as he spoke, but the effect was ruined by his grin.

"You don't appear to be too concerned," Lyon remarked dryly.

"These ladies are only after marriage, not our lives," Rhone said. "You don't have to play the game if you don't want to. Besides, I'm only an insignificant earl. You, on the other hand, must certainly marry again if the line is to continue forward."

"You know damn well I'm never going to marry again,"

Lyon answered. His voice had turned as hard as the marble he was leaning against. "Drop this subject, Rhone. I've no sense of humor when it comes to the issue of marriage."

"You've no sense of humor at all," Rhone pronounced in such a cheerful tone of voice Lyon couldn't help but grin.

Rhone was about to continue his list of Lyon's other faults when a rather attractive redheaded lady happened to catch his concentration. He gave her his full attention until he spotted Lyon's little sister making her way over to them.

"Better get rid of your frown," Rhone advised. "Diana's coming over. Lord, she just elbowed the Countess Seringham."

Lyon sighed, then forced a smile.

When Diana came to an abrupt stop in front of her brother, her short-cropped brown curls continued to float around her cherublike face. Her brown eyes sparkled with excitement. "Oh, Lyon, I'm so happy to see you smiling. Why, I do believe you're enjoying yourself."

She didn't wait for her brother to reply to her observation but turned to curtsy in front of Rhone. "It's so good to see you again," she said, sounding quite breathless.

Rhone inclined his head in greeting.

"Isn't it remarkable I was able to plead Lyon into coming this evening? He really doesn't like parties very much, Rhone."

"He doesn't?" Rhone asked, sounding so disbelieving Lyon actually laughed.

"Don't jest with her," Lyon said. "Are you enjoying yourself, Diana?" he asked his sister.

"Oh, yes," Diana answered. "Mama will be pleased. I do hope she's still awake when we get home so I can tell her all about tonight. I've just learned Princess Christina will be making an appearance, too. I confess I'm most curious to meet her. Why, I've heard the most wonderful stories about her."

"Who is Princess Christina?" Lyon asked.

It was Rhone who hastened to answer his question. "You've been secluded too long, Lyon, or you surely would have heard of her. Though I haven't actually met the lady,

I've been told she's very beautiful. There's an air of mystery surrounding her, too. Her father was ruler of some little principality near Austria's border. He was unseated during a rather nasty revolution," Rhone continued. "Lady Christina, if we use the title she gained from her mother, has traveled all over the world. Brummel met her and was immediately infatuated. He was the first to call her Princess. The woman neither accepted nor rejected that title."

"What happened to her mother?" Diana asked.

She looked quite spellbound by the story about the princess. Rhone smiled at her eagerness. "A tragedy, I'm told. The mother was weakheaded, and she—"

"What do you mean by weakheaded?" Diana interrupted to ask.

"Insane," Rhone explained. "When the mother learned she was going to have a child, she ran off. Until three months ago, everyone believed both mother and babe were dead."

"What happened to Princess Christina's father?" Diana asked.

"He left England shortly after his wife disappeared. No one has heard of him since. Probably dead by now," Rhone ended with a shrug.

"Oh, the poor Princess," Diana whispered. "Does she have anyone to call family now, or is she all alone?"

"For God's sake, Diana, you don't even know the woman and you look ready to weep for her," Lyon said.

"Well, it is such a sad story," Diana said, defending herself. She turned back to Rhone and added, "I remember how unbearable it was for all of us when James died. Mother still hasn't recovered. She stays hidden in her room pretending all sorts of ills, when it's truly grief that keeps her there."

Rhone took one look at Lyon's cold expression and immediately hastened to turn the topic around. "Yes, well, we all miss James," he lied, his tone brisk. "I'm anxious to meet Princess Christina, too, Diana. No one has been able to glean a scrap of information about her past. That does make for a mystery to be solved, now doesn't it?"

When Rhone gave Diana a wink, she blushed. Lyon's sister was still such an innocent. She was fetching enough, too, now that Rhone paused to really take a good look at her. Diana had filled out nicely since he'd last seen her. That realization actually irritated Rhone, though for the life of him he couldn't understand why. "Brat," he suddenly blurted out, "you do look pretty tonight." Rhone grimaced over the roughness he'd heard in his own voice.

Diana didn't seem to notice. She smiled over his compliment, affected another curtsy, and said, "Thank you, Rhone. It is kind of you to notice."

Rhone frowned at Lyon. "Her gown is cut entirely too low. What could you have been thinking of to allow her in public this way? You'd better keep a close eye on her."

"If I keep my eye on you, Diana will be safe enough," Lyon answered.

"All the same, I really think . . ." The sentence trailed off, for Rhone had just glanced toward the entrance of the salon. He let out a low whistle. Diana quickly turned around to see what held Rhone so enthralled.

"Princess Christina." Diana whispered the obvious, her voice filled with awe.

Lyon was the last to react. When he saw the vision standing across the room, he literally jerked away from the mantel. His body instinctively assumed a battle stance, his muscles tensed, ready.

He was slow to regain control. He realized his hands were actually fisted at his sides and his legs were braced apart for a fight, and he forced himself to relax. The abrupt movement made his knee start throbbing again. Lyon couldn't do anything about the pain now, or the furious pounding in his chest.

And no matter how valiantly he tried, he couldn't seem to take his gaze away from the Princess.

She really was lovely. She was dressed in silver from head to toe. The color belonged to an angel and highlighted the paler threads of her blond hair.

Without a doubt, she was the most beautiful woman he'd ever seen. Her skin appeared to be flawless, and even from the distance separating them Lyon could see the color of her eyes. They were the most startling shade of blue.

Princess Christina neither smiled nor frowned. Her expression showed only mild curiosity. The woman obviously understood her own appeal, Lyon concluded, hoping his cynical nature would save him from heart failure. He wasn't at all pleased about the way his body continued to respond to her.

"Brummel was right," Rhone announced. "The lady is enchanting."

"Oh, I do hope I'll be able to meet her," Diana said. She whispered as though they were in church. "Just look at everyone, Rhone. They are all taken with her. Do you think the Princess will be agreeable to an introduction?"

"Hush, Diana," Rhone said. "Princess Christina wouldn't dare ignore you. You seem to forget just who your brother is."

Diana gave Rhone a timid nod. "Sweetling, straighten your shoulders and quit wringing your hands. You'll give yourself spots. We'll find someone to give us a proper introduction."

Rhone knew Lyon's little sister hadn't heard the last of his remarks. She'd already picked up her skirts and headed for the entrance. "Now what do we do?" he asked when Lyon grabbed hold of his arm to stop him from chasing after Diana.

"We wait and see," Lyon advised. His voice sounded with irritation.

"Your sister is too impetuous," Rhone muttered, shaking his head. "She's ignoring all her lessons in—"

"It's high time Diana learned the lesson of discretion."

"Let us hope it isn't too painful for her."

Lyon didn't remark on that hope. He continued to give his attention to the beautiful Princess. An elderly couple approached the woman just as Diana came barreling to a halt a bare inch or so in front of them.

Diana almost knocked Christina to her knees. Rhone let out a long groan. The elderly couple didn't even try to hide their displeasure when they were so rudely cut off. Both turned away, staring at each other in obvious embarrassment.

"Oh, God, Diana just cut in front of the Duke and Duchess," Rhone said.

Lyon was infuriated with his sister. He was about to go after her to save her from further humiliation when the Princess took matters into her own hands. Rather nicely, too. She greeted Lyon's sister with what appeared to be a sincere smile, then took hold of Diana's hands when she spoke to her. Lyon thought the Princess was deliberately giving the impression to all those watching that she and Diana were close friends.

He watched the way Christina motioned Diana over to her side so that both could greet the Duke and Duchess of Devenwood. The Princess included Diana in the brief conversation, too, effectively smoothing over the mistake his sister had made.

Rhone sighed with relief. "Well, what do you know? She's still holding Diana's hand, too. A clever ploy to keep Diana from accidentally belting her one, I would imagine."

Lyon rested his shoulder against the mantel again, smiling over Rhone's observation. "Diana does like to use her hands when she speaks," he admitted.

"The Princess has a good heart. God's truth, I believe I'm in love."

"You're always in love," Lyon answered.

He wasn't able to keep the irritation out of his voice. Odd, but for some reason Rhone's jest bothered him. He didn't particularly want Princess Christina added to Rhone's list of future conquests. It was a ridiculous notion, Lyon realized. Why did he care if his friend chased after the woman or not?

He sighed when he realized he didn't have a ready answer. He did care, however. Fiercely so. And that honest admission soured Lyon's mood all the more. Damn, he was too old and too tired for an infatuation.

Christina didn't have any idea of the stir she was causing. She patiently waited in the center of the doorway for her Aunt Patricia to finish her conversation with their host. An eager young lady stood beside her, chattering away at such an incredible pace Christina couldn't quite keep up with her. She pretended interest, smiled when it seemed appropriate, and nodded whenever the lady named Diana paused for breath.

Lady Diana announced she was going to fetch her friends for an introduction. Christina was left alone again. She turned to look at all the people openly gawking at her, a serene smile on her face.

She didn't think she was ever going to get used to them. The English were such a peculiar lot. Though she'd been living in London for almost three months now, she was still perplexed by the odd rituals these whites seemed so determined to endure.

The men were just as foolish as their women. They all looked alike, too, dressed as they were in identical black garb. Their white neck wraps were starched to the point of giving the impression they were being strangled to death, an impression strengthened by their red, ruddy cheeks. No, Christina silently amended, they weren't called neck wraps . . . cravats, she told herself. Yes, that was the proper name for a neck wrap. She mustn't forget again.

There was so much to remember. Christina had studied diligently since arriving on her Aunt Patricia's doorstep in Boston a year ago. She already spoke French and English. The missionary Black Wolf had captured years before had taught her very well.

Her lessons in Boston centered on the behavior expected of a gentle lady. Christina tried to please her aunt, and to ease some of her fears, too. The sour woman was Christina's only link with her mother's family. Later, however, when Christina had conquered the written word well enough to understand the meaning in her mother's diary, her motives had changed. Dramatically. It was now imperative Christina win a temporary place in this bizarre society. She couldn't make any mistakes until her promise was carried out.

"Are you ready, Christina?"

The question was issued by Aunt Patricia. The old woman

came to Christina's side and grabbed hold of her arm in a clawlike grip.

"As ready as I shall ever be," Christina answered. She smiled at her guardian, then turned and walked into the throng of strangers.

Lyon watched her intently. He noticed how protective the princess appeared to be toward the wrinkle-faced woman clinging to her arm; noticed, too, how very correct the beautiful woman was in all her actions. Why, it was almost like a routine of some sort, Lyon thought. The Princess greeted each new introduction with a practiced smile that didn't quite reach her eyes. Next followed a brief conversation, and last, a brisk, efficient dismissal.

Lyon couldn't help but be impressed. The lady was good, all right. No wonder Brummel was so taken with her. The Princess followed all the rules of proper behavior. But Rhone was wrong. She wasn't all that different. No, she appeared to be just as rigid, just as polished, and certainly just as superficial as all the other ladies of the ton. Brummel embraced superficiality with a passion. Lyon detested it.

He wasn't disappointed by his conclusions about the Princess. The opposite was true for he'd felt off balance from the moment he'd first looked at the woman. Now his equilibrium was returning full force. He actually smiled with relief. Then he saw Rhone elbow his way through the crush of guests to get to the Princess. Lyon would have wagered his numerous estates that the woman would pay Rhone far more attention than the other men. Everyone in London knew of Rhone's family, and though he wasn't the most titled gentleman at the party, he was certainly one of the wealthiest.

Lyon would have lost his bet. Rhone didn't fare any better than all the others. A spark of perverse satisfaction forced a reluctant grin onto Lyon's face.

"You're losing your touch," Lyon remarked when Rhone returned to his side.

"What do you mean?" Rhone asked, pretending bewilderment.

Lyon wasn't buying it for a minute. He could see the faint blush on Rhone's face.

He really was starting to enjoy himself, Lyon realized. He decided then to rub salt in Rhone's wounds like any good friend would. "Was it my imagination, or did Princess Christina give you the same treatment she's given every other man in the room? She really didn't seem too impressed with your charms, old boy."

"You won't do any better," Rhone pronounced. "She really is a mystery. I specifically remember asking her several pertinent questions, yet when I walked away—"

"You mean when *she* walked away, don't you?"

Rhone gave Lyon a good frown, then shrugged. "Well, yes, when she walked away I realized I hadn't gotten a single answer out of her. At least I don't think I did."

"You were too interested in her appearance," Lyon answered. "A pretty face always did ruin your concentration."

"Oh?" Rhone said, drawing out the sound. "Well, old boy, let's see how many answers you gain. I'll put a bottle of my finest brandy up against one of yours."

"You're on," Lyon announced. He glanced around the room and found Princess Christina immediately. He had the advantage of being taller than everyone else in the room, and the object of his quest was the only blond-haired woman there.

She was standing next to his father's old friend, Sir Reynolds. Lyon was happy to see that Christina's dour-looking guardian had taken a chair across the room.

When Lyon was finally able to catch Sir Reynolds's attention, he motioned with an arrogant tilt of his head for an immediate introduction.

Sir Reynolds nodded—a little too enthusiastically for Lyon's liking—then leaned down and whispered to the Princess. Christina's back faced Lyon, but he saw her give an almost imperceptible nod. Long minutes elapsed before the heavyset woman speaking to the Princess paused for air. Sir Reynolds seized the opportunity to say goodbye. Lyon concluded his hasty explanation must have included his name, because the woman gave him a frightened look, picked up her skirts, and went scurrying in the opposite direction. She moved like a fat mouse with a cat on her tail.

Lyon's smile widened. His boast to Rhone hadn't been in vain. He really hadn't lost his touch.

He dismissed the silly woman from his mind when Princess Christina came to stand directly in front of him. Sir Reynolds hovered at her side like a nervous guardian angel. Lyon slowly pulled himself away from his lazy repose, patiently waiting for her to execute the perfect little curtsy he'd seen her give everyone else.

Her head was bowed, but even so he could tell she wasn't quite flawless after all. He could see the sprinkle of freckles across the bridge of her nose. The marks made her look less like a porcelain doll and far more touchable.

The woman barely reached his shoulders. She was too delicate-looking and much too thin for his liking, he decided. Then she looked up at him. Her gaze was direct, unwavering, captivating.

Lyon couldn't remember his own name.

He knew he'd eventually thank God for Sir Reynolds's intervention. He could hear the man's voice drone on and on as he listed Lyon's numerous titles. The long list gave Lyon time to recover.

He'd never been this rattled. It was her innocent gaze that held him so spellbound. Her eyes, too, he grudgingly admitted. They were unlike any shade of blue he'd ever seen.

He knew he had to get hold of himself. Lyon deliberately dropped his own gaze, settled on her mouth, and realized his mistake at once. He could feel himself reacting physically again.

Sir Reynolds finally ended his litany by stating, "I believe, my dear, you've already been introduced to the Earl of Rhone."

"Yes," Rhone interjected, smiling at Christina.

"Lyon, may I present Princess Christina to you?" Sir Reynolds said, sounding terribly formal.

Her eyes gave her away. Something said during the

introduction had unsettled her. She quickly recovered, though, and Lyon knew that if he hadn't been watching her so closely, he would have missed the surprise in her gaze.

"I'm honored to meet you, sir," Christina whispered.

Her voice appealed to him. It was soft, sensual. The unusual accent was noticeable, too. Lyon had traveled extensively, yet couldn't put his finger on the origin. That intrigued him almost as much as his senseless urge to grab hold of her, drag her off into the night, and seduce her.

Thank God she couldn't know what was going on inside his mind. She'd go screaming for a safe haven then, no doubt. Lyon didn't want to frighten her, though. Not just yet.

"Rhone has been Lyon's friend for many years," Sir Reynolds interjected into the awkward silence.

"I'm his only friend," Rhone commented with a grin.

Lyon felt Rhone nudge him. "Isn't that true?"

He ignored the question. "And are you a Princess?" he asked Christina.

"It would seem to many that I am," she replied.

She hadn't quite answered his question, Lyon realized. Rhone coughed—a ruse to cover his amusement, Lyon supposed with a frown.

Christina turned to Rhone. "Are you enjoying yourself this evening?"

"Immensely," Rhone announced. He looked at Lyon and said, "Your questions?"

"Questions?" Christina asked, frowning now.

"I was just wondering where you call home," Lyon said.

"With my Aunt Patricia," Christina replied.

"Lyon, surely you remember Lord Alfred Cummings," Sir Reynolds interjected with a great show of enthusiasm. "He was an acquaintance of your father's."

"I do recall the name," Lyon answered. He tried yet couldn't seem to take his gaze away from Christina long enough to spare a glance for Reynolds. It was probably rude, Lyon thought, even as he realized he wasn't going to do anything about it.

"Well, now," Sir Reynolds continued, "Alfred was appointed to the colonies years back. He died in Boston, God rest his soul, just two or three years ago, and the Countess returned home to England with her lovely niece."

"Ah, then you've been in England two years?" Lyon asked.

"No."

It took Lyon a full minute before he realized she wasn't going to expound upon her abrupt answer. "Then you were raised in the colonies." It was a statement, not a question, and Lyon was already nodding.

"No."

"Were you born there?"

"No," Christina answered, staring up at him with a hint of a smile on her face.

"But you lived in Boston?"

"Yes."

"Yes?"

He really hadn't meant to raise his voice, but Princess Christina was proving to be extremely exasperating. Rhone's choked laughter wasn't helping matters much either.

Lyon immediately regretted letting her see his irritation, certain she'd try to bolt at the first opportunity. He knew how intimidating he could be.

"Sir, are you displeased with me because I wasn't born in the colonies?" Christina suddenly asked. "Your frown does suggest as much."

He heard the amusement in her voice. There was a definite sparkle in her eyes, too. It was apparent she wasn't the least bit intimidated. If he hadn't known better, he would have thought she was actually laughing at him.

"Of course I'm not displeased," Lyon announced. "But are you going to answer all my questions with a yes or no?" he inquired.

"It would seem so," Christina said. She gave him a genuine smile and waited for his reaction.

Lyon's irritation vanished. Her bluntness was refreshing, her smile captivating. He didn't try to contain his laughter.

The booming sound ricocheted around the room, drawing startled expressions from some of the guests.

"When you laugh, sir, you sound like a lion," Christina said.

Her comment nudged him off center. It was such an odd remark to make. "And have you heard the roar of lions, Christina?" he asked, dropping her formal title.

"Oh, many times," Christina answered before she thought better of it.

She actually sounded like she meant what she said. That, of course, didn't make any sense at all. "Where would you have heard such a sound?"

The smile abruptly left her face. She'd inadvertently been drawn into revealing more than caution dictated.

Lyon waited for her to answer him. Christina gave him a wary look, then turned to Sir Reynolds. She bid him goodnight, explaining that she and her aunt had promised to make an appearance at another function before quitting the evening. She turned back to Lyon and Rhone and dismissed them both with cool efficiency worthy of a queen.

Lyon wasn't a man used to being dismissed.

Princess Christina was gone before he could mention that fact to her.

She knew she had to get away from him. She could feel her composure faltering. Her guardian was seated in a chair against the wall. Christina forced herself to walk with a dignified stride until she reached her aunt's side.

"I believe we should prepare to leave now," she whispered.

The Countess had lived with her niece long enough to know something was amiss. Her advanced years hadn't affected her keen mind or her physical shape. She all but bounded out of her chair, anchored herself to Christina's arm, and headed for the door.

Lyon stood with Rhone and Sir Reynolds. All three men watched Christina and her aunt make a hasty farewell to their host. "I'll be over tomorrow to get that bottle of brandy," Rhone announced with a nudge to get Lyon's attention.

"Rhone, if you jam your elbow into my ribs one more time, I swear I'll break it," Lyon muttered.

Rhone didn't look worried by the threat. He whacked his friend on the shoulder. "I believe I shall go and guard your sister for you, Lyon. You don't seem capable of the task."

As soon as Rhone left his side, Lyon turned to Sir Reynolds. "What do you know about Patricia Cummings?" he asked. "The truth, if you please, and no fancy fencing."

"You insult me, Lyon," Sir Reynolds announced, grinning a contradiction to his comment.

"You're known for your diplomacy," Lyon answered. "Now, about Christina's guardian. What can you tell me about her? Surely you knew her when you were younger."

"Of course," Reynolds said. "We were always invited to the same functions. I know my comments won't go any further, so I'll give the black truth to you, Lyon. The woman's evil. I didn't like her back then, and I don't like her now. Her beauty used to make up for her . . . attitude," he said. "She married Alfred when his older brother took ill. She believed he'd die at any moment. Patricia was like a vulture, waiting to inherit the estates. Alfred's brother outfoxed her, though. Lived a good ten years beyond everyone's expectations. Alfred was forced to take an appointment to the colonies, else be packed off to debtor's prison."

"What about Patricia's father? Didn't he attempt to settle his son-in-law's debts? I would have thought the embarrassment would have swayed him, unless, of course, he didn't have enough money."

"Oh, he was plenty rich enough," Sir Reynolds announced. "But he'd already washed his hands of his daughter."

"Because she married Alfred, perchance?"

"No, that isn't how the rumor goes," Reynolds said, shaking his head. "Patricia was always an abrasive, greedy woman. She was responsible for many cruelties. One of her little jests ended in tragedy. The young lady made the butt of her joke killed herself. I don't wish to go into further detail, Lyon, but let it suffice to say she doesn't appear to have changed her colors over the years. Did you notice the way she watched her niece? Gave me the shudders."

Lyon was surprised by the vehemence in Sir Reynolds's voice. His father's old friend was known for his calm, easygoing disposition. Yet now he was literally shaking with anger. "Were you the victim of one of her cruelties?" he asked.

"I was," Reynolds admitted. "The niece seems to be such a gentle, vulnerable little flower. She wasn't raised by her aunt. I'm sure of it. I pity the poor child, though. She's going to have a time of it trying to please the old bitch. The Countess will no doubt sell her to the highest bidder."

"I've never heard you speak in such a manner," Lyon said, matching Reynolds's whisper. "One last question, sir, for I can tell this conversation distresses you."

Sir Reynolds nodded.

"You said the Countess's father was a rich man. Who gained his estates?"

"No one knows. The father settled his affections on the younger daughter. Her name was Jessica."

"Jessica was Christina's mother?"

"Yes."

"And was she as demented as everyone believes?"

"I don't know, Lyon. I met Jessica several times. She seemed to be the opposite of her sister. She was sweet-tempered, shy—terribly shy. When she married, her father was extremely pleased. He strutted around like a rooster. His daughter, you see, had captured a king. I can still remember the glorious balls held in their honor. The opulence was staggering. Something blackened, though. No one really knows what happened." The elderly man let out a long sigh. "A mystery, Lyon, that will never be solved, I imagine."

Though he'd promised to curtail his questions, Lyon was too curious to drop the topic just yet. "Did you know Christina's father then? A king, you say, yet I've never heard of him."

"I met him, but I never really got to know him well. His name was Edward," Reynolds remembered with a nod.

"Don't recall his last name. I liked him. Everyone did. He was most considerate. And he didn't hold with pomp. Instead of lording it over us, he insisted everyone call him baron instead of king. He'd lost his kingdom, you see."

Lyon nodded. "It's a riddle, isn't it?" he remarked. "This Jessica does intrigue me."

"Why is that?"

"She married a king and then ran away from him."

"Jessica's reasons went to the grave with her," Sir Reynolds said. "I believe she died shortly after Christina was born. No one knows more than what I've just related to you, Lyon. And after your rather one-sided conversation with the lovely Princess, it would seem evident to me she's going to keep her secrets."

"Only if I allow it," Lyon said, grinning over the arrogance in his remark.

"Ah, then you have taken an interest in the Princess?" Sir Reynolds asked.

"Mild curiosity," Lyon answered with a deliberate shrug.

"Is that the truth, Lyon, or are you giving me fancy fencing now?"

"It is the truth."

"I see," Reynolds said, smiling enough to make Lyon think he didn't really see at all.

"Do you happen to know where Christina and her guardian were going when they left here? I heard Christina tell you they had one more stop to make before finishing the evening."

"Lord Baker's house," Reynolds said. "Do you plan to drop in?" he asked, his voice bland.

"Reynolds, don't make more out of this than it really is," Lyon said. "I merely wish to find out more about the Princess. By morning my curiosity will be appeased."

The briskness in Lyon's voice suggested to Reynolds that he stop his questions. "I haven't greeted your sister yet. I believe I'll go and say hello to her."

"You'll have to be quick about it," Lyon announced. "Diana and I are going to be leaving in just a few minutes."

Lyon followed Reynolds over to the crush of guests. He

allowed Diana several minutes to visit and then announced it was time to leave,

Diana's disappointment was obvious. "Don't look so sad," Sir Reynolds said. "I believe you aren't going home just yet." Sir Reynolds started chuckling.

Lyon wasn't the least amused. "Yes, well, Diana, I had thought to stop by Baker's place before taking you home."

"But Lyon, you declined that invitation," Diana argued. "You said he was such a bore."

"I've changed my mind."

"He isn't a bore?" Diana asked, looking completely bewildered.

"For God's sake, Diana," Lyon muttered, giving Reynolds a glance.

The harshness in Lyon's voice startled Diana. Her worried frown said as much.

"Come on, Diana. We don't want to be late," Lyon advised, softening his tone.

"Late? Lyon, Lord Baker doesn't even know we're going to attend his party. How can we be late?"

When her brother merely shrugged, Diana turned to Sir Reynolds. "Do you know what has come over my brother?" she asked.

"An attack of mild curiosity, my dear," Sir Reynolds answered. He turned to Lyon and said, "If you'll forgive an old man's interference, I would like to suggest that your sister stay here for a bit longer. I would be honored to see her home."

"Oh, yes, Lyon, please, may I stay?" Diana asked.

She sounded like an eager little girl. Lyon wouldn't have been surprised if she started clapping her hands. "Do you have a particular reason to stay?" he asked.

When his sister started blushing, Lyon had his answer. "What is this man's name?" he demanded.

"Lyon," Diana whispered, looking mortified. "Don't embarrass me in front of Sir Reynolds," she admonished.

Lyon sighed in exasperation. His sister had just repeated his opinion that Baker was a bore, and now she had the audacity to tell him he was embarrassing her. He gave her a good frown. "We're going to discuss this later, then," he announced. "Thank you, Reynolds, for keeping a close watch on Diana."

"Lyon, I don't need a keeper," Diana protested.

"You've yet to prove that," Lyon said before he nodded farewell to Sir Reynolds and left the room.

He was suddenly most eager to get to the bore's house.

Chapter Three

We stayed in England longer than Edward really wished so that my father could join in my birthday celebration. Edward was so very thoughtful of my dear papa's feelings.

The day after I turned seventeen, we sailed for my husband's home. I wept, yet remember thinking I was being terribly selfish. I knew I was going to miss my father. My duty was to follow my husband, of course.

After the tears were spent, I became excited about my future. You see, Christina, I thought Edward was taking me to Camelot.

Journal entry
August 10, 1795

Christina was feeling ill. She felt close to suffocating and kept telling herself her panic would dissipate just as soon as the horrible carriage ride was over.

How she hated the closeness inside the wobbly vehicle. The curtains were drawn, the doors bolted, the air dense and thick with her Aunt Patricia's heavy perfume. Christina's hands were fisted at her sides, hidden from her aunt's view by the folds of her gown. Her shoulders were pressed against the padded brown leather backrest.

The Countess didn't realize her niece was having any difficulty. As soon as the door was closed, she started in with her questions, never once allowing her niece time to give answers. The aunt laced each question with sharp, biting remarks about the guests they'd just left at Lord Carlson's townhouse. The Countess seemed to derive great pleasure in defaming others. Her face would twist into a sinister look, her thin lips would pucker, and her eyes would turn as gray as frostbite.

Christina believed the eyes reflected the thoughts of the soul. The Countess certainly proved that truth. She was such an angry, bitter, self-serving woman. Foolish, too, Christina thought, for she didn't even try to hide her flaws from her niece. Such stupidity amazed Christina. To show weakness was to give another power. Aunt Patricia didn't seem to understand that primitive law, however. She actually liked to talk about all the injustices done to her. Constantly.

Christina no longer paid any attention to her guardian's contrary disposition. She'd adopted a protective attitude toward the woman, too. The Countess was family, and while that probably should have been reason enough, there was another motive as well. Her aunt reminded Christina of Laughing Brook, the crazed old squaw who used to chase after all the children with her whipping stick. Laughing Brook couldn't help the way she was, and neither could the Countess.

"Didn't you hear me, Christina?" The Countess snapped, drawing Christina from her thoughts. "I asked you what made you want to leave Carlson's party so suddenly."

"I met a man," Christina said. "He wasn't at all like the others. They call him the Lion."

"You speak of the Marquess of Lyonwood," Patricia said, nodding her head. "And he frightened you, is that it? Well, do not let it bother you. He frightens everyone, even me. He's a rude, impossible man, but then his position does allow for insolence, I suppose. The ugly scar on his forehead gives him a sinister look."

"Oh, no, he didn't frighten me," Christina confessed. "Quite the contrary, Aunt. I was, of course, attracted to his mark, but when I heard Sir Reynolds call him Lion, I was immediately so homesick I could barely think what to say."

"How many times must I tell you those savages should mean nothing to you?" Patricia screeched. "After all I've sacrificed so that you can take your rightful place in society and claim my inheritance . . ."

The Countess caught her blunder. She gave her niece a piercing look to measure her reaction, then said, "You simply must not think about those people. The past must be forgotten."

"Why do they call him Lion?" Christina asked, smoothly changing the topic. She slowly moved her arm away from her aunt's painful grip. "I'm only curious," she explained, "for you did say the English didn't name themselves after animals or—"

"No, of course not, you stupid chit," Aunt Patricia muttered. "The Marquess isn't named after an animal. The spelling isn't the same." The Countess slowly spelled Lyon's name. Her voice lost some of its brittle edge when she continued, "It is in deference to his title that he's called Lyonwood. Closer friends are permitted to shorten the name, of course."

"He won't suit?" Christina asked, frowning.

"He most certainly will not," the Countess answered. "He's too shrewd, too rich. You'll have to stay away from him. Is that understood?"

"Of course."

The Countess nodded. "Why you would be attracted to him is beyond my comprehension. He wouldn't be the least manageable."

"I wasn't truly attracted to him," Christina answered. She lied, of course, but only because she didn't wish to goad her aunt into another burst of anger. And she really couldn't make her aunt understand anyway. How could she reason with a woman who believed a warrior's mark was a detraction? With that feeble mind-set, Christina's aunt would be appalled if she gave her the truth.

Oh, yes, the lion did appeal to her. The golden chips in his dark brown eyes pleased her. His powerful build was that of a warrior, and she was naturally drawn to his strength. There was an aura of authority surrounding him. He was aptly named, for he did remind her of a lion. Christina had noticed his lazy, almost bored attitude, yet she instinctively knew he could move with bold speed if given enough provocation.

Yes, he was attractive. Christina liked looking at him well enough.

But she loved his scent. And what would her aunt think of that admission, Christina wondered with a bit of a smile. Why, she'd probably install another chain on her bedroom door.

No, the Countess wouldn't understand her attraction. The old shaman from her village would understand, though. He'd be very pleased, too.

"We needn't worry that Lyon will show you the least interest," Aunt Patricia announced. "The man only escorts paramours. His latest attraction, according to the whispers I overheard, is a woman called Lady Cecille." The Countess let out an inelegant snort before continuing, "Lady indeed. Whore is the real name for the bitch. She married a man twice and half her age and no doubt began her affairs before the wedding was over."

"Doesn't this woman's husband mind that she—"

"The old goat died," her aunt said. "Not that long ago, I heard. Rumor has it Lady Cecille has her cap set for Lyon as her next husband."

"I don't think he'd marry a woman of ill repute," Christina said, shaking her head for emphasis. "But if she is called Lady, then she must not be a paramour. Isn't that right?" she asked, frowning over the confusion in her mind.

"She's accepted by the ton because of her title. Many of the married women do have affairs. All the husbands certainly keep mistresses," Aunt Patricia said. "The morals disgust me, but men will always follow their baser instincts, won't they?"

Her tone of voice didn't suggest she wanted Christina's opinion. "Yes, Aunt," she answered with a sigh.

"Lyon is rarely seen in public these days," the Countess continued. "Ever since his wife died he has set himself apart."

"Perhaps he still mourns his wife. He seemed vulnerable to me."

"Ha," the aunt sneered. "Lyon has been called many things, but never was the word vulnerable put to his name. I can't imagine any man mourning over the loss of a wife. Why, they're all too busy chasing after their own pleasures to care about anyone else."

The carriage came to a halt in front of the Bakers' residence, forcing an end to the conversation. Christina was acutely relieved when the door to the carriage was finally opened by the footman. She took several deep breaths as she followed her aunt up the steps to the brick-faced townhouse.

A soft, sultry breeze cooled her face. Christina wished she could pull all the pins out of her hair and let the heavy curls down. Her aunt wouldn't allow her to leave it unbound, however. Fashion ordered either short, cropped curls or intricately designed coronets. Since Christina refused to cut her unruly hair, she was forced to put up with the torture of the pins.

"I trust this won't be too much for you," the Countess sarcastically remarked before striking the door.

"I won't fail you," Christina replied, knowing those were the only words her aunt wanted to hear. "You really mustn't worry. I'm strong enough to face anyone, even a lion."

Her jest didn't take. The Countess puckered her lips while she gave her niece a thorough once-over. "Yes, you are strong. It's obvious you haven't inherited any of your mother's odious traits. Thank God for that blessing. Jessica was such a spineless woman."

It was difficult, but Christina held her anger. She couldn't let her aunt know how the foul words about Jessica upset her. Though she'd lived with her aunt for over a year now, she still found it difficult to believe that one sister could be so disloyal to another. The Countess wasn't aware her sister had kept a journal. Christina wasn't going to tell her about the diary—not just yet, anyway—but she wondered what her aunt's reaction would be if she was confronted with the truth. It wouldn't make any difference, Christina decided then. Her aunt's mind was too twisted to accept any changes in her opinions.

The pretense was becoming unbearable. Christina wasn't gifted with a patient nature. Both Merry and Black Wolf had cautioned her to keep a firm hold on her temper. They'd warned her about the whites, too. Her parents knew she'd have to walk the path alone. Black Wolf feared for her safety. Merry feared for her heart. Yet both ignored her pleas to stay with them. There was a promise to be kept, no matter how many lives were lost, no matter how many hearts were broken.

And if she survived, she could go home.

Christina realized she was frowning. She immediately regained her smile just as the door was opened by Lord Baker's butler. The smile stayed firmly in place throughout the lengthy introductions. There were only twenty guests in attendance, most of them elderly, and Christina was given hardly a moment's respite from the seemingly contagious topic of current illnesses until the call for refreshments was given.

The Countess reluctantly left Christina's side when Lord Baker offered her his arm. Christina was able to discourage three well-meaning gentlemen from ushering her into the dining room by pretending an errand in the washroom above the stairs. When she returned to the first floor, she saw that the drawing room was empty of guests. The solitude proved irresistible. Christina glanced over her shoulder to make certain she wasn't being observed, then hurried to the opposite end of the long, narrow room. She'd noticed a balcony beyond a pair of French doors nestled inside an arched alcove. Christina only wanted to steal a few precious minutes of blissful quiet before someone came looking for her.

Her hope was in vain. She'd just made it to the alcove when she suddenly felt someone watching her. Christina stiffened, confused by the feeling of danger that swept over her, then slowly turned around to face the threat.

The Marquess of Lyonwood was standing there, lounging against the entrance, staring at her.

The lion was stalking her. She shook her head, denying her own fanciful notions, yet took an instinctive step back at the same time. The scent of danger was still there, permeating the air, making her wary, confused.

Lyon watched her for a good long while. His expression was intense, almost brooding. Christina felt trapped by his dark gaze. When he suddenly straightened away from the wall and started toward her, she took another cautious step back.

He moved like a predator. He didn't stop when he reached her but forced her with his measured steps to back up through the archway and into the night.

"What are you doing, sir?" Christina whispered, trying to sound appalled and not too worried. "This isn't at all proper, is it?"

"No."

"Why, you've forgotten to make your presence known to our host," Christina stammered. "Did you forget your duty?"

"No."

She tried then to walk around him. Lyon wouldn't let her escape. His big hands settled on her shoulders, and he continued his determined pace. "I know you didn't speak to Lord Baker," Christina said. "Did you?"

"No."

"Oh," Christina replied, sounding quite breathless. "It is a rudeness, that."

"Yes."

"I really must go back inside now, my lord," she said. She was growing alarmed by his abrupt answers. His nearness was driving her to distraction, too. He'd confuse her if she let him, she told herself. Then she'd forget all her training.

"Will you unhand me, sir?" she demanded.

59

"No."

Christina suddenly understood what he was doing. Though she tried, she couldn't contain her smile. "You're trying to be as abrupt as I was with you, aren't you, Lyon?"

"I am being abrupt," he replied. "Do you like having all your questions answered with a simple yes or no?"

"It is efficient," Christina said, staring intently at his chest.

She'd mispronounced the word "efficient." Her accent had become more noticeable, too. Lyon assumed she was frightened, for he'd also caught the worry in her voice. He slowly forced her chin up, demanding without words that she look at him. "Don't be afraid of me, Christina," he whispered.

She didn't answer him. Lyon stared into her eyes a long minute before the truth settled in his mind. "I don't worry you at all, do I?" he asked.

She thought he sounded disappointed. "No," she admitted with a smile. She tried to shrug his hand away from her chin, and when he wouldn't let go of her she took another step back, only to find a weak railing blocking her.

She was good and trapped, and Lyon smiled over it. "Will you please let me go back inside?" she asked.

"First we're going to have a normal conversation," Lyon announced. "This is how it works, Christina. I'll ask you questions, and you may ask me questions. Neither of us will give abrupt one-word answers."

"Why?"

"So that we may get to know each other better," Lyon said.

He looked determined enough to stay on Lord Baker's balcony for the rest of the night if he needed to. Christina decided she had to gain the upper hand as soon as possible.

"Are you angry because I'm not afraid of you?" she asked.

"No," Lyon answered, giving her a lazy grin. "I'm not angry at all."

"Oh, yes you are," Christina said. "I can feel the anger inside you. And your strength. I think you might be just as strong as a lion."

He shook his head. "You say the oddest things," he remarked. He couldn't seem to stop touching her. His thumb slowly brushed her full lower lip. Her softness fascinated him, beckoned him.

"I don't mean to say odd things," Christina said, frowning now. "It is very difficult to banter with you." She turned her face away from him and whispered, "My Aunt Patricia doesn't want me in your company, Lyon. If she realizes I'm outside with you, she'll be most displeased."

Lyon raised an eyebrow over that announcement. "She's going to have to be displeased then, isn't she?"

"She says you're too shrewd," Christina told him.

"And that is a fault?" Lyon asked, frowning.

"Too wealthy, too," Christina added, nodding her head when he gave her an incredulous look.

"What's wrong with being wealthy?" Lyon asked.

"You wouldn't be manageable." Christina quoted her aunt's opinion.

"Damn right."

"See, you agree with my Aunt Patricia after all," Christina returned. "You aren't like the others, are you, Lyon?"

"What others?"

Christina decided to ignore that question. "I'm not a paramour, sir. Aunt tells me you're only interested in loose women."

"You believe her?" he asked. His hands caressed her shoulders again, and he was starting to have difficulty remembering what they were talking about. He could feel the heat of her through her gown. It was a wonderful distraction.

How he wanted to taste her! She was boldly staring up into his eyes now, with such an innocent look on her face, too. She was trying to make a mockery out of all his beliefs about women, Lyon decided. He, of course, knew better. Yet she intrigued him enough to play the game for just a little longer. There wasn't any harm in that, he told himself.

"No," Christina said, interrupting his thoughts.

"No, what?" Lyon asked, trying to remember what he'd said to her.

"No, I don't believe my aunt was correct. You're obviously attracted to me, Lyon, and I'm not a loose woman."

Lyon laughed softly. The sound was like a caress. Christina could feel her pulse quicken. She understood the danger now. Lyon's appeal could break through all her barriers. She knew, with a certainty that chilled her, he would be able to cut through her pretense. "I really must go back inside now," she blurted out.

"Do you know how much you confuse me?" Lyon asked, ignoring her demand to leave him. "You're very good at your craft, Christina."

"I don't understand."

"Oh, I think you do," Lyon drawled out. "I don't know how you've done it, but you've got me acting like a schoolboy. You've such a mysterious air about you. Deliberate, isn't it? Do you think I'll be less interested in you if I know more about you?"

Less interested? Christina felt like laughing. Why, the man would be appalled if he knew the truth. Yes, her aunt was right after all. The Marquess of Lyonwood was entirely too cunning to fool for long.

"Don't look so worried, my sweet," Lyon whispered.

She could see the amusement in his eyes. "Don't call me that," she said. Her voice shook, but it was only because of the strain of the pretense. "It isn't a proper law," she added, nodding vigorously.

"Proper law?" Lyon didn't know what she was talking about. His frustration turned to irritation. He forced himself to take a deep, calming breath. "Let's start over, Christina. I'll ask you a simple question, and you may give me a direct answer," he announced. "First, however, kindly explain what you mean when you say calling you sweet isn't a proper law."

"You remind me of someone from my past, Lyon. And I'm too homesick to continue this discussion." Her confession came out in a sad, forlorn whisper.

"You were in love with another man?" Lyon asked, unable to keep the anger out of his voice.

"No."

He waited, and when she didn't expound on her answer he let out a long sigh. "Oh, no, you don't," he said. "You will explain," he added, tightening his grip on her shoulders. "Christina, I've known you less than two hours, and you've got me tied in knots already. It isn't an easy admission to make," he added. "Can we not stay on one topic?"

"I don't think we can," Christina answered. "When I'm near you, I forget all the laws."

Lyon thought she sounded as bewildered as he felt. They'd circled back to her laws again, too. She wasn't making any sense. "I'll win, you know," he told her. "I always do. You can push me off center as many times as you like, but I'll always . . ."

He'd lost his train of thought when Christina suddenly reached up and trailed the tips of her fingers across the ragged line of his scar. The gentle touch sent shock waves all the way to his heart.

"You have the mark of a warrior, Lyon."

His hands dropped to his sides. He took a step back, thinking to put some distance between them so he could cool the fire rushing through his veins. From the innocent look in her eyes, he knew she didn't have any idea of the effect she was having on him.

It had happened so suddenly, so overwhelmingly. Lyon hadn't realized desire could explode so quickly.

Christina took advantage of the separation. She bowed her head and edged her way around him. "We must never touch each other again," she said before turning her back on him and walking away.

She had reached the alcove when his voice stopped her. "And do you find warriors with scars unappealing?"

Christina turned, so swiftly her skirt swirled around her ankles. She looked astonished by his question.

"Unappealing? Surely you jest with me," she said.

"I never jest," Lyon answered. His voice sounded bored, but the look in his eyes told her of his vulnerability.

She knew she must reveal this one truth. "I find you almost too appealing to deny."

She couldn't quite look into his eyes when she made her

confession, overcome by shyness because of her bold admission. She thought she might be blushing, too, and that thought irritated her enough to turn her back on Lyon once again.

He moved with the speed of a lion. One minute he was standing across the balcony, and the next he had her pinned against the brick wall adjacent to the alcove. His body kept her right where he wanted her. The lower half of Christina's body was trapped by his legs, and his hands were anchored on her shoulders. When he suddenly reached over to shut the doors, his thighs brushed intimately against hers. The touch unsettled both of them. Christina pushed herself up against the wall, trying to break the contact. Lyon's reaction was just the opposite. He leaned closer, wanting the touch again.

Lyon knew he was embarrassing her. He could see her blush, even in the soft moonlit night. "You're like a fragile little flower," he whispered while his hands caressed her shoulders, her neck. "Your skin feels like hot silk."

Her blush deepened. Lyon smiled over it. "Open your eyes, Christina. Look at me," he commanded in a voice as gentle as the breeze.

His tender words sent shivers down her arms. Love words, almost identical in meaning to the words Black Wolf always gave Merry when he thought they were alone. Lyon was trying to gentle her in much the same way. Did that mean he wanted to mate with her? Christina almost blurted out that question, then realized she shouldn't. Lyon was an Englishman, she reminded herself. The laws weren't the same.

Heaven help her, she mustn't forget. "I would never flirt with a lion," she blurted. "It would be dangerous."

Lyon's hands circled her neck. He wasn't sure if he wanted to kiss her or strangle her. The woman certainly did confuse him with her ridiculous comments. He could feel the frantic pulse of her heartbeat under his fingers. "Your eyes don't show any fear, but your heart tells the truth. Are you afraid of your attraction to me?"

"What an arrogant man you are," Christina said. "Why,

I'm so frightened I believe I might swoon if you don't unhand me this very minute."

Lyon laughed, letting her know he didn't believe her lie. He leaned down until his mouth was just a breath away from hers. "Didn't you tell me I was too irresistible to deny, Christina?"

"No," she whispered. "I said you were almost too irresistible to deny, Lyon. Almost. There is a difference."

She tried to smile yet failed the task completely. Christina was simply too occupied fighting the nearly overwhelming urge to melt against him, to hold him tightly, to learn his touch, his taste. She wanted his scent to mate with her own.

She knew it was a forbidden, dangerous longing. It was one thing to tease a cub and quite another to play with a fully grown lion. The dark look in Lyon's eyes told her he'd be just as determined as a hungry lion, too. He'd consume her if she didn't protect herself.

"Lyon," she whispered, torn between desire and the need for caution. "You really must help fight this attraction. I'll forget everything if you don't cooperate."

He didn't know what she was talking about. What did she think she'd forget? Perhaps he hadn't heard her correctly. Her accent had become so pronounced it was difficult to be certain. "I'm going to kiss you, Christina," he said, catching hold of her chin when she started to shake her head.

"One kiss," he promised. He nuzzled his chin against the top of her head, inhaled her sweet scent, and let out a soft, satisfied sigh. Then he took hold of her hands and slipped them around his neck.

God, she was soft. His hands slid down her arms, causing goosebumps he could feel. Pleased with her reaction to his touch, he settled his hands possessively on her hips and pulled her closer.

He was taking entirely too long getting on with it. Christina couldn't fight her attraction any longer. One small touch would certainly satisfy her curiosity. Then she'd go back inside and force herself to forget all about Lyon.

Christina leaned up on her tiptoes and quickly brushed

her mouth against his chin. She placed a chaste kiss on his mouth next, felt him stiffen in reaction. Christina drew back, saw him smile, and knew her boldness had pleased him.

His smile abruptly faded when she traced his lower lip with the tip of her tongue. Lyon reacted as though he'd just been hit by lightning. He dragged her up against him until her thighs were flattened against his own. He didn't care if his arousal frightened her or not. His arms circled her in a determined grip that didn't allow any leverage. Christina wasn't going to bolt until he let her.

She suddenly tried to turn her head away, and the tremor he felt rush through her made him think she might be having second thoughts. "Lyon, please, we will—"

His mouth found her, effectively silencing her protests. He teased and tantalized, coaching her to open her mouth for him. Christina responded to his gentle prodding. Her fingers slid into his hair as a passionate tremor coursed through his body. Lyon groaned into her mouth, then thrust his tongue deeply inside, demanding with his husky growl that she mate with him.

Christina forgot caution. Her hands clung to Lyon's shoulders. Her hips moved instinctively until she was cuddling his heat with her own. A whimper of pleasure escaped her when Lyon began to move against her hips. Christina used her tongue to explore the wonderful textures of Lyon's warm mouth, mimicking him.

A fire raged in his loins. Lyon's mouth slanted over hers once again in a hot, wild kiss that held nothing back. Christina's uninhibited response was a blissful torment he wanted never to end. The way she kissed him made him think she wasn't innocent of men after all. Lyon told himself he didn't care. The desire to bed her at the first possible moment overrode all other considerations.

Lyon had never experienced such raw desire. Christina made a soft moan deep in her throat. The sound nearly drove him beyond common sense. He knew he was about to lose all control and abruptly ended the kiss. "This isn't the time or the place, love," he told her in a ragged whisper.

He took a deep breath and tried desperately not to stare at her mouth. So soft, so exciting. She looked as though she'd just been thoroughly kissed, which of course she had, and Lyon could tell she was having as much difficulty regaining control as he was.

That fact pleased him immensely. He had to peel her hands away from his shoulders, too, for Christina didn't seem capable of doing more than staring up at him. Her eyes had turned a deep indigo blue. Passion's color, Lyon thought as he kissed her fingertips and then let go of her hands.

"I'm going to learn all of your secrets, Christina," Lyon whispered, thinking of the pleasure they could give each other in bed.

His promise penetrated with the swiftness of a dagger. Christina believed he'd just promised to find out about her past. "Leave me alone, Lyon," she whispered. She scooted around him, walked inside the archway, and then turned to look at him again. "Your curiosity could get you killed."

"Killed?"

She shook her head to let him know she wasn't going to expound upon that comment. "We satisfied each other by sharing one kiss. It was enough."

"Enough?"

His bellow followed her inside the drawing room. Christina grimaced at the anger she'd heard in his voice. Her heart was pounding, and she thanked the gods that the guests were still in the dining room. There was an empty chair next to her aunt. Christina immediately sat down and tried to concentrate on the boring conversation the Countess was having with their host and hostess.

Minutes later Lyon appeared in the entrance. Lord Baker was beside himself with excitement. It was obvious that he and everyone else in the dining room believed the Marquess of Lyonwood had only just arrived.

Christina acknowledged Lyon with a curt nod, then turned her back on him. The rude gesture delighted the Countess. The old woman actually reached out to pat

Christina's hand. It was the first show of affection she'd ever given her niece.

Lyon ignored Christina just as thoroughly. He was, of course, the center of attention, for his title and his wealth set him above the others. The men immediately surrounded him. Most of the women also left their chairs. They stood together like a covey of quail, bobbing their heads and eyelashes in unison whenever Lyon happened to glance their way.

When Christina couldn't stand the disgusting display any longer, she returned to the drawing room.

Lyon was trapped by their eager host into a discussion about crop rotation. He listened rather than advised, using the time to regain control of his temper. Though nothing showed on his face, inside he was shaking with fury.

Hell, she'd dismissed him again. Twice in one evening. Had to be some sort of record in that feat, he told himself. She was good, too. Why, she'd made him believe she was as hot as he was. Quite a little temptress, he decided.

Lyon was feeling as though he'd just been tossed into a snowbank. Christina was right, too. She had satisfied his curiosity. The problem, he grudgingly admitted, was the taste of her. Hot, wild honey. He hadn't gotten enough. And while Lord Baker enthusiastically spoke about the merits of barley, Lyon heard again the soft whimpers Christina had given him. It was all surely an act on her part, but the memory still made his blood run heavy.

Christina's aunt had followed her into the drawing room. The Countess stayed right by her niece's side, making snide remarks about the ill-tasting food of which she'd just eaten a horrendously large portion. Christina thought she was safe enough until Lyon happened to walk into the room at the very moment the Countess left to go upstairs to the wash-room to repair her appearance.

Christina was suddenly vulnerable again. Lyon was strid-ing toward her, and though he smiled at the other guests, she could certainly see the anger in his eyes. She immediately hurried over to Lord Baker and spoke to him, warily watching Lyon out of the corner of her eye.

"You have such a lovely home," Christina blurted out to the host.

"Thank you, my dear. It is comfortable for my needs," Lord Baker stated, his chest puffing out with new importance. He began to explain where he'd picked up various pieces of art littering the shelves in the room. Christina tried to pay attention to what he was telling her. She noticed Lyon hesitate, and she smiled over it.

"My wife actually made most of the selections. She has a keen eye for quality," Lord Baker commented.

"What?" Christina asked, puzzled by the way Lord Baker was staring at her. He did seem to expect some sort of answer. It was unfortunate, for she didn't have the faintest idea what they were talking about.

Lyon was getting closer. Christina blamed her lack of concentration solely on him, of course. She knew she'd make a fool of herself in front of her host if she didn't try to pay attention. She deliberately turned her back on Lyon and smiled again at her host. "Where did you find that lovely pink vase you've placed on your mantel?" she asked.

Lord Baker puffed up again. Christina thought he looked like a fat rabbit. "The most valuable piece in my collection," he announced. "And the only one I picked out on my own. Cost more than all my wife's jewels put together," he whispered with a nod. "Had to be firm with Martha, too. My wife declared it simply didn't work."

"Oh, I think it's very beautiful," Christina said.

"Baker, I'd like to speak to Princess Christina for a moment. In privacy, if you wouldn't mind." Lyon spoke right behind her. Christina knew if she took a step back she'd touch his chest. The thought was so unsettling she couldn't seem to come up with a quick denial.

"Certainly," Lord Baker announced. He gave Lyon a speculative look. Matching in his mind, Lyon decided. The rumor that he'd taken an interest in Christina would certainly be all over London by noon tomorrow. Odd, but that realization didn't bother Lyon too much. If it kept all the other dandies at bay, then perhaps the rumor would work to his advantage.

"Certainly not," Christina suddenly blurted out. She smiled at Lord Baker to soften her denial while she prayed he'd come to her rescue.

It was an empty prayer. Lord Baker looked startled and confused until Lyon interjected in a smooth, lying voice, "Christina does have the most wonderful sense of humor. When you get to know her better, I'm sure you'll agree, Baker."

Their host was fooled by Lyon's chuckle. Christina wasn't. Lyon's unbreakable hold on her hand told her he wasn't really amused at all.

He was determined to win. Christina thought he'd probably cause a scene if she tried to deny his request again. The man didn't seem to care what others thought of him. It was a trait she couldn't help but admire.

Lyon didn't have to use pretense, she reminded herself. His title assured compliance. Why, he was as arrogant and as confident as the chief of the Dakotas.

Christina tried to disengage herself from his hold when she turned to confront him. Lyon was smiling at Lord Baker, yet increasing the pressure in his grip at the same time. He was telling her without words not to argue, she supposed. Then he turned and started to pull her with him.

She didn't struggle but straightened her shoulders and followed him. Everyone was staring at them, and for that reason she forced herself to smile and to act as though it was nothing at all to be dragged across the room by a man she'd only just met. When she heard one woman whisper in a loud voice that she and the Marquess made a striking couple, she lost her smile. Yes, she did feel like hitting Lyon, but it was certainly uncomplimentary of the woman to make such a remark. She knew Lyon had also heard the comment. His arrogant grin said as much. Did that mean he wanted to strike her?

Lyon stopped when they reached the alcove. Christina was so relieved he hadn't dragged her outside, she began to relax. They were still in full view of the other guests—a blessing, because Christina knew Lyon wouldn't try to kiss her senseless with an audience watching his every move. No, tender embraces and soft words belonged to moments of privacy, when a man and woman were alone.

After nodding to several gentlemen, Lyon turned back to Christina. He stood close enough to touch if she took just one step forward. Though he'd let go of her hand, his head was inclined toward hers. Christina deliberately kept her head bowed, refusing to look up into his eyes. She thought she probably appeared to be very humble and submissive. It was an appearance she wished to give her audience, yet it irritated her all the same.

Another lie, another pretense. How her brother, White Eagle, would laugh if he could see her now. He knew, as well as everyone else back home, that there wasn't a submissive bone in Christina's body.

Lyon seemed patient enough to stare at her all evening. Christina decided he wasn't going to speak to her until she gave him her full attention. She captured her tranquil smile and finally looked up at him.

He was angry with her, all right. The gold chips were missing. "Your eyes have turned as black as a Crow's," she blurted out.

He didn't even blink over her bizarre comment. "Not this time, Christina," he said in a furious whisper. "Compliments won't get me off balance again, my little temptress. I swear to God, if you ever again dismiss me so casually, I'm going to—"

"Oh, it wasn't a compliment," Christina interrupted, letting him see her irritation. "How presumptuous of you to think that it was. The Crow is our enemy."

Heaven help her, she'd done it again. Lyon could so easily make her forget herself. Christina fought the urge to pick up her skirts and run for the front door. But she suddenly realized he couldn't possibly understand her comment. The confused look on his face told her she'd swayed his attention, too.

"Birds are your enemies?" he asked in a voice that sounded incredulous.

Christina smiled. "Whatever are you talking about?" she asked, feigning innocence. "Did you wish to speak to me about birds?"

"Christina." He'd growled her name. "You could make a saint lose his temper."

She thought he looked ready to pounce on her, so she took a protective step back and then said, "But you aren't a saint, are you, Lyon?"

A sudden shout drew Lyon's full attention. Christina also heard the sound, yet when she tried to turn around, Lyon grabbed hold of her and roughly pushed her behind his back. His strength amazed her. He'd moved so quickly Christina hadn't even guessed his intent until the deed was accomplished.

His broad shoulders blocked her view. Christina could tell by his rigid stance that there was danger. And if she hadn't known better, she would have thought he was trying to protect her.

She was highly curious. She hadn't sensed any threat, yet when she peeked out from Lyon's side she could see armed men standing in the entrance. Her eyes widened with surprise. The evening had certainly taken another bizarre twist. First she'd encountered a lion, and now it appeared that they were about to be robbed by bandits. Why, it was turning out to be an extremely interesting evening after all.

Christina wanted to get a better look at the mischief makers. Lyon, however, had other ideas. As soon as she moved to his side he pushed her behind him again.

He was protecting her. A warm feeling swept over Christina. She was pleased with his determination and actually smiled over it. She decided to let him have his way, then stood on her tiptoes, braced her hands against Lyon's back, and peeked over his shoulder so she could see what was going on.

There were five of them. Four held knives. Poor workmanship, Christina noted with a shake of her head. The fifth man held a pistol in his right hand. All wore masks that covered the lower portion of their faces. The man with the

pistol—obviously the leader in Christina's judgment—
shouted orders from the entrance. His voice was strained
into a deep, guttural tone. Christina immediately assumed
he was known by some of the guests. He wouldn't have
disguised his voice unless he thought he'd be recognized.
And while he was dressed like the others in peasant garb and
an ill-fitting hat, his boots weren't the same at all. They were
old and scruffy, like the boots the others wore, but the
quality of the leather was apparent to Christina.

And then the leader turned and looked across the room.
His eyes widened in surprise. Christina let out an involun-
tary gasp. Good Lord, she'd just met the man not an hour
past.

Lyon heard her indrawn breath. The scowl increased on
his face, for he immediately assumed Christina was terrified. He backed up a space, pushing Christina further into
the shadows. His intent was to block her inside the alcove,
and if the danger increased, he'd shove her out the doorway.

Lord Baker's wife swooned when one of the bandits
demanded her diamond necklace. She conveniently landed
on the settee. Christina was desperately trying not to laugh.
Swooning was such a delightful pretense.

All of a sudden, Christina's aunt walked into the middle
of the commotion. The Countess didn't seem to compre-
hend the fact that there was a robbery going on. When the
leader turned and aimed his pistol in her direction, Christina immediately retaliated.

Crazed or not, Aunt Patricia was family. No one was
going to harm her.

It happened too quickly for anyone to react. Lyon heard
the whistle of the knife seconds before the bandit's howl of
pain. He'd seen the glint of metal fly by his right shoulder.
He turned, trying to protect Christina from the new threat,
but didn't see anyone standing behind her. Whoever had
thrown the weapon had vanished out the doorway to the
balcony, he concluded.

Poor Christina. She tried to look dignified. Her hands
were demurely folded together, and she gave him only a

curious look. She even looked behind her when Lyon did, yet she didn't seem to understand there might be jeopardy there, lurking in the shadows.

Lyon quickly pushed her into the corner so that the wall protected her back. When he was satisfied no one could get to her from behind, he turned back to face the bandits. His shoulders pressed Christina against the wall.

She didn't argue over the confinement. She knew what he was doing. Lyon was still protecting her and was making sure no one was going to come back in through the archway. A noble consideration, Christina thought.

There wasn't any need, of course, for there had never been anyone behind her. She couldn't very well tell Lyon that, however, and his concern for her safety did please her immensely.

The leader had disappeared out the front door. The other bandits threatened the guests by waving their knives in front of them as they backed out of the room.

Both pistol and knife lay on the floor.

Lyon turned to Christina. "Are you all right?" he demanded.

He sounded so concerned. Christina decided to look frightened. She nodded, and when Lyon placed his hands on her shoulders and pulled her toward him she could feel the anger in him.

"Are you angry with me?" she asked.

He was surprised by her question. "No," he announced. His voice was so harsh, he thought he might not have convinced her. "Of course I'm not angry with you, love."

Christina smiled over the forced gentleness in his tone. "Then you may quit squeezing my shoulders," she told him.

He immediately let go of her. "You're angry because you couldn't fight the mischief makers, aren't you, Lyon?"

"Mischief makers? My dear, their intent was a little more serious," Lyon said.

"But you did want to fight them, didn't you?"

"Yes," he admitted with a grin. "I was aching to get in the middle of it. Some habits die hard," he added.

"You'll always be a warrior, Lyon."

"What?"

Oh dear, he was looking confused again. Christina hastened to say, "There are too many old people here. It wouldn't have been safe for you to interfere. Someone might have been hurt."

"Is your concern only for the old men and women?" he asked.

"Yes."

Lyon frowned over her answer. Then she realized he wanted her to be concerned for his safety, too. Didn't he realize it would have been an insult for her to show concern for him? Why, that would mean she didn't have enough faith in his ability! Still, he was English, she reminded herself. And they were a strange breed.

"I wouldn't worry for you, Lyon. You would have held your own."

"You have that much faith in me, do you?"

She smiled over the arrogance in his tone. "Oh, yes," she whispered, giving him the praise he seemed to need. She was about to add a bit more when a loud wail interrupted her.

"Our hostess is coming out of her swoon," Lyon announced. "Stay here, Christina. I'll be back in a minute."

She did as he ordered, though she kept her attention directed on him. Her heart started pounding when Lyon knelt down and picked up her knife. She took a deep breath, held it, and then sighed with relief when he put the knife on the table and turned his attention to the pistol.

The chaos surrounding her was confusing. Everyone was suddenly talking at the same time. Perhaps she should try to swoon after all, Christina considered. No, the settee was already taken, and the floor didn't look all that appealing. She settled on wringing her hands. It was the best she could do to look upset.

Two gentlemen were in deep discussion. One motioned Lyon over to join them. As soon as he moved toward the dining room Christina edged her way over to the table. She made certain no one was paying her any attention, then she cleaned and sheathed her knife.

She hurried over to stand beside her aunt. The Countess

was administering blistering advice to the distressed woman draped on the settee.

"I believe we've had enough excitement for one evening," Christina told her guardian when she was finally able to catch her attention.

"Yes," the Countess answered. "We'd better be on our way."

Lyon was blocked in the dining room, listening to absurd suggestions as to how two ancient gentlemen thought to trap Jack and his band.

After ten minutes or so, he'd had his fill. His attention kept returning to the unusual dagger he'd held in his hands. He'd never seen the like before. The weapon was crudely made, yet toned to needle-point sharpness. The handle was flat. Whoever owned the knife certainly hadn't purchased it in England.

Lyon decided to take the weapon with him. He was highly curious and determined to find the man who'd thrown it.

"I'll leave you gentlemen to think your plans through," Lyon announced. "I believe I'll see Princess Christina and her guardian safely home. If you'll excuse me?"

He didn't give them time to start in again but turned and hurried back inside the drawing room. He remembered telling Christina to wait for him until he returned. He shouldn't have left her alone, assuming she was still frightened enough to need his comfort. He sincerely hoped she was, for the thought of offering her solace was very appealing.

Lyon was already planning how he'd get Christina away from her guardian. He just wanted to steal a few minutes so he could kiss her once more.

"Well, hell." Lyon muttered the obscenity when he realized Christina had vanished. He glanced over at the table where he'd left the knife, then let out another foul expletive.

The knife had vanished, too. Lyon's mood blackened. He considered questioning the guests, but they were all still occupied rehashing their reactions to the robbery. He decided not to bother.

Lyon turned to look again at the alcove where he and

Christina had stood together during the robbery. A sudden revelation popped into his mind. No, he told himself. It wasn't possible.

Then he strolled over to the alcove and continued on until he was standing next to the balcony railing.

A good twenty feet separated the balcony from the sloping terrace below. Impossible to scale. The railing was shaky, too weak to hold rope and man.

His mind immediately jumped to a ludicrous conclusion.

Lyon shook his head. "Impossible," he muttered out loud. He decided to put that puzzle aside and concentrate on the real worry now.

Lyon left Baker's house in a black mood. He was too angry to speak just yet. He determined to wait until tomorrow.

Then he was going to have a long, hard talk with Rhone.

Chapter Four

Edward always wore white. Colors displeased him. He preferred me to wear long, flowing Grecian-styled gowns of white also. The palace walls were whitewashed once a month, and all the furnishings were devoid of even a splash of color. While Edward's peculiarity amused me, I did comply with his wishes. He was so good to me. I could have anything I wanted and wasn't allowed to lift a finger in labor. He only bound me to one rule. Edward made me promise never to leave the pristine palace grounds, explaining it was for my protection.

I kept my promise for almost six months. Then I began to hear rumors about the conditions outside my walls. I believed Edward's enemies spread the rumors of brutality solely to cause unrest.

My maid and I changed into peasant clothing and set out on foot for the nearest village. I looked upon the outing as an adventure.

God help me, I walked into purgatory.

Journal entry
August 15, 1795

T he solicitors in care of the Earl of Acton's estate called upon Countess Patricia Cummings Tuesday morning at ten o'clock. Misters Henderson and Borton were prompt to the minute.

The Countess could barely contain her enthusiasm. She ushered both gray-haired gentlemen into her study, shut the door behind her, and took her place behind the scarred desk.

"You'll have to forgive such shabby furnishings," she said. She paused to give both men a brittle smile before continuing. "I was forced to use the last of my reserves to dress my niece, Christina, for the season ahead of us, and there just wasn't anything left over. Why, I've had to turn down many requests for visitations with my niece—too embarrassed, you understand, to let anyone see the way we're living. Christina has caused a sensation. I'll marry her well."

The Countess suddenly realized she was rambling. She gave a dainty little cough to cover her embarrassment. "Yes, well, I'm certain you both know this townhouse is only on loan to us for another month. You did receive the bid for purchase, did you not?"

Henderson and Borton nodded in unison. Borton turned to his associate and gave him an odd, uncomfortable look. He poked at his cravat. The Countess narrowed her eyes over the rudeness. "When will my money be transferred into my hands?" she demanded. "I can't go on much longer without proper funds."

"But it isn't your money, Countess," Borton announced after receiving a nod from his associate. "Surely you realize that fact."

Borton blanched over the horrid frown the Countess gave him. He couldn't continue to look at her. "Will you explain, Henderson?" he asked, staring at the floor.

"Certainly," Henderson said. "Countess, if we might have a word in privacy with your niece, I'm certain this misunderstanding will be cleared up."

Henderson obviously wasn't intimidated by the Countess's visible anger. His voice was as smooth as good gin. He continued to smile all through the foul woman's tantrum. Borton was impressed.

Patricia slammed her fists down on the desk. "What does Christina have to do with this meeting? I am her guardian, and therefore I control her funds. Isn't that the truth?" she screeched.

Before Henderson could answer, Patricia slapped the desk again. "I do control the money, don't I?"

"No, madam. You do not."

Christina heard her aunt's bellow all the way upstairs. She immediately left her bedroom and hurried down the steps to see what had caused the Countess such an upset. Christina had learned the difference between her aunt's screams long ago. This one resembled the protest of a trapped owl, telling Christina her Aunt Patricia wasn't frightened. Just furious.

She reached the library door before she realized she was barefoot. Lord, that would certainly push her aunt into a tither, Christina thought. She hurried back upstairs, found her impractical shoes, and quickly put them on.

Christina counted five more shrieks before she was once again downstairs. She didn't bother to knock on the library door, knowing her aunt's shouts would drown out the sound. She threw the door open and hurried inside.

"Is there something I can do to help, Aunt?" Christina asked.

"This is your niece?" Henderson asked as he hurried out of his chair.

"Christina, go back to your room. I'll deal with these scoundrels."

"We'll not speak to you of the conditions set down in writing by your father, Countess," Borton said. "It is you who must leave us alone with your niece. Those were your father's wishes as spelled out in his will."

"How could such a condition exist?" the Countess shouted. "My father didn't even know Jessica was carrying a child. He couldn't have known about her. I made certain."

"Your sister wrote to your father, madam, and told him about his grandchild. I believe she sent the letter when she was staying with you. And she'd also left a message for him. The Earl found it a year after her disappearance."

"Jessica couldn't have written to him," Patricia announced with an inelegant snort. "You're lying. I would have known. I looked through each letter."

"You mean you destroyed each letter, don't you, Countess?" Henderson asked, matching Patricia's glare. "You didn't want your father to know about his heir, did you?"

Aunt Patricia's face turned as red as fire. "You can't know that," she muttered.

Christina was concerned about her aunt's extreme anger. She walked over to her side and put her hand on the old woman's shoulder. "It doesn't matter how my grandfather learned about me. The past is behind us, gentlemen. Let it rest."

Both men hastily nodded. "A sensible request, my dear," Henderson commented. "Now, according to the conditions of the will, we must explain the finances to you in privacy."

Christina increased her grip on her aunt's shoulder when she saw she was about to object. "If I request that the Countess remain, will you agree?" she asked.

"Of course," Borton said after receiving another nod from his partner.

"Then kindly sit down and begin your explanation," Christina instructed. She felt the tension leave her Aunt Patricia and slowly let go of her.

"A man by name of Captain Hammershield delivered your mother's letter to the Earl of Acton," Henderson began. "We have the letter in our file, and the one Jessica left behind in our files, if you wish to challenge this, Countess," the solicitor added. "I need not go into the other details of the letters, for as you say, Princess Christina, the past is behind us. Your grandfather fashioned a new will immediately. He had turned his back on you, Countess, and was so infuriated with his other daughter's behavior that he decided to put his fortune in holding for his only grandchild."

Borton leaned forward to interject, "He didn't know if you were going to be a boy or girl. There are conditions in both events, of course, but we will only explain the conditions for a granddaughter, you see."

"What did my mother do to cause her father to change his mind about her? I thought they were very close to each other," Christina said.

"Yes, whatever did my sainted sister do to turn Father against her?" Patricia asked, a sneer in her voice.

"Jessica humiliated her father when she left her husband. Princess Christina, your grandfather was most upset. He liked his son-in-law and thought his daughter was acting . . . out of sorts," he ended with a shrug to cover his embarrassment.

"What you're sniffing around and refusing to say is that my father at last realized Jessica was crazy," the Countess announced.

"That is the sad truth," Borton said. He gave Christina a sympathetic look.

"So the money goes directly to Christina?" the Countess asked.

Henderson saw the shrewd look that came into the woman's eyes. He almost laughed. The Earl of Acton had been right about this daughter, the solicitor decided. Henderson decided to rush through the rest of the stipulations, concerned that the old woman would ruin his midday meal if he had to look at her much longer.

"The funds were placed in abeyance until your nineteenth birthday, Princess Christina. If you marry before that day, the funds will be given to your husband."

"That is less than two months away," the Countess remarked. "She will not marry so soon. And so, as guardian—"

"Please listen to the rest of the stipulations," Henderson requested in a hard voice. "While the Earl liked his son-in-law, he decided to proceed with caution, in the event that his daughter's accusations about her husband turned out to have a drop of credibility."

"Yes, yes," Borton eagerly interjected. "The Earl was a most cautious man. For that reason, he added further controls to the distribution of his vast fortune."

"Will you get on with it?" the Countess demanded. "Spell out the damned conditions before you make me as demented as Jessica was."

The Countess was getting all worked up again. Christina supported her demand, though in a much softer tone of voice. "I would also like to hear the rest of this, if you will please continue."

"Certainly," Henderson agreed. He deliberately avoided looking at the Princess now, certain he'd lose his train of thought if he paused to appreciate the lovely shade of her blue eyes. He found it amazing that the two women were actually related to each other. The Countess was an ugly old bitch, in looks and manners, yet the lovely young woman standing next to her was as pretty as an angel and seemed to be just as sweet-tempered.

Henderson focused his attention on the desktop and continued. "In the event you reach nineteen and are unmarried, your father will oversee your inheritance. Princess Christina, your father was informed of the conditions of the will before he left England in search of your mother. He understood he wouldn't have access to the money until—"

"He can't still be alive," the Countess exclaimed. "No one's heard of him in years."

"Oh, but he is alive," Borton said. "We received a missive from him just a week past. He's currently living in the north of France and plans to return to claim the money on the day of his daughter's nineteenth birthday."

"Does he know Christina is alive? That she's here, in London?" the Countess asked. Her voice shook with anger.

"No, and we didn't feel the need to so inform him," Henderson said. "Princess Christina's birthday is less than two months off now. Of course, if you wish us to try to notify your father, Princess, before—"

"No." Christina controlled her voice. She felt like shouting the denial, however, and could barely catch her breath over the tightness in her chest. "It will be a happy surprise for him, don't you agree, gentlemen?" she added with a smile.

Both men smiled back in agreement. "Gentlemen, we

have tired my aunt," Christina announced. "As I understand this will, I can never control my own money. If I marry, my husband will direct the funds, and if I do not, then my father will have free hand with the inheritance."

"Yes," Borton answered. "Your grandfather would not allow a woman to have such power over his money."

"All this time I believed I would . . ." The Countess crumbled against her chair. "My father has won."

Christina thought her aunt might start weeping. She dismissed the two gentlemen a few minutes later. In a magnanimous gesture, Henderson told Christina he'd release a sum of money to tide her over until her father returned to gain guardianship.

Christina was humble in her gratitude. She saw the solicitors out the front door, then returned to the library to speak to her aunt.

The Countess didn't realize how upset her niece was. "I've lost everything," she wailed as soon as Christina rushed back into the room. "Damn my father's soul to hell," she shouted.

"Please don't get upset again," Christina said. "It cannot be at all good for your health."

"I've lost everything, and you dare to tell me not to get upset?" the Countess screeched. "You're going to have to plead on my behalf to your father, Christina. He'll give me money if you ask. Edward didn't like me. I should have been nicer to him, I suppose, but I was so jealous of Jessica's good fortune in capturing him I could barely be civil to the man. Why he chose her over me still doesn't make any sense. Jessica was such a mouse. I was far better-looking."

Christina didn't answer her aunt's mutterings. She started to pace in front of the desk, her mind filled with the problem ahead of her.

"Were you surprised to learn that your father is still alive?" the Countess asked.

"No," Christina answered. "I never believed he'd died."

"You're going to have to take care of me, Christina," the aunt whined. "Whatever will I do if your father doesn't support me? How will I get along? I shall be the laugh of the *ton*," she cried.

"I've promised to take care of you, Aunt," Christina said. "Remember how I gave you my word before we left Boston? I shall see my promise carried through."

"Your father might not agree with your noble intentions, Christina. He'll have control of *my* money, the bastard, and I'm sure he'll refuse to give me a single shilling."

Christina came to an abrupt halt in front of her aunt. "Giving my father control of the money does not suit my purposes," she announced. "I'll not let it happen."

Patricia Cummings had never seen her niece look so angry. She nodded, then smiled, for she assumed the stupid chit was infuriated on her behalf. "You're a dear girl to be so concerned about my welfare. Of course, your concern isn't misplaced. A grave injustice was done to me by my father, and I did use the last of my own accounts to see you properly attired. It was all for nought," the Countess added. "I should have stayed in the Godforsaken colonies."

Christina was irritated by the self-pity she heard in her aunt's voice. She took a deep breath, hoping to regain her patience, and said, "All is not lost. The solution to our problem is obvious to me. I will marry before my father returns to England."

Christina's calmly stated announcement gained her aunt's full attention. The old woman's eyes widened, and she actually straightened in her chair. "We don't know when Edward will arrive. He could walk into this very room as early as tomorrow," she said.

Christina shook her head. "No, I don't think so. Remember, he must surely believe I didn't survive. Everyone else seemed very surprised to see me. And I plan to marry as soon as possible."

"How could we make the arrangements in time? We don't even have a suitable man in mind."

"Make a list of those I must consider," Christina advised.

"This isn't at all proper," the Countess protested.

Christina was going to argue when she noticed the gleam

settle in her aunt's gaze. She knew then that she was giving the idea consideration. Christina goaded her into complete agreement. "We must move quickly if we are to be successful."

"Why? Why would you sacrifice yourself this way?" Patricia gave her niece a suspicious look. "And why would you rather have the money in your husband's hands instead of your father's?"

"Aunt, as I said before, it doesn't suit my purposes to let my father have any money. Now, what other objections must you raise before you see the wisdom of my plan?"

"Your father might have gained a new fortune by now. He may not even want the money."

"You know better," Christina said. "I doubt that he's rich. Why would he keep in correspondence with the solicitors if he was so wealthy? Oh, he'll come back to England, Aunt Patricia."

"If you claim Edward will want the inheritance, I won't argue with you," the Countess said.

"Good," Christina said. "I think you are one of the most clever women I've ever known," she praised. "Surely you can come up with a plausible reason for my hasty marriage."

"Yes," the Countess agreed. "I am clever." Her shoulders straightened until her spine looked ready to snap. "Just how will your marriage help me?" she demanded.

"We will ask the man I marry to sign over a large amount to you. He must sign the papers before we are wed."

"Then it will have to be someone manageable," the Countess muttered. "There are plenty of that kind around. I'll have to think of a good reason for the rush. Leave me now, Christina, while I make a list of possible husbands for you. With your looks, we can get just about anyone to agree to my conditions."

"I would like the Marquess of Lyonwood placed at the top of your list," Christina announced, bracing herself for her aunt's displeasure.

"You can't be serious," the Countess stammered. "He's rich, doesn't need the money, and simply isn't the type to cooperate with my plans."

"If I can get him to sign your papers, then will it be all right for me to wed with him for the short time I'm in England?"

"To wed with him isn't proper English, Christina. Oh, very well, since you're willing to make this necessary sacrifice, I'll allow you to approach the disgusting man. He won't agree, of course, but you have my permission to try."

"Thank you," Christina said.

"You're still set on returning to those savages?"

"They are not savages," Christina whispered. "And I will return to my family. Once you have the money in your hands, it shouldn't matter to you."

"Well, you certainly shouldn't mention that fact to the man we choose to marry you. It would surely set him against you, Christina."

"Yes, Aunt," Christina answered.

"Get out of here and change that gown," the Countess snapped. "You look positively ugly in that color of yellow. Your hair needs tending, too. Do something about it at once."

Christina immediately left the library, ignoring the ridiculous criticisms of her appearance.

By the time she shut the bedroom door behind her she'd shed the pretense. Christina was visibly shaking. Her stomach felt as though it was twisted into knots, and her head was pounding.

Though it was difficult to admit, Christina was honest enough to realize she was really frightened. She didn't like the strange feeling at all.

She understood the reason. The jackal was returning to England. He'd try to kill her. Christina didn't doubt her father's determination. Jackals didn't change their nature over the years.

Christina was going to give Edward a second chance to murder her. God willing, she'd kill him first.

Chapter Five

There really are demons living on this earth, Christina. I didn't know such evil men existed until I saw innocent children who'd been tortured, mutilated, destroyed, just to gain their parents' obedience. An army of enforcers slaughtered defenseless peasants. My husband was a dictator; anyone believed to have a subversive thought was murdered. The dead, the dying littered the alleys. Carts would come to collect the bodies every night. The stench that would make us close our doors in the palace each sunset wasn't due to excess garbage . . . no, no, the odor came from the burial fires.

The people were kept hungry so they would be too weak to rebel. Even the water was rationed. I was so sickened by the atrocities I couldn't think clearly. Mylala, my faithful maid, cautioned me against confronting Edward. She feared for my safety.

I should have listened to her, child. Yes, I acted the part of a naive fool, for I went to challenge my husband.

Learn from my mistakes, Christina. It's the only way you'll survive.

Journal entry
October 12, 1795

Lyon was slouched behind his desk, a full goblet of brandy in his hand and a hot container of water balanced on his knee.

Odd, but the injury hadn't given him any notice until this evening. It was well past four o'clock in the morning now. The nagging pain—and the dreams, of course—had forced him back to his study to work on the problems of his estates. He wouldn't retire until dawn was well upon the city of London . . . when his mind was too fatigued to remember.

He was feeling out of sorts. An old warrior, he thought with a smile. Wasn't that what Christina had called him? Warrior, yes, he remembered her calling him that . . . old, no, he didn't recall that mention.

The past had caught up with the Marquess. His years working for his country had taken a toll. He was a man who was feared still—had become legend, in fact, in many disreputable circles of French society. Lyon had always been given the most difficult, delicate missions. He was never called until the atrocity had been done, the evidence judged. His duty was solitary, his reputation unblemished by failure. The Marquess of Lyonwood was considered to be the most dangerous man in England. Some claimed the world.

No matter where the traitor hid, Lyon could ferret him out and dispatch him with quiet, deadly efficiency.

He'd never failed in his duty. Never.

The results of his loyalty were twofold. Lyon was given knighthood for his courage, nightmares for his sins. It was an easy enough retirement to accept. Since he lived alone, no one ever knew his torment. When the nightmares visited, and he once again saw the faces of those he'd eliminated, no one was there to witness his agony.

Lyon rarely thought about James or Lettie anymore, though he continued to shake his head over the irony of it all. While he was abroad defending his homeland against betrayers, his brother was home in England betraying him.

No, he didn't think about James much, and since meeting

Princess Christina his mind had been in such a turmoil he could barely think with much reason at all.

He was a man given to intrigue. A good puzzle held his attention until he'd resolved it. Christina, however, still proved too elusive to understand. He didn't know what her game was . . . yet. When she didn't openly flirt with him— or Rhone either, for that matter—his interest had picked up. Lyon kept mulling over the strange conversation he'd had with the lady, but after a while he gave up. He'd have to see her again, he told himself. She still hadn't given him enough clues to satisfy him.

And where in God's name would she have heard the roar of lions?

Lyon knew he was becoming obsessed with finding out about her past. His determination didn't make much sense to him. Christina was affecting him in ways he'd thought impossible. He'd never felt so overwhelmed by a woman before. The admission bothered him far more than the nagging pain in his knee.

He would learn all her secrets. She was sure to have them—every woman did—and then his curiosity would be satisfied. Yes, then he'd dismiss her.

The obsession would end.

With that decision reached, Lyon dispatched notes to the gossip leaders of the ton. He was, of course, discreet in his requests for information about the Princess, using his sister Diana and her introduction into society as his main reason for wanting to know the ins and outs of "business."

He wasn't the least concerned about his deceitful endeavor. And in the end, when all the letters had been answered, Lyon was more frustrated than ever. According to all those in the know, Princess Christina didn't have a past.

The woman hadn't even existed until two months ago.

Lyon wasn't about to accept such a conclusion. His patience was running thin. He wanted real answers . . . and he wanted to see Christina again. He had thought to corner her at Creston's ball the following Saturday, then decided against waiting.

Ignoring good manners altogether, he called upon No. 6

Baker Street at the unholy hour of nine o'clock in the morning. Lyon hadn't bothered to send a note begging an audience, certain the ill-tempered Countess would have denied him entrance if she'd been given advance warning.

Luck was on Lyon's side. An extremely feeble old man with a mop of stark yellow hair opened the door for him. His clothing indicated that he was the butler, and his manner resembled that of an uncivil pontiff.

"The Countess has just left for an appointment, sir, and won't return home for a good hour or more."

Lyon held his grin. "I don't want to see the Countess," he told the butler.

"Then who exactly did you want to see?" the servant asked in a haughty tone of voice.

Lyon let his exasperation show. The old man guarded the entrance like a gargoyle. Lyon brushed past him before he could issue a protest, calling over his shoulder, "I wish to speak to Princess Christina." He deliberately used his most intimidating voice to gain compliance. "Now."

A sudden grin transformed the servant's dour expression into wrinkles of delight. "The Countess ain't going to like it," he announced as he shuffled ahead of Lyon to the double doors on the left of the entryway. "She'll be displeased, she will."

"You don't seem too disturbed by that eventuality," Lyon remarked dryly when the butler let out a loud cackle.

"I won't be telling her about your visit, sir," the butler said. He drew himself up and turned toward the staircase. "You can wait in there," he said with a wave of his hand. "I'll go and inform the Princess of your wish to speak to her."

"Perhaps it would be better if you don't tell your mistress who her caller is," Lyon instructed, thinking Christina just might decide against seeing him. "I'd like to surprise her," he added.

"Since you ain't given me your name, it'll be easy enough to comply with your wishes."

It seemed to Lyon that it took an eternity for the butler to make it across the hallway. He leaned against the door frame and watched the old man. A sudden question made him call out, "If you don't know who I am, how can you be so sure the Countess will be displeased?"

The butler let out another crackle of laughter that sounded very like a long nail being dragged across a chalkboard. The effort nearly toppled him to the floor. He grabbed hold of the bannister before giving Lyon an answer. "It doesn't matter who you be, sir. The Countess don't like anyone. Nothing ever makes the old bat happy." The butler continued up the stairs in his slow, sluggish stride.

Lyon would have sworn it took the old man ten minutes to gain three steps.

"I take it the Countess wasn't the one who employed you," Lyon remarked.

"No, sir," the servant answered between wheezes. "It was Princess Christina who found me in the gutter, so to speak. She picked me up, dusted me off, and fixed me up real nice in new clothes. I was a butler many years ago, afore hard times caught me." The old man took a deep breath, then added, "The Princess don't like me calling her aunt an old bat, though. Says it ain't dignified."

"It might not be dignified, my good man, but old bat really does describe the Countess rather well."

The butler nodded, then grabbed hold of the bannister again. He stayed in that position a long moment. Lyon thought the man was trying to catch his breath. He was wrong in that conclusion, however. The butler finally let go of the railing, then cupped his hands to the sides of his mouth and literally bellowed his announcement up the stairwell. "You got yourself a visitor, Princess. I put him in the drawing room."

Lyon couldn't believe what he'd just witnessed. When the servant repeated the scream, he started laughing.

The butler turned back to explain to Lyon. "She don't want me overdoing," he said. "Got to save me strength for the old bat's orders."

Lyon nodded. The butler shouted to his mistress again. Christina suddenly appeared at the top of the steps, drawing Lyon's full attention. He wasn't ever going to get used to looking at her, he decided. She kept getting prettier. Her hair wasn't pinned atop her head today. Glorious. It was the only word that came to mind, for the thick, silvery mass of curls framing the angelic face defied any other description.

When she started down the steps, Lyon saw that the length of hair ended against the swell of her slender hips.

She was dressed in a pale pink gown. The scoop neckline showed only a hint of the swell of her bosom. There was something a little unusual about the modest ensemble, but Lyon was too distracted watching her smile at her butler to decide what seemed out of place to him.

She hadn't seen him yet. "Thank you, Elbert. Now go and sit down. The Countess will be home soon, and you'll have to be on your feet again."

"You're too good to me," Elbert whispered.

"It is good of you to think so," she said before continuing on down the steps. She spotted Lyon leaning against the entrance to the salon.

He knew she was surprised. Her eyes widened. "Oh, dear, the Countess is going to be—"

"Displeased," Lyon finished her comment with an exasperated sigh.

Elbert had obviously heard the remark. His scratchy laughter followed Christina into the drawing room. Lyon followed her, pausing long enough to shut the door behind him. "Believe it or not, Christina, I'm considered pleasing enough by the rest of the town. Why your aunt takes exception to me is beyond my comprehension."

Christina smiled over the irritation she'd caught in Lyon's voice. He sounded like a little boy in need of assurance. She sat down in the center of the gold brocade settee so Lyon couldn't sit beside her, motioned for him to take the chair adjacent to her, and then said, "Of course you're pleasing. Do not let my aunt's opinions upset you. Though it is rude of me to admit, your feelings are surely at stake, and so I will confess that my aunt doesn't really like too many people."

"You mistake my comment," Lyon drawled out. "I don't give a damn what your aunt thinks of me. I just find it puzzling that I . . ."

She was giving him a wary look, and he paused in his reply to change the topic. "Are you unhappy I called?" he asked, frowning over his own question.

Christina shook her head. "Good day to you," she suddenly blurted, trying to remember her manners. It was a problem for her, of course, because Lyon was looking wonderfully handsome again. He was dressed in buckskin riding pants that were the color of a young deer. The material clung to his powerful thighs. His shirt was white, probably made of silk, Christina thought, and partially covered by a forest-in-autumn-colored brown jacket that nicely matched the color of his shiny Hessian boots.

She realized she was staring at him, yet decided to excuse her ill conduct because he was looking at her with much the same intensity.

"I like looking at you."

"I like looking at you, too," Lyon answered with a chuckle.

Christina folded her hands in her lap. "Was there a specific reason for your sporadic visitation?" she asked.

"Sporadic? I don't understand . . ."

"Spontaneous," Christina said hastily.

"I see."

"Well, sir? Was there a specific reason?"

"I don't remember," Lyon answered, grinning at her.

She gave him a hesitant smile back. "Would you care for refreshment?"

"No, thank you," Lyon answered.

"Well, then, kindly explain what it is you don't remember," she instructed.

She gave him an expectant look, as if what she'd just requested was the most logical thing in the world. "How can I explain what it is I don't remember?" he asked. "You're back to making little sense again, aren't you?"

His smile could melt snow. Christina was having difficulty sitting still. All she wanted to think about was the way Lyon had kissed her, and all she wanted to do was find a way to get him to kiss her again.

It was, of course, an unladylike thought. "The weather has turned warm, hasn't it? Some people say it's the warmest autumn in many years," she added, staring intently down at her hands.

Lyon smiled over her obvious nervousness. He slowly stretched out his long legs, settling in for a confrontation. It was going to be easy work finding out his answers if Christina remained this ill at ease.

The tips of Lyon's boots touched the hem of her gown. She immediately scooted back against the settee, glanced down at the floor, and let out a small gasp. "Would you care for refreshments?" she asked in a surprisingly loud voice, jerking her gaze back to him. She wiggled to the edge of the settee again.

She was as skittish as an abandoned kitten. "You've already asked me that question," Lyon reminded her. "No, I don't care for refreshments. Do I make you uncomfortable?" he added, grinning enough to let her know he'd be happy if he did.

"Why would you think that?" Christina asked.

"You're sitting on the edge of the cushion, looking ready to run at any second, my sweet."

"My name is Christina, not sweet," she said. "And of course I'm uncomfortable. You'd make a buffalo nervous."

"A buffalo?"

"You'd make anyone nervous when you frown," Christina explained with a dainty shrug.

"Good."

"Good? Why, Lyon, you do say the oddest things."

"I say . . ." Lyon shouted with laughter. "Christina, you haven't made any sense since the moment I met you. Every time I see you I promise myself I'll get a normal conversation out of you, and then—"

"Lyon, you're being fanciful," Christina interrupted. "This is only the second—no, the third time I've seen you, if you count two times in one evening—"

"You're doing it again," Lyon said.

"Doing what?"

"Trying to push me off center."

"I couldn't push you anywhere. You're too big. I know my strengths, Lyon."

"Do you take everything in literal meaning?"

"I don't know. Do I?"

"Yes."

"Perhaps you're the one who has trouble making sense. Yes," Christina added with a quick nod. "You see, Lyon, you don't ask logical questions."

She laughed when he glared. "Why are you here?" she asked again.

She was back to staring at her hands again. A faint blush covered her cheeks. She was suddenly embarrassed about something.

He didn't have any idea what or why. That didn't surprise him, though. The unusual was becoming commonplace where Christina was concerned. Lyon thought he was ready for just about anything now. He was confident he'd have her game found out before the end of their visit.

"I really do know why you came to see me," Christina whispered timidly.

"Oh?" Lyon asked. "What is that reason?"

"You like being with me," she answered, daring a quick look up to see his reaction. When he didn't seem irritated by her honesty, she warmed to her topic.

"Lyon? Do you believe in destiny?"

Oh, dear, he was looking confused again. Christina let out a long sigh. "Well, you do admit you like being with me, don't you?" she coached.

"Yes, but God only knows why," Lyon confessed. He leaned forward and rested his elbows on his knees.

"Yes, the Great Spirit does know why."

"Great Spirit?" Lyon shook his head. "Lord, I'm starting to sound like an echo. All right, I'll ask. Who is this Great Spirit?"

"God, of course. Different cultures have their own names for the All Powerful, Lyon. Surely you know that. You aren't a heathen, are you?" She sounded quite appalled at that possibility.

"No, I'm not a heathen."

"Well, you needn't get irritated with me. I only asked."

He stared at her a long, silent minute. Then he stood up. Before Christina knew what he was going to do, he'd pulled her up into his arms. He hugged her to him and rested his chin against the top of her head. "I'm either going to strangle you or kiss you," he announced. "The choice is yours."

Christina sighed. "I would prefer that you kiss me. But first, please answer my question, Lyon. It's important to me."

"What question?"

"I asked you if you believed in destiny," she said. She pulled away from him and looked up at his face. "You really do have trouble holding a thought, don't you?"

She had the gall to sound disgruntled. "I don't have any trouble holding a thought," he muttered.

Christina didn't look like she believed him. She was a witch, trying to cast her magical spell on him. Lyon felt as besotted as a silly, worthless fop and as puny as an infant when her gaze was directed on him so enchantingly.

"Well?"

"Well what?" Lyon asked. He shook his head over his ridiculous reaction to the nymph glaring up at him. A lock of hair fell forward, concealing a part of his scar. Christina quit trying to pull away from him and reached up to smooth the lock back in place. The gentle touch jarred him back to her question.

"No, I don't believe in destiny."

"That's a pity."

She acted as though he'd just confessed a grave, unforgivable sin. "All right," he announced. "I know better than to ask, but God help me, I'm going to anyway. Why is it a pity?"

"Dare you laugh at me?" she asked when she saw his smile.

"Never," he lied.

"Well, I guess it really doesn't matter."

"That I laugh at you?"

"No, it doesn't matter if you believe in destiny," Christina answered.

"Why doesn't it matter?"

"Because what will happen will happen whether you believe or not. See how simple it is?"

"Ah," Lyon said, drawing the sound out. "You're a philosopher, I see."

She stiffened in his arms and glared at him again. The change in her mood happened so swiftly that Lyon was thrown off center. "Did I just say something to upset you?" he asked.

"I'm not a flirt. How can you so easily slander me? Why, I've been honest with you all during this conversation. I came right out and said I liked looking at you, and that I'd like you to kiss me. A philosopher, indeed."

The woman was making him daft. "Christina, a philosopher is a man who devotes his mind to the study of various beliefs. It was not slander for me to call you such."

"Spell this word, please," she said, looking extremely suspicious.

Lyon did as she requested. "Oh, I see now," she said. "I believe I've confused philanderer with this man who studies. Yes, that's what I've done. Don't look so confused, Lyon. It was an easy mistake to make."

"Easy?" He told himself not to ask. Curiosity won out again. "Why is it easy?"

"Because the words are close in spelling," she answered.

She sounded as though she was instructing a simple-minded child. He took immediate exception to her manner. "That is without a doubt the most illogical explanation I've ever heard. Unless of course . . . you've only just learned to speak English, haven't you, Christina?"

Because he seemed so pleased by his conclusion, Christina really didn't have the heart to tell him no, she hadn't just learned English. She'd been speaking the difficult language for several years now.

"Yes, Lyon," she lied. "I speak many languages and sometimes confuse my words. I'm not at all a bluenose, though. And I only seem to forget the laws when I'm with you. I do prefer to speak French. It's a much easier language, you see."

It all fell into place in Lyon's head. He'd solved the puzzle. "No wonder I had difficulty understanding you, Christina. It's because you've just learned our language, isn't that so?"

He was so happy he'd reasoned it all out, he'd just repeated his statement.

Christina shook her head. "I don't think so, Lyon. No one else seems to have the least bit of trouble understanding me. Have you been speaking English long?"

He hugged her again and laughed over the outrageous way she'd just turned the tables on him. In the corner of his mind was the thought that he could be content standing in the center of her salon holding her for the rest of the morning.

"Lyon? Would it make you unhappy if I really was a bluestocking? Aunt says it's not at all fashionable to even admit to reading. For that reason I must also pretend to be uninformed."

"Must also pretend?" Lyon asked, homing in on that odd remark.

"I really do like to read," Christina confessed, ignoring his question. "My favorite is the story of your King Arthur. Have you read it, by chance?"

"Yes, love, I have. Sir Thomas Mallory wrote it," Lyon said. "Now I know where you get your fantasies. Knights, warriors—both are the same. You have a very romantic nature, Christina."

"I do?" Christina asked, smiling. "That's good to know," she added when Lyon nodded. "Being romantic is a nice quality for a gentle lady to have, isn't it, Lyon?"

"Yes, it is," he drawled.

"Of course, we mustn't let Aunt Patricia know of this inclination, for it would surely—"

"Let me guess," Lyon interrupted. "It would displease her, right?"

"Yes, I fear it would. You'd better go home now. When you remember what it was you wanted to speak to me about, you may call again."

Lyon wasn't going anywhere. He told himself he couldn't take much more of her conversation, though. He decided to kiss her just to gain a moment's peace. Then he'd have her submissive enough to answer a few pertinent questions, providing of course that he could remember what those questions were. He'd already gained quite a bit of information about her. Christina had obviously been raised in France, or in a French-speaking neighborhood. Now he wanted to find out why she guarded that simple truth so ferociously. Was she ashamed, embarrassed? Perhaps the war was the reason for her reticence.

Lyon caressed her back to distract her from dismissing him again. Then he leaned down and tenderly nuzzled her lips while his hands continued to stroke her, gentle her. Christina moved into his embrace again. Her hands slowly found their way up around his neck.

She obviously liked the distraction. When Lyon finally quit teasing her and claimed her mouth completely, she was leaning up on her tiptoes. Her fingers threaded through his hair, sending a shudder through him. Lyon lifted her off the floor, bringing her mouth level with his own.

It was a strange sensation to be held in such a way, though not nearly as strange as the way Lyon was affecting her senses. His scent drove her wild. It was so masculine, so earthy. Desire swept through her in waves of heat when Lyon's tongue slid inside her mouth to deepen the intimacy.

It didn't take Christina any time at all to become as bold as Lyon was. Her tongue mated with his, timidly at first, and then with growing ardor. She knew he liked her boldness, for his mouth slanted almost savagely over hers and she could hear his groan of pleasure.

Christina was the most responsive woman Lyon had ever encountered. Her wild enthusiasm stunned him. He was a man conditioned to the game of innocence most women played. Christina, however, was refreshingly honest with her desire. She aroused him quickly, too. Lyon was actually shaking when he dragged his mouth away. His breath was choppy, uneven.

She didn't want to let go of him. Christina wrapped her arms around his waist and gave him a suprisingly strong hug. "You do like kissing me, don't you, Lyon?"

How could she dare to sound timid now, after the way she'd just kissed him? Hell, her tongue had been wilder than his. "You know damn well I like kissing you," he growled against her ear. "Is this part of the charade, Christina? You needn't be coy with me. I honestly don't care how many men you've taken to your bed. I still want you."

Christina slowly lifted her gaze to stare into his eyes. She could see the passion there, the possessiveness. Her throat was suddenly so constricted she could barely speak. Lyon was being just as forceful as a warrior.

God help her, she could easily fall in love with the Englishman.

Lyon reacted to the fear in her eyes. He assumed she was frightened because he'd guessed the truth. He captured a handful of her hair, twisted it around his fist, and then pulled her back up against his chest until her breasts were flattened against him. Then he gently forced her head further back. He leaned down, and when his mouth was just a breath away he said, "It doesn't matter to me. I give you this promise, Christina. When you're in my bed, you won't be thinking about anyone but me."

He kissed her again, sealing his vow. The kiss was unashamedly erotic. Ravenous. Entirely too short-lived. Just when she began to respond, Lyon pulled away.

His gaze immediately captured her full attention. "All I've been able to think about is how good we're going to be together. You've thought about it, too, haven't you, Christina?" Lyon asked, his voice husky with arousal.

He was already prepared for her denial. He was expecting the ordinary. That was his mistake, he realized, and certainly the reason he was so stunned when she answered him. "Oh, yes, I have thought about mating with you. It would be wonderful, wouldn't it?"

Before he could reply, Christina moved out of his arms.

She slowly walked across the room. Her stride was every bit as sassy as the smile she gave him over her shoulder when she tossed her hair behind her. When she'd opened the doors to the foyer, she turned back to him. "You have to go home now, Lyon. Good day."

It was happening again. Damn if she wasn't dismissing him. "Christina," Lyon growled, "come back here. I'm not finished with you yet. I want to ask you something."

"Ask me what?" Christina responded, edging out of the room.

"Quit looking so suspicious," Lyon muttered. He folded his arms across his chest and frowned at her. "First I would like to ask you if you'd like to go to the opera next—"

Christina stopped him by shaking her head. "The Countess would forbid your escort."

She had the audacity to smile over her denial. Lyon sighed in reaction.

"You're like a chameleon, do you know that? One second you're frowning and the next you're smiling. Do you think you'll ever make sense to me?" Lyon asked.

"I believe you've just insulted me."

"I have not insulted you," Lyon muttered, ignoring the amusement he heard in her voice. Lord, she was giving him such an innocent look now. It was enough to set his teeth grinding. "You're deliberately trying to make me daft, aren't you?"

"If you think calling me a lizard will win my affections, you're sadly mistaken."

He ignored that comment. "Will you go riding with me in the park tomorrow?"

"Oh, I don't ride."

"You don't?" he asked. "Have you never learned? I'd be happy to offer you instruction, Christina. With a gentle mount . . . *now* what have I said? You dare to laugh?"

Christina struggled to contain her amusement. "Oh, I'm not laughing at you," she lied. "I just don't like to ride."

"Why is that?" Lyon asked.

"The saddle is too much of a distraction," Christina confessed. She turned and hurried across the foyer. Lyon rushed after her, but Christina was already halfway up the steps before he'd reached the bannister.

"The saddle is a distraction?" he called after her, certain he hadn't heard her correctly.

"Yes, Lyon."

God's truth, he didn't have an easy argument for that ridiculous statement.

He gave up. Christina had just won this battle.

The war, however, was still to be decided.

Lyon stood there, shaking his head. He decided to be content watching the gentle sway of her hips, and it wasn't until she was out of sight that he suddenly realized what it was that had bothered him when he first saw her.

Princess Christina was barefoot.

The Countess Patricia was in high spirits when she returned home from her appointment. Calling upon a possible suitor for her niece had been an improper undertaking, yes, but the outcome had been so satisfying, the Countess snickered away any worry of being found out.

Emmett Splickler was everything the Countess had hoped he'd be. She'd prayed Emmett had inherited his father's nasty disposition. Patricia hadn't been disappointed. Emmett was a spineless halfwit, pint-sized in stature and greed. Very like his father, Emmett's crotch controlled his mind. His lust to bed Christina was soon obvious. Why, the man positively drooled when the Countess explained the reason for her visit. From the moment she'd mentioned marriage to Christina, the stupid man became jelly in her hands. He agreed to sign over anything and everything in order to get his prize.

The Countess knew Christina wasn't going to take to Emmett. The man was too much of a weakling. To placate her niece, Patricia had made a list of possible candidates. She'd even put the odious Marquess of Lyonwood at the top of the lines. It was all a farce, of course, but the Countess wanted Christina docile and unsuspecting for what was to come.

The Countess wasn't about to leave anything to chance.

Under no circumstances would she allow her niece to wed someone as honorable as Lyon.

The reason was very simple. Patricia didn't want just a substantial portion of her father's estate. She meant to have it all.

The plan she laid out for Splickler was shameful, even by a serpent's measure. Emmett had blanched when she calmly told him he'd have to kidnap her niece, haul her off to Gretna Green, and force her to marry him there. He could or could not rape the girl before or after the marriage certificate was signed. It made no matter to the Countess.

Emmett was more frightened of being found out than she was. When she told him to include two or three other men to help restrain Christina, the stupid man quit his complaining and grasped the plan wholeheartedly. She'd noticed the bulge grow between his legs, knew his mind had returned to the picture of bedding her niece, assumed then he'd be desperate enough to do what was required.

The worries exhausted the Countess. There was always the remote possibility that Emmett's cowardice was greater than his lust to bed Christina. The plan could fail if there was any interference.

For that reason, Patricia knew she was going to have to get rid of Christina's filthy Indian family. If her niece didn't marry Emmett, and she ended up with someone as strong-willed as Lyon, the union couldn't possibly last long. Christina's upbringing was bound to come out sooner or later. She wouldn't be able to hide her savage instincts forever. And what normal husband would put up with her disgusting ideas about love and honor? He'd be horrified by her true nature, of course. Though it wouldn't be possible for him to set her aside, for divorce was an unheard-of undertaking, he certainly would turn his back on her and turn to another woman for his needs.

Such rejection might well send Christina scurrying back to the savages who'd raised her. The stupid chit still insisted on returning home. The Countess couldn't let that happen. Christina had become her means of getting back into the ton. Even those who remembered her past indiscretions were so taken with Christina that they forced themselves to include the Countess again.

Last of all her worries was Edward. Christina's father wasn't going to take it kindly that she'd outwitted him. As goodnatured as she remembered him to be, Edward would probably still try to get his hands on a share of the fortune. Christina would certainly be able to control her father, the Countess believed.

Oh, yes, it was imperative that the little bitch remain in England until the Countess was finished with her. Imperative indeed.

Chapter Six

Edward kept his private quarters in a separate building adjacent to the main wing of the palace. I decided not to wait to tell him what his men were doing. You see, child, I couldn't believe my husband was responsible. I wanted to place the blame on his officers.

When I entered Edward's office by the side door, I was too stunned by what I saw to make my presence known. My husband was with his lover. They'd shed their clothes and were cavorting like animals on the floor. His mistress's name was Nicolle. She rode Edward like a stallion. My husband was shouting crude words of encouragement, his eyes tightly closed in ecstasy.

The woman must have sensed my presence. She suddenly turned her head to look at me. I was sure she'd cry out my presence to Edward. She didn't. No, Nicolle continued her obscene gyrations, but she was smiling at me all the while. I thought it was a smile of victory.

I don't remember how long I stood there. When I returned to my own rooms, I began to plan my escape.

Journal entry
August 20, 1795

Lyon, whatever is the matter with you? Why, you actually smiled at Matthews. Didn't I hear you ask after his mother, too? You aren't feeling well, are you?"

The questions were issued by Lyon's sister, Lady Diana, who was now chasing her brother up the stairs to the bedrooms.

Lyon paused to turn back to Diana. "You aren't happy when I'm frowning, and now you seem upset because I'm smiling. Make up your mind on the matter of my disposition and I shall try to accommodate you."

Diana's eyes widened over the teasing tone in her brother's voice. "You are sick, aren't you? Is your knee paining you again? Don't look at me as though I've grown another head. It isn't at all usual for you to smile, especially when you come to visit Mama. I know how tiring she can be. Remember, brother, I live with her. You only have to visit her once a week. I know Mama can't help the way she is, but there are times I wish you'd let me move into your townhouse. Is that shameful of me to admit?"

"Being honest with your brother is not shameful. You've had a time of it since James died, haven't you?"

The sympathy in Lyon's voice made Diana's eyes fill with tears. Lyon hid his exasperation. His sister was such an emotional whirlwind when it came to matters of family. Lyon was quite the opposite. It was difficult for him to show outward affection. He briefly considered putting his arm around his sister's shoulders to offer her sympathy, then pushed the awkward notion aside. She'd probably be so astonished by the gesture she'd break down into full-blown weeping.

Lyon wasn't up to tears today. It was quite enough he was going to endure another god-awful visit with his mother.

"I really thought Mama was going to get better when you made her servants open her townhouse for my season, Lyon, but she hasn't left her room since the day we arrived in London."

He merely nodded, then continued toward his destination. "Mama isn't the least bit better," Diana whispered. She trailed behind her brother's shadow. "I try to talk to her about the parties I've attended. She doesn't listen, though. She only wants to talk about James."

"Go back downstairs and wait for me, Diana. There's something I wish to discuss with you. And quit looking so worried," he added with a wink. "I promise I won't upset our mother. I'll be on my best behavior."

"You will?" Diana's voice squeaked. "You aren't feeling well, are you?"

Lyon started laughing. "God, have I really been such an ogre?"

Before Diana could think of a tactful answer that wouldn't be an outright lie, Lyon opened the door to his mother's quarters. He used the heel of his boot to close the door, then proceeded across the dark, stuffy room.

The Marchioness was reclining on top of her black satin covers. She was, as usual, dressed in black, from the silk cap covering her gray hair to the cotton stockings covering her feet. Lyon wouldn't have been able to find her if it weren't for her pasty white complexion glaring out from the shroud of black.

It was a fact that the Marchioness mourned with true dedication. Lyon thought she took to the task with as much intensity as a spoiled child took to tantrums. God only knew the woman had done it long enough to have become a master.

It was enough to make a dead man sit up and take notice. James had been gone for over three years now, but his mother continued to act as though the freakish accident had just taken place the day before.

"Good afternoon, Mother." Lyon gave his standard greeting, then sat down in the chair adjacent to the bed.

"Good afternoon, Lyon."

The visit was now over. They wouldn't speak again until Lyon took his leave. The reason was simple. Lyon refused to talk about James, and his mother refused to talk about any other topic. The silence would be maintained during the half hour Lyon stayed. To pass the time, he struck light to the candles and read *The Morning Herald.*

The ritual never varied.

He was usually in a foul mood when the ordeal was over. Today, however, he wasn't too irritated by his mother's shameful behavior.

Diana was waiting in the foyer. When she saw the smile was still on her brother's face, her worry about his health intensified. Why, he was acting so strangely!

Her mind leapt from one horrid conclusion to another. "You're going to send Mama and me back to the country, aren't you, Lyon? Oh, please, do reconsider," Diana wailed. "I know Uncle Milton has been a disappointment, but he can't help being bedridden with his liver again. And I do so want to go to Creston's ball."

"Diana, I shall be honored to take you to Creston's bash. And I never considered sending you home, sweet. You've had your presentation, and you'll certainly have the rest of the season. Have I ever gone back on my word?"

"Well . . . no," Diana admitted. "But you've never smiled this much either. Oh, I don't know what to think. You're always in a terrible mood after you've seen Mama. Was she more agreeable today, Lyon?"

"No," Lyon said. "And that's what I wanted to discuss with you, Diana. You need someone here to show you the way to go around. Since Milton isn't able and his wife won't go anywhere without him, I've decided to send for Aunt Harriett. Does that meet with your—"

"Oh, yes, Lyon," Diana interrupted. She clasped her hands together. "You know how much I love Father's sister. She has such a wonderful sense of humor. Will she agree, Lyon?"

"Of course," Lyon answered. "I'll send for her immediately. Now then, I'd like a favor."

"Anything, Lyon. I'll—"

"Send a note to Princess Christina inviting her here for tea. Make it for the day after tomorrow."

Diana broke into giggles. "Now I understand your strange behavior. You're smitten with the Princess, aren't you?"

"Smitten? What a stupid word," Lyon answered. His voice sounded with irritation. "No, I'm not smitten."

"I shall be pleased to invite the Princess. I can't help but wonder why you don't just send a note requesting an audience, though."

"Christina's aunt doesn't find me suitable," Lyon announced.

"The Marquess of Lyonwood isn't suitable?" Diana looked horrified. "Lyon, you have more titles than most men in England. You can't be serious."

"By the way, don't tell Christina I'll be here. Let her think it will be just the two of you."

"What if she requests that I come to her home instead?"

"She won't," Lyon advised.

"You seem very certain."

"I don't think she has enough money to entertain," Lyon said. "Keep this a secret, Diana, but I believe the Princess is in dire financial straits. The townhouse is a bit shabby—so are the furnishings—and I've heard the Countess had denied everyone who has requested entrance."

"Oh, the poor dear," Diana announced, shaking her head. "But why don't you want her to know you'll be here?"

"Never mind."

"I see," Diana said.

Lyon could tell from her expression she didn't see at all.

"I do like the Princess," Diana gushed when Lyon glared at her.

"You didn't come away confused?"

"I don't understand," Diana said. "Whatever do you mean?"

"When you spoke to her," Lyon explained. "Did she make sense with her answers?"

"Well, of course she made sense."

Lyon hid his exasperation. It had been a foolish question to put to someone as scatterbrained as his little sister. Diana's disposition had always been as flighty as the wind. He loved her, yet knew he'd go to his grave without having any understanding of what went on inside her mind. "I imagine you two will become fast friends," Lyon predicted.

"Would that upset you?"

"Of course not," Lyon answered. He gave Diana a curt nod, then started out the door.

"Well, why are you frowning again?" Diana called after him.

Lyon didn't bother to answer his sister. He mounted his black steed and went riding in the countryside. The brisk exercise was just what he needed to clear his mind. He was usually able to dispatch all unnecessary information and target in on the pertinent facts. Once he'd thrown out the insignificant, he was certain he'd be able to figure out his attraction to the most unusual woman in all of England. He was going to use cold reason to come to terms with his unreasonable affliction.

And it was an affliction, Lyon decided. To let Christina affect his every thought, his every action, was simply unacceptable. Confusing, too.

As confusing as being told he made her as nervous as a buffalo.

And where in God's name had she seen buffaloes?

The Earl of Rhone paced the carpet in front of his desk. His library was in shambles, but Rhone wouldn't let any of the servants inside to clean. Since being wounded, he'd been in too much discomfort to think about such mundane matters as household chores.

The injury was healing. Rhone had poured hot water over the opening, then wrapped his wrist in clean white gauze. Even though he wore an oversized jacket from his father's closet so that he could conceal the bandage, he was determined to stay hidden inside his townhouse until the wound was completely healed. He wasn't about to take any chances of being found out. There was too much work still to be done.

Rhone's primary concern was Princess Christina. He thought she might have recognized him. The way she'd stared at him and the funny, surprised look on her face did suggest she had known who was behind the mask.

Did Lyon know? Rhone mulled over that worry a long

while, then concluded his friend had been too occupied with protecting the little Princess to take a good look at him.

And just who in God's name had thrown the knife at him? Why, he'd been so surprised, he'd dropped his pistol. Whoever it was had a lousy aim, Rhone decided, and he'd thank God for that small blessing. Damn, he could have been killed.

He was going to have to be more careful. Rhone had no intention of quitting his activity. There were four names on his list, and every one of them was going to be tormented. It was the least he could do to ease his father's humiliation.

A servant's hesitant knock on the door broke Rhone's pacing. "Yes?" he bellowed, letting his irritation carry through the door. He had specifically ordered his staff not to interrupt him.

"The Marquess of Lyonwood is here to see you, my lord."

Rhone rushed over to take his seat behind the desk. He rested his good arm on a stack of papers, hid his injured hand in his lap, then called out in a surly voice, "Send him in."

Lyon strolled into the room with a bottle of brandy tucked under his arm. He placed the gift on the desk, then sat down in a leather chair in front of Rhone. After casually propping his feet on the desktop, he said, "You look like hell."

Rhone shrugged. "You never were a diplomat," he remarked. "What's the brandy for?"

"Our wager," Lyon reminded him.

"Oh, yes. Princess Christina," Rhone grinned. "She never did answer any of your questions, did she?"

"It doesn't matter. I've already found out quite enough about her. She was raised somewhere in France, or thereabouts," he stated. "There are a few little nagging inconsistences, but I'll have them worked out in short time."

"Why the interest, Lyon?"

"I'm not sure anymore. In the beginning I thought it was just curiosity, but now—"

"In the beginning. Lyon, you sound as though you'd known the woman for months."

Lyon shrugged. He reached over to the sideboard, extracted two glasses, and poured each of them a drink. Lyon waited until Rhone was in the process of swallowing a hefty portion before asking his question. "How's the hand, Jack?"

Needless to say, Lyon was immensely satisfied with his friend's reaction. Rhone started choking and coughing and trying to effect a denial all at the same time. It was laughable. Damning, too, Lyon thought with a sigh.

He waited until his friend had regained some control before speaking again. "Why didn't you tell me you were in such financial trouble? Why didn't you come to me?"

"Financial trouble? I don't know what you're talking about," Rhone protested. It was a weak lie. "Hell," he muttered. "It's always been impossible to lie to you."

"Have you lost your mind? Do you have a passion to live in Newgate prison, Rhone? You know it's only a matter of time before you're found out."

"Lyon, let me explain," Rhone stammered. "My father has lost everything. I've used my own estates, put them up as promise against the rest of the notes, but . . ."

"You and your father are free of debt as of yesterday eve," Lyon said. "Get angry and then get over it, Rhone," Lyon demanded, his voice edged with steel. "I paid off the moneylenders. In your name, by the way."

"How dare you involve—" Rhone bellowed. His face was flushed a bright red.

"Someone sure as hell had to intervene," Lyon announced. "Your father means as much to me as he does to you, Rhone. God only knows the number of times he put himself in front of my father to protect me when I was young."

Rhone nodded. Some of the fight went out of him. "I'll pay you back, Lyon, just as soon—"

"You will not pay me back," Lyon roared. He was suddenly furious with his friend. He took a deep, settling breath before continuing. "Do you remember what I was like when Lettie died?" he asked.

Rhone was surprised by the change in topic. He slowly nodded. "I remember."

"You stood by me then, Rhone. You're the only one who

knows about James. Have I ever asked to pay you back for your friendship?"

"Of course not. I would have been insulted."

A long moment stretched between the two men. Then Rhone actually grinned. "May I at least tell my father that you—"

"No," Lyon interrupted, his voice soft. "I don't want him to realize I know what happened to him. Let him think his son is the only one who knows, that you came to his assistance."

"But Lyon, surely—"

"Let it rest, Rhone. Your father is a proud man. Don't take that away from him."

Rhone nodded again. "Tell me what you know about my father's problems."

"I recognized you at Baker's, of course," Lyon began, smiling over the start that statement gave his friend. "It was foolish of you to—"

"You weren't supposed to be there," Rhone muttered. "Why did you attend his party? You can't stand Baker any more than I can."

Lyon chuckled. "The most carefully laid plans," he drawled. "For all his good points, your father is still a little naive, isn't he, Rhone? Baker and his cohorts took advantage, of course. Baker would have been the one to set up the games. Let's see if I have this straight. He would have included Buckley, Stanton, and Wellingham in the farce, too. They're all bastards. Did I get all the names, Rhone?"

His friend was astonished. "How did you learn all this?"

"Do you honestly think I wouldn't know about their little club? Your father isn't the only one to fall victim to their scheme."

"Does everyone know?"

"No," Lyon answered. "There isn't a hint of a scandal about your father. I would have heard of it."

"You've been out of circulation, Lyon. How can you be so sure?"

Lyon gave Rhone a look of exasperation. "With my line of work, you can seriously ask me that question?"

Rhone grinned. "I thought you might have gotten a little rusty," he said. "Father is still hiding in his country home. He's so ashamed of his own gullibility he won't show his face. He'll be relieved to learn no one is the wiser."

"Yes, he can come out of hiding now. And you can give up this foolish plan of yours. You'll eventually get caught."

"You'd never turn me in." Rhone's voice was filled with conviction.

"No, I wouldn't," Lyon acknowledged. "How was it done, Rhone? Did Baker mark the cards?"

"Yes. They are all blatant cheats, which of course is all the more humiliating for my father. He's feeling duped."

"He *was* duped," Lyon said. "Will you give it up, Rhone?"

Rhone let out a harsh groan. "Damn it all, Lyon. I'm itching to get even."

Lyon took a drink of his brandy. "Ah," he drawled. "Now you've touched on my area of expertise. Perhaps, Rhone, a game of chance is what is needed."

Lyon grinned when Rhone finally caught his meaning. "You mean to give them a dose of their own medicine, to cheat the cheaters?"

"It would be easy enough to accomplish."

Rhone slapped his hand on the tabletop, then let out a groan. "I keep forgetting about this injury," he excused. "Count me in, Lyon. I'll leave the details to you. As you just admitted, you're better versed in trickery than I am."

Lyon laughed. "I'll take that as a compliment."

Another knock sounded at the door, interrupting their conversation. "Now what is it?" Rhone shouted.

"I'm sorry to disturb you, my lord, but Princess Christina is here to see you," the servant shouted back.

The announcement gave Rhone a start. Lyon didn't look too happy with the news either. He glared at Rhone. "Have you been after Christina, Rhone? Did you invite her here?"

"No," Rhone answered. "My charms must have impressed her after all, Lyon." He grinned when Lyon's scowl increased. "So it is as I guessed. You're more than mildly interested in our little Princess."

"She isn't our little Princess," Lyon snapped. "She belongs to me. Understood?"

Rhone nodded. "I was only jesting," he said with a sigh. "Send her in," he bellowed to his servant.

Lyon didn't move from his position. Christina hurried into the library as soon as the door was opened for her. She spotted Lyon immediately and came to an abrupt stop. "Oh, I didn't mean to interrupt your conference, sir. I shall come back later, Rhone."

Christina frowned at Lyon, turned, and started back out the door.

Lyon let out a long, controlled sigh. He carefully put his glass down on the desk, then stood up. Christina saw him out of the corner of her eye. She ignored Rhone's pleas for her to stay and continued to move toward the front door.

Lyon trapped her just as she reached for the handle. His hands settled on the door on either side of Christina's face. Her back touched his chest. Lyon smiled when he saw how rigid her shoulders became. "I really must insist you stay," he whispered against her ear.

A tremor of warmth shook Christina. She slowly edged around until she was facing Lyon. "And I really must insist upon leaving, sir," she whispered.

She pushed one hand against his chest, hoping to dislodge him.

He didn't budge. He gave her a rascal's grin, then leaned down and kissed her.

Rhone's deep chuckle interrupted his desire to continue.

Christina immediately blushed over the intimacy. Didn't the man realize he wasn't supposed to show affection in front of others? She guessed he didn't. Lyon winked at her before grabbing hold of her hand and dragging her back inside the library.

She was wearing a light blue gown. Lyon deliberately checked to see if she'd remembered to put her shoes on. He wasn't disappointed to see she had.

Rhone hurried back to his chair. He hid his bandaged arm in his lap.

Christina refused to sit down. She stood beside Lyon,

trying to ignore him altogether. He put his booted feet back up on the edge of Rhone's desk and reached for his glass. She gave him a disgruntled look. If the man was any more relaxed, he'd fall asleep.

It soon became awkward. Rhone was looking at her expectantly. Christina clutched the blue receptacle in her left hand and kept trying to pull her other hand out of Lyon's hold. He'd forgotten to let go of her.

"Was there something in particular you wished to speak to me about?" Rhone prodded gently. He tried to put Christina at ease. The poor woman looked terribly worried.

"I'd hoped to find you alone," Christina announced. She gave Lyon a meaningful look. "Were you about to take your leave, Lyon?"

"No."

His abrupt answer was given in such a cheerful voice, Christina smiled. "I would like to speak to Rhone in private, if you don't mind."

"Ah, sweet, but I do mind," Lyon drawled out. He increased his grip on her hand, then suddenly jerked her off balance.

She landed right where he wanted her. Christina immediately started to struggle out of his lap. Lyon circled her waist with one arm, anchoring her to him.

Rhone was amazed. He'd never seen Lyon act in such a spontaneous manner. To show such open possessiveness was certainly out of character. "Princess Christina? You may speak freely in front of Lyon," Rhone advised.

"I may?" Christina asked. "Then he knows?"

When Christina hesitated, Rhone announced, "Lyon is privy to all my secrets, my dear. Now what is it you wanted to say to me?"

"Well, I was wondering, sir, how you're feeling."

Rhone blinked several times. "Why, I'm feeling very well," he replied awkwardly. "That is all you wanted to ask me?"

The two of them were dancing around the real issue, to Lyon's way of thinking. "Rhone, Christina wants to know how your injury is doing. Isn't that right, Christina?"

"Oh, then you do know?" Christina asked, turning to look at Lyon.

"*You* know?" Rhone's voice cracked.

"She knows," Lyon confirmed, chuckling over the flabbergasted look on Rhone's face.

"Well, hell, who *doesn't* know?"

"You sound pathetic," Lyon told his friend.

"It was the color of your eyes, Rhone," Christina explained, giving him her attention again. "They're an unusual shade of green, and very easy to remember." She paused to give him a sympathetic look. "And you did look right at me. I really didn't mean to recognize you. It just happened," she ended with a delicate shrug.

"Are we putting all our cards on the table?" Rhone asked, leaning forward to give Christina an intent look.

"I don't understand," Christina said. "I don't have any cards with me."

"Christina takes everything you say in its literal sense, Rhone. It's a trait guaranteed to make you daft. Believe me, I know."

"That is most uncharitable of you, Lyon," Christina announced, glaring at him. "I don't know what you mean when you say I'm literal. Is it yet another insult I should take exception to, perchance?"

"Rhone is asking you if he may speak freely," Lyon told Christina. "Hell, I feel like an interpreter."

"Of course you may speak freely to me," Christina announced. "No one's holding a knife to your neck, Rhone. I've some medicine with me. I'd like to tend your injury, Rhone. You probably haven't had proper care."

"I couldn't very well call upon my physician, now could I?" Rhone said.

"Oh, no, you'd be found out," Christina said. She scooted off Lyon's lap and went to Rhone's side. Rhone didn't protest when she began to unwrap his badly fashioned bandage.

Both men watched as Christina opened a small jar of horrid-smelling salve. "My God, what's in there? Dead leaves?"

"Yes," Christina answered. "Among other things."

"I was jesting," Rhone said.

"I wasn't."

"The smell will keep me hidden," Rhone muttered. "What else is in there?" he asked, taking another sniff of the foul medicine.

"You don't want to know," Christina answered.

"It's best not to ask Christina questions, Rhone. The answers will only confuse you."

Rhone took Lyon's advice. He watched Christina pat a large amount of the brown-colored salve on the cut, then rewrap the arm. "You have a nice scent, Rhone. Of course, the salve will soon remove it."

"I have a nice scent?" Rhone looked as though he'd just been handed England's crown. He thought he should return her compliment. "You smell like flowers," he told her, then promptly laughed over saying such a thing. It was the truth, but certainly ungentlemanly of him to comment upon. "You're the one with the unusual eyes, Christina. They're the most wonderful color of blue."

"That's quite enough," Lyon interjected. "Christina, hurry up and finish your task."

"Why?" Christina asked.

"He doesn't want you standing so close to me," Rhone explained.

"Give it up, Rhone." Lyon's voice had turned hard. "You aren't going to pursue Christina, so you can save your charms for someone else."

"Lady Diana would like your charms very much, Rhone," Christina interjected. She smiled at the reaction her comment caused in both men. Rhone looked perplexed. Lyon looked appalled. "Lyon, you don't own me. It is therefore unreasonable of you to dictate to other gentlemen. If I wanted Rhone's attention, I would let him know it."

"Why do you suggest Lyon's sister would like my attention?" Rhone asked. He was highly curious about her strange remark.

Christina replaced the jar in her receptacle before answering. "You English are so narrow-minded in your thinking sometimes. It's obvious Lady Diana is taken with you, Rhone. You only have to look at her to see the adoration in her eyes. And if you count the way you look after her, why, you'd realize you were meant for each other."

"Oh, God." It was Lyon who groaned out the words.

Both Christina and Rhone ignored him. "How can you be so certain?" Rhone asked. "You only met her once, and you couldn't have spent more than fifteen minutes with her. No, I think you're imagining this infatuation. Diana's just a child, Christina."

"Believe what you will," Christina answered. "What will happen will happen."

"I beg your pardon?"

Rhone looked confused again. Lyon shook his head. It was good to know he wasn't the only one dimwitted around Christina. "Destiny, Rhone," Lyon interjected.

"I really must leave now. Aunt Patricia believes I'm resting in my room," she confessed. "You will have to share my confidence, Rhone. Or should I call you Jack now?"

"No."

"I was only jesting, sir. Do not be so distressed," Christina said.

Rhone sighed. He reached out to take hold of Christina's hand, thinking to keep her by his side while he thanked her properly for tending his injury.

Christina moved so quickly Rhone was left reaching for air. Before he could blink, she was standing next to Lyon's chair again.

Lyon was just as surprised. He was arrogantly pleased, too, for even though Christina probably wasn't aware of what she'd done, she had instinctively moved back to him. There was some kind of little victory in that choice, wasn't there?

"Christina, if you recognized me, why didn't you tell Baker and the others?" Rhone asked.

She took exception to his question. "They'll have to find out on their own," she said. "I would never break a confidence, Rhone."

"But I didn't ask you to keep this confidence," Rhone stammered.

"Don't try to understand her, Rhone. It will be your undoing," Lyon advised with a grin.

"Then please answer me this," Rhone asked. "Did you see who threw the knife at me?"

"No, Rhone. In truth, I was too frightened to look behind me. If Lyon hadn't been there to protect me, I think I would have swooned."

Lyon patted her hand. "The pistol wasn't loaded," Rhone protested. "Did you think I'd actually hurt someone?"

Lyon prayed for patience. "I cannot believe you set out to rob Baker with an empty pistol."

"Why would you use an empty weapon?" Christina asked.

"I wanted to scare them, not kill them," Rhone muttered. "Will you two quit looking at me like that? The plan did work, I might remind you."

"You just did remind us," Christina announced.

"Lyon, will you be able to find out who injured me?" Rhone asked.

"Eventually."

Christina frowned. Lyon sounded too certain. "Why does it matter?"

"Lyon likes a good puzzle," Rhone announced. "As I recall, Baker's balcony is a good fifty feet from the terrace below. Whoever it was had to be—"

"Twenty feet, Rhone," Lyon interjected. "And the balcony couldn't be scaled. The railing was too weak."

"Then whoever it was must have been hiding behind you . . . somewhere," Rhone said with a shrug. "No, that doesn't make sense. Well, thank God he had a lousy aim."

"Why do you say that?" Christina asked.

"Because he didn't kill me."

"Oh, I think his aim was quite on target," she announced. "If he'd wanted to kill you, I think he might have. Perhaps he meant to make you drop your weapon."

Christina suddenly realized she was sounding too sure of herself. Lyon was staring at her with a strange, intent expression on his face. "It was just a possibility I was giving you," she added quickly. "I could be wrong, of course. His aim could have been faulty."

"Why did you come over here to tend Rhone's injury?" Lyon asked.

"Yes, why did you?" Rhone asked also.

"Now I am insulted," Christina announced. "You were hurt, and I only thought to help you."

"That was your only motive?" Lyon asked.

"Well, there was another reason as well," Christina admitted. She walked over to the door before explaining. "Didn't you tell me you were Lyon's only friend?"

"I might have made that remark," Rhone admitted.

"You did," Christina said. "I never forget anything," she boasted. "And it seemed to me that Lyon is a man in need of friends. I shall continue to keep your secret, Rhone, and you must promise not to tell anyone I came to see you. The Countess would be upset."

"He doesn't suit either?" Lyon asked, sounding vastly amused.

"I don't suit?" Rhone asked. "Suit what?"

Christina ignored the question and started out the doorway.

"Christina."

Lyon's soft voice stopped her. "Yes, Lyon?"

"I didn't promise."

"You didn't?"

"No."

"Oh, but you'd never . . . you don't even like the Countess. You wouldn't bother to tell her . . ."

"I'm seeing you home, love."

"I'm not your love."

"Yes, you are."

"I really prefer to walk."

"Rhone, what do you think the Countess will say when I inform her that her niece is strolling around town, paying calls on—"

"You don't fight with an ounce of dignity, Lyon. It's a sorry trait."

"I've never fought fair."

Her sigh of defeat echoed throughout the library. "I shall wait for you in the hall, you despicable man." Christina slammed the door shut to emphasize her irritation.

"She isn't at all what she appears to be," Rhone remarked. "She called us English, Lyon, as if we were foreigners. Doesn't make sense, does it?"

"Nothing Christina says makes sense, unless you remember she wasn't raised here." He stood up, stretched to his full height, and started for the door. "Enjoy the brandy, Rhone, while I go back into battle."

"Battle? What are you talking about?"

"Not what, Rhone. Who. Christina, to be exact."

Rhone's laughter followed Lyon out the door. Christina was standing next to the front door. Her arms were folded across her chest. She wasn't trying to hide her irritation.

"Ready, Christina?"

"No. I hate carriages, Lyon. Please let me walk home. It's only a few short streets away from here."

"Of course you hate carriages," Lyon said. His voice was filled with amusement. "Now, why didn't I realize that sooner, I wonder?" he asked as he took hold of her elbow. He half led, half dragged Christina to his vehicle. Once they were seated across from each other, Lyon asked, "Are carriages as much a distraction as saddles, perchance?"

"Oh, no," Christina answered. "I don't like being confined like this. It's suffocating. You weren't going to tell the Countess I left without permission, were you, Lyon?"

"No," he admitted. "Are you afraid of the Countess, Christina?"

"I'm not afraid of her," Christina said. "It's just that she is my only family now, and I don't like to upset her."

"Were you born in France, Christina?" Lyon asked. He leaned forward to take hold of her hands.

His voice coached, his smile soothed. Christina wasn't fooled for a moment. She knew he thought to catch her off guard. "When your mind is set on finding something out, you really don't give up, do you, Lyon?"

"That's about right, my dear."

"You're shameful," Christina confessed. "Quit smiling. I've insulted you, haven't I?"

"Were you born in France?"

"Yes," she lied. "Now, are you satisfied? Will you quit your endless questions, please?"

"Why does it bother you to be questioned about your past?" Lyon asked.

"I merely try to protect my privacy," she answered.

"Did you live with your mother?"

He was like a dog after a meaty bone, Christina decided. And he wasn't going to let up. It was time to soothe his curiosity. "A very kind couple by the name of Summerton raised me. They were English but enjoyed traveling. I've been all over the world, Lyon. Mr. Summerton preferred to speak French, and I'm more comfortable with that language."

The tension slowly ebbed away from her shoulders. She could tell by Lyon's sympathetic expression that he believed her. "The Countess can be difficult, as you well know. She had a falling out with the Summertons and refuses to let me speak of them. She wants everyone to think I was raised by her, I suppose. Lying is very difficult for me," she added with a straight face. "Since Aunt Patricia won't let me tell the truth, and I'm not any good telling lies, I decided it would be best to say nothing at all about my past. There, are you satisfied?"

Lyon leaned back against the upholstery. He nodded, obviously satisfied with her confession. "How did you meet up with these Summertons?"

"They were dear friends of my mother," Christina said. She gave him another smile. "When I turned two years of age, my mother took ill. She gave me to the Summertons because she trusted them, you see. My mother didn't want her sister, the Countess, to become my guardian. And the Summertons weren't able to have children."

"Your mother was a shrewd woman," Lyon remarked. "The old bat would have ruined you, Christina."

"Oh, my, did Elbert call my aunt an old bat in front of

you? I really must have another firm talk with him. He seems to have taken an extreme dislike to her."

"Love, everyone dislikes your aunt."

"Are you finished with your questions now?" Christina asked.

"Where did you hear the sound of lions, Christina, and where did you see buffaloes?"

The man had the memory of a child given the promise of candy. He didn't forget anything. "I did spend a good deal of time in France, because of Mr. Summerton's work, but he was very devoted to his wife—and to me, for he did think of me as his daughter. And so he took both of us with him when he went on his trips. Lyon, I really don't want to answer any more of your questions."

"Just one more, Christina. Will you let me escort you to Creston's ball on Saturday? It will be very proper. Diana will be with us."

"You know my aunt won't allow it," Christina protested.

The carriage came to a halt in front of Christina's home. Lyon opened the door, dismounted, and turned to lift Christina to the ground. He held her a bit longer than necessary, but Christina didn't take exception. "Simply tell your aunt that arrangements have already been made. I'll call for you at nine."

"I do suppose it will be all right. Aunt Patricia need never know. She's going to the country to visit a sick friend. If I don't mention the ball, I really won't have to lie. It isn't quite the same if the Countess believes I mean to stay home, is it? Or is it still a lie by deliberate silence, I wonder."

Lyon smiled. "You really do have trouble telling a lie, don't you, sweet? It is a noble trait," he added.

Heaven help her, she really mustn't laugh. Lyon would certainly grow suspicious then. "Yes, it is difficult for me," she confessed.

"You don't know how it pleases me to find a woman with such high standards, Christina."

"Thank you, Lyon. May I put a question to you now?"

Elbert opened the door just then. Christina became

distracted. She smiled at the butler, then waved him inside. "I shall see the door closed, Elbert. Thank you."

Lyon patiently waited until Christina turned back to him. "Your question?" he gently prodded.

"Oh, yes," Christina said. "First of all, I would like to ask you if you will be attending Sir Hunt's party Thursday evening."

"Are you going?"

"Yes."

"Then I shall be there."

"There is one more question, please."

"Yes?" Lyon asked, smiling. Christina was acting terribly shy all of a sudden. A faint blush covered her cheeks, and she couldn't quite meet his gaze.

"Will you marry me, Lyon? For just a little while?"

"What?"

He really hadn't meant to shout, but the woman did say the damnedest things. He couldn't have heard her correctly. Marriage? For just a while? No, he had misunderstood. "What did you say?" he asked again, calming his voice.

"Will you marry me? Think about it, Lyon, and do let me know. Good day, sir."

The door closed before the Marquess of Lyonwood could summon a reaction.

Chapter Seven

It took over three weeks before Mylala was able to find a captain willing to take the risk of helping us escape. I don't know what I would have done without my loyal maid. She put her family and her friends in jeopardy to aid me. I listened to her advice, for she had been in my husband's household for several years and knew his ways.

I had to act as though nothing had changed. Yes, I played the loving wife, but every night I prayed for Edward's death. Mylala suggested that I not take any possessions with me. When the call came for me to go, I would simply walk away with only the clothes on my back.

Two nights before word came from the captain, I went to see Edward in his quarters. I entered by the side door again, very quietly, as a precaution against finding Nicolle with him again. Edward was alone. He was sitting at his desk, holding a large, sparkling sapphire in his hands. On the desk top were over twenty other gems. Edward was fondling them in much the same way he fondled Nicolle. I stood there, in the shadows, watching him. The madman actually spoke to the jewels. After another few minutes, he wrapped the gems in a cloth and put them back in a small black lacquered box.

There was a false panel built into the wall. Edward slid the box into the dark crevice.

I went back to my rooms and related what I'd seen to my maid. She told me she'd heard a rumor that the treasury was barren. We came to the conclusion that the revolution was closer to reality than we'd believed. My husband had converted the coins into jewels, for they would be much easier to carry with him when he left his country.

I vowed to steal the jewels. I wanted to hurt Edward in any way that I could. Mylala cautioned me against such a plan, but I was past caring. The jewels belonged to the people. I promised myself that one day I'd find a way to give the jewels back.

God, I was so noble, but so very, very naive. I really thought I would get away with it.

Journal entry
September 1, 1795

The early morning hours belonged to Christina. It was a peaceful, quiet time of day, for the Countess rarely made an appearance or a demand before noon. Christina's aunt preferred to take her morning meal of biscuits and tea in bed, and only broke that ritual when an important visitation couldn't be rescheduled.

Christina was usually dressed and finished with her duties before the full light of dawn warmed the city. She and her aunt shared a lady's maid between them, but Beatrice had quite enough to do filling the Countess's orders. For that reason, Christina took care of her clothes and her bedroom. In truth, she was happy with the arrangement. She didn't have to keep up a pretense when she was alone in her room. Since Beatrice rarely interrupted her, Christina didn't have to wrinkle the covers on her bed every morning to give the appearance she'd actually slept there.

Once she bolted the door against intruders, she could let

her defenses slide. Every night she carried her blanket across the room to sleep on the floor in front of the double windows.

She didn't have to be strong when she was alone. She could cry, just as long as she was quiet about it. It was a weakness to shed tears, yet since no one was there to witness her distress, Christina felt little shame.

The tiny garden hidden behind the kitchens was Christina's other private domain. She usually spent most of the morning hours there. She blocked out the noise of the city and the stench of discarded garbage, slipped off her shoes, and wiggled her toes in the rich brown dirt. When the droplets of dew had been snatched away by the sun, Christina would return to the erupting chaos inside the house.

The precious reunion with the sun helped her endure the rest of the day. She could usually worry through any perplexing problem in such a tranquil setting too. However, since meeting the Marquess of Lyonwood, Christina hadn't been able to concentrate on much of anything. Her every thought belonged to him.

She'd been attracted to him from the moment of their meeting. When Sir Reynolds had called him Lyon, she'd been nudged into awareness. Then she'd looked up into his eyes, and her heart had been captured. The vulnerability she'd seen there, in his dark gaze, had made her want to reach out to him.

He was a man in need of attention. Christina thought he might be just as lonely as she was. She didn't understand why she'd come away with that impression, however. Lyon was surrounded by his family, embraced by the ton, envied, and somewhat feared. Yes, the ton bowed to him because of his title and his wealth. They were superficial reasons, to Christina's way of viewing matters, but Lyon had been raised in such a fashion.

He was different, though. She'd noticed he didn't bend to any of their laws. No, Lyon seemed determined to make his own.

Christina knew it hadn't been proper to ask him to marry her. According to the laws, it was the man's place to offer for his woman, not the other way around. She'd given the matter considerable thought, then reached the decision that she'd simply have to break this one law in order to be wed before her father returned to England.

Still, her timing might not have been perfect. She knew she'd stunned him with her hastily blurted question. The astonished look on his face worried her. She couldn't make up her mind if he was getting ready to shout with laughter or explode with anger.

Once he'd gotten over his initial reaction, however, Christina was certain he'd say yes. Why, he'd already admitted how much he liked being with her, how much he liked touching her. Life in this strange country would be so much more bearable with Lyon by her side.

And it would only be for a little while . . . he wouldn't have to be saddled with her forever, as the Countess liked to say.

Besides, she told herself, he really wouldn't be given a choice, would he?

She was the lioness of the Dakota. Lyon simply had to marry her.

It was his destiny.

Thursday evening didn't arrive soon enough to suit the Marquess of Lyonwood. By the time he entered Sir Hunt's townhouse, he was fighting mad.

Lyon had alternated between absolute fury and total disappointment whenever he thought about Christina's outrageous proposal. Well, he sure as hell had her game now, didn't he? She was after marriage, all right—marriage and money, just like every other woman in the kingdom.

He was just as angry with himself. His instincts had certainly been sleeping. He should have known what she was up to from the very beginning. God's truth, he'd done exactly what he accused Rhone of doing—he'd fallen victim to a pretty face and a clever flirtation.

Lyon was disgusted enough to want to bellow. And he was

going to set Christina straight at the first opportunity. He wasn't about to get married again. Once had been enough. Oh, he meant to have Christina, but on his terms, and certainly without benefit of clergy to muck up the waters. All women changed once wedded. Experience had taught him that much.

It was unfortunate that the first person he ran into when he entered Hunt's salon was his sister, Diana. She spotted him immediately, picked up her skirts, and charged over to curtsy in front of him.

Hell, he was going to have to be civil.

"Lyon, thank you for asking Sir Reynolds to escort me. He is such a kind man. Aunt Harriett will be arriving Monday next, and you won't have to be bothered with the duty any longer. Do you like my new gown?" she asked, straightening the folds of her yellow skirt.

"You look very pretty," Lyon announced, barely giving her a glance.

There was such a crowd, Lyon was having difficulty finding Christina. Though he was much taller than the other guests, he still hadn't been able to spot the golden crown of curls he was looking for.

"Green is a nice color for me, isn't it, Lyon?"

"Yes."

Diana laughed, drawing Lyon's attention. "My gown is yellow, Lyon. I knew you weren't paying me the least notice."

"I'm in no mood for games, Diana. Go and circulate through the crush like a good girl."

"She isn't here, Lyon."

"She isn't?" Lyon asked, sounding distracted.

Diana's giggles increased. "Princess Christina hasn't arrived yet. I had the most wonderful visit with her yesterday."

"Where did you see her?" Lyon asked. His voice was a bit sharper than he intended.

Diana didn't take exception. "For tea. Mother didn't join us, of course. Neither did you, by the way. Did you actually forget you asked me to invite her, Lyon?"

Lyon shook his head. "I decided against intruding," he lied. He really had forgotten the appointment, but he placed the blame for his ill discipline on Christina's shoulders. Since receiving her proposal of marriage, he hadn't been able to think about anything else.

Diana gave her brother a puzzled look. "It isn't like you to forget anything," she announced. When he didn't comment on that fact, she said, "Well, I was happy to have the time alone with her. Princess Christina is a fascinating woman. Do you believe in destiny, Lyon?"

"Oh, God."

"You needn't groan," Diana chided.

"I do not believe in destiny."

"Now you're shouting. Lyon, everyone is giving us worried looks. Do force a smile. I believe in destiny."

"Of course you do."

"Now why would that displease you?" Diana asked. She continued on before her brother could form an answer. "The princess makes such refreshing observations about people. She never says anything unkind, either. She's such a delicate, dainty woman. Why, I feel very protective around her. She's so gentle, so—"

"Was the old bat with her?" Lyon interrupted impatiently. He wasn't in the mood to hear about Christina's qualities. No, he was still too angry with her.

"I beg your pardon?" Diana asked.

"The Countess," Lyon explained. "Did she join you?"

Diana tried not to laugh. "No, she wasn't with Christina. I made an unkind remark about her aunt, though of course I didn't call her an old bat, and my comment was quite by accident. Christina was very gracious when she told me it was impolite to speak of the elderly in such a fashion. I was humbled by her gentle rebuke, Lyon, and then found myself telling her all about Mama and how she still grieves for our James."

"Family matters shouldn't be discussed with outsiders," Lyon said. "I really would appreciate it if you'd—"

"She says it's all your fault about Mama being—"

"What?" Lyon asked.

"Please let me finish before you sanction me," Diana advised. "Christina said the strangest thing. Yes, she did."

"Of course she did," Lyon returned with a long sigh.

Lord, it was contagious. One afternoon with Princess Christina had turned Diana completely senseless.

"I didn't understand what she meant, but she did say—rather firmly, too—that it was all your fault, and that it was up to you to direct Mama into returning to her family. Those were her very words."

Diana could tell by Lyon's expression he was just as puzzled as she was. "I tell you, Lyon, it was as though she was repeating a rule from her memory. I didn't want her to think me unschooled, so I didn't question her further. But I didn't understand what she was telling me. Princess Christina acted like her advice made perfect sense. . . ."

"Nothing the woman says or does makes any sense," Lyon announced. "Diana, go back to Sir Reynolds's side. He'll introduce you around. I've still to speak to our host."

"Lady Cecille is here, Lyon," Diana whispered. "You can't miss her. She's dressed in bright, shameful red."

"Shameful red?" Lyon grinned over the absurd description.

"You aren't still involved with the woman, are you, Lyon? Princess Christina would surely be put off if she thought you were seeing a woman of such stained reputation."

"No, I'm not involved with Cecille," Lyon muttered. "And how did you find out—"

"I listen to the rumors, just like everyone else," Diana admitted with a blush. "I'll leave you to your grumpy mood, Lyon. You may lecture me later." She started to turn away from him, then paused. "Lyon? Is Rhone going to be here tonight?"

He caught the eagerness in her voice. "It shouldn't matter to you if Rhone shows up or not, Diana. He's too old for you."

"Old? Lyon, he's your age exactly, and you're only nine years my senior."

"Don't argue with me, Diana."

She dared to frown at her brother before giving in to his advice. When Diana finally left him alone, Lyon leaned against the bannister in the foyer, waiting for Christina.

His host found him and dragged him across the salon and into a heated debate about government issues. Lyon patiently listened, though he kept glancing toward the entrance.

Christina finally arrived. She walked into the salon, flanked by their hostess and the Countess, just as Lady Cecille touched Lyon's arm.

"Darling, it is wonderful to see you again."

Lyon felt like growling. He slowly turned around to acknowledge his former mistress.

What in God's name had he ever seen in the woman? The difference between Cecille and Christina was stunning. Lyon felt like taking a step back.

Cecille was a tall woman, somewhat stately, and terribly vulgar. She wore her dark brown hair piled high atop her head. Her cheeks were tinged with pink paint, as were her full, pouting lips.

Christina never pouted. She didn't pretend coyness either, Lyon decided. His disgust with Cecille was a sour taste in his mouth. Cecille was trying to be provocative now. She deliberately lowered her eyelashes to half mast. "I've sent you notes asking you to call, Lyon," she whispered as she increased her hold on his arm. "It's been such an unbearably long while since we shared a night together. I've missed you."

Lyon was thankful the men he was speaking to had walked away. He slowly removed Cecille's hand. "We've had this discussion, Cecille. It's over. Accept it and find someone else."

Cecille ignored the harshness in Lyon's voice. "I don't believe you, Lyon. It was good between us. You're only being stubborn."

Lyon dismissed Cecille from his mind. He didn't want to waste his anger on her. No, he told himself, he was saving all of it for Princess Christina. He turned to find the woman he sought to reject and spotted her immediately. She was standing next to their host, smiling sweetly up at him. She looked entirely too pretty tonight. Her gown was the color of blue ice. The neckline was low-cut, showing a generous amount of her full, creamy-looking bosom. The gown wasn't as indecently fashioned as Cecille's, but Lyon still didn't like it. Hunt was giving Christina's chest lecherous looks. Lyon thought he just might kill him.

There were too many dandies at the party, too. Lyon looked around the room, glaring at all the men openly coveting his Christina. He knew he wasn't making any sense. He wasn't going to marry Christina, but he wasn't willing to let anyone else have her, either. No, he wasn't making any sense at all. It was Christina's fault, of course. The woman had made him crazy.

Cecille stood beside Lyon, watching him. It didn't take her long to realize he was mesmerized by the Princess. Cecille was irritated. She wasn't about to let anyone compete for Lyon's attention. No one was going to interfere with her plan to marry him. Lyon was a stubborn man, but Cecille was certain enough of her own considerable charms to believe she'd eventually get her way. She always did. Yes, Lyon would come around, provided she didn't prod too obviously.

From the way Lyon kept his gaze directed on the beautiful woman, Cecille knew she'd better act quickly. The little Princess could cause trouble. Cecille made up her mind to have a talk with the chit as soon as possible.

She had to wait a good hour before she gained a proper introduction. During that time she heard several comments about Lyon's preoccupation with the woman. There was actual speculation that Lyon was going to offer for her. Cecille turned from irritated to incensed. It was obviously far more serious than she'd first guessed.

She waited for her opportunity. When Christina finally stood alone, Cecille nudged her arm and begged for a private audience in their host's library to discuss an issue of high importance.

The innocent little Princess looked confused by her request. Cecille smiled as sweetly as she could manage. She felt like gloating. In just a few minutes she'd have the silly girl terrified enough to do anything she suggested.

The library was located in the back of the main floor. They entered the chamber from the hallway.

Three high-backed chairs were angled in front of a long desk. Christina sat down, folded her arms in her lap, and smiled up at Lady Cecille expectantly.

Cecille didn't sit down. She wanted the advantage of towering over her adversary.

"What is it you wish to say to me?" Christina asked, her voice soft.

"The Marquess of Lyonwood," Cecille announced. The sweetness was missing from her voice now. "Lyon belongs to me, Princess. Leave him alone."

Lyon had just opened the side door to the library in time to overhear Cecille's demand. It wasn't by accident that he happened upon the conversation, nor was it coincidence he'd chosen to go around to the door connecting the kitchens to the study. Lyon remembered from past meetings with Sir Hunt that there were two doors leading to the library. And he'd kept his attention on Christina since the minute she'd entered the townhouse. When Cecille had taken hold of Christina's arm and led her down the hallway, Lyon was right behind her.

Neither Christina nor Cecille noticed him. Lyon knew it was bad form to listen in on their private conversation, yet he believed his motives were pure enough. He knew what Cecille was capable of. She could make mutton out of a gentle little lamb. Gentle Christina wasn't up to handling anyone as cunning, as vicious as Cecille. Lyon only wanted to protect Christina. The beautiful woman was simply too naive for her own good.

"Has Lyon offered for you, then?" Christina suddenly asked.

"No," Cecille snapped out. "Don't give me that innocent look, Princess. You know he hasn't offered for me yet. But he will," she added with a sneer. "We're intimate friends. Do you know what that means? He comes to my bed almost every night. Do you get my meaning?" she asked in a malicious voice.

"Oh, yes," Christina answered. "You're his paramour."

Cecille gasped. She folded her arms across her chest and glared down at her prey. "I'm going to marry him."

"No, I don't think you are, Lady Cecille," Christina answered. "Was that all you wanted to say to me? And you really don't have to raise your voice. My hearing is sound."

"You still don't understand, do you? You're either stupid or a real bitch, do you know that? I'm going to ruin you if you get in my way," Cecille announced.

Lyon was puzzled. He'd thought to intervene the moment Cecille started her insults, but the look on Christina's face kept him from moving.

Christina seemed to be totally unaffected by the discussion. She actually smiled up at Cecille, then asked in an extremely casual voice, "How could you ruin me?"

"I'll make up stories about you. It won't matter if they're true or not. Yes," Cecille rushed on, "I'll tell everyone you've slept with several men. Your reputation will be in tatters when I'm done with you. Give Lyon up, Christina. He'd tire of you soon anyway. Your looks are nothing in comparison to mine. Lyon will always come back to me. My beauty captivates him. You will immediately let him know you aren't interested in him. Then ignore him completely. Otherwise—"

"Say what you will," Christina said. "I don't care what your people think of me."

Cecille was infuriated by the amusement in Christina's voice. "You are a stupid woman," she shouted.

"Please don't get so bothered, Lady Cecille. It's upsetting your complexion. Why, your face is full of splotches."

"You . . . you . . ." Cecille paused to take a deep, calming breath. "You're lying. You have to care what others think. And your aunt will certainly care, I can promise you that. She can't be as ignorant as you are. Ah, I see I've finally gotten your attention. Yes, the Countess will be ruined by the scandal I'm going to weave."

Christina straightened in her chair. She frowned up at Cecille. "Are you saying your made-up stories will upset my aunt?"

"God, you really are a simple one, aren't you? Of course she'll be upset. When I'm finished, she won't be able to show her face in public. Just you wait and see."

Cecille could smell victory. She turned her back on Christina to circle the chair as she began to detail the vile lies she would spread.

Lyon had heard enough. He turned to pull the door wide open, determined to walk into the library and end Cecille's terror tactics at once.

It was time to protect his angel from the serpent.

She must have moved with incredible speed. Lyon had only taken his gaze off Christina for a second or two, but when he glanced back, the scene he witnessed so astonished him that he couldn't move.

He had trouble believing what he was seeing. Christina had Cecille pinned up against the wall. His former mistress wasn't making a sound of protest over the violation. She couldn't. Christina's left hand was anchored around the woman's neck, holding her in place. From the way Cecille's eyes were beginning to bulge, Lyon thought Christina just might be strangling her to death.

Cecille outweighed Christina by a good twenty pounds. She was much taller, too, yet Christina acted as though she was holding up a trinket for closer observation.

The little angel Lyon wanted to protect used only one hand to secure Cecille. She held a dagger in her other hand. The tip of the blade rested against Cecille's cheek.

The victim had just turned victor.

Christina slowly increased her hold on Cecille's neck, then let her see the tip of her knife. "Do you know what my people do to vain, deceitful women?" she asked in a soft whisper. "They carve marks all over their faces, Cecille."

Cecille started whimpering. Christina pricked her skin

with the tip of the knife. A drop of blood appeared on her cheek. Christina nodded with satisfaction. She had Lady Cecille's full attention now. The woman looked terrified. "If you tell one lie, I'll hear about it. Then I'm going to hunt you down, Cecille. There isn't a rock large enough for you to crawl under, nor enough men in England to see to your protection. I'll come to you during the night, when you're sleeping. And when you open your eyes, you'll see this blade again. Oh, yes, I'll get to you, I promise. And when I do," Christina added, pausing to dramatically drag the flat of her blade across the woman's face, "I'm going to cut your skin into ribbons. Do you understand me?"

Christina let up on her hold only long enough for Cecille to gulp air and nod. Then she squeezed her up against the wall again. "The Countess is my family. No one upsets her. And no one is going to believe you if you think to tell them I just threatened you. Now get out of here and go home. Though it is unkind of me to say so, you really do look a fright."

With those words of dismissal, Christina moved away from the disgusting woman.

Lady Cecille didn't possess an ounce of dignity. She was weeping all over her gown. She had obviously believed every word of Christina's threats.

Lord, she was a silly woman. Christina had difficulty maintaining her stern expression. She wanted to laugh. She couldn't, of course, and she kept her gaze locked on the terrified woman a long moment before she took pity on her. Lady Cecille couldn't seem to move. "You may leave now," Christina announced.

Cecille nodded. She slowly backed away from Christina until she reached the exit. Her hands shook when she lifted her skirt all the way up to her knobby knees, then she flung the door wide and ran with enough speed to suggest she thought demons were chasing her.

Christina let out a long, weary sigh. She replaced the dagger in the sheath above her ankle, straightened the folds of her gown, then daintily patted her hair into place. "Such a silly woman," she whispered to herself before walking out of the room.

Lyon had to sit down. He waited until Christina was out of sight before he went over to Hunt's desk and leaned against it. He tried to pour himself a drink of his host's whiskey from the cart to the side of the desk, but he quickly discarded that idea. God help him, he was laughing too hard to get the deed done.

So much for his conclusion that Christina was just like every other woman. She certainly wasn't raised in France, either. Lyon shook his head. She gave the appearance of being helpless . . . or had he drawn that conclusion on his own, he wondered. It was an easy mistake to make, he realized. Christina was so feminine, so dainty, so damned innocent-looking . . . and she wore a knife strapped to her leg.

It was identical to the knife he'd held in his hands the night of Baker's party, the knife that had wounded Rhone. What a cunning little liar she was. Lyon remembered how he'd turned to see who'd thrown the weapon. Christina had looked so frightened. Hell, the woman had turned around to look behind her, too. She'd gone right along with his thought that someone lurked behind them in the shadows. Then, when he was locked in conversation with the gentlemen, she'd quietly snatched her weapon back.

Lyon's instincts were wide awake now. His temper began to simmer, too. Hadn't she told him the night of the robbery she was so frightened she thought she might swoon?

No wonder she'd gone to Rhone to take care of his injury. Guilt, Lyon decided.

He wasn't laughing now. Lyon thought he just might throttle the woman.

"Has trouble telling a lie, does she?" he muttered to himself. Oh, yes, she'd looked him right in the eye when she told him that story. It was very difficult for her . . . yes, she'd said that, too.

He *was* going to throttle her. But first he was going to have a long talk with her . . . his little warrior had a large amount of explaining to do.

Lyon slammed his empty glass down on the tray and went in search of Christina.

"Are you enjoying yourself?"

Christina visibly jumped. She whirled around to confront Lyon. "Where did you just come from?" she asked, sounding highly suspicious. She glanced around him to look at the library door.

Lyon knew exactly what she was thinking. She looked worried. He forced himself to look calm. "In the library."

"No, I just came from the library, Lyon. You couldn't have been in there," she announced, shaking her head.

He almost said that he wasn't the one who lied, then caught himself. "Oh, but I was in the library, my sweet."

His announcement gave her a start. "Was there anyone else in there?" she asked, trying to sound only mildly curious.

Lyon knew she was testing him.

"I mean to ask, sir, that is, did you happen to notice if anyone else was in the library?"

He took his sweet time nodding. Christina decided he looked just like a mischievous devil. He was dressed like one, too. Lyon's formal attire was all of black, save for the white cravat, of course. The clothing fit him well. The man was too handsome for her peace of mind.

She was certain Lyon hadn't seen or heard anything. He was looking down at her with such a tender expression in his eyes. Christina felt safe enough. Lyon wasn't acting the least appalled. But why had he lied to her? Christina decided he must have seen her go inside the study with Lady Cecille. The poor man was probably worried that his paramour had told Christina something he didn't want repeated. Yes, she told herself, he was just prodding for information.

It was a plausible explanation. Still, one did need to be absolutely certain. Christina lowered her gaze to stare at his waistcoat. She forced a casual voice and asked, "You didn't perchance overlisten to my conversation with Lady Cecille, did you?"

"The word is eavesdropping, Christina, not overlistening."

His voice was strained. She thought he might be trying not to laugh at her. Christina didn't know if it was her question or her mispronunciation that had caused the change. She was too irritated with him for lying to her to take great exception, however. "Thank you, Lyon, for instructing me. Eavesdropping, yes, I do recall that word."

Lyon wouldn't have been surprised if she'd started wringing her hands. She was upset, all right, for she'd just spoken to him in French. He doubted she was even aware she'd slipped into the foreign language.

He decided to answer her in kind. "I am always happy to instruct you, love."

She didn't notice. "But you didn't eavesdrop, did you?"

"Why, Christina, what an unkind question to put to me. Of course not."

She tried not to let her relief show.

"And you know I'd never lie to you, my sweet. You've always been so open, so honest with me, haven't you?"

"Yes, I have," Christina returned, giving him a quick smile. "It is the only way to be with each other, Lyon. Surely you realize that."

Lyon clasped his hands behind his back so he wouldn't be able to give in to his urge to grab her by her throat. She seemed very relaxed with him now, very sure of herself. "Did you learn the value of honesty from the Summertons?" he asked.

"Who?"

His grip on his control intensified. "The Summertons," Lyon repeated, trying to control his anger. "Remember, love, the people who raised you?"

She couldn't quite look him in the eye when she answered him. He was such a good, trusting man. It was becoming a little bit of a strain to lie to him. "Yes, the Summertons did teach me to be honest in all endeavors," she announced. "I simply can't help myself. I'm not any good at fabrications."

He was going to strangle her.

"Did I hear you say you were in the study with Lady Cecille?"

Her guess had been right all along. Lyon was worried about the conversation. He had seen her go inside the library with Lady Cecille. Christina decided to put his fears to rest. "I was," she said. "Lady Cecille seems to be a dear woman, Lyon. She had some rather pleasing remarks to make about you."

No, he wasn't going to strangle her. He thought he'd beat her first. "I'm pleased to hear it," Lyon said. His voice was as smooth as a soft wind. The effort made his throat ache. "What exactly did she say?"

"Oh, this and that."

"What specific this and that?" Lyon insisted. His hands had moved to rest on Christina's shoulders, and it was all he could do not to shake the sincerity right out of her.

"Well, she did mention that we made a lovely couple," Christina said.

She was back to staring at his waistcoat again. While she appreciated the fact that the English tended to be somewhat naive, she was beginning to feel ashamed of herself for lying so blatantly to Lyon.

"Did she mention destiny, perchance?" Lyon asked.

She hadn't noticed the edge in his voice. "No, I don't recall Lady Cecille mentioning destiny. That does remind me, though, of my question. Have you given my proposal consideration?"

"I have."

"Lyon, why are you speaking French to me? We're in England, and you really should speak the language of your own people."

"It seemed appropriate," Lyon muttered.

"Oh," Christina said. She tried to shrug his hands away from her shoulders. They were still alone in the hallway, but there was always the chance someone could come along and see them. "Are you going to mate with . . . I mean, are you going to marry me?"

"Yes, I'm going to mate with you. As for marriage, I fear I will have to decline your proposal."

Christina wasn't given time to react to Lyon's announcement. Sir Reynolds called out, interrupting them. Lyon let go of her shoulders, then pulled her around and up against his side. He trapped her with one hand wrapped around her waist.

"Lyon, I've been looking all over this house for you. Do you approve of my taking your sister over to Kimble's do? We'd stay here until dinner hour is over, of course."

"Certainly," Lyon said. "And I appreciate your taking Diana under your wing, sir."

"Glad to do it," Reynolds said. "Good evening, Princess Christina. I trust you are well?"

"Yes, thank you," Christina answered. She tried to curtsy, but Lyon wouldn't let up on his hold. She settled on a smile instead. It was a puny half effort at best, for Lyon's answer had just settled in her mind.

Though she told herself it didn't matter, that she'd surely find someone else to marry, she knew she was lying to herself. It did matter. Lord, she felt close to weeping.

"My dear," Sir Reynolds said, addressing Christina, "I've agreed to see you home. Your aunt pleaded fatigue and has taken your carriage. She explained she was leaving for the countryside tomorrow. I was given to understand you won't be going with her."

"Yes, that is correct," Christina answered. "My aunt is going to visit a friend who has taken ill. She prefers that I stay in London. I will have to wait for another opportunity to see your lovely countryside."

"I forget you've only been here a very short while," Sir Reynolds said. "But you're surely not on your own for an entire week, are you? Do you wish me to lend my arm Saturday eve? You do intend to go to Creston's ball, of course. Or do you already have an escort?"

"I shall not be going," Christina interjected, her voice firm.

"Yes, you will," Lyon said. He squeezed her waist before adding, "You promised."

"I've changed my mind. Sir Reynolds, I'm also fatigued. I'd be pleased if you'd—"

"I'll take you home." Lyon's voice was hard with anger.

Sir Reynolds could feel the tension between the two. They'd obviously had a falling out, he decided. From the way Princess Christina was trying to get out of his embrace, and the determined way Lyon wasn't letting her, it was very apparent. Why, he could almost see the sparks between them.

Determined to douse the argument and aid Lyon at the same time, he asked him, "Are you sure you wish to see Princess Christina home?"

"Yes," Lyon snapped. "When must she get there, Reynolds? Did the Countess set the hour?"

"No, she assumed Christina would accompany your sister and me to Kimble's. You've at least two hours before the Countess takes notice," he added with a grin.

"Please don't discuss me as if I were not present," Christina said. "I really am tired now and would prefer—"

"That we leave immediately." Lyon finished the sentence for her, increasing his hold on her waist until she could barely catch her breath.

"Perhaps you might consider leaving by the back door," Sir Reynolds suggested in a conspiratorial whisper. "I shall make certain everyone believes Princess Christina left with her aunt, you see, and will of course offer your regrets to our host as well."

"A good idea," Lyon announced with a grin. "Of course, Reynolds, we must keep this deception between the three of us. Christina has such difficulty telling a lie. As long as she doesn't have to fabricate a story to her aunt, her honor will remain unblemished. Isn't that right, love?"

She gave him a good long frown. And she really wished he'd quit dragging up the issue of her honesty. It was making her terribly uncomfortable. Lyon looked sincere enough for her to believe he actually admired her.

It no longer signified what he thought, she told herself when Lyon started dragging her toward the back of the house. He'd just rejected her offer of marriage. No, it didn't matter what he thought of her anymore.

She wouldn't see him again after this evening. Heaven help her, her eyes were filling with tears. "You've just broken another law," she muttered into his back. She tried to sound angry instead of desolate. "My aunt will be outraged if she hears of this trickery."

"Speak English, sweetheart."

"What?"

Lyon didn't say another word until he had Christina settled inside his carriage. He sat down next to her, then stretched his long legs out in front of him.

The carriage was much bigger than the one Aunt Patricia had rented, and much more elegant in detail.

Christina still hated it. Large or small, elegant or not, it made no difference to her. "Don't you have any of those open carriages like the ones I've seen in Hyde Park, Lyon? And please quit trying to crush me. Do move over."

"Yes, I have an open carriage. It's called a phaeton. One doesn't use a phaeton after dark, however," he explained with exasperation. His patience was wearing thin. Lyon was itching to get the truth out of her, not discuss such mundane matters as carriages.

"One should," Christina muttered. "Oh, God, I shouldn't admit this to you, but I won't be seeing you again, so it really doesn't matter. I can't stand the darkness. May we open the drapes covering the windows, please? I can't seem to catch my breath."

The panic in her voice turned his attention. His anger quickly dissipated when he felt her tremble against his side.

Lyon immediately pulled the drapes back, then put his arm around her shoulders.

"I've just handed you a weapon to use against me, haven't I?"

He didn't know what she was talking about. The light filtering in through the windows was sufficient for him to see the fear in her eyes, though. He noticed that her hands were fisted in her lap.

"You really are frightened, aren't you?" he asked as he pulled her up against him.

Christina reacted to the gentleness in his voice. "It isn't really fear," she whispered. "I just get a tightness here, in my chest," she explained. She took hold of his hand and placed it against her heart. "Can you feel how my heart is pounding?"

He could have answered her if he'd been able to find his voice. The simple touch had sent his senses reeling.

"I'll try to take your mind off your worry, love," he whispered when he could speak again. He leaned down and kissed her. The intimacy was slow, languid, consuming, until Christina reached up to brush her fingertips across his cheek.

A shudder rushed through him. His heart was pounding now. "Do you know what a witch you are?" he asked when he pulled away. "Do you have any idea what I want to do to you, Christina?" His fingers slid just inside the top of her gown to gently caress her softness.

He whispered erotic, forbidden longings into her ear. "I can't wait much longer, my love. I want you under me. Naked. Begging. God, I want to be inside you. You want me just as much, don't you, Christina?"

He didn't wait for her answer but claimed her soft lips for another deep kiss. His mouth moved hungrily over hers, his tongue delving inside, deeper and deeper with each new penetration, until she was reaching for his tongue with her own whenever he deliberately withdrew.

Christina didn't know how it happened, but she suddenly realized she was sitting on his lap with her arms wrapped around his neck. "Lyon, you mustn't say such things to me." Her protest sounded like a ragged moan. "We cannot share the same blankets unless we're wed," she added before she cupped the sides of his face and kissed him again.

She forgot all about the closeness inside the carriage, forgot all her worries and his rejection of her proposal. His kisses were robbing her of all thoughts.

Her breasts ached for more of his touch. She moved, restlessly, erotically, against his arousal. Lyon trailed wet kisses down the side of her neck, pausing to tease her earlobe with his warm breath, his velvet tongue. His knuckles brushed against her nipples, once, twice, and then again, until a fever began to burn inside her.

She tried to stop him when he pushed the top of her gown down, exposing her breasts. "No, Lyon, we mustn't—"

"Let me, Christina," Lyon demanded, his voice harsh with need. His mouth found her breasts before she could protest again, and then she was too weak, too overwhelmed by what he was doing to her to protest at all.

"I love the taste of you," he whispered. "God, you're so soft." His tongue caressed the nipple of one breast while his hand stroked the other. Christina clung to him, her eyes tightly closed. A soft whimper escaped when he took the nipple into his mouth and began to suckle. An aching tightness made her move against Lyon again. He groaned, telling her how much pleasure her instinctive motion had given him.

Christina never wanted the sweet torture to end.

It was Lyon's driver who saved her from disgrace. His shout that they'd gained their destination penetrated her sensual haze. "Dear God, we are home!" Her announcement came out in a strained voice.

Lyon wasn't as quick to recover. It took a moment for her announcement to settle in his mind. His breathing was harsh, ragged. He leaned back against the cushion and took a deep breath while he fought to regain some semblance of control.

Christina had adjusted her gown to cover her breasts and moved to sit beside him. She dropped her hand on his thigh. Lyon reacted as though she'd just stabbed him. He pushed her hand away. "Are you angry with me?" she whispered.

His eyes were closed now. The muscle was flexing in the side of his cheek, though, and she thought he really was angry with her. She clasped her hands together in her lap, trying to stop herself from trembling. "Please don't be angry with me."

"Damn it, Christina. Give me a minute to calm down," Lyon snapped.

Christina bowed her head in shame. "I'm so sorry, Lyon. I didn't mean for our kisses to go so far, but you made me weak and I forgot all about stopping."

"It was my fault, not yours." Lyon muttered his round-about apology. He finally opened his eyes and glanced down at her. Hell, she looked so dejected. Lyon tried to put his arm around her again, but she scooted over into the corner. "Sweetheart, it's all right." He forced a smile when she looked up at him. "Do you want me to come inside with you?"

She shook her head. "No, the Countess is a light sleeper. She'd know," Christina whispered.

Lyon didn't want to leave her. Not yet . . . not like this. He was feeling extremely guilty because she was looking so ashamed. If she started to cry, he didn't know how he'd be able to comfort her.

"Hell," he muttered to himself. Every time he touched her he went a little crazy. If he tried to offer her solace, he'd probably make it worse.

Lyon threw open the door and helped Christina to the ground. "When will I see you again?" he asked her. They were in the midst of a struggle, and he wasn't certain she heard him. Christina was trying to push his hands away, and he was trying to hug her. "Christina, when will I see you again?"

She refused to answer him until he let go of her.

Lyon refused to let go of her until she answered him. "We'll stand here all night," he told her when she kept pushing against his shoulders.

Christina suddenly threw her arms around his neck and hugged him. "I blame myself, Lyon. It was wrong of me to ask you to marry with me. I was being very selfish."

Her words so surprised him, he let go of her. Christina kept her head bowed so he couldn't see her distress, yet was powerless to keep her voice from trembling. "Please forgive me."

"Let me explain," Lyon whispered. He tried to pull her

back into his arms. Christina evaded him again by taking a quick step back. "Marriage changes a person. It isn't a rejection of you, Christina, but I—"

She shook her head. "Do not say another word. You might have fallen in love with me, Lyon. When the time came for me to go home, you would have had a broken heart. It is better for me to choose someone else, someone I don't care about."

"Christina, you *are* home. You aren't going anywhere," Lyon said. "Why can't we go along the way we—"

"You're very like Rhone, do you know that?"

Her question confused him. Christina hurried up the steps to her townhouse. When she turned back to look at Lyon, he could see how upset she was. Tears streamed down her cheeks. "Your friend only steals jewels, Lyon. Your sin is greater. If I let you, you'd steal my heart. I cannot allow that to happen. Goodbye, Lyon. I must never see you again."

With those parting words, Christina went inside the house. The door closed softly behind her.

Lyon was left standing on the stoop. "The hell you will forget me," he bellowed.

Lyon was furious. He thought he had to be the most frustrated man in England. How in God's name had he ever allowed himself to get involved with such a confusing woman?

She'd had the audacity to tell him he might fall in love with her.

Lyon knew the truth. Heaven help him, he was already in love with her.

Needless to say, that admission didn't sit well. Lyon almost ripped the door off the carriage when he climbed back inside. He shouted the order to his driver to take him home, then began to list all the reasons he should stay away from Christina.

The woman was a blatant liar.

He despised liars.

God only knew how many hearts she'd broken.

Destiny . . . he decided he hated that word.

By the time he arrived home, he'd accepted the fact that none of his reasonable arguments made any difference. He was stuck with Christina whether he wanted to be or not.

Chapter Eight

Mylala wouldn't leave her homeland. She wouldn't leave her family. While I understood her reasons, I was afraid for her. She promised me she'd take every precaution. My maid planned to hide in the hills until Edward was unseated from power or fled the country. Her family would look after her. I gave her all my own treasury, though it was a pittance by England's standards. We wept together before we parted, like true sisters who knew they'd never see each other again.

Yes, she was my sister, in spirit and heart. I'd never had a confidant. My own sister, Patricia, could never be trusted. Be warned, child. If Patricia is still alive when you've grown up, and you meet up with her one day, protect yourself. Don't put your faith in her, Christina. My sister loves deception. She feeds on others' pain.

Do you know, she really should have married Edward. They would have been very compatible. They are so very much alike.

Journal entry
September 3, 1795

Lyon spent most of Friday afternoon sitting in the Bleak Bryan tavern, located in a particularly seedy section of the city. Lyon wasn't there to drink, of course, but to glean information from the captains and shipmates who favored the tavern.

He moved easily in and out of such a setting. Though dressed in quality buckskins and riding jacket, he didn't need to worry about being set upon. Lyon was always given a wide berth. Everyone in this area knew his reputation well. They feared him, yet respected him, and entered into conversation only when he motioned to them for an audience.

Lyon sat with his back against the wall. Bryan, a retired shipmate from the moment he lost his hand in a knife fight, sat beside him. Lyon had purchased the tavern and set Bryan up in business as a reward for past loyalty.

He questioned one man after another, refusing to become impatient when the hours stretched or the shipmates lied in order to get another free glass of ale. A newcomer strutted over to the table and demanded his share of the bounty. The big man lifted the seaman Lyon was questioning by his neck and carelessly threw him to the side.

Bryan smiled. He still enjoyed a good fight. "Have you never met the Marquess of Lyonwood, then?" he asked the stranger.

The seaman shook his head, took his seat, and then reached for the pitcher of ale. "Don't give a belch who he be," the man muttered menacingly. "I'm wanting my due."

Bryan's eyes sparkled with amusement. He turned to Lyon and said, "He's wanting his due."

Lyon shrugged. He knew what was expected of him. Every face in the tavern was looking at him. There were appearances to keep up, and if he wanted a peaceful afternoon, he'd have to take care of this little matter.

He waited until the seaman had put the pitcher back on the table, then slammed the heel of his boot into the man's groin.

It happened too quickly for the seaman to protect himself. Before he could scream in pain, Lyon had him by the throat. He squeezed hard, then flung the big man backwards.

The crowd roared their approval. Lyon ignored them. He tilted his chair back against the wall, never taking his gaze off the man writhing in agony on the floor.

"You got your due, you horse's arse. Now crawl on out of here. I run a respectable tavern," Bryan bellowed between bouts of laughter.

A thin, jittery man drew Lyon's attention then. "Sir, I hear you're wanting information about ships from the colonies," he stammered out.

"Take a seat, Mick," Bryan instructed. "He's a good, honest man, Lyon," Bryan continued, nodding at his friend.

Lyon waited while the seaman exchanged news with Bryan. He continued to watch the man he'd just injured until the door slammed shut behind him.

Then his thoughts returned to Christina and his mission.

Lyon had decided to start over. He was finished forming his own conclusions based on logical assumptions. Logic didn't work where Christina was concerned. He threw out all her explanations about her past. The only fact he knew to be truthful was that the Countess had returned to England approximately three months ago.

Someone had to remember the old bat. The woman was foul enough to have drawn attention to herself by complaining about something to someone. She wouldn't have been an appreciative passenger.

Mick, as it turned out, remembered the woman. Rather well. "Captain Curtiss weren't a fair man with me, sir. I would have chosen to slop the decks or empty the pots rather than fetch and carry for the Cummings woman. Gawd, she kept me legs running day and night."

"Was she traveling alone?" Lyon asked. He didn't let Mick know how excited he was to finally have real information, thinking the man might lace his answers in order to please him into giving him more ale.

"Of a sort," Mick announced.

"Of a sort? That don't make sense, Mick. Tell the man straight," Bryan advised.

"I mean to say, sir, she came on board with a gentleman and a pretty little lady. I only got a quick glance at the lovey, though. She wore a cape with the hood over her head, but before the Countess pushed her below deck she looked right at me and smiled. Yes, sir, she did."

"Did you happen to notice the color of her eyes?" Lyon asked.

"Blue they were, as blue as my ocean."

"Tell me what you remember about the man traveling with the Countess," Lyon instructed. He motioned for Bryan to refill Mick's glass.

"He weren't family," Mick explained after taking a swig of ale. "A missionary, he told some of the men. Sounded Frenchy to me, but he told us he lived in a wilderness past the colonies. He was going back to France to see his relatives. Even though he was French, I liked him. Because of the way he protected the little lass. He was old enough to be her father—treated her like he was, too. Since the Cummings woman stayed below most of the voyage, the missionary man would take the pretty for a stroll on the decks."

Mick paused to wipe his mouth with the back of his hand. "The old woman was a strange bird. She didn't have nothing to do with the other two. Even demanded to have an extra chain put on the inside of her door. Captain Curtiss tried to calm her fears by telling her none of us would touch her. Gawd almighty, we couldn't stomach to look at her, and why she'd be thinking we'd want to bother her didn't make a spit of sense. It took a while, sir, but some of us did finally figure out her scheme. She was bolting her door against the little miss. Yes, sir, she was. The missionary man was overheard telling the little lady not to feel sad 'cause her aunt was afraid of her. Don't that beat all?"

Lyon smiled at Mick. It was all the encouragement the seaman needed to continue. "She was such a sweet little thing. 'Course, she did throw Louie overboard. Flipped him right over her shoulder, she did. Couldn't believe it—no, sir, couldn't believe it. Louie had it coming, though. Why, he snuck up behind her and grabbed her. That's when I seen the color of her hair. Real light yellow. She'd always been wearing that hood, even in the heat of the afternoons. Must have been mighty uncomfortable."

"She threw a man overboard?" Bryan asked the question. He knew he shouldn't interfere in Lyon's questions, but he was too astonished by Mick's casually given remark to keep silent. "Enough about the hood, man, tell me more about this girl."

"Well, it were a good thing for Louie the wind weren't up. We fished him out of the water without too much backache. He left the miss alone after that surprise. Come to think on it, most o' the men did."

"When will Captain Curtiss be returning to London?" Lyon asked.

"Not for another month or two," Mick said. "Would you be wanting to speak to the missionary man, too?"

"I would," Lyon answered, keeping his expression impassive. He sounded almost bored.

"He's coming back to London real soon. He told us he was only going to stay in France a short while, then planned on giving the little miss a nice visit before going back to the colonies. He was real protective toward the girl. Worried about her, too. Don't blame him none. That old . . ."

"Bat?" Lyon supplied.

"Yes, she was an old bat," Mick said with a snicker.

"Do you remember the missionary's name, Mick? There's an extra pound for you if you can give me his name."

"It's right on the tip of me tongue," Mick said, frowning intently. "When it comes to me, I'll tell you, Bryan. You'll keep the coins safe for me, won't you?"

"Question some of your shipmates," Bryan suggested. "Surely one of them will recall the man's name."

Mick was in such a hurry to gain his reward, he immediately left the tavern to go search for his companions.

"Is this government business?" Bryan asked when they were once again alone.

"No," Lyon answered. "A personal concern."

"It's the lady, isn't it? Don't need to pretend with me, Lyon. I'd be interested in her, too, if I were young enough."

Lyon smiled. "You've never even seen her," he reminded his friend.

"Makes no matter. Mick said she was a slip of a girl with blue eyes and yellow hair. Sounds pretty enough for my tastes, but that isn't the true reason I'd chase after her skirts. Have you ever met Louie?"

"No."

"He's as big as I am, though he weighs a few stones more. Any lady who could toss him overboard has to be mighty interesting. Lord, I wish I'd been there to see it. Never could like Louie. There's a rank smell coming from him. His mind's as sour as his body. Damn, I wish I'd seen him hit the water."

Lyon spent a few more minutes exchanging bits of news with Bryan, then stood to take his leave. "You know where to find me, Bryan."

The tavern owner walked Lyon to the curb. "How's Rhone getting on?" he asked. "Up to his usual antics?"

"Afraid so," Lyon drawled. "That reminds me, Bryan. Would you have the back room ready for Friday after next? Rhone and I are setting up a card game. I'll give you the details later."

Bryan gave Lyon a speculative look. "Always trying to outguess me, aren't you, Bryan?" Lyon asked.

"My thoughts are always on my face," Bryan answered, with a grin. "It's why I'd never make it in your line of work," he added.

Bryan held the door of the carriage open for Lyon. He waited until the Marquess was about to close the door behind him before calling out his ritual farewell. "Guard your back, my friend." On the spur of the moment, he included another caution. "And your heart, Lyon. Don't let any pretties throw you overboard."

That suggestion had come a little too late, to Lyon's way of thinking. Christina had already caught him off guard. He'd vowed long ago not to get emotionally involved with another woman for as long as he lived. He was going to keep his relationships short and sweet.

So much for that vow, Lyon thought with a sigh. He couldn't guard his heart now. It already belonged to her.

His mind returned to the puzzle of Christina's bizarre remarks. He remembered she'd told him that his curiosity could get him killed. Was she lying or was she serious? Lyon couldn't decide.

Christina had been truthful when she announced she wasn't going to stay in London long, that she meant to return home. At least she looked like she was telling the truth.

He wasn't about to let her go anywhere. Christina was going to belong to him. But he wasn't taking any chances. If she did manage to get away from him, his job of hunting her down would be much easier if he knew exactly where her home was.

"She isn't going anywhere," Lyon muttered to himself. No, he wasn't going to let her out of his sight.

With a growl of new frustration, Lyon accepted the truth. There was only one way he could keep Christina by his side.

Hell, he was going to have to marry her.

"Where in God's name have you been? I've been sitting in your library for hours."

Rhone bellowed the question as soon as Lyon strode into the foyer of his townhouse. "I have messengers searching the town for you, Lyon."

"I wasn't aware I had to account to you, Rhone," Lyon answered. He threw off his jacket and walked into the study. "Shut the door, Rhone. What do you think you're doing? You shouldn't be out in public. Someone might notice the bandage. You took a needless chance. Your man would have found me soon enough."

"Well, where have you been? It's almost dark outside," Rhone muttered. He collapsed in the first available chair.

"You're beginning to sound like a nagging wife," Lyon said with a chuckle. "What's the problem? Is your father having more difficulties?"

"No, and you sure as hell won't be laughing when I tell you why I've been looking all over London for you. Better put your jacket back on, my friend. You've work to do."

The seriousness in Rhone's tone gained Lyon's complete attention. He leaned against the desk top, folded his arms across his chest, and said, "Explain yourself."

"It's Christina, Lyon. She's in trouble."

Lyon reacted as though he'd just been hit by lightning. He bounded away from the desk and had Rhone by his shoulders before his friend could take a new breath. "There's still plenty of time, Lyon. I was just worried you might have taken off for your country home. We've got until midnight before they come after her . . . for God's sake, man, unhand me."

Lyon immediately let Rhone fall back into his chair. "Who are they?" he demanded.

His expression had turned deadly. Rhone was immensely thankful Lyon was his friend and not his enemy. "Splickler and some men he hired."

Lyon gave Rhone a brisk nod, then walked back out into the foyer. He shouted for his carriage to be brought around front again.

Rhone followed Lyon out the front door. "Wouldn't your steed get you there quicker?"

"I'll need the carriage later."

"What for?"

"Splickler."

The way he'd said the bastard's name told Rhone all he needed or wanted to know. He waited until they were both settled inside the conveyance to give his full explanation. "One of my men—or rather one of Jack's men—was offered a sizable amount to help take Christina to Gretna Green. Splickler thinks to force a marriage, you see. I went to meet with my men to tell them there wasn't going to be another raid. One of them is a decent enough fellow—for a bandit—by the name of Ben. He told me he'd been asked by Splickler and agreed to go along. Ben thought it was a rather amusing way to make some easy money."

The look on Lyon's face was chilling.

"Splickler hired Ben and three others. I paid Ben so he'd pretend to be in on the scheme. He won't help Splickler, if we can count on his word."

"You're certain it's set for midnight?" Lyon asked.

"Yes," Rhone answered with a nod. "There's still plenty of time, Lyon." He let out a long sigh. "I do feel relieved you're going to take care of the matter," he admitted.

"Oh, yes, I'll take care of the matter."

Lyon's voice was whisper-soft. It sent a chill down Rhone's spine. "You know, Lyon, I always thought Splickler was a snake, but I didn't think he had enough rattle in him to do something this obscene. If anyone finds out about this plot of his, Christina's reputation might very well suffer."

"No one's going to find out. I'll see to it."

Rhone nodded again. "Could someone have put Splickler up to this, Lyon? The man isn't smart enough to make change."

"Oh, yes, someone put him up to it, all right. The Countess. I'd stake my life on it."

"Good God, Lyon, she's Christina's aunt. You can't believe—"

"I do believe it," Lyon muttered. "She left Christina all alone. A little too convenient, wouldn't you agree?"

"Do you have an extra pistol for me?" Rhone asked.

"Never use them."

"Why not?" Rhone asked, appalled.

"Too much noise," Lyon answered. "Besides, there are only four of them, if we can believe your friend's count."

"But there are five."

"Splickler doesn't count. He'll run at the first sign of trouble. I'll find him later."

"I don't doubt that," Rhone answered.

"Rhone, when we reach Christina's townhouse, I'll have my man take you home. I don't want my carriage sitting out front. Splickler would see it. We don't want him to change his plans. I'll have my driver return for me an hour after midnight."

"I insist on lending a hand," Rhone muttered.

"You've only got one good hand to lend," Lyon answered, smiling.

"How can you be so glib?"

"The word is controlled, Rhone. Controlled."

Lyon was out of the carriage giving fresh instructions to his driver before the vehicle had rocked to a full stop. "Damn it, Lyon. I could be of help," Rhone shouted.

"You'd be more of a hindrance than a help. Go home. I'll send word to you when it's over."

Lord, he acted so unaffected by what was taking place. Rhone knew better, though. He almost felt a little sorry for the stupid, greedy men who'd joined with Splickler. The poor fools were about to find out just how the Marquess of Lyonwood had earned his reputation.

Damn, he really hated to miss the action. "I'm sure as certain not going to," Rhone muttered to himself. He waited for his opportunity. When the carriage slowed to round the corner, Rhone jumped to the street. He landed on his knees, cursed himself for his clumsiness, then brushed himself off and started walking towards Christina's house.

Lyon was going to get his good hand whether he wanted it or not.

The Marquess was shaking mad. He knew he'd calm down as soon as he saw Christina and knew she was all right. She was taking her sweet time opening the door for him. His nerves were at the snapping point. Lyon was about to break the lock with one of the special tools he always carried with him for just such an eventuality when he heard the sound of chain being slipped from the bar.

Though he'd held his temper in front of Rhone, the minute Christina opened the door he exploded with anger. "What in God's name do you think you're doing opening the door with just a robe on? Hell, you didn't even find out who it was, Christina!"

Christina clutched the lapels of her robe together and backed out of Lyon's way. The man literally charged into the foyer like a crazed stallion.

"What are you doing here?" she asked.

"Why didn't Elbert answer the door?" Lyon demanded. He stared at the top of her head, knowing full well that the sight of her dressed in such scanty attire, with her hair unbound in lovely disarray, would make him lose his train of thought.

"Elbert's visiting his mother," Christina explained. "Lyon, isn't it terribly late to be paying a call?"

"His what?" Lyon's anger suddenly evaporated.

"His mama. And just why is that so amusing, I wonder?" she asked. "You're the lizard, Lyon. You shout at me, then turn to laughing in the blink of an eye."

"Chameleon, Christina, not lizard," Lyon instructed. "Elbert has to be at least eighty if he's a day. How can his mother still be alive?"

"Oh, I've met her, Lyon. She's a dear woman. Looks just like Elbert, too. Well, are you going to tell me why you're here?"

"Go upstairs and get dressed. I can't think with you strutting around like that."

"I'm not strutting," Christina protested. "I'm standing perfectly still."

"We're going to have company in a little while."

"We are?" Christina shook her head. "I didn't invite anyone. I'm really not in the mood to entertain, Lyon. I had only just begun to mourn you, and now here you are—"

"Mourn me?" Lyon repeated, matching her frown. "What the hell are you mourning me for?"

"Never mind," Christina said. "And quit losing your temper. Who is coming to pay a call?"

Lyon had to take a deep breath to regain his control. He then explained all about Splickler and his men. He deliberately left out mention of the Countess's involvement, for he didn't want Christina too upset. He decided to wait, thinking to take care of one problem at a time.

"What is it you want me to do?" Christina asked. She bolted the front door and walked over to stand directly in front of him.

Lyon inhaled the scent of flowers. He reached out to take her into his arms. "You smell good," he told her.

His hands cupped the sides of her angelic face. Lord, she was staring up at him with such trust in her eyes.

"You must tell me what to do," Christina whispered again.

"Kiss me," Lyon commanded. He lowered his head to steal a quick kiss.

"I was talking about the mischief makers," Christina said when he'd pulled away. "You really can't hold a thought for more than a minute, can you, Lyon? Does the flaw run in your family?"

Lyon shook his head. "Of course I can hold a thought. I've been thinking about getting you into my arms since the moment you opened the door. You don't have anything on underneath this flimsy little robe, do you?"

She would have shaken her head if he hadn't been holding her so securely. "I just finished my bath," she explained, smiling over the fact that he'd just admitted wanting to touch her.

He was such an honest man. Christina leaned up on her tiptoes to give him what he wanted. She thought only to imitate the same quick kiss he'd given her. Lyon had other notions. His thumb nudged her chin down just enough for his tongue to thrust inside her mouth in search of hers.

Christina held onto the lapels of his jacket, fearing her knees were about to buckle. When she was certain she wouldn't disgrace herself by falling down, she returned his kiss with equal fervor.

The way she responded to him made him half-crazed. His mouth slanted over hers, powerfully, possessively. Christina wasn't able to hold back. That fact aroused Lyon almost as much as her whispered moans, her soft lips, her wild tongue.

Yes, he was thoroughly satisfied with her response. He was fast coming to the conclusion that it was the only time she was honest with him.

Lyon reluctantly pulled away from her. "You've made my hands tremble," Christina said. "I won't be much help to you if they knock on my door now."

"Too bad you aren't talented with a knife," Lyon remarked.

He waited for the lie, knowing full well she couldn't admit to such training.

"Yes, it is too bad," Christina answered. "But knives are for men. Women would harm themselves. I don't have a pistol, either. Perhaps you're disappointed I'm so poorly educated?"

He could tell by the way she'd asked the question she was hoping for agreement.

"Not at all, sweet," Lyon answered, his voice smooth. He draped his arm around her shoulder and started up the steps. "It's a man's duty to protect his little woman."

"Yes, that's the way in most cultures," Christina returned. Her voice turned hesitant, almost shy, when she added, "Still, you wouldn't take great exception if this same little woman did know how to defend herself. Would you? I mean to say, you wouldn't think it was unladylike . . . or would you?"

"Is this your room?" Lyon asked, deliberately evading her question. He pushed the door of the first bedroom open, took in the dark colors and the rank odor of old perfume, and knew before Christina answered him that he'd breached the Countess's quarters.

The room was dark enough to please a spider. Or an old bat, Lyon thought with a frown.

"This is my aunt's room," Christina said. She peeked inside. "It's awfully gloomy, isn't it?"

"You seem surprised. Haven't you ever been inside?"

"No."

Lyon was pulling the door closed when he saw the number of bolts and chains attached to the inside. "Your aunt must be an uneasy sleeper," he remarked. "Against whom does she lock her door, Christina?"

He knew the answer and was already getting angry. Lyon remembered the seaman's remark about the Countess being frightened of the pretty little miss.

The locks were on the wrong side of the door, as far as Lyon was concerned. Christina should be protecting herself against the Countess, and not the other way around.

What kind of life had Christina been forced to live since

returning to her family and her homeland? She must surely be lonely. And what kind of woman would shun her only relative?

"My aunt doesn't like to be disturbed when she sleeps," Christina explained.

Lyon reacted to the sadness in her voice by hugging her close to him. "You haven't had an easy time of it since coming home, have you, love?"

He could feel her shrug against him. "My room is at the end of the hall. Is that what you're looking for?"

"Yes," he answered. "But I want to check all the windows, too."

"I have two windows in my room," Christina said. She pulled away from him, took hold of his hand, and hurried into her room.

Lyon took in everything in one quick glance. The bedroom was sparse by most women's standards, immensely appealing by his own. Trinkets didn't litter the two chest tops. No, there wasn't any clutter. A single chair, angled in the corner, a privacy screen behind it, a canopy bed with a bright white coverlet, and two small chests were the only pieces of furniture in the large square room.

Christina obviously liked order. The room was spotless, save for the single blanket someone had dropped on the floor by the window.

"The garden's right below my windows," Christina said. "The wall would be easy to scale. The greenery reaches the ledge. I think the vines are sturdy enough to hold a man."

"I'd rather they didn't come in through the windows," Lyon remarked, almost absentmindedly. He tested the frames, then looked down at the garden. He wished the moon wasn't so accommodating this evening. There was too much light.

Lyon glanced over at Christina. His expression and his attitude had changed. Drastically.

Christina felt like smiling. He really was a warrior. His face was just as impassive as a brave's. She couldn't tell what he was thinking now, and the rigidity of his bearing indicated to her he was preparing for battle.

"The drawing room only has two front windows, as I recall. Is there another entrance besides the one from the foyer?"

"No," Christina answered.

"Good. Get dressed, Christina. You can wait in there until this is over. I'll make it safe enough."

"How?"

"By blocking the windows and the doors," Lyon explained.

"No. I mean, I don't wish to be locked inside anywhere, Lyon."

The vehemence in her tone surprised him. Then he remembered how uncomfortable she'd been inside the closed carriage. His heart went out to her. "If I fashion a lock on the inside of the door so you'll know you could get out if you—"

"Oh, yes, that would do nicely," Christina interrupted with a brisk nod. She looked very relieved. "Thank you for understanding."

"Now why are you frowning?" Lyon asked, clearly exasperated.

"I've just realized you have another weapon to use against me if you become angry with me," she admitted. "I've just shown you a weakness," she added with a shrug.

"No, you've just insulted me," Lyon returned. "I don't know too many men, or women either, who would like to be locked in a room, Christina. Now quit trying to distract me. Get dressed."

She hurried to do his bidding. "I don't think I want to wait in the drawing room at all," she muttered to herself as she grabbed the first gown she could lay her hands on and moved behind the screen to change. She realized what a poor selection she'd made after she'd shed her robe and put the royal blue dress on.

"Lyon? The fastenings are in the back," she called out. "I can't do them up properly."

Lyon turned from the window to find Christina holding the front of her dress against her chest.

When she turned to give him her back, the first thing he noticed was her flawless skin. In the candlelight she looked too enticing for his peace of mind.

The second thing he took notice of was that she wasn't wearing a damn thing underneath. He wasn't unaffected either. His hands shook when he bent to the task of securing her gown, his fingers awkward because he wanted to caress her smooth skin.

"Where's your maid, Christina?" he asked, hoping conversation would pull him away from the ungentlemanly thought of carrying her over to the bed and seducing her.

"I'm alone for the week. I let Beatrice have the time away."

Her casually spoken comment irritated him. "For God's sake, no gentle lady stays all by herself," he muttered.

"I do well enough for myself. I'm most self-serving."

"Self-sufficient," Lyon said with a sigh. He was having difficulty catching the last button. Her silky hair kept getting in his way.

"I beg your pardon?"

Lyon lifted her hair and draped it over her shoulder. He smiled when he saw the goosebumps on her skin. "Self-sufficient, my sweet, not self-serving."

"There is a difference?" she asked, trying to turn around to look at him.

"Stand still," Lyon ordered. "Yes, there is a difference. Your aunt is self-serving. You're self-sufficient."

"Do you know I never make mistakes except when I'm with you, Lyon? It is therefore all your fault I get confused."

He didn't want to waste time arguing with her. "Come along," he ordered after he'd finished fastening her gown. He took hold of her hand and pulled her behind him.

Christina had to run to keep up with him. "I haven't braided my hair," she said quickly. "I really must, Lyon. It could be used against me. Surely you realize that."

He didn't realize, knew he shouldn't ask, but did anyway. "Why is your hair a weapon?"

"The men could catch hold of me if they grabbed my hair,

unless of course I'm as quick as a panther, as fearless as a wolf, as cunning as a bear."

The woman was getting carried away. Lyon let her see his exasperation when they'd reached the drawing room.

"Will you be all right sitting in the dark?" Lyon asked. He walked over to the front windows, pulled the braided cord from one side of the drape, and handed it to Christina.

"I'm not afraid of the dark," she answered, looking disgruntled. "What a silly question to put to me."

"Tie this rope around the door handles, Christina. Make it good and tight. If anyone tries to break in, I'll hear the noise. All right?"

Lyon checked the windows. Age had sealed them tight. "Yes, Lyon, I'll not let you down," Christina said from behind him.

"Now listen well, my little warrior," Lyon said in a hard voice. He took hold of her shoulders to give her a squeeze. "You're going to wait inside this room until the danger is over. Do you understand me?"

His voice had been harsh, angry. It didn't seem to worry Christina, though. She was still smiling up at him. "I really would like to help you, Lyon. After all, I would remind you that they are my attackers. Surely you will allow me to do my part."

"Surely I will not," Lyon roared. "You'd just get in my way, Christina," he added in a softer voice.

"Very well," Christina said. She turned to the small oval mirror hanging on the wall adjacent to the windows and began the task of braiding her hair. She looked so graceful, so feminine. When she lifted her arms, her gown edged up above her ankles.

"You've forgotten to put your shoes on," Lyon said, a smile in his voice. "Again."

"Again? Whatever do you mean?" Christina asked, turning back to him.

He shook his head. "Never mind. You might as well leave your hair alone. You aren't going to get involved."

Her smile reeked of sincerity. Lyon was immediately suspicious. "Give me your word, Christina. Now."

"What word?" she asked, feigning innocence. She turned away from his glare and started braiding her hair again.

Lyon held his patience. The little innocent didn't realize he could see her reflection in the mirror. She wasn't looking sincere now, only very, very determined.

He would gain her promise, even if he had to shake it out of her. Her safety was his primary concern, of course. Lyon wasn't about to let anything happen to her. But there was another reason as well. Though it was insignificant in comparison with the first, it still worried him. In truth, he didn't want her to watch him. There was a real possibility Christina would become more frightened of him than of Splickler and his men by the time the night was over.

Lyon didn't fight fair, or honorably either. Christina couldn't have heard about his past. Now that he realized how much he cared about her, he wanted to protect her from the world in general, bastards like Splickler in particular . . . but protect her from knowing about his dark side, too. He didn't want to disillusion her. She believed he was simply the Marquess of Lyonwood, nothing more, nothing less. God help him, he meant to keep her innocent.

He thought he'd lose her if she knew the truth.

"I promise I won't interfere until you ask me to," Christina said, interrupting his dour thoughts. "Mrs. Smitherson did show me how to defend myself," she hastened to add when he gave her a dark look. "I would know what to do."

"Summerton," Lyon answered on a long, drawn-out sigh. "The people who raised you were called Summerton."

His mood was just like the wind, Christina decided. Completely unpredictable. He wasn't smiling now but looking as though he was contemplating murder.

"You act as though we have all the time in the world before our visitors arrive," Christina remarked. "Won't they be here soon?" she asked, hoping to turn his attention away from whatever sinister thought had him glaring so.

"Not for a while yet," Lyon answered. "Stay here while I have a look around."

Christina nodded. The minute he was out of sight she ran

upstairs to fetch a ribbon for her hair. And her knife, of course. Lyon was going to get her help whether he wanted it or not.

She was back inside the drawing room, sitting demurely on the worn settee, her knife hidden under the cushion, when Lyon returned.

"I've decided to make it easy for Splickler."

"How?"

"Left the back door unlatched."

"That was most accommodating of you."

Lyon smiled over the praise in her voice. He walked over to stand directly in front of her. His big hands rested on his hips, his legs were braced apart, and Christina was given the disadvantage of having to tilt her head back as far as she could just to see his face. Since he was smiling again, she assumed his mood had lightened. "If you're sure they'll come through the garden, why let them inside the house at all? Why not greet them outside?"

"Greet them?" Lyon shook his head. "Christina, they aren't coming here to speak to you. There might very well be a fight."

He hated to worry her but knew she needed to understand. "Well, of course there will be a fight," Christina answered. "That's the reason I prefer you to meet them outside, Lyon. I'm the one who'll have to clean up the mess, after all."

He hadn't thought of that. And when he realized she thoroughly understood what was going to happen, he was immensely relieved. "You're very brave," he told her. "The moon, however, gives too much light. I memorized every detail of the room they'll enter before I put out the candles. They'll have the disadvantage."

"They'll also have to come through one at a time," Christina interjected. "A very cunning idea, Lyon. But what if they climb the vines instead of trying the door?"

"They won't, sweetheart."

He seemed so certain, Christina decided not to worry about it. She watched him walk over to the doors. "Time to put out the candles, love. Tie the rope around the doorknobs

first, all right? You aren't frightened, are you? I'll take care
of you. I promise."

"I trust you, Lyon."

Her answer warmed him. "And I trust you to stay here."

"Lyon?"

"Yes, Christina?"

"Be careful."

"I will."

"Oh, and Lyon?"

"Yes?"

"You'll try not to make too much of a mess, won't you?"

"I'll try."

He winked at her before closing the door behind him.
Christina tied the rope around the two door handles,
forming a tight double knot. She blew out the candles and
settled down to wait.

The minutes dragged by at a turtle's pace. Christina kept
straining to hear sounds from the back of the house. For that
reason, she was quite unprepared to hear a scraping sound
coming from the front windows.

They weren't suppose to come through the front of the
house. Lyon was going to be disappointed. Christina felt like
instructing the villains to go around back, then realized how
foolish that suggestion would have been. She decided she'd
just have to wait it out in hopes they'd give up trying to
breach the windows and eventually try the back door.

"Christina?"

Her name was called out in a soft whisper, but she
recognized the voice all the same. The Earl of Rhone was
trying to get her attention.

She pulled the drape back and found Rhone hanging on
the ledge, grinning up at her. The smile didn't stay long—
nor did Rhone, for that matter. He suddenly lost his grip on
the ledge and disappeared. A soft thud came next, followed
by several indecent curses telling Christina the poor man
hadn't landed on his feet.

She was going to have to fetch him out of the hedges, she
decided. He was making such a commotion he was sure to
alert the mischief makers.

Rhone met her at the front door. He looked a sight, for his jacket was ripped away from his sleeve, his cravat was soiled and undone, and he was favoring one leg.

He was such a clumsy man, she thought, yet her heart warmed to him all the same. Lyon must have confided in him. Christina believed he'd ventured out to give his friend assistance. It was the only answer for such an unexpected visit. "You look as though you've already lost one fight. Rhone, behind you!"

A crash echoing from the back of the house nearly drowned out her voice. Rhone caught her warning, however. He reacted with good speed, wasted little time by turning around to face the threat, and used his right shoulder to shove the door into the face of a wiry-looking man trying to barrel through the opening. His legs were buckled to the task, his face red with exertion.

When it became evident he wasn't going to get the door closed without her help, Christina added her own strength.

"Lyon!"

Rhone's shout made her ears ring. "Go and hide someplace," Rhone gasped out to Christina, his voice strained.

"Christina. Go back inside the salon."

Lyon's voice came from behind her. Christina thought only to glance over her shoulder to explain that her weight was needed to get the door closed, but the sight that met her pushed her explanation out of her mind.

She slowly turned around and took a tentative step forward. She was too dazed to move more quickly.

The transformation in the Marquess held her spellbound. He didn't even resemble an Englishman now. His jacket was gone, his shirt torn to the waist. Blood trickled down his chin from a cut on the side of his mouth. It wasn't a significant wound, and it didn't frighten her. Neither did the splatter of blood on his sleeve, for she instinctively knew the blood wasn't his . . . no, she wasn't frightened of his appearance.

The look in his eyes was another matter. He looked ready to kill. Lyon appeared to be quite calm. His arms were folded across his chest, and his expression was almost bored. It was all a lie, of course. The truth was there, in his eyes.

"*Now!*"

His bellow shook her from her daze. Christina didn't even spare a backward glance for Rhone as she ran toward the drawing room.

"Get out of the way, Rhone."

Rhone didn't hesitate to follow Lyon's order. As soon as he jumped back, three men the size of giants lunged inside. They fell, one atop another. Rhone stood in the corner, hoping Lyon would ask for his help.

Lyon stood in the center of the foyer patiently waiting for the three cutthroats to get back on their feet. Rhone thought that was just a bit too accommodating of his friend.

He was outnumbered, outweighed, outweaponed. The men now crouched in front of him all held knives in their hands. One of the bastards clutched a dagger in each hand.

Someone started to snicker. Rhone smiled. The poor fool obviously didn't realize Lyon still had the advantage.

The fat man in the center suddenly lashed out at Lyon with his blade. Lyon's boot caught him under his chin. The force of the blow lifted the man high enough in the air for Lyon to slam his fists into the man's groin. The attacker blacked out before he hit the floor.

The other two attacked in unison just as another man came charging up the front steps. Rhone heard him coming, reached out, and kicked the door shut. The howl of pain radiating through the door told Rhone his timing had been excellent.

Rhone never took his gaze off Lyon. Though he'd seen him in battles before, Lyon's strength continued to impress him. Lyon used his elbow to crack one man's jaw while he anchored the other man's arm away from him. He dealt with him next, and when Rhone heard the snap of bone he knew Lyon had broken the man's wrist.

Bodies littered the entrance when Lyon was done. "Open the door, Rhone."

"Hell, you're not even out of breath," Rhone muttered. He got the door open, then moved out of the way as Lyon, showing not the least amount of effort, lifted each man and threw him out into the street.

"We work well together," Rhone commented.

"We?"

"I watch, you work," Rhone explained.

"I see."

"What happened to Splickler? Did he come in through the back door, or did he run away?"

Lyon grinned at Rhone, then nodded toward the pyramid of bodies at the bottom of the steps. "Splickler's on the bottom. I think you probably broke his nose when you slammed the door in his face."

"Then I did do my part," Rhone announced, puffing up like a cloud.

Lyon began to laugh. He whacked Rhone on the shoulder, then turned to find Christina standing in the center of the doorway.

She looked like she'd just seen a ghost. The color was gone from her cheeks, and her eyes were wide with fright. Lyon's heart lurched. God, she must have seen the fight. He took a step toward her but stopped when she took a step back.

He felt defeated. She was afraid of him. Lord, he'd meant to protect her, not terrify her.

Christina suddenly ran to him. She threw herself into his arms, very nearly knocking both of them to the floor. Lyon didn't understand what had caused the change in her attitude, yet he was thankful all the same. Relief washed the rigidity from his stance. He put his arms around her, rested his chin on the top of her head, and let out a long sigh. "I'm never going to understand you, am I?"

"I'm so happy you aren't angry with me."

Her voice was muffled against his chest, but he understood her. "Why would I be angry with you?"

"Because I broke my promise," Christina reminded him. "I left the salon to let Rhone in the front door."

Lyon looked over at his friend. "I specifically remember

telling you to go home." He frowned at his friend, then suddenly noticed his appearance. "What happened to you? I don't recall you getting in the fight."

"A little mishap," Rhone said.

"He fell in the hedge," Christina explained, smiling over the embarrassment she could see in Rhone's face. Why, the man was actually blushing.

"The hedge?" Lyon sounded incredulous.

"I think I'll walk home. Your carriage is probably waiting in front of my townhouse, Lyon. I'll have your driver bring it along for you. Good evening, Princess Christina."

"No, you really mustn't walk. Lyon, you should—"

"Let him walk. It's only a short distance away," Lyon interjected.

Christina didn't argue further. Someone was going to have to fetch the carriage, and she preferred that Rhone took care of the matter so that she could spend a few minutes alone with Lyon.

"Thank you for your assistance, Rhone. Lyon, what are you going to do about those men cluttering my walkway? And am I mistaken, or are there one or two in the back of the house as well?"

"There are two," Lyon said. "I threw them out back."

"They'll wake up and crawl home," Rhone advised. "Unless, of course, you—"

"I didn't," Lyon said.

"Didn't what?" Christina asked.

"Kill them," Rhone said.

"Rhone, don't frighten her," Lyon said.

"Goodness, I hope not. Think of the mess." Christina sounded appalled, but for all the wrong reasons. Both Lyon and Rhone started laughing.

"Shouldn't you be crying or something?" Rhone asked.

"Should I?"

"No, Christina, you shouldn't," Lyon said. "Now quit frowning."

"You aren't wearing any shoes, Christina," Rhone suddenly blurted out.

"Do be careful walking home," Christina answered, ignoring his comment about her bare feet. "Don't let anyone see your bandage. They might begin to wonder."

As soon as the door was bolted shut, Christina turned back to Lyon, only to find that he was already halfway up the stairs, taking them two at a time. "Where are you going?"

"To wash," Lyon called back. "Wasn't there a pitcher of water in your room, Christina?"

He was out of sight before she could give him a proper answer. Christina hurried up the steps after him.

When she caught up with him she wished she'd waited below the stairs. Lyon had already stripped out of his shirt. He was bent over the basin, splashing water on his face and arms.

Christina was suddenly overwhelmed by his size. She could see the sinewy strength in his upper arms, his shoulders; a pelt of golden hair covered his chest, narrowed to a line above the flat of his stomach, then disappeared below the waistband of his pants. She'd never seen the like. She was fascinated and wondered what it would be like to be held in his arms now.

He reached for the cloth. Christina took the strip of linen from his hands and began to pat his face dry. "Your skin is so dark, Lyon. Have you been working in the sun without your shirt on?" she asked.

"When I was on my ship I used to," Lyon answered.

"You have a ship?" Christina answered, sounding quite pleased.

"Had a ship," Lyon corrected. "Fire destroyed it, but I plan to build another."

"With your own hands, Lyon?"

Lyon smiled down at her. "No, love. I'll hire others to do the work."

"I liked the ship I was on when I came to England. I didn't like it much below the deck though. It was too confining," she admitted with a shrug.

Her voice trembled. So did her hands when she started to dry his shoulders. There were several glorious marks on him, and the sight of such handsome scars made her heartbeat quicken.

For the first time in his life, Lyon was actually feeling a little awkward. Christina was such a beautiful woman, while he was covered with marks. They were reminders of his black past, Lyon thought, but the ugly scars hadn't bothered him until this moment.

"I promise to take you on my new ship," he heard himself say.

"I would like that, Lyon," Christina answered. The towel dropped to the floor when she gently traced the long, curved scar on Lyon's chest. "You are so handsome," she whispered.

"I'm covered with flaws," Lyon whispered back. His voice sounded hoarse to him.

"Oh, no, they are marks of valor. They are beautiful."

She was looking up at him, staring into his eyes, and Lyon thought he'd never get used to her beauty.

"We should go back downstairs." Even as he said the words, he was pulling her into his arms. God help him, he couldn't stop himself. The realization that he was alone with her, that they were in fact in her bedroom, rocked all the gentlemanly thoughts out of his mind.

"Will you kiss me before we go downstairs?" she asked.

Lyon thought she looked as though she'd already been kissed. A faint blush covered her cheeks, and her eyes had turned a deep blue again.

The woman obviously didn't understand her own jeopardy. And if she only knew the wild thoughts rambling through his mind, her face would turn as white as the sheets.

She trusted him. She wouldn't have asked him to kiss her if she didn't trust him. Lyon was going to have to control his baser instincts. Yes, he was going to be a gentleman.

One kiss surely wouldn't hurt. He'd wanted to take her into his arms the moment the fight had ended. The anger had been flowing like lava through his veins. Oh, he'd wanted her then, with a primitive passion that had shaken him.

And then she'd backed away from him. The sudden remembrance gave him a start.

"Christina, are you afraid of me?"

She could tell he was serious. The worry in his gaze said he was. The question was puzzling. "Why would you think I'd be afraid of you?" she asked, trying not to laugh. He did look terribly concerned.

"After the fight, when you backed away from me . . ."

She did smile then, couldn't help herself. "Lyon, the little skirmish I witnessed couldn't possibly be called a fight . . . and you actually thought I was afraid?"

He was so surprised by her comment, he immediately defended himself. "Well, I'll admit that I didn't think it was much of a fight either, but when you stared at me with such a frightened look on your face I naturally assumed you were upset. Hell, Christina, most women would have been hysterical."

By the time he'd finished his statement, he'd gone from sounding very matter-of-fact to muttering with irritation.

"Was it my duty to weep, Lyon? I apologize if I've displeased you, but I've still to understand all your laws."

"You could make a duck daft," Lyon announced.

Because he was grinning down at her, Christina decided not to let her exasperation show. "You're the most confusing man," she remarked. "I have to keep reminding myself that you're English."

The temptation was too compelling. Before she could stop her inclination, she reached out to touch his chest. The heat in his skin felt good against her fingertips, the mat of hair crisp yet soft.

"I wasn't afraid of you, Lyon," Christina whispered, avoiding his eyes now. "I've never been afraid of you. How could I be? You're such a gentle, kind man."

He didn't know how to answer her. She sounded almost in awe of him. She was wrong, of course. He'd never been kind or gentle. A man could change, though. Lyon determined to be anything and everything Christina wanted him to be. By God, if she thought him gentle, then gentle he'd be.

"You really are a warrior, aren't you, Lyon?"

"Do you want me to be?" he asked, sounding confused.

"Oh, yes," Christina answered, daring a quick look up.

"Warriors aren't gentle," he reminded her.

She didn't want to press the issue because she knew he wouldn't understand. He was wrong, but it would be rude of her to set him straight. Her hands slipped around his neck, her fingers entwining in his soft, curly hair.

She felt him shudder; his muscles tightened.

Lyon would have spoken to her, but he was certain his voice would betray him. Her touch was driving him to distraction.

Gentle, he cautioned himself, I have to be gentle with her. He placed a kiss on her forehead. Christina closed her eyes and sighed, encouraging him. He kissed her on the bridge of her freckled nose next and finally reached her soft lips.

It was a very gentle kiss. Sweet. Undemanding.

Until her tongue touched his. The hunger inside him seemed to ignite. The feeling was so intoxicating, so over-powering, he forgot all about gentleness. His tongue penetrated her warmth, tasting, probing, taking.

When Christina pulled him closer, his demand increased until all he could think about was filling her . . . completely.

She wasn't resisting. No, her soft moans told him she didn't want him to stop. Her hips cuddled his arousal. He knew her action was instinctive, yet the way she slowly arched against him made him wild. She felt so good, so right.

Lyon dragged his mouth away from hers with a harsh groan. "I want to make love to you, Christina," he whispered against her ear. "If we're going to stop, it has to be now."

Christina's head fell back as Lyon rained wet kisses along the column of her throat. Her hands, still entwined in his hair, clenched, pulled, begged.

He knew he'd soon be past the caring point. Lyon tried to separate himself from the torment. "God, Christina, walk away from me. Now."

Walk away? Dear Lord, she could barely stand up. Every part of her body responded to his touch. She could hear the anger in his voice, could feel the tension in his powerful hold. Her mind tried to make sense out of the confusion of his reaction. "I don't want to stop, Lyon."

She knew he'd heard her. Lyon clasped her shoulders, squeezed until it was painful. Christina looked into his eyes, saw the desire there. The force of his passion overwhelmed her, robbed her of her own strength to think logically.

"Do you know what you're saying to me?"

She answered him the only way she knew how. Christina used her body to give him permission. She deliberately arched against him again, then pulled his head down toward her.

She kissed him with a passion that sent his senses reeling. Lyon was at first too stunned to do more than react to her boldness, but he soon became the aggressor again.

He wanted to pleasure her so completely that any memory of other men would be washed away. She would belong to him, now and forever.

Lyon fumbled with the fastenings at the back of her gown, his mouth fastened on hers. Christina heard the sound of material being ripped away. He suddenly pulled her hands away from him, then tore the gown completely free. The dress fell to the floor.

There were no undergarments to hinder his gaze. When he took a step back, Christina stood before him, her hands at her sides.

Her body belonged to him. He was her lion. Christina accepted the truth, repeated it again and again inside her mind, trying to overcome her shyness, her fear.

She couldn't shield her body from him . . . or her heart.

Both belonged to Lyon.

Lyon's gaze was ravenous as it swept over her. She was so perfectly formed, so very, very beautiful. Her skin was smooth, creamy-looking in the soft candlelight. Her breasts were high, full, taut. The nipples were erect, waiting for his touch. Her waist was so narrow, her stomach flat, her hips slender.

She was irresistible.

And she belonged to him.

Lyon's hands shook when he reached for her, drew her back into his arms.

Christina gasped from the initial contact of her bare breasts against his chest. His hair tickled her, his skin warmed her, and the way he controlled his strength as he held her close to him made her forget all her fears. She was innocent of men, yes, yet she knew with a certainty that made tears come to her eyes that Lyon would be gentle with her.

She kissed his throat where she could see the throbbing of his pulse, then rested her head in the crook of his shoulder, inhaling his wonderful masculine scent, waiting for him to show her what to do.

Lyon slowly untied the ribbon from the bottom of Christina's braid, then unwound the silky curls until a blanket of sunlight covered her back. He lifted her into his arms and carried her over to the bed, pausing only to pull the covers back before placing her in the center.

Christina tried to protest, to tell him it was her duty to undress him, but Lyon had already taken his shoes and socks off. Her voice became locked in her throat when he stripped out of the rest of his clothes, and all she could do was stare at him in wonder.

He was the most magnificent warrior she'd ever seen. The power was there, in his arms and legs. His thighs were muscular, strong, beautiful. His arousal was full, hard, and when he came to lie on top of her Christina instinctively opened herself to him. He settled himself between her thighs. Christina had barely accepted his weight before he captured her mouth for another searing kiss.

Christina wrapped her arms around his waist. His mouth had never felt so wonderful, his tongue never so exciting. His hands were never still, stroking, caressing, giving her shivers of pleasure. Their legs entwined, and when Lyon moved to take her breast into his mouth her toes brushed against his legs. Her moans of pleasure drove him wild. His hands fondled her breasts while his tongue swirled around one nipple and then the other. When he finally began to suckle, a white-hot knot of need started to burn inside her.

Christina's hips moved restlessly, rubbing against his arousal. She wanted to touch him, to worship his body the way he was worshipping hers, but the sensations coursing through her body were too new, too raw. She could only cling to him and beg him with her whimpers.

His hands settled between her thighs to tease her sensitive skin. His fingers soon made her wild with need, caressing the nub protected by her soft curls until she was moist with desire. His fingers penetrated her tight sheath just as his tongue thrust into her mouth.

Lyon could feel the incredible heat of her. He was nearly out of control now, for Christina was so unashamedly responsive to his touch. He couldn't wait much longer, knew he'd soon lose his control. He cautioned himself against hurrying her even as his thigh pushed her legs further apart.

"From this moment on you belong to me, Christina. Now and forever."

He entered her with a swift, determined thrust, lifting her hips with his hands to penetrate her completely.

She was a virgin. The realization came late. Lyon was fully embedded inside her now. He took a deep breath and tried not to move. The effort nearly killed him. Christina was so hot, so tight; she fit him perfectly.

His heart was slamming against his chest. His breath was harsh, choppy. "Why didn't you tell me?" he finally asked her. He propped himself up on his elbows to look down into her face. God, she hadn't made a sound. Had he hurt her? "Why didn't you tell me you haven't been with a man before?" he asked again, capturing her face with his hands.

"Please, Lyon, don't be angry," Christina whispered.

She knew she was going to start weeping. The fierce light in his eyes frightened her. Her body was throbbing with pain from his invasion, and every muscle was tense, tingling. "I'm sorry if I disappointed you," she apologized in a ragged voice. "But I didn't want you to stop. Could you be disappointed later, please?"

"I'm not disappointed," Lyon answered. "I'm very pleased." He was trying to keep his voice soft, gentle. It was an excruciating task, because his arousal was begging for release, and all he wanted to do was spill his seed into her.

He was going to make certain she found complete satisfaction first. "I'll try not to hurt you, Christina."

"You already did."

"Oh, God, I'm sorry. I'll stop," he promised, knowing full well he wouldn't.

"No," Christina protested. Her nails dug into his shoulders, keeping him inside her. "It will be better now, won't it?"

Lyon moved, groaning over the pleasure he gained. "Do you like that?" he asked.

"Oh, yes," Christina answered. She arched her hips up against him, pulling him higher inside her. "Do you like that?"

He might have nodded. She was too consumed by the waves of heat to notice. His mouth slanted over hers then, claiming her full attention.

Lyon tried to be tender, but she was making it an impossible quest. She kept moving against him restlessly, demandingly, urgently. Lyon's discipline deserted him.

"Easy, love, don't let me hurt you."

"Lyon!"

"Christina, why did you let me think you'd been with other men?"

Lyon was stretched out on his back, his hands behind his head. Christina was cuddled up against his side, one shapely leg draped over his thigh. Her face rested on his chest. "Let you think?" she asked him.

"You know my meaning," Lyon said, ignoring the laughter he'd heard in her voice.

"It seemed unimportant to argue with you. Your mind was set on the matter. Besides, you probably wouldn't have believed the truth anyway."

"I might have believed you," he protested. He knew he was lying. No, he wouldn't have believed her.

"Why did you think I'd—"

"It's the way you kissed me," Lyon explained, grinning.

"What is the matter with the way I kiss you? I was only imitating you."

"Oh, nothing's the matter, love. I like your . . . enthusiasm."

"Thank you, Lyon," Christina said, after she'd given him a good look to see if he was jesting with her or not. "I like the way you kiss, too."

"What else do you imitate?" Lyon asked.

Because he was teasing her, he was unprepared for her answer. "Oh, everything. I'm quite good at it, you know, especially if I like what I'm imitating."

"I'm sorry I hurt you, Christina," Lyon whispered. "If you'd told me you were a virgin before, I could have made it easier for you."

Lyon was feeling a bit guilty, but terribly arrogant, too.

She belonged to him. He hadn't realized just how possessive he could be. Lyon wanted to believe Christina wouldn't have given herself to him unless she loved him.

He knew she'd reached fulfillment. Lord, she'd cried out his name loud enough for the streetwalkers to hear. A smile settled on his face. She hadn't been the delicate little flower he'd thought she was. When she let go, she let go. Wild. Totally uncontrolled. And loud, Lyon admitted. His ears were still ringing from her lusty shouts. Lyon didn't think he could ever be happier. No, Christina hadn't held back. He had the scratches to prove it.

Now all he wanted to hear from her was the truth inside her heart. He wanted her to tell him how much she loved him.

Lyon let out a long sigh. He was acting just like a virgin on his wedding night. Uncertain. Vulnerable.

"Lyon, do all Englishmen have such hair on their bodies?"

Her question nudged him away from his thoughts. "Some do, others don't," he answered with a shrug that nearly pushed her off his chest. "Haven't you ever seen Mr. Summerton without his shirt on, love?" he teased.

"Who?"

He wasn't going to remind her again. If the woman couldn't keep her lies straight, he certainly wasn't going to help. Lyon was immediately irritated. He knew it was his own fault for bringing up the lie, but that didn't seem to matter. "Christina, now that we've become so intimate, you don't have to fabricate stories any longer. I want to know everything about you," he added, his voice a little more intense than he wished. "No matter what your childhood was like, I'll still care for you."

Christina didn't want to answer his questions. She didn't want to have to lie to him again . . . not now. A warm glow still surrounded her heart. Lyon had been such a tender lover. "Did I please you, Lyon?" she asked, trailing her fingers down his chest to distract him.

"Very much," he answered. He captured her hand when she'd reached his navel. "Honey, tell me about—"

"Aren't you going to ask me if you pleased me?" she asked, pulling her hand free of his grasp.

"No."

"Why not?"

Lyon took a deep breath. He could feel himself getting hard again. "Because I know I pleased you," he ground out. "Christina, stop that. It's too soon for you. We can't make love again."

Her hand touched his arousal, stealing the breath out of his protest. Lyon let out a low groan. His hand dropped to his side when she began to place wet kisses on the flat of his indrawn stomach. She moved lower to taste more of him.

"No more," Lyon commanded.

He pulled her by her hair, twisting the curls to get her attention. "If you want to tease, you'd better wait until tomorrow," he warned. "A man can only take so much, Christina."

"How much?" she whispered. Her mouth was getting closer to his hard shaft.

Lyon jerked her back up to his chest. "We only have this one night," Christina protested.

"No, Christina," Lyon said. "We have a lifetime."

She didn't answer him, but she knew he was wrong. Her

eyes filled with tears when she turned her face away from him. Christina was almost desperate to touch him again, to taste all of him. The memory of her Lyon would have to stay with her . . . forever.

She lowered her head to his stomach again. She kissed him there, moved to his thighs next, and finally between them.

His scent was just as intoxicating as the taste of him. She was only given a few minutes to learn his secrets, however, before Lyon dragged her up on top of him.

He kissed her hungrily as he rolled her to his side. Christina moved her leg over his thigh and begged him with her mouth and her hands to come to her.

She was more than ready for him. Lyon was shaken when he touched the sweet wetness between her thighs. He slowly penetrated her warmth, holding her hips in a fierce grip, determined not to let her hurt herself by pushing up against him too quickly.

She bit him on his shoulder in retaliation. Lyon was driving her mad. He slowly penetrated her, then withdrew just as slowly. It was agonizing. Maddening.

He had the patience and the endurance of a warrior. She thought she could withstand the sweet torment for the rest of her life. But Lyon was far more adept at the ways of loving than she was. When his hand slipped between them and he touched the heat of her in such a knowing way, her control completely vanished.

Her climax was unimaginable, consuming her. Christina clung to him, her face pillowed against the side of his neck, her eyes tightly closed against the hot sensations shooting through her body.

Lyon was no longer controlled. His thrusts became powerful. When she instinctively arched against him, tightened herself around him, he found his release. The force of his climax stunned him. Lyon felt it in the very depths of his soul.

He was at peace.

Several long minutes elapsed before he could slow his

racing heart or his ragged breath. He was too content to move.

Christina was crying. Lyon suddenly felt the wetness of her tears on his shoulder. The realization jarred him out of his haze. "Christina?" he whispered, hugging her close to him. "Did I hurt you again?"

"No."

"You're all right?"

She nodded against his chin.

"Then why are you crying?"

If he hadn't sounded so caring, she might have been able to restrain herself. There wasn't any need to be quiet about it now, since he knew she was weeping, and she was soon wailing, loud and undignified as a crazed old squaw.

Lyon was horrified. He rolled Christina on her back, brushed her hair out of her face, and gently wiped her tears away. "Tell me, love. What is it?"

"Nothing."

It was a ludicrous answer, of course, but Lyon held his patience. "I really didn't hurt you?" he asked, unable to keep fear out of his voice. "Please, Christina. Quit crying and tell me what's the matter."

"No."

His sigh was strong enough to dry the tears from her cheeks. Lyon cupped the sides of her face, his thumbs rubbing the soft skin below her chin. "I'm not going to move until you tell me what's bothering you, Christina. Your aunt will find us in just this position when she comes home next week."

She knew he meant what he said. He had a stubborn look on his face. The muscle in the side of his jaw flexed. "I've never felt the way you make me feel, Lyon. It frightened me," she admitted.

She started crying again. Dear God, how could she ever leave him? The full truth was unbearable. Shameful. Lyon probably loved her. No, she admitted, shaking her head. He loved a princess.

"Christina, you were a virgin. Of course you were frightened," he said. "Next time it won't be so terrifying for you. I promise you, my sweet."

"But there can't be a next time," Christina wailed. She pushed against Lyon's shoulders. He immediately shifted his weight, then rolled to his side.

"Of course there's going to be another time," he said. "We'll be married first, just as soon as possible. *Now* what have I said?"

He had to shout his question. Christina was making so much noise he knew she wouldn't have been able to hear him if he'd spoken in a normal tone of voice.

"You said you wouldn't marry me."

Ah, so that was the reason. "I've changed my mind," Lyon announced. He smiled, for he understood her real anxiety now. He was also very pleased with himself. Lord, he'd just said the word marriage without blanching. Even more amazing was the fact that he really wanted to marry her.

The turnabout stunned him.

Christina struggled to sit up. She threw her hair over her shoulder when she turned to look at Lyon. She stared at him a long while and tried to form an explanation that wouldn't sound confusing. Christina finally decided to say as little as possible. "I've changed my mind, too. I can't marry you."

She jumped off the bed before Lyon could stop her, then hurried over to her chest to get her robe. "At first I thought I could, because I knew you'd be able to make my stay in England so much more bearable, but that was when I thought I'd be able to leave you."

"Damn it, Christina, if this is some kind of game you're playing, I would advise you to stop."

"It isn't a game," Christina protested. She tied the belt around her waist, pausing to wipe the fresh tears away from her face, then walked back over to stand at the foot of the bed. Her head was bowed. "You want to marry Princess Christina," she said. "Not me."

"You're not making any sense," Lyon muttered. He got out of bed and walked over to stand behind her.

He hadn't the faintest idea what was going through her mind, and he told himself it didn't matter.

"You can tell me all the lies you want to, but the way you just gave yourself to me was honest enough. You want me as much as I want you."

He was about to pull her up against him when her next comment gave him pause. "It doesn't matter."

The sadness in her voice tore at him. "This isn't a game, is it? You really think you aren't going to marry me."

"I can't."

Her simple answer made him livid. "The hell you can't. We're getting married, Christina, just as soon as I can make the arrangements. God's truth, if you shake your head at me one more time I'm going to beat you."

"You needn't shout at me," Christina said. "It's almost dawn, Lyon. We are both too tired for this discussion."

"Why did you ask me to marry you," he asked, "and then change your mind?"

"I thought I'd be able to marry you for just a little while and then—"

"Marriage is forever, Christina."

"According to your laws, not mine," she answered. She took a step away from him. "I'm too upset to speak of this tonight, and I'm afraid you'll never understand anyway—"

Lyon reached out to pull her up against his chest. His hands circled her waist. "Did you know before we made love that you weren't going to marry me?"

Christina closed her eyes against the anger in his voice. "You had already declined my proposal," she said. "And yes, I knew I wouldn't marry you."

"Then why did you give yourself to me?" he asked, sounding incredulous.

"You fought for my honor. You protected me," she answered.

He was infuriated over her perplexed tone of voice. She acted as though he should have understood. "Then it's damned fortunate someone else didn't—"

"No, I wouldn't have slept with any other Englishman. Our destiny is—"

"Your destiny is to become my wife, understand, Christina?" he shouted.

Christina pulled away from him, somewhat surprised he'd let her go. "I hate England, do you understand me?" she shouted back at him. "I couldn't survive here. The people are so strange. They run from one tiny little box to another. And there are so many of them, a person has no room to breathe. I couldn't—"

"What little boxes?" Lyon asked.

"The houses, Lyon. No one ever stays outside. They scurry like mice from one place to another. I couldn't live like that. I couldn't breathe. And I don't like the English people, either. What say you to that full truth, Lyon? Do you think me daft? Perhaps I'm as crazy as everyone here believes my mother was."

"Why don't you like the people?" he asked. His voice had turned soft, soothing. Christina thought he really might be thinking she'd just lost her mind.

"I don't like the way they act," she announced. "The women take lovers after they've pledged themselves to a mate. They treat their old like discarded garbage. That is their most appalling flaw," Christina said. "The old should be honored, not ignored. And their children, Lyon. I hear about the little ones, but I've yet to see one. The mothers lock their children away in their schoolrooms. Don't they understand the children are the heartbeat of the family? No, Lyon, I could not survive here."

She paused to take a deep breath, then suddenly realized Lyon didn't look very upset about her comments. "Why aren't you angry?" she asked.

He grabbed her when she tried to step away from him again, wrapped his arms around her, and held her close to him. "First of all, I agree with most of what you've just said. Second, all during your irate protest you kept saying 'they,' not 'you.' You didn't include me with the others, and as long as it's the other English you dislike, that's quite all right with me. You told me once you thought I was different. It's why you've been drawn to me, isn't it? It doesn't really matter," he added with a sigh. "You and I are both English. You can't change that fact, Christina, just as you can't change the fact that you belong to me now."

"I'm not English where it matters most, Lyon."

"And where might that be?" Lyon asked.

"In my heart."

He smiled. She sounded like a small child in need of comfort. She happened to pull away from him just at that moment, saw his smile, and was infuriated. "How dare you laugh at me when I tell you what is in my heart?" she shouted.

"I dare, all right," Lyon shouted back. "I dare because this is the first time you've ever been completely honest with me. I dare because I'm trying to understand you, Christina," he added, taking a menacing step toward her. "I dare because I happen to care about you. God only knows why, but I do care."

Christina turned her back on him. "I'll not continue this discussion," she announced. She picked up his pants and threw them at him. "Get dressed and go home. I'm afraid you'll just have to walk, because I don't have a servant available to fetch your carriage for you."

She glanced back at him, took in his startled expression. A sudden thought made her gasp. "Your carriage isn't waiting out front, is it?"

"Oh, hell," he muttered. He had his pants on in quick time, then strode out of the bedroom, barechested and barefooted, still muttering under his breath.

Christina ran after him. "If anyone sees your carriage . . . well, I can certainly count on someone telling my aunt, can't I?"

"You don't care what the English think, remember?" Lyon shouted back. He threw the front door open, then turned to give her a good glare. "You would have to live on the main street," he said, sounding as if her choice of townhouses had been a deliberate provocation somehow.

Lyon turned to yell instructions to his driver after making that accusation. "Go and wake up the servants, man. Bring half the number over here. They'll stay with Princess Christina until her aunt returns from the country."

He'd been forced by circumstances to bellow his orders. His driver wouldn't have heard him otherwise. No, the parade of carriages coming down the street was making too much of a clatter.

He knew he should have felt a shred of shame for what he was deliberately doing. When he spotted the first carriage rounding the corner, the very least he could have done was wave his driver away and shut the door.

"Thompson's party must have just let out," he remarked in a casual voice to the horrified woman hovering behind his back.

Lyon actually smiled when he heard her gasp, pleased she understood the ramifications well enough. Then he leaned against the door frame and waved at the startled occupants of the first carriage.

"Good eve, Hudson, Lady Margaret," he shouted, totally unconcerned that his pants were only partially buttoned.

Over his shoulder he told Christina, "Lady Margaret looks like she's about to fall out of the carriage, love. She's hanging halfway out the window."

"Lyon, how could you?" Christina asked, clearly appalled by his conduct.

"Destiny, my dear."

"What?"

He waved to three more carriages before he finally closed the door. "That ought to do it," he remarked, more to himself than to the outraged woman looking ready to kill him. "Now, what were you saying about not marrying me, my sweet?"

"You are a man without shame," she shouted when she could find her voice.

"No, Christina. I've just sealed your fate, so to speak. You still do believe in destiny, don't you?"

"I'm not going to marry you, no matter what scandal you weave."

If she hadn't been so infuriated, she might have tried to explain again. But Lyon was grinning at her with such a

192

victorious, arrogant look on his face, she decided to keep the full truth to herself.

He drained the anger right out of her. Lyon suddenly pulled her into his arms and kissed her soundly. When he finally let go of her, she was too weak to protest.

"You will marry me."

He started back up the stairs in search of his shoes.

Christina held on to the bannister, watching him. "Do you think ruining my reputation will matter, Lyon?"

"It's a nice start," Lyon called back. "Remember, what will be is going to be. Your words, Christina, not mine."

"I'll tell you what's going to be," she shouted. "I won't be in England long enough to care about my reputation. Don't you understand, Lyon? I have to go home."

She knew he'd heard her. She'd shouted loud enough to rattle the walls. Lyon disappeared around the corner, but Christina patiently waited for him to come back downstairs. She wasn't about to go chasing after him again. No, she knew she'd end up back in bed with him if she went up the stairs. God help her, she'd probably be the one to suggest it. Lyon was simply too appealing, and she was too weak-hearted to fight him.

Besides, she told herself, she hated him. The man had the morals of a rattlesnake.

He was dressed when he came downstairs. He was ignoring her, too. Lyon didn't speak another word until his carriage had returned with two big men and one heavyset maid. Then he spoke to his staff, giving them his orders.

Christina was infuriated with his high-handed manner. When he instructed the men to see to her protection, to let no one enter her home without his permission, she decided to protest.

The look he gave her made her reconsider. She was seeing a different side of Lyon's character now. He was very like Black Wolf when he was addressing his warriors. Lyon was just as cold, as rigid, as commanding. Christina instinctively knew it would be better not to argue with him now.

She decided to ignore him just as thoroughly as he was ignoring her. That decision was short-lived, however. Christina was staring into the fireplace, trying to pretend the man didn't even exist, when she heard a rather descriptive curse. She turned just in time to see Lyon jump up from the settee.

He'd sat on her knife.

"Serves you justice," she muttered when he held the blade up and glared at it.

She tried to snatch her weapon away from him, but Lyon wouldn't let her have it. "It belongs to me," she announced.

"And you belong to me, you little warrior," Lyon snapped out. "Admit it, Christina, now, or I swear to the Great Spirit I'll show you how a real warrior uses a knife."

Their gazes held a long, ponderous moment. "You really don't know what you're trying to catch, do you? Very well, Lyon. For now—until you change your mind, that is—I will belong to you. Does that satisfy you?"

Lyon dropped the knife and pulled Christina into his arms. He then proceeded to show her just how immensely satisfied he really was.

Chapter Nine

Edward had left to put down a resistance in the West. When the captain of my ship came for me, I made him wait outside my husband's office while I went inside to steal the jewels. I briefly considered leaving a note for Edward, then decided against it.

We set sail immediately, but I didn't begin to feel safe until we were two days out to sea. I stayed below in my cabin most of the time, for I was terribly ill. I couldn't hold any food in my stomach, and I believed it was the weather that was the cause.

It wasn't until a week had passed that the truth settled in my mind. I was carrying Edward's child.

God forgive me, Christina, but I prayed for your death.

> *Journal entry*
> *September 7, 1795*

Monday was a trial of endurance for Christina. Although she protested vehemently, Lyon's servants had her possessions packed up and transferred to his mother's townhouse by noon.

Christina kept insisting that she wasn't going anywhere, that the Countess would be home Monday next, and that she would take care of herself until that time. No one paid her the least attention. They followed the instructions from their employer, of course, and though they were friendly enough, one and all suggested she mention her distress to the Marquess of Lyonwood.

Although Christina had not seen Lyon since Friday evening, his presence was certainly felt. He hadn't allowed her to attend Creston's ball, or to go anywhere else, for that matter. Christina thought he kept her closeted inside her townhouse so she wouldn't be able to run away.

There was also the possibility that he was trying to protect her feelings, Christina realized. He might not want her to hear any of the whispers circling the ton about her liaison with Lyon. It was a scandal, to be sure, but a scandal Lyon had personally caused.

Perhaps Lyon thought she'd be upset about the slurs against her character. She was unmarried, Lyon had been undressed, and half the ton had witnessed the scene. Oh, there was a scandal floating about; Christina had heard Colette, the lady's maid Lyon had thrust upon her, tell one of the other servants a juicy bit of gossip she'd overheard when she'd gone to do the marketing with the cook.

Christina had a splitting headache by midafternoon. It came upon her all at once when she happened to notice the wedding announcement in the newspapers. Lyon had had the gall to post his intention to marry Princess Christina the following Saturday.

Colette caught her tearing up the paper. "Oh, my lady, isn't it romantic the way the Marquess flaunts tradition? Why, he's doing everything to his liking and doesn't care what others will say."

Christina didn't think it was romantic at all. She felt like screaming. She went upstairs to her bedroom, thinking to find a few minutes' peace, but she'd barely closed the door behind her when she was once again interrupted.

A visitor was waiting for her in the drawing room. Since Lyon had ordered that no one was to be allowed entrance, Christina naturally assumed he was the one waiting for her.

She was fighting mad when she stormed into the salon. "If you think you can . . ."

Her shout tapered off as soon as she saw the elderly woman sitting in the gold wing-back chair. "If I think what, my dear?" the woman asked, looking perplexed.

Christina was embarrassed by her outburst. The woman smiled at her then. Some of the awkwardness left her. Christina could tell the stranger was kind. There were laugh wrinkles around her eyes and her mouth. The top of her gray-haired bun was level with the top of the chair, indicating she was an extremely tall woman. She wasn't very attractive. Her hooked nose took up a good portion of her face, and she had a slight yet noticeable line of hair above her thin upper lip. She was a heavy-bosomed woman with wide shoulders.

She seemed to be about the Countess's age. "I do apologize for shouting at you, madam, but I believed you were Lyon," Christina explained after making a low curtsy.

"How very bold of you, child."

"Bold? I don't understand," Christina said.

"To raise your voice to my nephew. Proves you've got spirit," the woman announced with a brisk nod. She motioned for Christina to sit down. "I've known Lyon since he was a little boy, and I've never had the courage to shout at him. Now, allow me to introduce myself," she continued. "I'm Lyon's aunt. Aunt Harriett, to be correct. I'm his father's younger sister, you see, and since you'll soon be the new Marchionness of Lyonwood, you might as well call me Aunt Harriett from the beginning. Are you ready to come home with me now, Christina, or do you need a little more time to prepare? I shall be happy to wait in here, if you could order me a spot of tea. My, it has gone warm again today, hasn't it?" she asked.

Christina didn't know how to answer her. She watched her take a small fluted fan from her lap, open it with a quick flip of her wrist, and begin to wave it a bit violently in front of her face.

Because of the woman's advanced years, Christina naturally took a submissive attitude. The elders were to be respected and—whenever possible—obeyed without a word of protest. It was the way of the Dakota, the way Christina was raised.

Christina bowed her head and said, "I am honored to meet you, Aunt Harriett. If you have the patience to listen to me, I would like to explain that there seems to be a misunderstanding."

"Misunderstanding?" Harriett asked. Her voice sounded with amusement. She pointed her fan at Christina. "My dear, may I be open with you? Lyon has ordered me to see you settled in his mother's townhouse. We both know he'll have his way, regardless of your feelings. Don't look so crestfallen, child. He only has your best interests at heart."

"Yes, madam."

"Do you want to marry Lyon?"

Her blunt question demanded an answer. She was staring intently at Christina. Very much like a hawk, Christina thought.

"Well, child?"

Christina tried to think of a way to soften the truth. "What I would like to do and what I must do are two separate issues. I'm trying to protect Lyon from making a terrible mistake, madam."

"Marriage would be a mistake, you say?" Aunt Harriett asked.

"If he marries me, yes," Christina admitted.

"I've always been known for my bluntness, Christina, so I'm going to ask you right out. Do you love my nephew?"

Christina could feel herself blushing. She looked up at Aunt Harriett for a long moment.

"You don't need to answer me, child. I can see you do."

"I am trying not to love him," Christina whispered.

Aunt Harriett started fanning herself again. "I certainly don't understand that remark. No, I don't. Lyon did tell me you've only just learned the English language, and that you might not make sense all the time. Now, don't get red in the face, Christina, he meant no criticism. Do you have any idea how remarkable it is that this union will be based on love?"

"When I first met Lyon, I believed we were meant to be together . . . for a short time. Yes," she added when Aunt Harriett gave her a puzzled look. "I believed it was our destiny."

"Destiny?" Aunt Harriett smiled. "What a romantic notion, Christina. I believe you're just what my nephew needs. He's such an intense, angry man most of the time. Now please explain what you meant by saying it would be for only a short while. Do you believe you'd fall out of love so quickly? That is a bit of a shallow constitution, isn't it?"

Christina wasn't sure what the woman meant by her remark. "Lyon would like to marry a princess. I would like to go home. It is really very simple."

The look on Aunt Harriett's face indicated she didn't think it was simple at all.

"Then Lyon will have to go home with you," Aunt Harriett announced. "I'm sure he'd insist upon visiting your homeland."

The absurd suggestion made Christina smile.

"See? I've lightened your worry already," Aunt Harriett said. "Why, of course, Lyon will take you home for a visitation."

Christina knew it was pointless to argue with the kind woman's expectations, and it would have been rude to disagree openly with her. After ordering refreshments, Christina spent the next hour listening to Aunt Harriett tell amusing stories about her family.

She learned that Lyon's father had died in his sleep. Lyon was away at school when the tragedy happened, and Christina thought it sad indeed that he hadn't been by his father's side. She also learned that Lyon's wife, Lettie, had died in childbirth. The story was so sad, Christina had to fight back her tears.

And when the hour was up, Christina went with Aunt Harriett to Lyon's mother's home.

She'd been inside the beautiful townhouse once before, when she'd visited Lady Diana by request, and for that reason the sight of such luxury didn't quite take her breath away.

The entrance blazed with candlelight. The receiving room was on the left. It was a good three times the size of all the others Christina had seen. The dining room was on the right. A long, narrow table took up most of the room, polished to such a sheen one could actually see his face in the reflection. There were sixteen chairs lining each side.

Christina assumed there were that many relatives living with Lyon's mother. Lyon had provided well for his family. There were servants rushing around, fetching and carrying. Aunt Harriett had told her that Lyon paid for it all.

Lady Diana rushed down the steps to greet Christina. "Lyon is waiting for you upstairs in the library," she announced, tugging on Christina's arm. "Oh, you do look lovely in pink, Christina. It's such a soft color," she added. "Do you know, I wish I were as delicate in stature as you are. Why, I feel like an elephant when I'm standing next to you."

Diana continued her chatter, so Christina assumed she wasn't supposed to comment on that observation.

Lady Diana led her up the stairs and into the library. It was a bright, airy room, but that was all Christina noticed when she walked inside. Lyon captured her full attention. He was standing by the windows, his back to her. A surge of anger washed over her. Christina was suddenly infuriated with Lyon's high-handed manner in taking over her life. She knew she was going to shout at him. The urge was making her throat ache.

She kept her intention hidden from his sister, even managed a weak smile when she said, "Lady Diana? May I have a few minutes alone with your brother?"

"Oh, I really don't know if that's a good idea. Aunt Harriett says you can't be unchaperoned for a single minute. She'd heard the rumors, you see," Diana whispered to Christina. "Still, she's downstairs now, and if you give me your promise that it will only be for a few minutes, no one will—"

"Diana, close the door behind you."

Lyon had turned around. He was staring at Christina when he gave the order to his sister.

Christina held his gaze. She wasn't going to be intimidated by him. And she certainly wasn't going to take any time at all to notice how ruggedly handsome he looked today. He was wearing a dark blue riding jacket. The fit made his shoulders look bigger than she'd remembered them to be.

Christina suddenly realized he was frowning at her. Why, he was actually angry with her. The observation didn't sit well. Christina was at first so astonished she could barely speak. How dare he be angry? He was the one causing all the mischief.

"I understand you accepted Baron Thorp's request to accompany you to Westley's affair, Christina. Is that true?"

"How did you hear that?" Christina asked.

"Is it true?"

He hadn't raised his voice, but the harshness was there in his tone.

"Yes, Lyon, I did agree to the baron's request. He asked me last week. We're going to this Westley's lawn party, whatever in heaven's name that is, and I don't particularly care if you're angry or not. It would be rude of me to cancel his escort now. I did give my word."

"You aren't going anywhere unless you're by my side, Christina," Lyon said. He took a deep breath before continuing. "One does not accompany other men when one is about to be married. It's becoming obvious to me that you don't grasp the situation, love. We are getting married Saturday, and I'll be damned if you'll have another escort the day before."

Lyon had tried to hold his temper, but by the time he ended his comments he was shouting.

"I shall not marry you," Christina shouted, matching his tone. "No, we shouldn't get married. Can't you see I'm trying to protect you? You don't know anything about me. You want a princess, for God's sake."

"Christina, if you don't start making sense . . ."

Lyon suddenly moved and had her in his arms before she could take a step back. Christina didn't try to struggle. "If you weren't so stubborn, Lyon, you'd realize I was right. I

201

should find someone else. If Thorp doesn't agree to my proposal, I could ask someone else, even Splickler."

He had to force himself to take another deep breath. "Listen carefully, Christina. No one's going to touch you but me. Splickler's not going to be able to walk for a month, and I forsee a long voyage coming Thorp's way. Believe me when I tell you that every man you settle on will meet with a few unpleasant surprises."

"You wouldn't dare. You're a Marquess. You can't just go around frightening people. Why can't Splickler walk?" she suddenly asked. "I remember quite specifically that Rhone shut the door on his nose. You're exaggerating. You wouldn't—"

"Oh, but I would."

"Dare you smile at me while you make such obscene remarks?"

"I dare to do whatever I want to do, Christina." He rubbed his thumb across her mouth. Christina felt like biting him.

Then her shoulders sagged in defeat. All the man had to do was touch her, and her rational thoughts went flying out the window. God help her, she could feel the shivers gathering in her stomach now.

She let him kiss her, even opened her mouth for his tongue, then let him coach all the anger out of her.

Lyon didn't let up on his tender assault until Christina was responding to him with equal ardor. He ended the intimacy only after she'd put her arms around his shoulders and was clinging to him.

"The only time you're honest with me is when you kiss me, Christina. For now, that's quite enough."

Christina rested her head against his chest. "I will not give my heart to you, Lyon. I will not love you."

He rubbed his chin against the top of her head. "Yes, you will, my sweet."

"You're very sure of yourself," she muttered.

"You gave yourself to me, Christina. Of course I'm sure."

A loud knock on the door interrupted them. "Lyon, unhand that maiden immediately. Do you hear me?"

The question was unnecessary. Aunt Harriett had shouted loud enough for the neighbors to hear.

"How did she know you were holding me, Lyon? Does she have the sight?" Christina asked, her voice filled with awe.

"The what?" Lyon asked.

"Open this door. Now."

"The sight," Christina whispered between Aunt Harriett's bellows. "She can see through the door, Lyon."

Lyon laughed. The booming sound made her ears tingle. "No, my love. My Aunt Harriett just knows me very well. She assumed I'd be holding you."

She looked disappointed. When Aunt Harriett shouted again, Christina turned to go to the door. "If you give me one or two promises, I'll wed you Saturday," she said.

Lyon shook his head. The little innocent still didn't understand. Promises or not, he was going to marry her.

"Well?" she asked.

"What promises?"

Christina turned and found Lyon standing with his arms folded across his chest, waiting. His manner seemed condescending to her. "One, you must promise to let me go home when my task is done here. Two, you must promise not to fall in love with me."

"One, Christina, you aren't going anywhere. Marriage is forever. Get that little fact in your head. Two, I don't have the faintest idea why you wouldn't want me to love you, but I'll try to accommodate you."

"I knew you'd be difficult. I just knew it," Christina muttered.

The door suddenly opened behind her. "Well, why didn't you tell me it wasn't latched?" Aunt Harriett demanded. "Did you get this misunderstanding straightened out, Christina?" she asked.

"I have decided to marry Lyon for a little while."

"A long while," Lyon muttered.

The woman was as dense as fog. Lyon felt like shaking her.

"Good. Now come along with me, Christina, and I'll show you your room. It's next to my bedroom," she added, with a long, meaningful look in Lyon's direction. "There will be no private meetings during the night while I'm about."

"She'll be there in just a minute," Lyon said. "Christina, answer me one question before you leave."

"I shall wait right outside this door," Aunt Harriett announced before pulling the door closed.

"What is your question?" Christina asked.

"Are you going to change your mind before Saturday? Do I have to keep you guarded inside the townhouse until then?"

"You're smiling as though you'd like to do just that," Christina announced. "No, I won't change my mind. You're going to be very sorry, Lyon," she added in a sympathetic voice. "I'm not at all what you think I am."

"I know exactly what I'm getting," Lyon said, trying not to laugh. She was giving him a forlorn look, telling him without words that she felt sorry for him.

"You're marrying me because you realize how good it was when we slept together," he announced.

It was an arrogant statement, and he really didn't think she'd bother to answer him.

"No."

Christina opened the door, smiled at Aunt Harriett, then turned to give Lyon her full answer. "The full truth, Lyon?"

"That would be nice for a change," Lyon answered with a drawl.

"In front of your dear Aunt Harriett?" she qualified, giving the perplexed woman a quick smile.

Aunt Harriett let out a sigh, then pulled the door closed again. Christina could hear her muttering something about not needing her fan what with the door flapping back and forth in her face, but she didn't understand what the older lady meant.

"Answer me, Christina, with your full truth."

His sudden impatience irritated her. "Very well. I'm marrying you because of the way you fought the mischief makers."

"What does that have to do with marriage?" he asked.

"Oh, everything."

"Christina, will you make sense for once in your life?" Lyon demanded.

She realized then she should simply have lied to him again. The truth was often more upsetting, more complex than a simple fabrication. Still, it was a little too late to fashion another lie now. Lyon looked as if he wanted to shout. "I'm trying to make sense, Lyon. You see, even though the battle wasn't much to boast about, you did fight like a warrior."

"And?"

"Well, it's perfectly clear to me."

"Christina." His voice was low, angry.

"You aren't going to be an easy man to kill. There, now you have the full truth. Does it satisfy you?"

Lyon nodded, giving her the impression he understood what she was talking about. He knew in that moment that nothing the woman ever said to him in the future would confuse him. No, he'd just reached his limit. A man could only take so many surprises, he told himself.

Then he tried to concentrate on the new puzzle she'd handed him. "Are you telling me you'll try to kill me once we're wed, but because I can defend myself, you might not be able to accomplish the deed? And that is why you're marrying me?"

He had to shake his head when he'd finished his illogical conclusions.

"Of course not," Christina answered. "How shameful of you to think I'd want to harm you. You've a devious mind, Lyon."

"All right," he said, clasping his hands behind his back. "I apologize for jumping to such unsavory conclusions."

Christina looked suspicious. "Well, I would hope so," she muttered. "I shall accept your apology," she added grudgingly. "You look contrite enough to make me believe you're sincere."

Lyon vowed he wasn't going to lose his patience. He wasn't as certain about his mind, however. Christina was making mincemeat out of all his thoughts. God help him, he was going to get a clear answer out of her, no matter how long it took. "Christina," he began, keeping his voice soothing enough to lull an infant, "since you've decided I'm not an easy man to kill—and I do appreciate your faith in me, by the way—do you happen to know who's going to try?"

"Try what?"

"To kill me."

The man really needed to learn how to control his temper. Christina had just opened the door again. She smiled at Aunt Harriett, saw the poor woman was about to speak, but shut the door in her face before she could get a word out. She didn't want the woman to overhear her answer.

"My father. He's coming back to England. He'll try to kill me. I promise to protect you, Lyon, for as long as I'm here. When I go away again, he'll leave you alone."

"Christina, if he's going to try to kill you, why do you think to protect me?"

"Oh, he'll have to kill you first. It's the only way he'll be able to get to me," she reasoned. "You're a very possessive man, Lyon. Yes, you are," she added when she thought he was about to protest. "You'll guard me."

Lyon was suddenly feeling extremely pleased but didn't have the faintest idea why. Had she just given him a compliment? He couldn't be sure.

He decided to make certain. "Then you trust me," he announced.

She looked astonished. "Trust a white man? Never."

Christina jerked the door open and set about smoothing the bluster out of Aunt Harriett. It was a difficult undertaking, for her mind was still occupied with Lyon's outrageous conclusion. Trust him? Where in God's name had he come by that ridiculous notion?

"It's about time, young lady. A woman could grow old waiting for you."

"Aunt Harriett, I appreciate your patience. And you were so right. A good talk with Lyon has resolved all my worries. Will you show me to my room now? I would like to help the maid unpack my gowns. Do you think there's enough room here for my aunt when she returns to London next week? The Countess will be displeased when she learns I've moved away."

Her ploy worked. Aunt Harriett immediately lost her puzzled expression. The urge to take charge overrode all other considerations. "Of course I was right. Now come along with me. Did you know Diana has invited several people over for the afternoon? Quite a number have already arrived. They're all very anxious to meet you, Christina."

The door clicked shut on Aunt Harriett's enthusiastic remarks.

Lyon walked back over to the windows. He saw the gathering in the garden below, then dismissed the guests from his mind.

The puzzle was taking shape. Lyon concentrated on the new item he believed to be true. Christina did think her father was going to come back to England.

To kill her.

The frightened look in her eyes, the way her voice had trembled, told him she was, for once, giving him the truth. She knew far more than she was telling, however. Lyon guessed the only reason she'd admitted that much to him was to put him on his guard.

She was trying to protect him. He didn't know if he should feel insulted or happy. She had taken on his duty. But she was right. He was possessive. Christina belonged to him, and he wasn't about to let anyone harm her. They'd have to kill him first in order to get to her.

How had she ever come by such conclusions about her father? Lyon remembered how emphatic Sir Reynolds had been when he told him Christina had never even met her father.

None of it made sense, unless Christina's mother had lived longer than anyone believed and had handed down her fears to her daughter . . . or possibly left the fears with someone else.

Who had raised Christina? It surely wasn't the

Summertons, Lyon thought with a smile. What a little liar she was. Though he should have been furious with her for deceiving him, he was actually amused. He sensed she'd fabricated the story just to placate him.

How simple it would be if only she'd tell him the whole truth. Christina wouldn't, of course, but at least now he understood her reason. She didn't trust him.

No, he corrected himself, she didn't trust white men.

She'd meant to say Englishmen . . . or had she?

The key to the riddle rested in the missionary's hands. Lyon knew he'd have to be patient. Bryan had sent him a note telling him that Mick had remembered the man's name. He was called Claude Deavenrue.

Lyon had immediately dispatched two of his loyal men in search of Deavenrue. Although he knew the missionary had told Mick he was going to stop in England on his way back from France to pay Christina a visit, Lyon wasn't about to put his faith in that possibility. There was always the chance Deavenrue might change his mind, or that Mick had been wrong in what he'd heard.

No, Lyon wasn't taking any risks. It had suddenly become imperative that he speak to the missionary as soon as possible. His reasons for finding out about Christina's past had changed, however. A feeling of unease had settled in his mind. She was in danger. He wasn't certain if her father was the true threat, but all his instincts were telling him to beware. The urge to protect Christina fairly overwhelmed him. Lyon had learned long ago to trust his instincts. The scar on his forehead had been the result of one of those foolish instances when he hadn't heeded their warning.

Lyon hoped the missionary would be able to shed some light on the mystery, to tell him enough about Christina's past to help him protect her. Lyon had already drawn his own conclusions. From all her comments, he decided she was probably raised by one of those courageous frontier families he'd heard about. He even pictured Christina inside a small log cabin somewhere in the wilderness beyond the colonies. That would explain the facts that she liked to go barefooted, loved the outdoors, had heard the sounds of mountain lions, and had possibly seen a buffalo or two.

Yes, that explanation made good sense to Lyon, but he wasn't going to hold firm to that easy conclusion until he had confirmation from Deavenrue.

Lyon let out a long, weary sigh. He was satisfied that he was doing all he could for the moment. Then his mind turned to another troubling thought. Christina kept insisting she was going to go home.

Lyon vowed to find a reason to make her want to stay.

A loud knock on the door interrupted Lyon's thoughts. "Have time for us, Lyon?" Rhone asked from the doorway. "Lord, you're scowling like a devil," he remarked in a cheerful voice. "Don't let it put you off, Andrew," he told the young man standing beside him. "Lyon is always in a foul mood. Had another recent conversation with Christina, perchance?" he asked, his voice as bland as the color of his beige jacket. When Lyon nodded, Rhone started chuckling. "Andrew has yet to meet your intended, Lyon. I thought you would like to do the introductions."

"Good to see you again, Andrew," Lyon said, trying to sound as if he meant it. He hadn't wanted to be interrupted; he didn't want to be civil, and he glared just that message to Rhone.

His friend was tugging on the sleeve of his jacket, probably trying to keep his bandage concealed, Lyon thought. The man had no business being out and about yet. Lyon would have pointed out that fact if they'd been alone. Then he decided Rhone had deliberately dragged Andrew with him up to the library to avoid an argument.

"The ladies are outside in the garden," Rhone said, ignoring the black look his friend was giving him. He strolled over to the windows where Lyon stood, then motioned for Andrew to follow.

Rhone's companion made a wide berth around Lyon to

stand beside Rhone. His face was red, his manner timid. "Perhaps I should wait downstairs," Andrew remarked with a noticeable stammer. "We have intruded upon the Marquess," he ended in a whisper to Rhone.

"There's Christina, Andrew," Rhone announced, pretending he hadn't heard his complaint. "She's standing between two other ladies, in front of the hedges. I don't recognize the pretty one speaking to her now," Rhone continued. "Do you know who the other blonde is, Lyon?"

Lyon looked down at the flutter of activity below. His sister had obviously invited half the ton to her afternoon party, he decided.

He found Christina almost immediately. He thought she looked confused by all the attention she was getting. The women all appeared to be talking to her at the same time.

Then one of the gentlemen began to sing a ballad. Everyone immediately turned toward the sound. The doors to the music room had been opened, and someone was playing the spinet in the background.

Christina liked music. The fact was obvious to Lyon. The way her gown floated around her ankles indicated she was enjoying the song. Her hips were keeping gentle rhythm.

She was so enchanting. Her smile of pleasure made Lyon feel at peace again. Christina looked quite mesmerized. Lyon watched as she reached out and tore a leaf from the hedge, then began to twirl it between her fingers as she continued to sway to the music.

He thought she didn't even realize what she was doing. Her gaze was directed on the gentleman singing the song, her manner relaxed, unguarded.

Lyon knew she wasn't aware she was being watched, either. She wouldn't have eaten the leaf otherwise, or reached for another.

"Sir, which one is Princess Christina?" Andrew asked Lyon, just as Rhone started in choking on his laughter.

Rhone had obviously been watching Christina, too.

"Sir?"

"The blond-headed one," Lyon muttered, shaking his head. He watched in growing disbelief as Christina daintily popped another leaf into her mouth.

"Which blond-headed one?" Andrew persisted.

"The one eating the shrubs."

Chapter Ten

Father was overjoyed to see me. He thought Edward had approved of my visit, and I didn't tell him the truth for several days. I was too exhausted from my journey, and knew I had to regain my strength before explaining all that had happened to me.

Father was driving me mad. He'd come into my room, sit on the side of my bed, and talk of nothing but Edward. He seemed convinced that I didn't yet realize how fortunate I was to have married such a fine man.

When I could listen no more, I began to sob. The story poured out of me in incoherent snatches. I remember I screamed at my father, too. He thought I'd lost my mind to make up such lies about my husband.

I did try to speak to him again. But his mind was set in Edward's favor. Then I heard from one of the servants that he'd sent a message to my husband to come and fetch me home.

In desperation, I wrote the full story down on paper, including the fact that I was carrying his grandchild. I hid the letter in my father's winter chest, hoping he wouldn't find it until long months had passed.

Christina, he would have believed my delicate condition was the reason for what he referred to as my nervous disposition.

I began to make my plans to go to my sister, Patricia. She was living with her husband in the colonies. I didn't dare take the gems with me. Patricia was like a hound; she'd find them. She had such an inquisitive nature. For as long as I could remember, she'd read all my letters. No, I couldn't risk taking the jewels with me. They were too important. I'd taken them with the sole intent of seeing them returned to the poor in Edward's kingdom. He'd robbed them, and I was going to see justice done.

I hid the jewels in a box, then waited until the dead of night to go into the back garden. I buried the box in the flower bed, Christina.

Look for the blood roses. You'll find the box there.

> *Journal entry*
> *October 1, 1795*

The bride was nervous throughout the long wedding ceremony. Lyon stood by her side, holding her hand in a grip that didn't allow for any movement—or escape.

He was smiling enough to make her think he'd lost his mind. Yes, he was thoroughly enjoying himself. If Christina had been gifted with a suspicious nature, she might have concluded that her frightened state was the true reason for his happiness.

His mood did darken when she refused to repeat the vow "until death do we part," however. When she realized the holy man with the pointed velvet cap on his head wasn't going to continue along until he'd had his way, and Lyon started squeezing her hand until she thought the bones were going to snap, she finally whispered the required words.

She let Lyon see her displeasure for having to lie to a holy man, but he didn't appear to be bothered by her frown. He gave her a slow wink and a lazy grin. No, he hadn't been bothered much at all.

The man was simply too busy gloating.

Warriors did like to get their way, Christina knew. This one more than most, of course. He was a lion, after all, and he had just captured his lioness.

When they left the church, Christina clung to his arm for support. She was worried about her wedding gown, concerned that any abrupt movement would tear the delicate lace sewn into the neckline and the sleeves. Aunt Harriett had supervised the making of the gown, standing over three maids to see the task done to her satisfaction.

It was a beautiful dress, yet impractical. Lady Diana had told Christina she would only wear the garment once and must then put it aside.

It seemed such a waste. When she remarked on that fact to her new husband, he laughed, gave her another good squeeze, and told her not to be concerned. He had enough coins to keep her in new dresses every day for the rest of her life.

"Why is everyone shouting at us?" Christina asked. She stood next to Lyon on the top step outside the chapel. They faced a large crowd of people she'd never seen before, and they were making such a commotion she could barely hear Lyon's answer.

"They're cheering, love, not shouting." He leaned down and kissed her on her forehead. The cheers immediately intensified. "They're happy for us."

Christina looked up at him, thinking to tell him that it made little sense to her that complete strangers would be happy for them, but the tender expression in his eyes made her forget all about her protest, the crowd, the noise. She instinctively leaned into his side. Lyon put his arm around her waist. He seemed to know how much she needed his touch at that moment.

She quit trembling.

"My, it was a splendid ceremony." Aunt Harriett made her announcement from directly behind Christina. "Lyon, get her into the carriage. Christina, do be sure to wave to all the well-wishers. Your wedding is going to be the talk of the season. Smile, Christina. You're the new Marchioness of Lyonwood."

Lyon reluctantly let go of his bride. Aunt Harriett had taken hold of Christina's arm and was trying to direct her down the steps. Lyon knew his aunt would have her way, even if it meant a tug of war.

Christina was looking bewildered again. Little wonder, Lyon thought. His aunt was fluttering around them like a rather large bird of prey. She was dressed like one, too, in bright canary yellow, and kept flapping her lemon-colored fan in Christina's face while she barked her orders.

Diana stood behind Christina trying to undo the long folds in the wedding gown. Christina glanced behind her, smiled at Lyon's little sister, and then turned back to the crowd.

Lyon took hold of her hand and led her to the open carriage. Christina remembered to do what Aunt Harriett had instructed. She waved at all the strangers lining the streets.

"It's a pity your mama couldn't attend the ceremony," she whispered to Lyon when they were on their way. "And my Aunt Patricia is going to be angry," she added. "We really should have waited for her return from the country, Lyon."

"Angry because she missed the wedding or angry because you married me?" Lyon asked, his voice laced with amusement.

"Both, I fear," Christina answered. "Lyon, I do hope you'll get along with her when she comes to live with us."

"Are you out of your mind? The Countess will not be living with us, Christina," he said. His tone had taken on a hard edge. He took a deep breath, then started again. "We'll discuss your aunt later. All right?"

"As you wish," Christina answered. She was confused by his abrupt change in disposition, yet didn't question him. Later would be soon enough.

The reception had been hastily planned, but the result was

more than satisfactory. Candles blazed throughout the rooms, flowers lined the tables, and servants dressed in formal black scooted through the large crowd with silver trays laden with drinks. The guests spilled out into the gardens behind Lyon's mother's home, and the crush, as Aunt Harriett called it, proved that the party was a success.

Lyon took Christina upstairs to meet his mother. It wasn't a very pleasing first meeting. Lyon's mother didn't even look at her. She gave Lyon her blessing, then began to talk about her other son, James. Lyon dragged Christina out of the dark room during the middle of one of his mother's reminiscences. He was frowning, but once the door was shut behind them the smile slowly returned to his face.

Christina decided to speak to Lyon about his mama at the first possible opportunity. He'd been remiss in his duty, she thought, and then excused his conduct by telling herself he simply didn't understand what his duty was. Yes, she'd speak to him and set him straight.

"Don't frown so, Christina," Lyon said as they walked down the stairs again. "My mother is content."

"She'll be more content when she comes to live with us," Christina remarked. "I shall see to it."

"What?"

His incredulous shout drew several stares. Christina smiled up at her husband. "We shall speak of this matter later, Lyon," she instructed. "It is our wedding day, after all, and we really must be getting along. Oh, see how Rhone stands next to your sister? Do you notice the way he glares at the young men trying to get her attention?"

"You see only what you want to see," Lyon said. He pulled her up against his side when they reached the entrance, guarding her just like a warrior when they were once again surrounded by their guests.

"No, Lyon," Christina argued between introductions. "You're the one who sees only what you want to see," she explained. "You wanted to marry a princess, didn't you?"

Now what in heaven's name did she mean by that remark? Lyon thought to query her when her next question turned his attention. "Who is that shy man hovering in the doorway, Lyon? He can't seem to make up his mind if he should come inside or not."

Lyon turned to see Bryan, his friend. He caught his attention and motioned him over. "Bryan, I'm pleased you could make it. This is my wife, Christina," he added. "My dear, I'd like you to meet Bryan. He owns the Bleak Bryan tavern in another part of town."

Christina bowed, then reached out to take the timid man's hand. He offered her his left hand, thinking to save her embarrassment when she noticed his right hand was missing, but Christina clasped her hands around his scarred wrist and smiled so enchantingly that Bryan could barely get his breath. "I am honored to meet you, Bleak Bryan," she announced. "I've heard so much about you, sir. The tales of your boldness are quite wonderful."

Lyon was immediately puzzled. "My dear, I didn't speak of Bryan to you," he commented.

Bryan was blushing. He'd never had a lady of such quality pay him so much attention. He tugged his cravat, making a mess of the knot he had spent hours trying to perfect.

"I would certainly like to know where you've heard my name," he said.

"Oh, Rhone told me all about you," she answered with a smile. "He also said you would be giving your back room to Lyon next Friday eve for a game of chance."

Bryan nodded. Lyon frowned. "Rhone talks too much," he muttered.

"Is this the lady Mick told the story about, Lyon?" Bryan asked his friend. "No, she cannot be the same. Why, she doesn't look like she'd have the strength to throw a man . . ."

Bryan finally noticed Lyon was shaking his head.

"Who is Mick?" Christina asked.

"A shipmate who frequents my establishment," Bryan answered. His leathery face wrinkled into another smile. "He told the most remarkable story about—"

"Bryan, go and get something to eat," Lyon interjected.

217

"Ah, here comes Rhone now. Rhone? Take Bryan into the dining room."

Christina waited until she was once again alone with Lyon, then asked him why he'd suddenly become irritated. "Did I say something to upset you?"

Lyon shook his head. "I can't take much more of this crowd. Let's leave. I want to be alone with you."

"Now?"

"Now," he announced. To show her he meant exactly what he'd said, he took hold of her hand and started pulling her out the front doorway.

Aunt Harriett cut them off at the bottom step.

Christina had the good grace to look contrite. Lyon looked exasperated.

Aunt Harriett didn't budge from her position. She reminded Lyon of a centurion, for her hands were settled on her hips and her bosom was heaving forward like a solid plate of armor.

A smile suddenly softened her rigid stance. "I've put Christina's satchel inside your carriage, Lyon. You've lasted a good hour longer than I imagined you would."

Aunt Harriett wrapped Christina in a suffocatingly affectionate hug, then released her.

"Be gentle this night," she instructed Lyon.

"I shall."

It was Christina who gave the promise. Both Lyon and his aunt looked at her. "She means me, Christina," Lyon said dryly.

"You have only to remember that Lyon is your husband now, my dear," Aunt Harriett announced with a true blush. "Then all your fears will be put to rest."

Christina didn't have any idea what the woman was trying to tell her. She kept giving Christina knowing nods, and an intense hawklike stare as well.

Lyon suddenly swept her up into his arms and settled her on his lap inside the carriage. Christina wrapped her arms around her husband's neck, rested the side of her face against his shoulder, and sighed with pleasure.

He smiled against the top of her head.

Neither said a word for quite a while, content to hold each other and enjoy the blissful solitude.

Christina didn't know where he was taking her, and she didn't particularly care. They were finally alone, and that was all that mattered to her.

"Christina, you don't seem frightened of the closed quarters today," Lyon remarked. He trailed his chin across the top of her forehead in an affectionate caress. "Have you conquered this dislike?"

"I don't think I have," Christina answered. "But when you're holding me so close to you, and when I close my eyes, I do forget my worry."

It was because she trusted him, Lyon told himself. "I like it when you're honest with me, Christina," Lyon said. "And now that we're married, you must always tell me the truth," he added, thinking to ease into the topics of love and trust.

"Haven't I always told you the truth?" Christina asked. She leaned away from him to look up at his face. "Why are you looking so out of sorts? When have I ever lied to you?"

"The Summertons for one," Lyon drawled.

"Who?"

"Exactly," Lyon answered. "You told me the Summertons raised you, and we both know that was a lie."

"A fabrication," Christina corrected.

"There's a difference?"

"Sort of."

"That's not an answer, Christina," Lyon said. "It's an evasion."

"Oh."

"Well?"

"Well, what?" Christina asked. She tickled the back of his neck with her fingertips, trying to turn his attention. It was their wedding night, and she really didn't want to have to lie to him again.

"Are you going to tell me the truth about your past now? Since the Summertons don't exist . . ."

"You really are persistent," Christina muttered. She softened her rebuke with a quick smile. "Very well, Lyon. Since I am your wife, I do suppose I should tell you the full truth."

"Thank you."

"You're welcome, Lyon."

She settled herself against his shoulder again and closed her eyes. Lyon waited several long minutes before he realized she thought the discussion was over.

"Christina?" he asked, letting his exasperation show. "Who took care of you when you were a little girl?"

"The sisters."

"What sisters?"

Christina ignored the impatience in his voice. Her mind raced for a new fabrication. "Sister Vivien and Sister Jennifer mostly," she said. "I lived in a convent, you see, in France. It was a very secluded area. I don't remember who took me there. I was very young. The sisters were like mothers to me, Lyon. Each night they'd tell me wonderful stories about the places they'd seen."

"Buffalo stories?" Lyon asked, smiling over the sincerity in her voice.

"Why, as a matter of fact, yes," Christina answered, warming to her story. She made the decision not to feel guilty about deceiving her husband. Her motives were pure enough. Lyon would only be upset by the truth.

He was English, after all.

"Sister Frances drew a picture of a buffalo for me. Have you ever seen one, Lyon?"

"No," he answered. "Now tell me more about this convent," Lyon persisted. His hands caressed her back in a soothing motion.

"Well, as I said, it was in a very isolated spot. A giant wall surrounded the buildings. I was allowed to run barefoot most of the time, for we never had visitors. I was terribly spoiled, but I was still a sweet-tempered child. Sister Mary told me she knew my mother, and that is why they took me in. I was the only child there, of course."

"How did you learn to defend yourself?" he asked, his voice mild.

"Sister Vivien believed that a woman should know how to protect herself. There weren't any men around to protect us. It was a reasonable decision."

Christina's explanation made good sense. She'd answered his question about her confusion with the English laws, the reason she preferred to go shoeless, and where she'd seen a buffalo. Oh, yes, the explanation tied up some of the dangling strings all right. It was convincing and logical.

He wasn't buying it for a minute.

Lyon leaned back against the upholstery and smiled. He accepted the fact that time was needed for Christina to learn to trust him with the truth. He'd probably know all there was to know about her before she finally got around to telling him, of course.

Lyon realized the irony. He was determined that Christina would never find out about his past activities. He meant to keep his sins from her, yet he persisted, like a hound after a meaty rabbit, in prodding her into telling him all about herself.

He wasn't, however, the one insisting he was going home. She was. And Lyon knew full well the mythical convent wasn't her real destination.

She wasn't going anywhere.

"Lyon, you're squeezing the breath right out of me," Christina protested.

He immediately softened his hold.

They arrived at their destination. Lyon carried her up the steps to his townhouse, through the empty foyer, and up the winding staircase. Christina barely opened her eyes to look around.

His bedroom had been made ready for them. Several candles burned with soft light on the bedside tables. The covers had been drawn back on the huge bed. A fire blazed in the hearth across the room, taking the chill out of the night air.

Lyon placed her on the bed and stood there smiling at her for the longest time. "I've sent my staff on ahead to open the country home, Christina. We're all alone," he explained as he knelt down and reached for her shoes.

"It's our wedding night," Christina said. "I must undress you first. It is the way it should be done, Lyon."

She flipped her shoes off, then stood beside her husband. After she'd untied the knot of his cravat, she stood back to help him with his jacket.

When his shirt had been removed and her fingers slipped into the waistband of his pants, Lyon couldn't stand still any longer. Christina smiled when she noticed how his stomach muscles reacted to her touch. She would have continued undressing him, but Lyon wrapped his arms around her waist, pulled her up against his chest, and claimed her mouth in a hot, sensual kiss.

For long sweet minutes they teased each other with their hands, their tongues, their whispered words of pleasure.

Lyon had vowed to go slowly this night, to give Christina pleasure first, and he knew that if he didn't pull away and help her get undressed soon he'd end up ripping another gown off her.

She was trembling when he dragged his mouth away from hers. Her voice had deserted her, and she had to nudge him toward the side of the bed. When he sat down, she pulled off his shoes and socks.

She stood on the platform between Lyon's legs and slowly worked the fastenings free on her sleeves. It was an awkward task because she couldn't seem to take her gaze away from Lyon to watch what she was doing.

"You'll have to help me with the back of my gown," she said, smiling because her voice sounded so strained to her.

When she turned around, Lyon pulled her down onto his lap. She fought the urge to lean against him, impatient now to get her scratchy gown out of the way. Her hands reached to her coronet, but she'd only pulled one pin free before Lyon pushed her hands away and took over the task. "Let me," he said, his voice husky.

The heavy curls unwound until the rich, sun-kissed locks fell to her waist. Christina sighed with pleasure. Lyon's fingers were making her shiver. He slowly lifted the mass to drape it over her shoulder, paused to kiss the back of her neck, and then began the arduous task of unhooking the tiny fastenings.

His heart was slamming against his chest. The scent of her was so appealing, so wonderfully feminine. He wanted to bury his face in her golden curls; he would have given in to his urge if she hadn't moved against his arousal so impatiently, so enticingly.

Lyon was finally able to get her gown open to her waist. She was wearing a white chemise, but the silk material easily tore free when he slipped his hands inside. He found her breasts and cupped their fullness as he pulled her forcefully back against his chest.

Christina arched against him. His thumbs slid over her nipples, making her breath catch in her throat. Her skin tingled when she rubbed her back against the warm pelt of hair on his chest.

"You feel so good, my love," Lyon whispered into her ear. He nuzzled her earlobe as he tugged on her gown, lifting her away from him only long enough to push the garment down over her hips.

Christina was too weak to help. Her hips moved against him. Lyon thought her motions were excruciatingly blissful. He kissed the side of her neck, then her shoulder. "Your skin is so smooth, so soft," he told her.

Christina tried to speak to him, to tell him how very much he pleased her, but his hand slid between her thighs, making her forget her own thoughts. His thumb teased her sensitive nub again and again until the sweet torture threatened to consume her. She called his name with a ragged moan when his fingers penetrated her, then tried to push his hand away. Lyon wouldn't cease his torment, and she was soon lost to the sensations coursing through her, unable to think much at all. She could only react to the incredible heat. "Lyon, I can't stop."

"Don't fight it, Christina," Lyon whispered. He increased his pressure until she found her release. Christina arched against him, called his name again.

He could feel the tremors flowing through her. Lyon

didn't remember taking the rest of his clothes off, didn't know if he'd been gentle or rough when he moved her from his lap to the center of the bed.

Her hair fanned out on top of the pillows, shining almost silver in the candlelight. She was so beautiful. She was still wearing her white stockings. He might have smiled, but the surge of white-hot desire consumed him and he couldn't be sure.

He came to her then, settling himself between her thighs, wrapping his arms around her. He captured her mouth in a searing kiss and thrust into her tight, moist heat just as his tongue thrust inside her mouth to mate with hers.

Christina put her legs around him, pulling him deeper inside. She met each thrust completely, forcefully, arching with demand when he withdrew.

They both found their release at the same moment.

"I love you, Christina."

Christina couldn't answer him. The sweet ecstasy overwhelmed her. She felt like liquid in his strong arms, could only hold onto him until the storm had passed.

Reality was slow to return to Lyon. He wanted never to move. His breathing was harsh, erratic. "Am I crushing you, love?" he asked when she tried to move.

"No," Christina answered. "But the bed seems to be swallowing me up."

Lyon leaned up on his elbows to take most of his weight off her. His legs were tangled with hers, and he shifted his thighs to ease the pressure.

His gaze was tender. "Say the words, Christina. I want to hear them."

Because he fully expected to hear her tell him that she loved him, he wasn't at all prepared for her tears. "My sweet?" he asked, catching the first drops that fell from her thick lashes with his fingertips. "Are you going to cry every time we make love?"

"I cannot seem to help myself," Christina whispered between sobs. "You make me feel so wonderful."

Lyon kissed her again. "You sound like you're confessing

a grave sin," he said. "Is it so terrible to feel wonderful?"

"No."

"I love you. In time you'll give me the words I want. You're very stubborn, do you know that?"

"You don't love me," Christina whispered. "You love—"

His hand covered her mouth. "If you tell me I love a princess, I'll—"

"You'll what?" Christina asked when he moved his hand away from her mouth.

"Be displeased," Lyon announced, giving her a lopsided grin.

Christina smiled at her husband. Lyon rolled to his side, then pulled her up against him. "Lyon?"

"Yes?"

"Will I always feel as though my soul has merged with yours?"

"I hope so," Lyon answered. "Very few people are able to share what we've—"

"It's destiny," Christina said. She wiped her tears away with the back of her hand. "You may laugh at me if you want, but it was our destiny to be with each other. Besides, no other woman would have you."

Lyon chuckled. "Is that so?" he asked.

"Oh, yes. You're a scoundrel. Why, you ruined my reputation just to get your way."

"But you don't care what others say about you, do you, Christina?"

"Sometimes I do," she confessed. "It's a sorry trait, isn't it? I care what you think of me."

"I'm glad," Lyon answered.

Christina closed her eyes with a sigh. The last thing she remembered was Lyon pulling the covers up over them.

Lyon thought she looked like a contented kitten, curled up against him. He knew he wouldn't be able to sleep for very long, and the familiar tension settled in the pit of his stomach. The nightmares would certainly visit him again. He hadn't missed a night in over two years. His worry was for Christina, of course. He didn't want to frighten her. No, he knew he'd have to go downstairs and meet his past there, in the privacy of his library.

He closed his eyes for a moment, wanting to savor her warmth just a little longer.

It was his last thought until morning light.

Chapter Eleven

The voyage to the colonies was very difficult. The ocean in winter was angry with giant swells. The bitterness of the frigid air kept me inside my cabin most of the time. I tied myself to my bed with rope the captain had supplied, for I would have been tossed around the room if I hadn't taken that precaution.

I wasn't sick in the mornings any longer, and my heart had softened toward you, Christina. I actually thought I'd be able to make a new beginning in the colonies.

I felt so free, so safe. Another ocean would soon separate me from Edward. You see, I didn't realize he'd come after me.

*Journal entry
October 3, 1795*

Morning sun flooded the bedroom before Lyon awakened. His first thought was an astonishing one. For the first time in over two years, he'd actually slept through the night. The pleasant realization didn't last long, however. Lyon rolled to his side to take his wife into his arms, and only then he realized she wasn't there.

He bolted out of the bed, then thanked God and his quick reflexes, for he'd just missed stepping on her.

She'd obviously fallen out of bed, and in her sound sleep she hadn't awakened enough to climb back in.

Lyon knelt down next to Christina. He must have slept like an innocent, too, he decided, because he hadn't heard her fall. She'd dragged one of the blankets with her, and she did look comfortable. Her breathing was deep, even. No, he didn't think the fall had harmed her.

He gently eased her into his arms. When he stood up, she instinctively cuddled against his chest.

You trust me when you're sleeping, he thought with a grin as her hands slipped around his waist and he caught her contented sigh.

Lyon stood there holding her for long, peaceful minutes, then placed her in the center of his bed. Her breathing hadn't changed, and he really didn't think he'd awakened her, but when he tried to move her hands away from his waist her grip increased.

Christina suddenly opened her eyes and smiled at him.

He smiled back a bit sheepishly, for the way she was watching him made him feel as though he'd just been caught in the act of doing something forbidden.

"You fell out of bed, sweetheart," he told her.

She thought his comment was vastly amusing. When he questioned her about her laughter, she shook her head, told him he probably wouldn't understand, and asked why he didn't just make love to her again and quit frowning so ferociously.

Lyon fell into her arms, and into her plan wholeheartedly.

Christina proved to be just as uninhibited in the morning light as she was during the dark hours of the night. And he was just as satisfied.

He stayed in bed with his hands behind his head, watching his wife as she straightened the room and got dressed. He was amazed by her lack of shyness. She didn't seem to be the least embarrassed by her nudity. She was dressed all too soon for his liking, in a pretty violet-colored walking gown, and when she began to brush the tangles from her hair, Lyon noticed the length didn't reach her hips now. No, her hair was waist-length.

"Christina, did you cut your hair?"

"Yes."

"Why? I like it long," Lyon said.

"You do?"

She turned from the mirror to smile at him. "Don't pin it up on top of your head, either," Lyon ordered. "I like it down."

"It isn't fashionable," Christina quoted. "But I shall bend to my husband's dictates," she added with a mock curtsy. "Lyon, are we leaving for your country home today?"

"Yes."

Christina tied a ribbon around her hair at the back of her neck, a frown of concentration on her face. "How long will it take us?" she asked.

"About three hours, a little longer perhaps," Lyon answered.

Then came a sound of someone banging on the front door. "Now who do you suppose that could be?" Christina asked.

"Someone with bad manners," Lyon muttered. He reluctantly got out of bed, reached for his clothing, then quickened his actions when his wife hurried out of the room. "Christina, don't you open that door until you know who it is," he bellowed after her.

He stumbled on a piece of sharp metal, let out a curse over his awkwardness, then glanced down to see the handle of Christina's knife protruding from the edge of the blanket she'd pulled to the floor with her. Now what in heaven's name was her knife doing there? Lyon shook his head. He determined to question her just as soon as he got rid of their unwanted visitors.

Christina had requested names as Lyon instructed before she unlocked the chains and opened the door.

Misters Borton and Henderson, her grandfather's solicitors, stood on the front stoop. They both looked terribly uncomfortable. Aunt Patricia was standing between the two men. She looked furious.

Christina wasn't given time to greet her guests properly or to get out of her aunt's way. The Countess slapped Christina across her face so forcefully that Christina stumbled backwards.

She would have fallen if Mr. Borton hadn't grabbed hold of her arm to steady her. Both solicitors were shouting at the Countess, and Henderson endeavored to restrain the wily old woman when she tried to strike Christina again.

"You filthy whore," the Countess screeched. "Did you think I wouldn't hear the stories of the vile things you did while I was away? And now you've gone and married the bastard!"

"Silence!"

Lyon's roar shook the walls. Borton and Henderson both took hesitant steps back. The Countess was too angry to show similar caution, however. She turned to glare up at the man who had ruined all her plans.

Christina also turned to look at her husband. The left side of her face was throbbing with pain, but she tried to smile at her husband, to tell him it was really all right.

Lyon was down the stairs and pulling Christina into his arms before she could begin her explanation. He tilted her face up for his scrutiny, then asked her in a voice chilled with his rage, "Who did this to you?"

She didn't have to answer. The solicitors interrupted each other as they hastened to explain that the Countess had struck her niece.

Lyon turned to Christina's aunt. "If you ever touch her again, you won't live to boast of it. Do you understand me?"

The aunt's eyes turned to slits, and her voice was filled with venom when she answered Lyon. "I know all about you. Yes, you would kill a defenseless woman, wouldn't you? Christina's going home with me now. This marriage will be annulled."

"It will not," Lyon answered.

"I'll go to the authorities," the Countess shouted, so forcefully that the veins stood out in the sides of her neck.

"Do that," Lyon answered, his voice soft. "And after you've spoken to them, I'll send your friend Splickler to tell them the rest of the story."

The Countess let out a shrill gasp. "You cannot prove—"

"Oh, but I already have," Lyon interjected. A smile that didn't quite reach his eyes changed his expression. "Splickler has conveniently written everything down on paper, Countess. If you want to make trouble, go right ahead."

"You can't believe I had anything to do with Splickler," the Countess said to Christina. "Why, I was visiting my friend in the country."

"You were staying all by yourself at the Platte Inn," Lyon answered.

"You had me followed?"

"I knew you'd lied to Christina," Lyon announced. "It's a fact you don't have any friends, Countess. I was immediately suspicious."

"Then you're the one who caused all the mishaps when I tried to return to London before the wedding. I would have stopped it. You knew that, didn't you, you—"

"Get out of here," Lyon commanded. "Say goodbye to your niece, Countess. You're never going to see her again. I'll see to it."

"Lyon," Christina whispered. She was about to soothe his anger. He gave her a gentle squeeze, however, and she assumed he didn't want her interference.

Christina wished he wouldn't get so upset on her behalf. It really wasn't necessary. She understood her aunt far better than Lyon did. She knew how greed motivated her aunt's every action.

"Christina, do you know you've married a cold-blooded murderer? Oh, yes," the Countess sneered. "England knighted him for his cold-blooded—"

"Madam, hold your tongue," Mr. Henderson said in a harsh whisper. "It was wartime," he added, with a sympathetic look at Christina.

Christina could feel the rage in her husband. His hold on her was rigid. She tried to think of a way to calm him and rid them of their uninvited guests. She slipped her hand under his jacket and began to stroke his back, trying to tell him without words that the angry comments didn't matter to her.

"Mr. Borton? Have you carried along the papers for me to sign?" she asked in a whisper.

"It is your husband who must sign the papers, my dear," Mr. Henderson answered. "My lord? If you would only give us a few minutes of your time, the funds will be handed over to you without further delay."

"Funds? What funds?" Lyon asked, shaking his head.

The Countess stomped on the floor. "Christina, if he doesn't give me my money, I'll make certain he never wants to touch you again. Yes, I'll tell him everything. Do you understand me?"

Christina's soothing strokes on Lyon's back weren't helping. She could feel his new fury. She gave him a squeeze.

Lyon had never harmed a woman, but he didn't think it was an odious thought to murder the evil woman defaming his wife. He was aching to throw her out the door.

"Did this woman come with you or does she have her own carriage?" Lyon asked the two gentlemen.

"Her conveyance is out front," Henderson answered with a nod.

Lyon turned back to the Countess. "If you aren't out of here in exactly thirty seconds, I'm going to throw you out."

"This isn't over," the Countess shouted at the Marquess. She glared at Christina. "No, this isn't over," she muttered again as she strode out the doorway.

Mr. Borton shut the door and sagged against the frame. Henderson poked at his collar. He held a satchel in his other hand. Suddenly he seemed to remember what his duty was, and he said, "Sir, I do apologize for rushing in on you this way, but the Countess was set on disrupting you."

"Who in God's name are you, man?" Lyon asked, his patience at an end.

"He is Mr. Henderson, Lyon, and the man holding up the door is Mr. Borton. They are my grandfather's solicitors. Let us get this over and done with, please, Lyon? If you'll take the gentlemen into the library, I shall fetch some soothing tea. My, it has been quite a morning, hasn't it, husband?"

Lyon stared down at his wife with an incredulous look on

his face. She acted as though nothing upsetting had taken place. Then he decided her calm manner was deliberate. "Are you trying to placate me?" he asked.

"Soothing your temper," Christina corrected. She smiled at her husband, then grimaced against the sting of her swelling skin.

Lyon noticed her discomfort. His grip tightened around her waist. She felt his anger again, had to sigh over it. "I shall go and make the tea now."

It wasn't as easy for Lyon to let go of his anger. He was abrupt when he motioned the men into his study, then took great pleasure in slamming the door shut behind him. "This had better be worth the interruption," he told the men.

Christina deliberately took her time so that Lyon would hear the facts of her grandfather's will before she interrupted.

She could tell, when Mr. Borton opened the door to her knock and took the tray from her, that the meeting hadn't gone well. No, he was looking very nervous. Christina glanced over to look at her husband and immediately understood Borton's worry. Lyon was scowling.

"Why didn't you tell me, Christina? Damn, you have more money than I do."

"And that displeases you?" she asked. She poured the tea, handed him the first cup, then continued her task until the solicitors had both been served.

"I don't believe your wife understood the exact amount left to her by her grandfather," Mr. Henderson said.

"Is it important, Lyon? It all belongs to you now, doesn't it? That is what you said earlier, Mr. Borton," Christina said. "Of course, we must make an allowance for Aunt Patricia. It must be substantial, too."

Lyon leaned back in his chair. He closed his eyes and prayed for patience. "Do you really think I'm going to provide for that . . . that . . ."

"She cannot help what she is," Christina interjected. "She's old, Lyon, and for that reason alone we must provide for her. It isn't necessary that you like her."

Christina smiled at their visitors. "At first I believed that

233

my aunt could come and live with us, but I see that wouldn't work. No, she would never get along with Lyon. Of course, if my husband doesn't agree to finance her, then I suppose she'll have to stay with us."

He knew exactly what she was doing. A slow smile pushed his frown away. His gentle little wife had a pure heart, and a mind worthy of a diplomat. She was manipulating him now, hinting at the ridiculous possibility that the Countess would have to live with them if he didn't provide for her.

At that moment though, with her smiling so innocently at him, he decided he didn't want to deny her anything.

"Henderson, if you've the stomach for it, I would like to put you and Borton in charge of the Countess's account. Let me know what is needed to keep Christina's aunt content enough to leave us alone."

While Christina patiently waited, the details were worked out. She then saw the gentlemen out the door and hurried back into the library.

"Thank you, husband, for being so understanding," she said as she walked over to stand beside him.

Lyon pulled her down into his lap. "You knew damn well I'd do anything to keep that old bat away from you. God's truth, I'd even quit the country if I had to."

"Thank you for not calling my aunt an old bat in front of our guests," Christina said.

"I was about to," Lyon answered, grinning. "You knew that, of course. It's the reason you interrupted me, wasn't it?"

Christina wrapped her arms around Lyon's neck. "Yes," she whispered. She leaned forward to nuzzle the base of his throat. "You are such a shrewd man."

Lyon's hand rested on her thigh. His other hand was busy pulling the ribbon out of her hair. "Christina, what weapon does the Countess hold over you?"

The softly spoken question caught her unprepared. "I don't understand your meaning, Lyon. My aunt doesn't have any weapons."

"Christina, I saw the fear in your eyes when the Countess said she'd tell me everything. What did she mean?"

He felt the sudden tension in her, knew then she understood exactly what the threat was. "You're going to have to tell me the truth, Christina. I can't protect you unless I know whatever secrets there are."

"I don't want to talk about it now, Lyon," she announced. She started to nibble on her husband's ear, hoping to distract him. "We are newly married, after all, and I'd rather be kissing you."

He told himself he wouldn't let her waylay his topic, tried to ignore the surge of desire hardening his loins when Christina moved against his arousal, but when she boldly whispered into his ear how much she wanted him to touch her he decided to give in to her demand before asking her any more questions.

His mouth had never felt as wonderful to Christina. The fear of his rejection when he learned all her secrets made her feel almost desperate to take and to give as much as she could now, before the truth was turned against her.

His kiss was magical, soon robbing her of all her frightening thoughts. Yes, it was magic, for Lyon made her feel so desirable, so loved.

The kiss exploded into raw passion. His breathing was harsh when he pulled away from her. "Let's go back upstairs," he rasped.

"Why?"

"Because I want to make love to you," Lyon answered, trying to smile over her innocent question. He was literally shaking with his need for her.

"I want to make love to you, too," Christina whispered between fervent kisses along his jaw. "Do we have to go back upstairs? I don't want to wait that long."

His laughter confused her until he lifted her off his lap and started undressing her. Then she decided he was pleased by her idea.

They came together in wild abandon, fell to the floor in one fluid motion.

Christina was stretched out on top of Lyon, her legs tangled with his. Her hair fell to the floor, on the sides of Lyon's profile, acting as a shield against the outside world.

She was content to stare into her husband's eyes for a long moment, to savor the anticipation of the splendor only he could give her. Lyon's hands stroked shivers down her spine. The heat of his arousal warmed her belly, and the hairs on his chest tickled her nipples into hardening.

"I'm shameless, for I can't seem to get enough of you," she whispered.

Lyon cupped her soft, rounded bottom in his hands. "I wouldn't want you any other way," he told her. "Kiss me, wife. Christina, all you have to do is look at me and I start throbbing."

Christina kissed his chin while she slowly, deliberately rubbed her breasts and her thighs against him.

He groaned with pleasure. His hands moved to the back of her head. He forced her mouth upward to seal it with his own. His tongue plunged hungrily inside to taste again the intoxicating sweetness she offered him.

Christina was more impatient than he was. She moved to straddle him, then slowly lowered herself until he was completely inside her. She leaned back, tossing her hair over her shoulder in an utterly wanton motion. Lyon pulled his legs up until his knees pressed against her smooth back. His hands fell to cup the sides of her hips. "Don't let me hurt you," he ground out. "Slow down, love. I won't be able to stop."

He quit his protests when he felt her tighten around him, knew she was about to find her own release. His hand slid into the silky triangle of curls nestled against him. His fingers stroked her there until the fire consumed her and she turned into liquid gold in his arms.

He spilled his seed into her with a harsh groan of blissful surrender, then pulled her down to cover his chest, to hold her close, to share the rapture.

It had never been this good. It kept getting better, too, Lyon realized when his mind could form a logical thought again. "You're a wild tigress," he whispered to Christina in a voice that sounded thoroughly satisfied.

Christina propped her chin on her hands and stared down at her husband. "No, I am your lioness," she whispered.

He didn't dare laugh. Christina had sounded so terribly serious, as if what she'd just told him was of high importance. He nodded, giving her his agreement while his fingers combed through the tumble of luxuriant curls covering her back. He lifted and then rearranged the strands in an absentminded fashion as he stared into his wife's magnificent blue eyes.

"Do you know, when you look at me like that I immediately lose my concentration," he told her.

"I'll take that as a compliment," Christina announced. She leaned down to kiss him again. "You feel so good inside me," she whispered against his mouth. "And now you must give me the soft words, Lyon."

He wasn't sure what she meant by soft words, but she looked serious again. She'd stacked her hands under her chin and was staring down at him with an expectant look on her face.

"What are soft words, Christina? Tell me and I'll give them to you."

"You must tell me what is inside your heart," she instructed.

"Ah," Lyon drawled. His eyes took on a tender look when he added, "I love you, Christina."

"And?"

"And what?" Lyon asked, exasperated. "Christina, I never thought I'd be able to love again. And to actually get married . . . you've made me change all my old ways. I do not tell you I love you on a whim, Christina."

"But I already know you love me," Christina answered. "I didn't want you to, but I do admit it still pleases me. Now you must praise me, Lyon. It's the way it's done."

"I don't understand," Lyon said. "That doesn't surprise me," he added with a wink. He looked around the room and saw the chaos their hastily discarded clothing had made. The fact that he was stretched out on the carpet in his library with his uninhibited wife draped over him, trying to have a logical conversation, vastly amused him. "Do you think you're always going to be so shameless, my sweet?"

"Do not change this topic, Lyon. You must tell me I'm as

beautiful as a flower in spring, as soft and delicate as a flower's petal. And why is that amusing to you? A woman must feel as desirable after loving as before, Lyon."

He quit smiling when he realized she was about to cry.

Lyon understood what she needed now. He could see the vulnerability in her eyes. He cupped the sides of her face and leaned up to kiss her. It was a soft, tender caress meant to remove her worry, her tears.

And then he wrapped his arms around her waist and gave her all the soft words she longed to hear.

Chapter Twelve

It wasn't a very joyful reunion with my sister. Patricia acted just like Father. She was happy to see me until she realized Edward wasn't with me. Patricia's husband, Alfred, was as kind as I remembered, and he made my stay as pleasant as he could. Patricia told me they'd broken all their engagements to stay home with me, but after a while I realized they didn't have any friends at all. Patricia hated the people of Boston, and I believed the feeling was reciprocated.

My sister longed to go back to England. She fashioned a ridiculous plan. Once she was convinced I meant to stay in the colonies and never return to my husband, she announced that I must give her my baby. She would pass the child off as her own.

She tried to make me believe she wanted to be a mother, that her life wouldn't be filled until she had a child to call her own. I knew the truth, of course. Patricia hadn't changed over the time we'd been separated. No, she wanted a grandchild to give our father. An heir. Father would forgive her transgressions; he'd want to provide well for his only grandchild.

I was vehemently against this deception, Christina. I knew greed was my sister's only reason. I told her I'd never give my *child away. Patricia ignored my protests. I saw her destroy a letter I'd given her husband to post to London for me. I was able to get one letter past her scrutiny, though, and I was also secure in the knowledge that my father would find the missive I'd left behind in his winter chest.*

Albert kept me supplied with the daily papers to keep my mind occupied while I awaited your birth, and it was quite by chance that I came upon an article about the frontier people.

Journal entry
October 5, 1795

Lyon and Christina set out for his country manor shortly after a picnic luncheon Christina had insisted upon. They ate crusty bread, cheese, sliced mutton, and plump apple tarts. The fare was spread out on a soft blanket Christina had dragged down from upstairs. Lyon had instinctively reached for his pants, thinking to get dressed first, but his wife had laughed at his modesty, and he'd been easily convinced there really wasn't any need to be in such a hurry.

They were both covered with a layer of dust by the time they arrived at their destination, thanks to Christina's plea to ride in an open carriage and Lyon's agreement to let her have her way.

During the journey he tried to bring up the subject of her father several times, but Christina easily evaded his questions. And once they'd put the city behind them, the beauty of the surrounding wilderness kept Christina fully occupied. Her amazement was obvious. It didn't take Lyon long to realize she had believed all of England was like London.

"Why would you ever want to go into the city when you could stay in such splendor?" Christina asked him.

Splendor? Lyon hadn't thought of the countryside in such a way. Yet the pleasure he could see in his wife's expression made him open his mind to the raw beauty around him.

"We take for granted what is familiar to us," Lyon excused.

"Look around you, Lyon. See God's gifts," Christina instructed.

"Will you promise me something, Christina?" Lyon asked.

"If I am able," she answered.

"Never change," he whispered.

He'd meant it as a compliment and was therefore confused by her reaction. Christina clasped her hands in her lap and bowed her head for a long minute. When she finally looked up at him again, she was frowning.

"My dear, I haven't asked you how to settle England's debts," Lyon remarked. "And my question was irrelevant anyway. I'll make certain you don't change."

"How will you do that?" Christina asked.

"Remove all temptations," Lyon announced with a nod.

"Temptations?"

"Never mind, my sweet. Quit frowning. It will be all right."

"Did Lettie change?"

She knew he didn't like her question. That irritated her, of course, for it was the very first question about his past she'd ever put to him. "Did you love your wife very much, Lyon?" she asked.

"Lettie's dead, Christina. You're all that matters to me now."

"Why is it quite all right for you to prod me about my past and not acceptable for me to ask you questions? Your scowl won't work with me, Lyon. Please answer me. Did you love Lettie?"

"It was a long time ago," Lyon said. "I thought I did . . . in the beginning . . ."

"Before she changed," Christina whispered. "She wasn't what you thought she should be, isn't that the way of it?"

"No, she wasn't." His voice had taken on the familiar chill.

"You still haven't forgiven her, have you, Lyon? Whatever did she do to hurt you so?"

"You're being fanciful," Lyon announced. "How in God's name did we get on this topic?"

"I'm trying to understand," Christina answered. "Your sister told me you loved Lettie. Is it so painful you cannot even speak her name?"

"Christina, would you prefer that I act like my mother? All she'll talk of is James," he added.

"Lyon, I'd like our time together to be filled with joy. If I knew how Lettie changed, perhaps I wouldn't make the same mistakes."

"I love you just the way you are. And I'm damned tired of hearing our marriage is only for a short duration. Get this through your head, woman. We're married until death separates us."

"Or until I change like Lettie did," Christina answered. Her voice was just as loud, just as angry as his had been.

"You aren't going to change."

Lyon suddenly realized he was shouting at her. "This is a ridiculous conversation. I love you."

"You love a princess."

"I don't give a damn if you're a princess or not. I love you."

"Ha."

"What in God's name is that supposed to mean?" Lyon reached out to pull her into his arms. "I cannot believe we're yelling at each other like this."

"Lyon, I'm not a princess."

She'd whispered the confession against his shoulder. Lord, she sounded so forlorn. Lyon's anger evaporated. "Good," he whispered.

"Why is it good?" Christina asked.

"Because now you can't tell me I love a princess," he reasoned with a smile in his voice. "I didn't marry you because of your title."

"Then why? You've told me I'm not at all sensible, that I try to make you daft—"

"Your money."

"What?" Christina pulled out of his arms to look into his face. There was a definite sparkle in his eyes. "You're jesting with me. You didn't know I had any money until after we'd wed."

242

"How astute of you to remember," Lyon said. He kissed the frown away from her face, then draped his arm around her shoulder.

Christina rested against his shoulder. The continuous clip of the horses and the rocking motion of the carriage made her sleepy and content.

"Lyon? You haven't asked me why I married you," she whispered several minutes later.

"I already know why you married me, love."

She smiled over his arrogant comment. "Then explain it to me, please. I still haven't come to understand it."

He gave her a squeeze to let her know he wasn't amused by her announcement. "First, there are the scars. You happen to love my flawed body."

"And how would you know that?" she asked, pretending outrage.

"You can't keep your hands off me," he told her. "Second, I remind you of a warrior."

Christina shook her head. "You haven't any humility," she told him. "And you *are* a warrior, Lyon. A vain one, yes, but a warrior all the same."

"Ah, vanity," Lyon drawled. "Does that mean you might have to use your knife on me?"

"What are you talking about?"

"Lady Cecille. You did threaten to—"

"So you *were* listening to our conversation in the library." Christina sounded stunned. "You lied to me. That is shameful."

"*I* lied to *you*?" Lyon's voice was incredulous. "You, of course, have always been honest with me."

"You will have to cast Lady Cecille aside," Christina announced, flipping the subject to avoid another argument. "I won't be wed to a roamer."

"A what?"

"A man who chases other women," Christina explained. "I shall be true to you, and you must be true to me. Even though it is fashionable in England to take a lover, you aren't going to have one. And that's that."

He was surprised by the vehemence in her tone. He hadn't

243

known she had such an assertive manner. In truth, her demand pleased him immensely. "You're a bossy bit of goods, do you know that?" he whispered. He kissed her again in a leisurely fashion.

Christina realized he hadn't given her his promise, but she decided not to press the issue. Later would be soon enough.

She was about to fall asleep when they reached Lyonwood. Lyon nudged her out of her sleepy state. "We're home, Christina."

The carriage rounded the curve in the road. The wilderness suddenly disappeared.

The land had been transformed into a lush, well-manicured lawn. There were sculptured bushes lining the circle drive of gravel, with wildflowers of bold colors woven between the trees. At the top of the gently sloping hill stood Lyon's magnificent home.

Christina thought it looked like a palace. The house was made of gray and brown stone, double storied, with windows one above the other all across the front of the house. Bright green ivy splattered the stones.

"Lyonwood is as handsome as its master," Christina whispered. "I shall never remember how to get around."

"You get around me well enough," Lyon remarked. "I'm sure you'll conquer your new home just as swiftly."

Christina smiled at his teasing manner. "How many of your family members live here with you? Will I meet all of your relatives today, do you suppose?"

"I suppose not," Lyon answered. "I live by myself." He laughed when he saw her astonished reaction. "Now, of course, my gentle little wife will live with me."

"How many bedchambers are there?"

"Just twelve," Lyon answered with a shrug. The carriage stopped in the center of the circle just as the front door opened. Lyon's butler, a stout, dark-haired young man by the name of Brown, led the parade of servants down the four steps. The staff lined up behind their leader. Their uniforms were starched, as well as their stance, and though they kept their expressions contained, every gaze was directed upon their new mistress.

Lyon refused assistance in helping his wife out of the carriage. Her hands were cold and her nose pink from the brisk, windy ride. He thought she might be a bit nervous meeting his servants for the first time, and so he kept her hand clasped in his.

It didn't take him long to realize she wasn't the least bit nervous. Her manner was worthy of a queen . . . or a princess, Lyon thought with a grin. There was an air of quiet dignity in her bearing. She was gracious as she greeted each one, attentive when she listened to their explanations of what their duties were.

She captivated them, of course, just as she'd captivated him. Even Brown, his dour-faced butler, was affected. When Christina took hold of his hand and announced that it was obvious to her he'd done his duty well, the man's face broke into a spontaneous smile.

"I shall not give you interference, Mr. Brown," she explained.

Brown looked relieved at that announcement. He turned then to address his employer. "My lord, we have prepared both your chamber and the adjoining one for the Marchioness."

Christina looked up at her husband, fully expecting him to set the man straight. When Lyon simply nodded and took hold of her elbow to walk up the steps, she forced a smile for the watching servants while she whispered her displeasure to her husband.

"I shall not have my own room, Lyon. I am your wife now. I must share your blankets. And I really don't want a lady's maid." Looking around, she added, "Heavens, Lyon, this entryway is larger than your whole townhouse."

Christina wouldn't have been surprised if she'd heard an echo. The entrance was gigantic. The floors were polished to a gleam. There was a large sitting room on the left, another of equal proportions on the right. A hallway began to the left of the circular staircase. Lyon explained that the dining room was adjacent to the sitting room, with the gardens behind. The kitchens, he added, were on the opposite side.

Their bedrooms were linked by a door. "I'll have your

clothes moved in here," Lyon told Christina when she gave him a good frown. He motioned to his bed with a raised eyebrow and asked her if she'd like to see if it was comfortable enough.

"You look just like a rascal," Christina laughed. "I should like a bath, Lyon, and then I would like to see your stables. You do keep horses here, don't you?"

"But you don't like to ride," Lyon reminded her.

"Never mind that," Christina answered.

"Christina, if you don't think you'll be happy with Kathleen, I will assign the task of lady's maid to another."

"Oh, Kathleen seems very capable," Christina answered. "I just don't want any maids."

"Well, you're having one," Lyon announced. "I won't always be here to fasten your gowns, love, so quit scowling at me."

Christina sauntered over to the windows. "You're a bossy bit of goods, do you know that, Lyon?" she announced.

Lyon grabbed her from behind. He placed a wet kiss on the column of her throat. "I really insist that you try the bed."

"Now?"

Christina turned to watch Lyon walk over to the door. When he turned the lock and faced her again she could see he wasn't jesting. He gave her his most intimidating look, then motioned her over with an arrogant nod of his head.

"I'm covered with dust."

"So am I."

She was already breathless, and he hadn't even touched her yet.

Christina kicked off her shoes and walked over to the bed. "Will you always be this demanding with your wife?" she asked him.

"Yes," Lyon answered. He discarded his jacket and his shoes, then went to Christina. "Will my wife always be this submissive?" he asked as he pulled her into his arms.

"It's the wife's duty, isn't it, to be submissive to her husband?" Christina asked.

"It is," Lyon answered. His hands moved to the fastenings on her dress. "Oh, yes, it definitely is."

"Then I shall be submissive, Lyon," Christina announced. "When it suits me."

"A man can't ask for more than that," Lyon said with a grin.

Christina threw her arms around his neck and kissed him passionately. She wasn't submissive now. Her tongue darted inside his mouth to rub against his. She knew he liked her aggressiveness. His hold tightened around her waist and he growled his pleasure.

"My love, I think I'm going to tear another gown," he whispered.

He didn't sound overly contrite. And his wife's soft laughter told him it really didn't matter to her.

The following two weeks were as wonderful and magical to Christina as the early pages of Sir Thomas Mallory's story of Camelot. The weather accommodated her fantasy, for it only rained during the black night hours.

Christina and Lyon spent most of the sun-filled days exploring the vast wilderness surrounding his home.

She was amazed that one man could own so much land.

He was astonished that one woman could know so much about it.

Christina gave him the gift of awareness and a new appreciation for the wonders of nature.

Lyon began to realize how important her freedom was to her. She was happiest when they were outside. Her joy was contagious. Lyon found himself laughing with just as much joy as he tramped through the jungle of bushes in pursuit of his wife.

They always ended their days in front of a peaceful stream they'd chanced upon quite by accident their first day out, and usually soaked their feet in the cool water while they ate the meal the cook had thoughtfully prepared for them.

On one such afternoon, Lyon decided to tease his wife. He plucked a leaf from the nearest shrub and pretended that he was going to eat it. Christina wasn't amused. She slapped the leaf out of his hand, admonished him for his ignorance, and then explained that the leaf was poisonous and that he shouldn't be putting plants in his mouth anyway. If he was that hungry, she'd be more than happy to give him her portion of their meal.

Friday morning arrived too soon for Lyon's liking. He had to return to London to meet with Rhone and their unknowing victims for a game of cards.

Lyon was extremely reluctant to leave his gentle little wife even for one evening.

Lyon awakened early to find his wife sound asleep on the floor again. He immediately lifted her into his arms and put her back in his bed. Her skin felt cold to him, and he used his hands and his mouth to warm her.

He was hard and throbbing when Christina finally opened her eyes. His mouth was fastened on her breast, his tongue like rough velvet as it brushed against her nipple. He began to suckle while his hands stoked the growing fire inside her.

He knew just where to touch, just how to drive her wild. His fingers slipped inside her, drawing a breathless moan from her, then withdrew to tease and torment, and then thrust inside again.

Christina wanted to touch him. "Lyon." She could barely get his name out. His mouth had moved to her stomach to place wet, hot kisses there while his fingers continued their magic.

She couldn't catch her breath. "Tell me you want this," Lyon demanded, his voice hoarse now. His head was slowly moving toward the junction of her legs. "Tell me, Christina," he whispered. His breath was warm against her sensitive skin. His fingers plunged deep and then withdrew to be replaced by his mouth, his tongue.

What he was doing to her made her forget to breathe. Her eyes were tightly closed and her hands clutched the sheets. The pressure grew inside her until it consumed her. Emotion swept through her like a blaze out of control.

"Lyon!"

"Do you like this, love?"

"Yes. Oh, God, yes . . . Lyon, I'm going to—"

"Let it happen, Christina," he demanded in a rough, husky voice.

He wouldn't let her hold on to her control. The tension was unbearable as the fire rushed through her body.

Christina arched against him, cried out his name in a soft gasp. The splendor still captivated her when Lyon plunged inside her.

He was too greedy to hold back. His breathing was ragged against her ear.

"You like this, don't you, love?" he demanded.

"Yes, Lyon," she whispered.

"Put your legs around me, take me . . ." The order ended on an intense groan. Christina had wrapped her arms and her legs around him, pulling him high inside her. Her nails raked his shoulders, her grip tight and sweet, as tight and sweet and hot as her sheath.

He grunted his satisfaction. Christina slowly moved her hips. "Do you like that, Lyon?" she whispered as she pushed up against him again.

He couldn't answer her. But his body showed her how very much he did like it. And when he spilled his seed into her, he thought he'd died and gone to heaven.

An hour later, Lyon walked with Christina down the steps, his arm draped around her shoulders possessively.

Brown was waiting at the bottom of the steps. After announcing that the stablemaster had Lyon's mount ready and waiting out front, the butler discreetly withdrew so that the Marquess could have another minute alone with his wife to give her a proper farewell.

"Christina, when you get over your fear of horses we'll go riding every—"

"I'm not afraid of horses," Christina interrupted. Her voice sounded outraged. "We've had this discussion before, Lyon. I fear the saddles, not the animals. There is a difference."

"You're not going to ride without a saddle," Lyon announced. "And that's that."

"You're too stubborn for my own good," she muttered.

"I don't want you to fall and break your pretty little neck."

Lyon opened the front door, grabbed hold of Christina's hand, and dragged her outside.

Christina was frowning. She thought he might have insulted her again. Then she reasoned he couldn't know how skilled she was with a good mount. Perhaps he hadn't slandered her after all but was truly concerned for her safety or, as he'd just put it, her pretty little neck.

She wondered what he'd think if he found out she went out riding most mornings. He'd be upset with her, she supposed. She had to sigh over that little deception, then cast her guilt aside. She was always back in his bed before he awakened and really wasn't worried he'd find out. Wendell, the stablemaster, wouldn't say anything to Lyon. No, Wendell was a man of few words. Besides, he thought she'd gained Lyon's permission.

"Christina, I'll be back home by noon tomorrow," Lyon said, interrupting her thoughts. He tilted her chin up and kissed her soundly.

When he started down the steps, Christina hurried after him. "I still don't understand why I can't go with you. I would like to see your sister, and your mama, too, Lyon."

"Next time, sweetheart. Diana will be going to Martin's party tonight."

"Will Aunt Harriett also be going?"

"Probably," Lyon answered.

"I could go with them," Christina suggested.

"I thought you liked it here in the country," Lyon returned. "You do, don't you?"

"Yes, very much. But I'm your wife, Lyon. I should do my duty with your relatives. Do you know, it's rather odd of me to admit, but I did enjoy some of the parties. There were some very nice people I would like to see again."

"No."

His voice was so firm, Christina was immediately perplexed. "Why don't you want me to go with you? Have I done something to displease you?"

Lyon reacted to the worry in her voice. He paused to look down at her, then gave in to his sudden urge to kiss her again. "Nothing you could ever do would displease me. If you want to attend some of the parties, you'll wait until I can go with you."

"May I play cards with you and the mischief makers?" she asked. "I've never played before, but I'm certain it wouldn't be too difficult to master."

Lyon hid his amusement. His wife was obviously serious in her request. The sincerity in her voice said as much. "I'll teach you another time, Christina. If you wish, I'll wait while you write a note to Diana and Aunt Harriett."

Christina could tell by his manner that he wasn't going to give in to her plea to go along. "I've already written to everyone, even Elbert and my Aunt Patricia," she informed him. "Brown sent a messenger with my letters yesterday."

They walked on, hand in hand. When they reached his mount, he turned. "I have to leave now, my sweet."

"I know."

She hadn't meant to sound so pitiful. The fact that Lyon was leaving was distressing, yes, but not nearly as much as his casual, dismissive attitude. She didn't think he was going to mind the separation at all. She, on the other hand, minded very much.

It wasn't like her to be so clinging. She couldn't seem to let go of his hand. What in heaven's name was the matter with her? Lord, she felt like crying. He was only going to be away for one night, she told herself, not an eternity.

Lyon kissed her on her forehead. "Do you have anything you wish to say to me before I leave, Christina?"

His voice coaxed a response. Christina dropped his hand. "No."

Lyon let out a long sigh. He took hold of her hand again and dragged her off to the side of the path so that the stablemaster wouldn't overhear him. "I'll miss you," he said.

His voice wasn't coaxing now, but brisk.

Christina smiled.

"Damn it, wife, I want the soft words," he muttered. He

251

immediately felt like a fool for making such a ridiculous confession.

"Damn it, Lyon, I want to go to London with you."

"Christina, you're staying here," Lyon bellowed. He drew a deep breath, then added in a furious whisper, "I love you, Christina. Now tell me you love me. I've waited all week to hear you admit it."

She gave him a disgruntled look. Lyon wasn't waylaid. "I'm waiting, Christina."

"Have a safe journey, Lyon."

Lyon hadn't realized how important it was for him to hear her tell him she loved him until his demand was so thoroughly ignored. He stood there feeling angry and defeated, his gaze brooding as he watched Christina walk away from him.

"Hell," he muttered to himself. He mounted his steed, accepted the reins from Wendell, yet seemed incapable of nudging his stallion into moving. He couldn't even tear his gaze off the stubborn woman strolling to the front door.

Christina couldn't dismiss him this time. Her hand shook when she took hold of the brass door handle. He was so horribly stubborn. He constantly prodded and nagged. He wouldn't let her shield her feelings from him. But he didn't understand the significance of what he was asking of her. Once she'd given him the words, there could be no going back.

No, she'd never be able to go home.

A half smile changed her expression. The truth was both painful and joyful. She'd never really been given a choice in the matter, had she? From the moment she'd met Lyon, her heart had known the truth. Why had it taken her mind so long to accept?

Christina looked over her shoulder. Tears clouded her vision. "Hurry home, Lyon. I will be waiting for you."

"Say the words, Christina." He'd shouted this time, and the look on his face showed his anger.

"I love you."

Several heartbeats passed before he acknowledged her admission. And then he gave her a curt nod. Oh, he was arrogant. But his expression was tender, caring, so very loving.

It was quite enough. Christina hid her smile. A feeling of contentment and joy filled her. She suddenly felt as light as the wind.

The truth had set her free.

Christina opened the door and started to walk inside when her husband's bellow stopped her. "Wife?"

"Yes, husband?"

"Tell me you trust me as well."

She turned around again. Her hands settled on her hips. She hoped he could see her exasperation. "Don't push me, Lyon. Savor one victory at a time, like any noble warrior would."

Lyon shouted with laughter. "Yes, Christina, one victory at a time. I've got you now, haven't I?" he asked, his voice and his eyes filled with merriment.

The man was gloating again.

Christina strolled over to the top step. "Yes, Lyon, you've got me. And when you come home from London, you're going to find out just exactly what you've gotten. No more pretenses, husband. No more lies."

"I couldn't be happier," Lyon remarked.

"Enjoy the feeling, Lyon. I fear it will not last long."

She'd called the warning over her shoulder. The front door slammed shut before Lyon could question her further.

Lyon felt as though a weight had been lifted from his shoulders—and from his heart. She loved him. "The rest will come, wife," he whispered to himself. "I'll see to it."

He'd never felt so confident, so very, very peaceful.

The feeling wasn't going to last long.

Chapter Thirteen

You were only three months old when I bundled you up and set out on another adventure. I left in the dead of night so that Patricia wouldn't be able to stop me. I didn't leave a note for her, for I believed she'd send men after me.

You were such a precious infant. Upon reflection, I think the journey was far more difficult for me than for you. You'd just begun to smile, and you were such a sweet-tempered little one.

I had made arrangements to travel with Jacob and Emily Jackson. I'd met them through Sunday church, you see, and took to them at once. They were a newly wedded couple who had sold their wedding gifts so that they'd have enough coins to go in search of a new life. They were very appreciative of my contributions. Emily took to you, too, Christina. She'd sing to you and rock you to sleep while I saw to the night meals.

Jacob was a man bitten by wanderlust. Every evening he'd tell us the most wonderful stories about the courageous people living in the Black Hills. His brother had already taken his family there and had sent Jacob word that he was prospering as a gentleman farmer.

Jacob's fever was contagious. I soon became as excited as he *was. Emily told me there were many unattached men working the raw land, that I would surely find a good man to marry. I led them to believe my husband had recently died, I admit to you, and I felt great shame for lying to them.*

I told myself over and over that the lie didn't count. Edward would never find me in this vast wilderness.

We joined another wagon train when we reached what I believed was the end of the earth. I fought my exhaustion. Emily was always so cheerful. And then, on a bleak, rainy afternoon, we finally reached the valley below the most magnificent mountains I'd ever seen.

I remember that it was a bitterly cold day. It didn't matter, though. We were free, Christina. Free. No one could hurt us now.

Journal entry
October 11, 1795

Lyon had been gone for over an hour when two letters arrived. Both were addressed to Christina, and both required her immediate attention.

After instructing Kathleen to take the messenger into the kitchens for refreshments, Christina took her letters into Lyon's study.

The first missive came from her Aunt Patricia. It was a hateful note, filled with defaming remarks about Lyon. The Countess told Christina she'd learned the truth about the Marquess and felt it was her duty to warn her niece that she was married to a murderer.

The Countess then demanded that Christina return to London immediately so that she could accompany her aunt to the various functions of the ton. She whined about the disgraceful fact that she hadn't received a single invitation since Christina's outrageous marriage.

Christina shook her head. It had been less than a month since the wedding, but her aunt was carrying on as though a full year had passed.

The Countess ended her list of complaints with the

statement that she was sending along a letter she'd received from the missionary Deavenrue.

She hoped Christina didn't find ill news.

Christina was immediately suspicious. It wasn't like her aunt to offer such a good-hearted remark. She thought the Countess might be up to her usual tricks. She was familiar with her former teacher's handwriting, however, and the flourishing style of his script on the envelope indicated that he had in fact written the letter. The seal on the back of the envelope hadn't been tampered with, either.

Convinced that the letter was really from her dear friend, Christina finally opened it.

Brown was the first to react to the heart-wrenching scream coming from the library. He rushed into the room and nearly lost his composure altogether when he saw his mistress had collapsed on the floor.

He shouted orders over his shoulder as he knelt down beside the Marchioness. Kathleen, Christina's maid, came running next. When she saw her mistress, she gave a yell. "Did she swoon? What made her cry out, Brown? Is she hurt?"

"Cease your questions, woman," Brown snapped. He carefully lifted his mistress into his arms, then noticed that she clutched a letter in her hands. He decided that whatever news she'd just received had caused her to faint. "Go and prepare your lady's bed, Kathleen," he whispered. "She doesn't weigh more than a feather. God help us all if she's ill."

Most of the staff had assembled, and they trailed silently behind Brown as he carried Christina up the winding staircase. Kathleen had hurried on ahead to turn down the bed, but Brown walked right past Christina's bedroom and continued on into his master's quarters.

"She'll find comfort here when she wakes up," he whispered to the cook. "They are a very close couple. She sleeps in here every night."

"Do we send for the Marquess?" Kathleen asked between sobs.

"Get Sophie," Brown ordered. "She'll know what to do about the swoon. Is the messenger still here?"

When Kathleen nodded, Brown said, "I shall send a message to the Marquess with him. Lewis," he commanded the gardener, "go and delay him."

Christina opened her eyes just as Brown was awkwardly pulling the covers over her. "Do not make a fuss over me, Brown."

"Are you in pain, milady?" Brown asked, his voice ragged with worry. "I've sent for Sophie. She'll know what to do," he added, trying to force the tremor out of his voice.

Christina struggled to sit up just as a large gray-headed woman came rushing into the room. She grabbed two pillows and tucked them behind Christina's back.

"What do you think it is, Sophie?" Kathleen asked. "She let out a horrible scream and then fainted dead away."

"I heard her," Sophie announced. She slapped the back of her hand against Christina's forehead. Her manner was brisk, her frown intense. "Best send for Winters, Brown. She feels fevered to me. Winters is your husband's physician," Sophie explained to Christina.

"I'm not ill," Christina protested. She was surprised her voice sounded so weak to her. "Brown, do not send for a physician. I'm quite all right now. But I must go to London immediately. Please bring the carriage around front for me. Kathleen, would you see to packing a few of my gowns for me?"

"Milady, you cannot leave this bed. You are ill whether you know it or not," Sophie exclaimed. "You're as pale as a cloud. Yes, you are."

"I must go to my husband," Christina argued. "He will know what to do."

"It was the letter that caused your swoon, wasn't it?" Kathleen asked, wringing her hands.

Brown turned to glare at the maid. Kathleen was immediately contrite. "I'm sorry for prying, milady, but we are all so concerned. You gave us all a scare, and we've come to care about you."

Christina tried to smile. "And I care about all of you," she said. "Yes, Kathleen, it was the letter."

"Was it bad news?" Kathleen asked.

"Of course it was bad news, you silly chit," Brown muttered. "Anyone with half a mind can see that it was," he added. "Milady, is there anything I can do to ease your distress?"

"Yes, Brown," Christina answered. "Don't fight me when I tell you I must leave for London at once. Please help me, Brown. I beg of you."

"I would do anything for you," Brown blurted out in a fervent voice. He blushed and added, "The Marquess will be upset by this change in orders, but if you are truly set on going, I shall send four strong men to accompany you. Kathleen, hurry and do your lady's bidding."

"Will I be going with you?" Kathleen asked her mistress.

"You will," Brown announced before Christina could dissuade her eager maid.

"I would like a few minutes alone," Christina whispered. "I must grieve in privacy."

They understood then. Someone close to their mistress had passed away.

Brown immediately ushered the servants out of the bedroom. He hesitated after closing the door behind him, then stood there, feeling impotent and unworthy, as he listened to his mistress's tormented sobs.

He didn't know how to help her. Brown straightened his shoulders and hurried down the hall. The welfare of his mistress rested on his shoulders now. He wasn't going to take any chances. He decided to send six men along instead of four to protect the Marchioness.

And though it was highly unusual for a butler to leave his post as guardian of the household, Brown didn't care. He wasn't going to leave his mistress's side until she was safely in her husband's arms. Yes, he would go along with the assembly. And if he could remember how to hang onto a mount, he just might lead them.

Christina had no idea of the worry she was causing her

staff. She huddled under the covers, hugging Lyon's pillow to her bosom, weeping softly.

When her tears were spent, she slowly climbed out of the bed and went in search of her scissors. She would cut her hair and begin the mourning ritual.

As of this moment, her Aunt Patricia was dead. Christina would never again acknowledge her existence.

The task of cutting several inches off the length of curls took little time. Kathleen rushed into the room with a pale green gown draped over her arm. Her eyes widened when she saw what her mistress had done to her hair, but she held her silence and assisted her mistress in changing her clothing.

"We will be ready to leave in ten minutes' time," Kathleen whispered to Christina before leaving her alone again.

Christina walked over to the windows to stare out at the land. She thought about her family. How Merry would love this country. Black Wolf would be impressed, too, though he'd never acknowledge it, of course. He was too arrogant to make such an admission. He'd be perplexed, too, if he knew that Lyon owned so much land.

White Eagle would be more impressed with Lyon's stables. The horses had been bred for strength and endurance, and the new foals, so feisty, so magnificent, were proof of Lyon's careful selection.

"They are not dead." Christina's voice was filled with anger.

She started to cry again. No, they weren't dead. The letter was a lie. She would have known, in her heart, if anything had harmed her family.

"I would have known," she whispered.

Yes, it was trickery. Christina didn't know how her aunt had accomplished the foul deed, but she was behind the deception. The evil woman wanted Christina to believe that her Indian family was dead.

Christina didn't understand the Countess's reasons.

Lyon would be able to explain. He was a cunning warrior who knew all the ways of the jackals in this world.

She felt a desperate need to get to her husband.

Christina would demand that he take her into his arms and tell her how much he loved her. And then she would make him kiss her. His touch would take the pain and the sorrow away.

She would demand and Lyon would give. It was his duty.

When Lyon arrived at his townhouse in London proper, Sir Fenton Richards was waiting on his doorstoop.

Richards wasn't smiling.

Lyon was immediately on his guard. "You've put on weight," he announced in lieu of a greeting.

"I have put on weight," Richards admitted with a grin. He patted his belly to emphasize just where the extra pounds had settled.

Lyon began to relax. His friend's manner told him all he needed to know. There had to be a problem, for Richards wouldn't have waited for him just to pay a social call. Yet his casual manner indicated it wasn't a terribly important problem.

Richards turned to bang on the door. It was immediately opened by a servant. Lyon motioned to his man to take the reins and see to his mount, then led his friend inside to the library.

Richards lumbered in behind him. He was a large man with a bushy beard and silver-tipped hair. He was softspoken, stoop-shouldered, and usually guarded in his expressions. Except when he was in Lyon's company. The older man could relax then, because his trust in his young friend was absolute.

"All hell has broken loose, and with a vengeance."

Lyon raised an eyebrow over the mildly given remark.

"Rhone is under house arrest," Richards announced. He settled himself in one of the two leather-backed chairs in front of Lyon's desk before adding, "I tried to intervene, but the charges had already been filed by Wellingham. It's up to you to take care of the matter now."

"How was he found out?" Lyon asked. He sat down

behind his desk and began to sift through the stack of letters and invitations piled in the center.

Richards chuckled. "You're taking our friend's demise well," he remarked.

"As you said, it's up to me now. I'll take care of the matter. Tell me what happened. How——"

"Wellingham noticed the bandage on Rhone's wrist. One guess led to another after that. Rhone takes too many chances," Richards announced. "It seems he ran into Wellingham on his way home from your wedding. I was sorry I missed the celebration, by the way," he added. "Couldn't be helped. I just got back to London the day before yesterday."

"It was a small affair," Lyon said. "You'll have to come to Lyonwood to meet my Christina," he added. "How's Rhone taking the situation?" he asked, turning the subject back to the immediate problem.

"With his usual flair for nonsense," Richards commented dryly. "Since he can't get out, he's had a party at his townhouse every night. There's another one scheduled for this eve, as a matter of fact. I thought I'd drop in."

Richards paused to give Lyon a long, meaningful look.

Lyon grinned. "I'll be there," he told his friend. "Don't bring any valuables with you, Richards. You wouldn't want to be robbed by Jack, would you?"

"Ah, then Jack will be making an appearance?"

"You may wager on it."

"Won't Rhone be amused?" Richards commented. He straightened in his chair, his manner suddenly brisk. "Now that Rhone's problem is taken care of, I'll move on to my other reason for coming to see you. Your wife's father, to be exact."

Richards had just captured Lyon's full attention. He pushed the letters aside and leaned forward.

"Did you know your wife's father is on his way to London?"

Lyon shook his head. "How would you know him?" he asked.

"His name is Edward Stalinsky, but of course you would know that," Richards said.

Lyon nodded. He did know his father-in-law's full name, but only because he'd watched Christina sign the marriage certificate. "Yes, Baron Stalinsky," he said, urging Richards along.

"He did a favor for us a very long time ago. The Brisbane affair. Do you remember hearing about that mishap?"

Mishap? Lyon shook his head. "I remember you called the Battle of Waterloo Napoleon's mishap," he said. "Tell me about this Brisbane business. I have no memory of it in my mind."

"You were a young lad. Still, I thought you might have heard of the matter sooner or later," Richards said, his voice whisper-soft. "I forget I'm a good twenty years your senior. I suppose I should let the younger ones take charge," he added with a sigh.

"You've tried to resign several times since I've worked for you," Lyon answered.

He was eager to hear Richards recount the happening to him and learn all he could about Christina's father, but he knew his friend well enough to understand he would take his usual slow time getting to it.

"I'm like an old hound," Richards said. "The scent of trouble still captures my mind. Brisbane was an Englishman," he continued, finally getting to the heart of the matter. "You might say he was our Benedict Arnold. He turned traitor, sold a few secrets, then his family began to worry his conscience. He had a wife and four little girls. He came to us and confessed his transgressions. We, or rather my predecessors, worked a promise with the man. We were after bigger fish, you see. With Brisbane's full cooperation, we set a trap to catch his superiors. Baron Stalinsky acted as our intermediary. I don't remember how he got involved," he added with a shrug. "The baron did all he could—took every precaution, I'm told—but the plan failed miserably all the same."

"How?" Lyon asked.

"Brisbane's wife and children were murdered. Their

throats were cut. The atrocity was made to look as if Brisbane had killed them and then turned the blade on himself."

"You don't believe that's what really happened, do you?" Lyon asked.

"No, of course not. I think one of Brisbane's superiors found out about the trap," Richards answered. "Either by chance or by payment."

"What about Baron Stalinsky? Did he continue to work with the government?"

"No. He married shortly after the Brisbane business and returned to his home. He was outraged by the horror he'd witnessed. He was the first to find the bodies, you see, and he refused to lend England a hand after that. Can't fault the man. I wasn't there, but I can imagine the nightmare Stalinsky walked into."

"Have you kept in touch with the Baron since that time?"

"None of us have," Richards said. "But several of his old friends have received notice from him that he'll be arriving in England soon."

"I wonder if he knows he has a daughter now."

"Good God. You mean to tell me he didn't know?" Richards asked.

"Father and daughter have never met. I believe the baron thought his wife and child had died years ago. For that matter, everyone I talked to thought the Baron had passed away, too. Sir Reynolds was one to make that speculation."

"Yes, there was surprise when the letters arrived," Richards said.

"I wonder what the baron has been up to all these years."

"I heard that a year or so later Stalinsky lost his kingdom. Then he vanished. We never had reason to keep track of the man," Richards added. A frown marred his expression. "Something's bothering you. What is it?"

"Do you have any reason at all to distrust the baron?"

"Ah, so that's the itch, is it?"

"Tell me everything you know about the man," Lyon ordered. "Everything you can remember. I realize it was a long time ago," he added.

"There's very little to tell. I was young and impressionable back then, but I do remember being in awe of the man. He wasn't much older than I was. He had a commanding presence. I envied him. Lyon, damn it all, you've got my guts churning. Now you tell me what you know about the baron," he ordered.

"I don't have any information to give you. I've never met him. Christina hasn't either, but she's afraid of him. When you meet my wife, you'll understand the full force of that comment. Christina isn't a woman who frightens easily."

"I already know that much about her," Richards said.

"How?"

"She married you, didn't she?"

Lyon grinned. "Yes, she did," he said. "Not very willingly, but . . ."

Richards snorted with laughter. "Perhaps she's afraid of her father because of the unusual circumstances," he said after a moment's pause. "Not to know one's father and then finally to meet him . . ."

"No," Lyon said, shaking his head. "Her fear is based on something else. She called him a jackal. Keep your guard up when you're with the baron, Richards. My instincts and Christina's fears are enough to sway my mind."

"You're that uneasy?"

"I am."

"Why hasn't Christina explained the real reasons for her fears, then?"

"She's very stubborn," Lyon announced with a smile that told Richards he thought that was a noble quality. "And she is just beginning to trust me. It's a fragile bond, Richards. For that reason, I'm not going to prod her. Christina will tell me when she's ready, and not a minute before."

"But you trust her judgment?" Richards asked. "You trust her?"

"I do." His answer was given without hesitation, his voice emphatic.

And then the full realization settled in his mind . . . and in his heart. He did trust her. Completely. "In all matters,"

Lyon acknowledged in a soft voice. "God only knows why, but I do," he told his friend before he started to laugh.

"And that's amusing?"

"Oh, yes. My little wife and I have been playing a game with each other," Lyon confessed. "It's amusing, you see, because neither one of us has realized it."

"I don't understand," Richards confessed.

"I'm only just beginning to understand," Lyon said. "Christina hides her past from me . . . just as I've been hiding my past from her. I think she believes I'll find her inferior in some way," he added. "I wouldn't, of course, but she needs to learn to trust me enough to believe it in her heart."

"I would be happy to investigate your wife's past for you," Richards volunteered.

"No. I sent men to France to make inquiries, but I'm going to call them home. I will not look into her past, and I don't want you to either, Richards. In time she'll tell me what she wants me to know."

"And will you tell her your secrets?" Richards asked. His voice was whisper-soft. "You have no cause to worry, Lyon. I've never been able to trust a man the way I trust you. Your loyalty to your country has always been absolute. That is why you were always given the most difficult assignments."

Lyon was surprised by the vehemence in his friend's voice. Richards wasn't a man given to compliments. In all their years working together, Lyon had never heard such praise.

"Now you've got me worried about Stalinsky," Richards continued. "I'll start looking into his affairs immediately. There's another problem, however," he added. He scratched his beard in an absentminded fashion. "The department had hopes that you'd give a reception honoring your father-in-law when he arrives. Heaven help us, there's already talk of knighthood. Some of the older gentlemen remember with exaggerated recall the noble deeds Baron Stalinsky accomplished for the good of England. I'm going to look into those deeds as well," he added with a brisk nod.

"A reception isn't going to sit well with Christina," Lyon said.

Richards gave a discreet cough, then said, "Lyon, I certainly don't want to be the one to tell you how to manage your marriage, but it would seem to me that you must simply question your wife about her father at the first opportunity. Order her to explain her fears to you. Make her answer your questions, son."

Question her? Lyon felt like laughing. Since the minute he'd met Christina he'd done nothing but question her. "There will be no questions. She'll tell me—"

"I know, I know," Richards interrupted with a long sigh. "In her own time."

"That's about it," Lyon answered. "Until then, it's my duty to keep her safe."

"Safe?"

"Christina believes her father will try to kill her."

"Oh, Lord."

"Exactly. And you can see how offended we both would be if the baron is knighted."

"Lyon, I insist that you question your wife. If there is danger—"

"I will deal with it. I will not question her again."

Richards ignored the irritation in his friend's tone. "I'm not one to judge, but I believe you have a very unusual marriage."

"I have a very unusual wife. You'll like her, Richards."

A sudden noise coming from the foyer interrupted the conversation. Lyon glanced up just as the library doors were thrown open.

Brown, his loyal butler, came rushing into the room.

Lyon bounded out of his chair. His heart started slamming against his chest and he felt as though the breath was being squeezed out of him.

Something had happened to Christina. She'd been hurt . . . taken . . .

The feeling of panic slowly dissipated. When Christina came flying into the room, her golden hair floating around her shoulders, Lyon literally fell back into his chair.

She was all right. Oh, her eyes were clouded with unshed tears, and her expression showed how troubled she was. She was upset, yes, but she hadn't been injured.

He started breathing again.

"Lyon, you just tell me how it was done," Christina demanded. She rushed right past Richards, didn't even seem to notice that anyone else was in the room, reached her husband's side, and thrust two envelopes into his hands. "I recognized his handwriting, and at first I thought it might be true. But in my heart I didn't feel it was so. I would have known if something had happened to them. I would have known."

Lyon grabbed hold of Christina's hands. "Sweetheart, calm down and start at the beginning."

"Read this letter first," Christina said. She pulled her hand away and motioned to the Countess's envelope. "Then you'll understand why I know it's trickery."

"The Marchioness fainted dead away, my lord," Brown called out.

Lyon turned his attention to his butler. Brown was still standing in the doorway.

"She what?" Lyon roared.

"She swooned," Brown said, nodding vigorously.

"Then why did you bring her to London?"

Lyon was suddenly infuriated. He glared at his butler, then turned to Christina. "You should be home in bed," he shouted.

"Don't yell at me," Christina ordered. Her voice was every bit as loud as Lyon's had been. "Brown knew better than to argue with me. I was determined to come to you, Lyon. Please read the letters. I know it is all a lie."

Lyon forced himself to calm down. Christina had started crying. He decided to get to the matter of her health after he'd dealt with her problem.

Lyon read the Countess's letter first. By the time he was finished with it his hands were shaking.

God help him, she'd learned the truth about him. The Countess had found out about his past and had recounted several damning details in her letter to her niece.

Now Christina wanted his denial. She'd come all the way to London to confront him, to hear him tell her that they were lies.

He wasn't going to lie to her. But the truth could destroy her.

No more lies, no more pretenses . . . hadn't she given him that promise just this morning?

She deserved equal measure. "Christina," Lyon began. He slowly lifted his gaze to hers, "We do what we must do when there is a threat, and I . . ."

He couldn't seem to finish his explanation.

Christina could see his pain, his anguish. The need to comfort him overrode all other considerations. She instinctively reached out to him.

And then the confusion of it all hit her. Her hand stilled in the air between them. "What are you talking about?"

"What?"

"Why are you looking at me like that?"

"I'm trying to explain," Lyon muttered. He turned to glare at Brown. The butler caught the message and immediately closed the door.

Lyon's gaze then settled on Richards. His friend rudely ignored the silent order and stayed right where he was.

"Lyon, answer me," Christina demanded.

"Christina, it's very difficult to explain with an audience listening," he said. He took a deep breath. "It's true. All of it. I did exactly what your aunt has told you. My motives were a hell of a lot cleaner, however, and I would . . ."

She finally understood. Christina closed her eyes and prayed for guidance. She knew she probably wasn't being a good wife now, that Lyon obviously felt the need to unburden himself of his secrets. He'd picked a strange time to share his worries with her, she thought. Although it was selfish of her to feel this way, she really wished he'd help her with her problem first.

When Christina closed her eyes, Lyon felt as though a knife had just been plunged into his heart. "My dear, I was a soldier. I did what I had to . . ."

She finally looked at him. Her gaze was direct and filled with tenderness.

He was too stunned to say another word.

"You are a warrior, Lyon. But you are also a gentle, loving man. You wouldn't have killed anyone who hadn't challenged you. No, you hunt only jackals."

He seemed to have trouble taking it all in. "Then why did you come to London to—"

"I knew you'd help me find the truth," Christina said.

"I'm trying to tell you the truth."

He was shouting again. Christina shook her head. "How can you tell me that when you haven't even read the other letter?"

"If you two will forgive an old man's interference," Richards interjected.

"What is it?" Lyon snapped.

"Who is that man?" Christina asked Lyon.

"Fenton Richards," Lyon said.

Christina recognized the name. She frowned at Lyon's guest and then said, "Lyon cannot come back to work for you. His leg still has not healed to my satisfaction. It may be long years before he mends completely," she added.

"Christina, how do you know about Richards?"

"Rhone," she answered. "And you do talk in your sleep some nights," she added. "I hadn't thought to mention that flaw to you in front of an outsider, but . . ."

"Oh, hell," Lyon muttered.

"Oh, my God," Richards whispered.

"Don't be concerned, sir," Christina told Richards. "I will keep his secrets safe."

Richards stared at her a long minute and then slowly nodded. "I believe you will," he acknowledged.

"How did you know about my leg?" Lyon asked, drawing Christina's attention again. "I haven't complained. It has healed, damn it. Did Rhone—"

"The first night I met you I could tell you were in pain. I could see it in your eyes. You kept leaning against the mantel, too. That was another sign. Later I did question

Rhone, and he confessed that you'd injured your knee. And it hasn't healed," she added with a hasty glance in Richards's direction.

Richards hid his smile. Lyon's wife was a charmer. "The two of you seem to be at cross purposes," he remarked. "Lyon, I don't think your wife is upset about the news in her aunt's letter. It's something else, isn't it, my dear?"

"Yes," Christina answered. "The Countess enclosed a letter from my good friend. The writing on his envelope is by his hand, I'm certain of it, and the writing on the paper looks the same, but—"

"You don't think it is. That's the trickery you're referring to?" Lyon asked.

She nodded. "See how the Countess ends her letter, Lyon? She tells me she hopes my friend hasn't sent ill news."

Her eyes filled with tears again. Lyon quickly read the letter from Deavenrue. He then held the envelope up next to the paper to compare the writing style. Christina held her breath and waited.

It didn't take him long to see the differences. "It's similar, but it isn't the same. Richards, you want to have a look at this?" Lyon asked. "Another opinion would make Christina rest easy."

Richards leapt out of his chair, his curiosity nearly out of control, and snatched the envelope and the letter. He soon saw the discrepancies. "Oh, yes. The letter was written by another hand. It is a deception."

He then read the contents. His gaze was sympathetic when he looked at Christina again. "These people in the wilderness . . . they were like family to you?"

Christina nodded. "What is spotted fever?" she asked, frowning. "The letter says they died of—"

"God only knows," Lyon said.

"Who is responsible for this?" Richards asked. "What kind of monster would do such a thing?"

"Christina's aunt." Lyon's voice sounded his anger.

Richards dropped the letter on the desk. "Forgive me for saying this, Christina, but I believe your aunt is a—"

"Think it but don't say it," Lyon interrupted before Richards could finish his sentence.

Christina sagged against Lyon's chair. Lyon put his arm around her waist. "I still don't understand how it was done. The seal wasn't disturbed."

Richards was the one who explained how easy it was to use steam to open an envelope. "An expert would have been able to tell, my dear," he said.

Richards left minutes later. As soon as the door closed behind him, Christina burst into tears. Lyon pulled her onto his lap. He hugged her close to him.

He didn't try to quiet her. She had a good store of tears, and it was quite a while before her racking sobs slowed down.

"I've gotten your shirt all wet," Christina whispered between hiccups.

She obviously wasn't ready to do anything about it. Christina cuddled up against his chest, tucked her head under his chin, and let out a weary sigh.

She didn't move again for a long time. Lyon thought she might have fallen asleep. He didn't mind. He'd hold her close for the rest of the afternoon, if that was what she needed. In truth, he thought it might take him that long to rid himself of his anger.

Richards had meant to call the Countess a bitch, Lyon decided. The old bat was that, all right, and more.

Christina's mind must have been following the same path, for she suddenly whispered, "Do you know that I used to believe all the English were like my aunt?"

He didn't answer her. But his breath caught in his throat, and he prayed his silence would encourage her to tell him more.

His patience was rewarded minutes later.

"My father hated the whites. And when I lived with the Countess in Boston, my only friend was Mr. Deavenrue. He is the one who took me to my aunt, and he would come every day to tutor me. I wasn't permitted to go outdoors. The Countess kept telling me she was ashamed of me. I was very confused. I didn't understand why she believed I was so unworthy."

"You aren't, my love," Lyon said emphatically. "You are very, very worthy."

Christina nodded. "It is good of you to notice," she said.

He smiled over the sincerity in her voice.

And then he waited for her to tell him more.

It seemed an eternity had passed before she spoke again. "She used to lock me in my room at night. I tried not to hate her for that."

Lyon closed his eyes and drew a shaky breath. He could feel her anguish. It washed over him like hot lava until his eyes smarted with tears.

"I couldn't stand being locked in like that. I finally put a stop to it."

"How, sweetheart?"

"I took the hinges off the door," Christina confessed. "The Countess started bolting her bedroom door then. She was afraid of me. I didn't mind that. She's old, Lyon, and for that reason I tried to respect her. It is what my mother would have wanted."

"Jessica?"

"No, I never knew Jessica."

"Then who?"

"Merry."

Lyon couldn't stop himself from asking her another question. "And does she also hate the whites?"

"Oh, no, Merry doesn't hate anyone."

"But the man you call Father does?"

He didn't think she was going to answer him. The silence stretched between them for long minutes.

He shouldn't have prodded her, he told himself. Damn, he'd only just vowed never to ask her any more questions.

"Yes, he does," Christina whispered. "But not me, of course. My father loves me with all his heart."

Christina waited for his reaction. Her heart pounded furiously.

Lyon didn't say a word. Christina decided then that he hadn't understood.

"I have a brother."

Nothing. Not a word, not a sigh, not even a mutter. "His name is White Eagle."

A slow smile settled on Lyon's face.

"Do you understand what I'm telling you, Lyon?" she asked.

He kissed the top of her head. "I understand," he whispered. He cupped the sides of her face and gently forced her mouth upward. He kissed her tenderly.

And then he soothed her fears away. "I understand that I am the most fortunate man in all the world. I never believed I'd find anyone I could love the way I love you, Christina. I owe your family a great debt, sweetheart. They kept you safe for me."

"You don't know them, and yet you sound as if you care about them," Christina whispered. Her voice shook with emotion.

"Of course I care," Lyon said. "Your mother must be a gentle, loving woman, and your father . . ."

"A proud warrior," Christina supplied. "As proud as you, Lyon."

"I love you, Christina. Did you really believe that your background would make me think you were less than—"

"I have never felt unworthy. Never. I am a lioness. In truth, I thought the English were unworthy . . . until I met you."

Lyon smiled. "You have gained some of your father's arrogance," he noted. "That pleases me."

"It isn't going to be easy for you, Lyon. I have different habits. I don't want to have to pretend any longer. At least not when we are alone . . ."

"Good. I don't want you to pretend whatever it is you pretend either," Lyon announced. He laughed then, for he didn't have the faintest idea what he'd just said.

"I love you, Lyon," Christina whispered. Her fingers caressed the nape of his neck. "Lyon? I want . . ."

"I do too," Lyon growled. He kissed her again, hungrily this time. His tongue plunged inside to taste, to stroke. Christina curled her arms around his neck. She'd meant to tell him she wanted to go home to Lyonwood, but his kiss soon pushed that thought aside. His mouth slanted over hers, again and again, until her breath was little more that a soft pant.

"Let's go upstairs, Lyon," she whispered between passionate kisses.

"There isn't time, Christina."

"Lyon!"

He tried to smile over the demand in her voice, but he was too occupied trying to hold onto his control. Christina was rubbing against his arousal, nipping his earlobe with her teeth, and stroking him wild with her hands.

He couldn't have made it up the stairs if his life had depended upon it.

Chapter Fourteen

He came during the night, while everyone was sleeping. The Jacksons had made their beds outside. It was bitterly cold, but Jacob wanted privacy, and for that reason he'd made a small tent.

I heard a strange sound, and when I looked outside the wagon I saw a man bent over Emily and Jacob. I called out to the man, still not realizing the danger. In my mind I thought it was Jacob's turn to take the watch.

The man stood and turned into the moonlight. The scream was trapped in my throat. Edward had come after me. He held a bloody knife in his hand.

I was so stunned and so terrified I could barely move. You were the one who forced me into action, Christina. Yes, for when you awakened and started to whimper, I came out of my stupor. I wasn't going to let Edward kill you.

I grabbed Jacob's hunting knife just as Edward climbed into the wagon. I screamed and thrust the blade in his face. Edward snarled in pain. The tip of the knife cut the edge of his eye. "Give me the jewels," he demanded as he knocked the weapon out of my hands.

The camp awakened to my screams. Edward heard the shouts of confusion behind him. He told me he'd come back to kill me. He looked over at the basket you slept in, Christina, then turned back to me. "I'll kill her first. You should have let Patricia have her," he added with a sneer before he slithered out of the wagon.

The Jacksons were dead. Their throats had been slashed. I told the wagonmaster I'd heard a sound and had seen a man leaning over Jacob and Emily.

A search was made of the camp. The light was poor, and Edward wasn't found.

Several hours later the camp again settled down. Three times the number of guards were posted as a precaution, and it had been decided that the burial for the Jacksons would take place at daybreak.

I waited, then bundled you up and calmly rode out of the camp. I didn't know where I was going, didn't care.

I had failed you, Christina. It was over. It was only a matter of time before Edward hunted us down.

Journal entry
October 20, 1795

It was early afternoon when Lyon kissed Christina goodbye. She assumed he was going to meet Rhone for their scheduled card game. Lyon, in his haste to make the necessary arrangements for Jack's arrival at Rhone's house, didn't take the time to set his wife straight. He told her only that the card game had been delayed and that he had important business to see to.

Christina had just changed into a deep blue dress when Kathleen announced that Lady Diana was downstairs waiting to see her.

"She's terribly upset about something," Kathleen told her mistress. "The poor dear is crying."

Christina hurried down the winding staircase. When Diana saw her, she blurted out the news about Rhone.

Christina led her sister-in-law into the drawing room, then sat down beside her and patted her hand while she poured out the full story.

"The poor man is innocent," Diana sobbed. "He's trying to be so noble, too. Did you know he is even having parties every night? Oh, if only Lyon will come home soon so that I can tell him what has happened. He will know what to do."

"I'm sure he'll find out very soon," Christina said. "This is all my fault," she added.

"How can it be your fault?" Diana asked.

Christina didn't answer her. She felt responsible for Rhone's problem. She was the one who'd wounded him, after all, and the guilt belonged on her shoulders.

"I must think of a way to . . . Diana, did you say Rhone is having a party tonight?"

"Yes. Aunt Harriett won't let me attend," Diana said. "We are already promised to another affair, but I would much rather go to Rhone's."

Christina hid her smile. "Of course you would," she said, patting Diana's hand again. "It's all going to be over by tomorrow," she added in a mock whisper.

"How could that be?" Diana whispered back. "Do you know something you aren't telling me?" she asked.

"Yes," Christina answered. She deliberately paused, then cast a glance over her shoulder. When she turned back to Diana, she said, "I have it on good authority that the real Jack is going out hunting tonight."

Diana's gasp told Christina she believed her. "You mustn't say a word to anyone, Diana, else Jack might find out and decide against going out."

Diana clasped her hands together. "I won't tell, I promise you," she said. "But how did you learn—"

"There isn't time to go into the details," Christina announced. "And I have an important errand to see to. May I ride with you back to your home and then borrow your carriage for a short spell?"

"Yes, of course," Diana responded. "I could go with you on your errand," she volunteered.

Christina shook her head. "Hurry, Diana. There's much to be done."

"There is?"

"Never mind. Now dry your eyes and come along."

Christina pulled Lyon's sister behind her. She turned Diana's attention away from the matter of Jack by asking several questions about her family.

"Was Lyon close to his brother James?" she asked.

"For a time. They were very competitive," Diana said. "Lyon would always best James—in riding, sword fighting, and . . . well, even with women," she added with a shrug. "James seemed obsessed with winning. He took chances."

"How did he die?"

"Fell from his mount. He didn't linger. His death was quick. Baron Winters, our family physician, said it was painless. I think he might have said that to ease Mama's mind."

"About your mother," Christina began, her voice hesitant. "Diana, I know you must be very very close to her, but I hope you won't argue with my plan."

"What plan?" Diana asked, frowning.

"I would like to take your mother with me tomorrow when I return to Lyonwood."

"Are you serious? Does Lyon know of this intention?"

"Quit looking so suspicious," Christina admonished with a small smile. "I do have your mama's best interests at heart. You have a season to see to, or I'd ask you to come along. I know the separation will be difficult for you. She is your mama, after all," she told her as she continued on.

Diana lowered her gaze to stare at her hands. She was ashamed of the acute relief she was feeling. Someone was finally going to take charge of her mama. "It is dreadful for me to admit this to you, but you are my sister now, and so I will confess I will not miss Mama at all."

Christina didn't know what to say. She opened the door of the carriage for her sister-in-law, then said, "Your mother has been a bit . . . difficult, then?"

"You've met her," Diana whispered. "All she wants to talk about is James. She doesn't care about me or Lyon.

James was her firstborn. Oh, I know you think less of me now. I shouldn't have told you that I—"

Christina reached out to take Diana's hands in hers. "You must always tell me the truth. It's the only way to go along, you see. Diana, I know you love your mama. You wouldn't be so angry with her if you didn't."

Diana's eyes widened. "I am angry," she announced.

"You must go inside now. I have to see to my errand," Christina said, changing the subject. "Please have the servants pack up your mother's things. I shall come and fetch her tomorrow morning."

Diana suddenly lunged at Christina, capturing her in an awkward hug. "I am so happy Lyon married you."

"I'm also happy that I married him," Christina told her.

Diana let go of Christina. She climbed out of the carriage, then turned to plead once more to go along on the mysterious errand. Christina again denied her request, then waited until she'd gone inside the townhouse before turning to the driver and giving him her destination.

"Do you know where the Bleak Bryan is located?" the driver responded. His eyes were bulging out of his face, and he swallowed several times.

"No, I don't know exactly where it's located. Do you, sir?"

"Well, yes, madam, I do," the driver stammered.

"Then that is all that matters, isn't it? Please take me there at once."

Christina got back inside the carriage and shut the door. The driver's pale face suddenly appeared at the open window. "You cannot be serious, madam. The Bleak Bryan is in the most unsavory part of London. Cutthroats and—"

"Bryan is a special friend of mine. I must go to him now, sir. What is your name?" she asked.

"Everet," the driver announced.

"Everet," Christina repeated. She gave him a smile meant to dazzle him, then said, "It is a very good name. Now then, Everet, I must tell you that I will be very unhappy if you don't do as I've requested. Yes, I will," she added in a firm voice.

Everet paused to scratch the bald spot on the top of his head before answering. "That's the rub of it, madam. You'll be unhappy if I don't take you to the Bleak Bryan tavern, but your husband, when he hears of it, will kill me. I'll be getting it no matter what I do. That's the rub, all right."

"Oh, I understand your hesitation now. You don't realize my husband has specifically requested that I make this visitation to Mr. Bryan. Put your fears aside, my good man. Lyon knows all about this."

Everet did look relieved. The Marchioness's sincerity was apparent to him. She was such an innocent little thing, Everet thought. Why, she wouldn't even know how to be devious.

The driver stammered out his apology, requested that Christina bolt her doors from the inside, and then hastened back up on his perch.

He drove the carriage at breakneck pace. Christina thought the man might be a little frightened.

Her conclusions were proven correct when they finally arrived at the tavern. When Everet helped her from the carriage, his hands were shaking. He kept glancing over his shoulder. "Please, madam, be quick with your business in there. I'll be waiting inside your carriage, if you don't mind," he whispered.

"Oh, you don't have to wait for me. I don't know how long my business will take. Go along home now, Everet. Mr. Bryan will see that I get home."

"But madam," Everet stammered out. "What if he ain't inside? What if he went on an errand of his own?"

"Then I shall have to wait for him," Christina announced. She started toward the door, calling her gratitude over her shoulder, and before Everet could get his wits about him to think what to do the Marchioness had disappeared inside the tavern.

She hadn't come unprepared. No, she wasn't as foolish as Everet's look suggested. Christina hid a small knife in her hand; her regular one was strapped above her ankle. She was far more comfortable with the larger knife, but she couldn't very well carry it in her hand. Why, she'd be giving the impression she wanted a confrontation.

From past experience, Christina had learned that most mischief makers were an ignorant breed. One had to be firm from the outset.

She stood inside the doorway for a long minute as she looked around the crowded area in search of the owner. There were at least twenty men sitting at the wooden tables and another few leaning against the warped bar that ran the length of the right side of the large room.

A man was standing behind the bar, staring gape-mouthed at her. Christina assumed the gentleman worked for the owner and immediately started over to him.

She didn't get more than halfway there before the first oaf tried to deter her. The man was rank with the smell of ale, his motion awkward when he tried to grab her.

Christina slapped his hand away with her blade. The man immediately let out a howl of pain. Everyone inside the tavern watched the big man lift his hand and stare at it in astonishment.

"You cut me!"

His bellow shook the rafters. "You cut me," he roared again as he started to lunge toward Christina.

Christina hadn't moved. She flashed the knife in front of his eyes. "Sit down or I shall have to hurt you again."

She really didn't have time for this, she told herself. There was so much to be seen to before Rhone's party.

"You cut me, you—"

"You tried to touch me," Christina answered. The tip of her knife rested against the befuddled man's throat. "And if you try again, you'll be drinking your ale from the hole I shall fashion in your neck."

She heard the snickers and turned her gaze to find the offender. "I have business to attend to with Mr. Bleak Bryan."

"Are you his lovey, then?" someone shouted out.

Christina let out a sigh of frustration. The mischief maker sitting next to her immediately thought to attack again.

She never even looked down at him as she pricked a narrow, shallow cut in his neck.

He howled again. Christina turned her gaze to the ceiling, praying for patience.

Yes, the mischief makers of the world were all the same. Ignorant.

"I'm the Marquess of Lyonwood's lovey," she told the group of men. "My husband's friend is the owner of this tavern. I have immediate business with the man, and my patience is wearing thin." She paused to scowl at the man holding his neck. "It is a paltry cut, sir, but if you do not cease this foolishness, I promise the next will be more painful."

Though Christina didn't realize it, the news that she was Lyon's wife had changed every man's opinion. "Leave her be, Arthur, if you want to live. She's the mistress of Lyonwood."

"Your name is Arthur?" Christina asked.

The man she'd just questioned was too terrified to answer her.

"Arthur is an appealing name, sir. Do you know the story of Camelot? No?" she asked when the man continued to stare at her stupidly. "Your mama must have read the tale then and named you after King Arthur," she decided for him.

Arthur wasn't listening to her. His mind was far away, captured by the nightmare of what the Marquess of Lyonwood was going to do to him when he heard of this foul incident. "I didn't mean nothing by trying to snatch you. I'm good as dead," he whined. "I didn't know—"

"That I was a married lady?" Christina asked. She let out a sigh. "Well, I suppose you couldn't have known I wasn't available, but it was rude of you to try to snatch a lady without gaining her permission first," she instructed. "But you're not going to die because of your ill manners, Arthur," she added in a gentle voice.

She turned to address her audience. "Does anyone else want to try to snatch me?"

Every single man inside the tavern shouted his denial. And they kept shaking their heads in unison.

It was an amusing sight, but Christina hid her smile. She didn't want them to think she was laughing at them.

"Is your promise true?" she demanded, just to make certain it was safe to put her knife away.

Christina did smile then. She couldn't help herself. The men's vigorous nods were too amusing a sight.

"Arthur, go and wash your cuts now," Christina instructed over her shoulder as she walked over to the bar to wait for the attendant. "I shall send medicine to soothe the sting just as soon as I'm finished here. Does anyone happen to know where Mr. Bleak Bryan is?" she asked the silent men.

"Connor went to fetch him, miss," a man called out.

Christina smiled at the thin little man. She noticed then that he was holding cards in his hand. "Are you having a game of chance?" she called out, biding her time until Bryan arrived and trying at the same time to ease the tension in the room. "I'm sorry if I interrupted you, sir."

"No, no," the man replied. "I couldn't get no one to play."

"Why is that?"

"Nitty is too lucky, miss," another shouted out.

"Are you a patient man, Nitty?" Christina asked.

"Don't rightly know, your grace," Nitty answered.

Christina decided against explaining that she shouldn't be addressed as "your grace." The man looked very nervous to her.

"Shall we find out?" Christina asked. Her husky laughter warmed smiles onto the men's faces. "I would like to learn to play cards, sir, and if you have the time and the inclination, now would be fine with me. I must wait to speak to the owner . . ."

"I would be honored to teach you the ways," Nitty announced. His shoulders straightened. "Poppy, clear a space for the lady," he ordered. "Get her a clean seat, Preston. What game were you wanting to learn, miss?" he asked.

"What game do men like to play?"

"Well now, your husband's game is poker, miss, but of course you wouldn't be wanting to learn—"

"Oh, but I would," Christina announced.

"Here, miss," another shouted. "I'll stake you to a few coins when you've caught on."

"Coins?"

"To bet with," another eager man said.

Christina couldn't believe how helpful the men were. The man named Poppy made a dramatic flourish with his arm as he bowed. "Your chair awaits, my lady," he announced. "Spit's dry now. It's clean as can be."

After taking her seat at the round table, Christina nodded to Nitty. "Do you know my husband, then?" she asked as she watched him flip the cards together. "You said poker was his game," she added as explanation for her question.

"We all know of him, miss," Poppy announced over her shoulder.

"Oh, that is nice," Christina said. "Now then, Nitty. Explain this game to me. Thank you for your coins, sir, and you as well, and . . . oh, I don't believe I need this much money, gentlemen," she added when the coins mounted into a heap in front of her. "You are all so very generous. My husband is fortunate to have such good friends."

Christina's husband was thinking much the same thought as he finished giving his orders to five seedy-looking but very loyal men behind the tavern. Bryan stood by his side, wishing with all his heart he could take part in the charade.

"Damn it all, Lyon, I wish I could be there to see Rhone's expression. Remember, lad," he told the man who was going to imitate Jack, "to stay in the background. Your eyes aren't as green as Rhone's are. Someone might notice."

"Bryan, you got to come back inside," the bartender nagged for the third time. "I'm telling you a fight is brewing. Didn't you hear the screams?"

"I only hear men having a good time, Connor. Whoever sparked the fight must have changed his mind. Now get back inside before I'm robbed blind."

Bryan scowled Connor inside, then stayed beside Lyon, listening to him advise the men.

A sudden roar of laughter caught his attention. Bryan nodded to Lyon and then strolled back inside the tavern to see what everyone was cheering about. He immediately noticed the crowd had gathered around the corner table, and he started forward just as several men shifted their positions. He was able to see the occupants of the table then. After a long disbelieving minute, Bryan turned tail and ran out the back door.

"Lyon, are you finished yet?"

"I was just leaving," Lyon answered. "Why? Do you have a problem?" he asked. The tone in Bryan's voice had put him on his guard. His friend sounded like he was strangling.

"It isn't my problem, it's yours," Bryan answered.

When Lyon tried to walk inside, Bryan blocked the entrance with his arm. "Are you still a betting man, Lyon?"

Lyon let Bryan see his exasperation. "I am."

"Then I'll wager you're about to get the surprise of your life," Bryan said. He moved to the side, then crooked his thumb. "Your surprise is waiting inside."

Lyon didn't have time for foolishness. He hurried inside, believing Bryan wanted him to disarm a man or two.

The crowd of men blocked his view of the table. "There's no danger here," he told Bryan. "What's the attraction, I wonder," he added. "Does Nitty have a new victim for his card tricks?"

"Oh, it's a card game all right," Bryan drawled out. "Frankie, how's the game going?"

"The little miss just bested Nitty with a paltry pair of tens," someone called out from the crowd.

"Ain't my fault," Nitty bellowed goodnaturedly. "She's got a quick mind. Why, she took to the game the way crabs takes—"

"Watch your mouth, Nitty," another man shouted. "The Marquess of Lyonwood's woman is respectable, you stupid little sod. Talk clean in front of her."

The Marquess of Lyonwood's woman.

He couldn't have heard what he thought he'd just heard. No, it couldn't be . . .

Lyon turned to Bryan. His friend was slowly nodding. Lyon still had trouble believing. He walked over to the crowd. Some of the more anxious men moved out of his way.

The cheering abruptly stopped. Christina wasn't aware of the tension in the atmosphere, or the fact that her husband was standing directly behind Nitty, staring at her.

She was concentrating on her hand, her frown intense. Nitty, on the other hand, was afraid to look behind him. He could see the expressions on the faces of the men who stood behind Christina. None of them looked too happy. "I believe I'll fold, miss."

Christina didn't look up, but she drummed her fingertips on the tabletop and stared at the five cards she held in her other hand. "No, Nitty, you can't fold now. You told me I had to put up or fold." She pushed the pile of coins into the center, then glanced up to smile at her new friend. "I shall see you."

Nitty dropped his cards on the table. "Uh, miss, you didn't have to put all the coins in the pot. I've got you beat with my three kings, you see, but you can have the coins back. It's only a teaching game."

The men nodded. Some grumbled their approval while others cast fearful glances in Lyon's direction.

Christina didn't dare look up from her hand. Nitty had warned her that the expressions on players' faces often revealed what they held in their hands. Since Nitty had already shown her his cards, she wasn't sure if that law still applied, but she wasn't about to take any chances . . . not with the wonderful cards she'd been dealt.

"Fair is fair, Nitty. Winner takes all. Didn't you say that?"

"I did, miss," Nitty stammered out.

Christina placed two sevens down on the table. She'd deliberately withheld the other three cards. "Gentlemen," she told the men hovering around her, "Prepare to collect your winnings."

"But miss, you've got to best my . . ."

Nitty stopped his explanation when Christina flipped over the other cards.

"Good God, she's got three aces," Nitty whispered. His voice was filled with relief. Lyon's woman had won the hand.

Christina's husky laughter wasn't echoed by her audience. They all watched the Marquess of Lyonwood, awaiting his judgment. He didn't look too happy. If the powerful Marquess wasn't amused, then neither were they.

Christina was busy stacking the coins in several piles. "Nitty? While we continue to wait for Mr. Bleak's return, I would like you to show me how to cheat. Then, you see, I'll know how it's done and won't be easily tricked."

Nitty didn't answer her request. Christina glanced up at her teacher.

The man looked terrified. The silence finally registered in her mind. She didn't understand until she looked up and found her husband staring down at her.

Her reaction was immediate, her surprise obvious. "Lyon, what are you doing here?"

Her sweet, welcoming smile infuriated him beyond measure. The woman appeared to be pleased to see him.

Christina's smile did falter as her husband continued to stand there staring at her without giving her a greeting.

A tremor of apprehension slowly straightened her shoulders. The truth finally settled in her mind. Lyon was furious. Christina frowned in confusion. "Lyon?" she asked, her voice hesitant. "Is something the matter?"

Lyon ignored her question. His cold gaze swept over the crowd of men.

"Out."

He cleared the tavern with one word. His voice had cracked like a whip. While Christina watched, the men rushed to do his bidding. Nitty tripped over his chair in his hurry to leave the tavern.

"You've forgotten your coins," Christina called after the men.

"Do not say another word."

Lyon had roared his command to her. Christina's eyes

widened in disbelief. She stood up to face her husband. "You dare to raise your voice to me in front of strangers? In front of our friend, Bleak Bryan?"

"I damn well do dare," Lyon bellowed.

The chilling rebuke stunned her. She turned to look at his friend, caught his sympathetic expression, and was suddenly so ashamed she wanted to weep.

"You are humiliating me in front of another warrior." Her voice trembled and she clasped her hands together.

He believed she was afraid of him. Her forlorn expression cut through his haze of anger. Lyon's expression slowly changed until he looked almost in control.

"Tell me what you're doing here," Lyon demanded. His voice was still harsh with his suppressed anger. Lyon considered that a victory of sorts over his temper, for he still felt the need to shout.

She hadn't understood the danger. Lyon kept repeating that statement inside his head until it became a litany. No, she hadn't realized what could have happened to her . . .

He was all too aware of the horrors awaiting a gentle lady in this part of London. Lyon forced himself to block the black possibilities from his thoughts, knowing he'd never regain control if he didn't.

Christina couldn't look at her husband. She stood with her head bowed, staring at the tabletop.

"Lyon, your wife must have had a terribly important reason for coming here," Bryan stated, trying to ease the tension between husband and wife.

Christina's head jerked up to look at Bryan. "My husband is angry because I came here?" she asked, her voice incredulous.

Bryan didn't know what to say to that absurd question. He decided to ask one of his own. "You didn't know what a sorry area this is?"

She had to take a deep breath before she spoke again. Her hands were fisted at her sides. "I will go wherever I wish to go . . . whenever I want."

Oh, hell, Bryan thought to himself, she's done it now. He gave Lyon a quick glance before looking back at Christina.

The sweet innocent didn't know her husband very well yet. Why, she'd just waved a red flag in front of his face.

Lyon wasn't over his initial anger. It helped little to prod him the way Christina was doing. Bryan rushed to intervene before Lyon had time to react to his wife's ill-chosen remark. "Why don't you both sit down? I'll leave you to your privacy . . ."

"Why? He already humiliated me in front of you," Christina whispered.

"Christina, we're going home. Now."

Lyon's voice had turned into a soft whisper. Bryan hoped Christina would realize that wasn't a good sign.

No, she hadn't realized. She turned to glare at her husband. Bryan had to shake his head over her indiscretion.

Lyon moved with the speed of lightning. Christina suddenly found herself pinned up against the back wall, her sides blocked by his hands. His face was only inches away from hers, and the heat of his anger was hot enough to burn.

"This is how it works in England, Christina. The wife does as her husband orders. She goes only where the husband allows her to go, only when he allows it. Got that?"

Bryan was pacing behind Lyon's back. His heart went out to the delicate flower Lyon had wed. The poor dear had to be terrified. Why, even he was a bit nervous. Lyon's temper still had the power to frighten him.

When Christina answered her husband, Bryan realized she wasn't frightened at all. "You have shamed me. Where I come from, that is sufficient reason for a wife to cut her hair, Lyon."

He was trying to calm down, but her absurd remark made him crazy. "What the hell does that mean?"

She didn't want to take the time to explain. No, Christina could feel her anger burning inside her. She wanted to scream at him. But she wanted to weep, too. That made little sense to her, but she was too upset to reason the contrary emotions clear. "When a woman cuts her hair, it is because she has lost someone. A wife cuts her hair when her husband dies . . . or when she casts him aside."

"That is the most ridiculous notion I've ever heard of,"

Lyon muttered. "Do you realize what you're implying? You're speaking of divorce."

The enormity of her folly and her outrageous remarks suddenly hit him full force. Lyon dropped his forehead on top of hers, closed his eyes, and started to laugh. Her blessed arrogance had pushed his anger away.

"I knew you'd change when you knew my past, you inferior Englishman," she raged against him. "You're nothing but a . . . stupid little sod," she announced, remembering one of the men's earlier comments to another.

"You and I are going to have a long talk," Lyon drawled. "Come along," he ordered as he grabbed hold of her hand and started to pull her after him.

"I have still to speak to Mr. Bleak," Christina said. "Unhand me, Lyon," she added, trying to jerk her hand away.

"Perhaps you didn't get it after all," Lyon remarked over his shoulder. "I just told you that a wife goes where her husband—"

"Lyon? I'm ready to kill with curiosity," Bryan interposed. He'd caught the irritation in his friend's voice and was trying to intervene before another conflict started. "I would like to know why your wife came here," he added with an embarrassed stammer.

Lyon paused at the door. "Tell him," he ordered Christina.

She wished she could deny his command so that he would realize she'd meant every word of what she'd said to him, but Rhone's well-being was at issue, so she put her pride aside. "Rhone is having a party tonight," she began. "I wanted to ask you if you could find some good men to act as mischief makers and—"

Christina never finished her explanation. Lyon dragged her out the door in the middle of her sentence. They walked halfway around the block before his carriage came into view. No wonder she hadn't known he was visiting Bryan, she thought to herself. The man had hidden his vehicle a good distance away.

She didn't understand his reason, yet she wasn't about to

question him. Her voice might betray her. Christina knew she was close to weeping. She didn't think she'd ever been this angry in all her life.

Neither said a word to the other until they were home. Lyon used the time to try to calm down. It was a difficult endeavor. He couldn't quit thinking about what could have happened to Christina. The unwanted images fueled his temper. God help him, his knees had nearly buckled under him when he'd first spotted Christina in the tavern.

She was playing cards with the worst thugs in London. She hadn't realized her jeopardy, of course; she couldn't have. She wouldn't have looked so pleased with herself if she had. And she had smiled at him. Lyon didn't think he'd ever been so furious . . . or so frightened.

"You're too damned innocent for your own good," he muttered after he'd jerked the door to the carriage open.

Christina wouldn't look at him. She kept her gaze directed on her lap, and when he made his unkind remark she merely shrugged her shoulders in indifference.

He offered her his hand when she climbed out of the vehicle. She ignored it.

It wasn't until she'd raced on ahead of him that he realized she'd cut a portion of her hair. The curls ended in the middle of her back now.

Brown met them at the door. After giving his butler instructions to watch over his wife, he chased after Christina. She was halfway up the staircase when he stopped her. "When I'm not too angry to speak of this matter, I will explain to you why—"

"I don't wish to hear your reasons," Christina interrupted.

Lyon closed his eyes and took a deep breath. "Don't you dare venture out again until tomorrow morning," he told her. "I have to go to Rhone's now."

"I see."

"No, I don't think you do see," Lyon muttered. "Christina, you went to Bryan to ask his help in finding men to masquerade as Jack and his friends, didn't you?"

She nodded.

"Wife, you have little faith in me," Lyon whispered, shaking his head.

Christina believed his comment was ridiculous. "Faith has nothing to do with my errand. I didn't know you'd been informed of Rhone's terror."

"Terror?"

"He's been barred inside his house," Christina explained. "Since he is your friend, I thought of a most cunning plan. You ruined it," she added.

"No, *you* would have ruined it," Lyon announced. "I've already taken care of the problem, Christina. Now give me your word that you'll stay inside."

"I have no other errands to take care of," Christina answered.

When he let go of her arm, Christina turned and rushed up the rest of the steps. Lyon was just walking out the front door when she called out to him.

"Lyon?"

"Yes."

"You're going to have to apologize. Will you do it now or when you return from Rhone's house?"

"Apologize?"

He'd shouted the word at her. Christina concluded he wasn't contrite. "Then you're going to have to start all over," she shouted back.

"What are you talking about? I don't have time for riddles," Lyon announced. "If anyone's going to apologize . . ."

He didn't bother to finish his demand, for his wife had turned her back on him and disappeared down the hallway.

She'd just dismissed him again. Lyon didn't think he was ever going to get used to that action.

He wasn't ever going to understand her, either. She had a devious mind. She'd come up with the same plan he had to help Rhone. He couldn't help being impressed.

Lord, the task ahead of him would certainly prove exhausting. He was going to have to go to great lengths to keep Christina safe. She'd get into quick trouble if he wasn't always by her side, watching over her. Christina didn't seem to understand caution. Hell, she didn't even know enough to be afraid of him when his temper exploded.

No woman had ever raised her voice to him . . . nor had many men, Lyon realized. Yet Christina certainly had. When he shouted at her, he got equal measure in return.

She was his equal in all things. Her passion matched his own, and in his heart, he knew she loved him just as much.

Yes, the next twenty years, God willing, were going to be exhausting.

And very, very satisfying.

Chapter Fifteen

I didn't want any more innocent people to die because of me. Edward would come after us. I knew I'd only been given a temporary stay of execution.

When dawn arrived, I'd only made it to the first peak. The wagon train was waking up. Would they send searchers out to find me?

I saw the Indians pouring down the hill then and thought to scream a warning, but I knew they wouldn't be able to hear me. Then another scream came from behind me. It was a woman's voice. Edward! He was there, I believed. Another innocent would die because of me. I grabbed the knife Jacob kept in his saddle pocket and ran toward the sound.

The sight that met me when I rushed through the trees broke through my cowardice, my fear. I saw a little boy, so battered, so bloody, crumbled like a fallen leaf on the ground. The woman who'd screamed was silent now. Her hands and feet had been bound.

Mother and child . . . like you and me, Christina . . . the attacker became Edward in my mind. I don't remember putting *you down on the ground, don't know if I made a sound as I ran forward and plunged my knife into his back.*

The knife must have pierced his heart, for the attacker didn't struggle.

I made certain he was dead, then turned to help the little boy. His whimpers of agony tore at me. I gently lifted the child into my arms to give him what little comfort I could. When I began to croon to him, his breathing deepened.

I suddenly felt someone watching me. I turned and saw that the Indian woman was staring at me.

Her name was Merry.

> *Journal entry*
> *November 1, 1795*

Lyon didn't return to his townhouse until the early hours of the morning. It had been a thoroughly satisfying evening all around. The look on Rhone's face when he was being robbed by the man pretending to be Jack would live in Lyon's memory a good long while.

Yes, it had all been worth his efforts. The charges against Rhone would be dropped by tomorrow at the latest. Everyone now believed Rhone's story that he'd injured his wrist by accident when he'd fallen on a piece of jagged glass.

Wellingham had been made to look like a fool. That thought pleased Lyon. He wasn't through with that bastard —or the other three, for that matter—but Lyon knew he'd have to wait before making their lives as miserable as he had planned. Rhone's father would be avenged. The four thieves were going to regret the day they'd decided to make Rhone's family their target. Lyon would see to it.

Christina was sound asleep on the floor next to his side of the bed. Lyon undressed quickly, then lifted his wife into his arms, careful to avoid being pricked by the knife under her blanket. Put her where she belonged—in his bed. He wrapped his arms around her until she was snuggled against his chest.

He'd have to do something about the soft mattresses, he

supposed. He smiled as he remembered Christina telling him on their wedding night that the bed was trying to swallow her up.

She hadn't fallen out of bed. No wonder she'd laughed when he'd announced that she had. Lyon fervently hoped she'd get used to the bed. He didn't relish the idea of bedding down on the ground, but he would do it, he realized with a sigh, if it was the only way he could hold her.

Compromise. The word whispered through his mind. It was a foreign concept to him. Until Christina. Perhaps now, he decided, it was time to practice it.

Lyon was eager for morning to come. After explaining his reason for being so angry with her when he'd found her at Bryan's tavern, he'd ease into the issue of her safety. He'd make her understand he only had her best interests at heart, and that she couldn't go flitting about town without proper escort.

And she would learn to compromise.

Lyon wasn't able to lecture his wife the following morning. She wasn't there to listen to him.

He didn't wake up until noon—an amazing fact, for he rarely slept more than three hours at a stretch. He felt rested, ready to take on the world. More exactly, he was ready to take on his wife, and he hurried in his dress so that he could go downstairs to begin her instruction.

Lyon had jumped to the erroneous conclusion that Christina would actually be waiting for him.

"What do you mean? She can't be gone!"

His bellow frightened the timid servant. "The Marchioness left several hours ago, my lord," he stammered out. "With Brown and the other men. Have you forgotten your orders to your wife? I heard the Marchioness tell Brown you had insisted she return to Lyonwood immediately."

"Yes, I did forget," Lyon muttered. He lied to his servant, of course. He hadn't given any such instructions. Yet he wasn't about to let a member of his staff know Christina wasn't telling the truth. It wasn't *her* character he was protecting but his own. Lyon didn't want anyone to know the lack of control he had over her.

It was humiliating. Lyon grumbled about that sorry fact until a sudden thought made him cheer up a bit. Christina must have been nervous to leave so quickly. Perhaps she'd realized the significance of her actions yesterday.

Lyon at first thought to go to Lyonwood immediately, then decided to let Christina stew in her own worries for most of the day. By the time he arrived home she might even be contrite.

Yes, time and silence were his allies. He hoped he'd have her apology by nightfall.

Lyon spent an hour going over estate details, then decided to stop by his mother's townhouse to tell Diana about Rhone.

He was given a surprise when he barged into the drawing room and found Rhone sitting on the settee with his arm draped around Diana.

"Am I interrupting?" he drawled.

His entrance didn't seem to bother either one of them. Diana's head continued to rest on Rhone's shoulder, and his friend didn't even glance up.

"Here's Lyon now, sweetling. Quit crying. He'll know what's to be done."

Lyon barked orders as he strode over to the fireplace. "Rhone, get your arm off my sister. Diana, sit up and behave with a little decorum, for God's sake. What are you crying about?"

His sister tried to comply with his command, but as soon as she straightened up Rhone pulled her back, forcing the side of her cheek onto his shoulder again.

"You stay right there. I'm comforting her, damn it, Lyon, and that's that."

Lyon decided he'd have to deal with his friend later. "Tell me why you're crying, Diana. Now. I'm in a hurry," he added.

"You don't need to raise your voice to her, Lyon." Rhone glared at his friend. "She's had an upset."

"Will one of you please tell me what the hell the upset was?"

"Mama." Diana wailed. She pulled away from Rhone to

dab at her eyes with her lace handkerchief. "Christina took her."

"She what?" Lyon asked, shaking his head in confusion.

"Your wife took your mother to Lyonwood with her," Rhone said.

"And that's why Diana's crying?" Lyon asked, trying to get to the bottom of the matter.

Rhone was trying not to laugh. His eyes sparkled with merriment. "It is," he said as he patted Diana's shoulder.

Lyon sat down across from his sister and waited for her to get hold of herself. She looked like a butterfly, he thought, dressed in a yellow gown with brown trim. Her tears were making a mess of the gown.

"Diana," he said in what he hoped was a soothing voice, "You needn't be afraid that I'm angry because my wife took our mother with her. That's why you're crying, isn't it?"

"No."

"You wanted Mother to stay here?"

When she shook her head and continued to sob, Lyon's patience wore out. "Well?"

"Mama didn't want to go," Diana cried. "Rhone, you tell him. You saw what happened. I just don't know what to think. And Aunt Harriett laughing like a loon the whole time. Oh, I didn't know what—"

"Rhone, do you care about Diana?"

"I do. Very much."

"Then I suggest you quiet her down before I strangle her. Diana, stop that snorting."

"I'll explain, my sweet," Rhone told Diana in a tender, soothing voice.

Lyon hid his exasperation. Rhone was acting like a lovesick puppy.

"Your mama denied Christina's request to go along with her to Lyonwood, you see. And that's when the fireworks began."

Rhone couldn't control his smile. Diana was weeping into his jacket now, so he felt safe grinning. "Your wife was very determined to take your mother with her. So determined, in fact, that she . . . well, she dragged your mother out of bed."

"You're jesting."

"Mama didn't want to go."

"Obviously," Lyon drawled. "Did Christina explain her reasons for being so forceful?"

A smile pulled at the corners of his mouth, but his sister was watching him intently, and he didn't want to upset her further by letting her see his amusement.

Rhone didn't help his determination to shield his sister's feelings. "You should have seen it, Lyon. Your mother is a strong woman. I never realized that fact. I thought she'd been languishing these past years, but she did put up quite a fight. Of course, that was only after . . ."

"After what?" Lyon asked, thoroughly puzzled by his wife's conduct.

"Mama told Christina she wanted to stay where she was. She had people coming to call, and she wanted to talk to them about James, of course," Diana said to Lyon.

"Yes, well, that's when Christina asked your mother if her heart had died."

"I don't understand," Lyon announced, shaking his head.

"I didn't either," Rhone answered. "Anyway, your mother said that since James had died, her heart was also dead . . . whatever in God's name that means."

Lyon smiled then. He couldn't help himself. "My mother is a professional mourner, Rhone. You know that well enough."

"Was," Rhone drawled out. "Christina had gotten your mother down into the entryway by this time. Your aunt, Diana, and I were standing there, watching the two ladies, wondering what was going on. Then Christina explained it all to us."

"She's going to kill Mama."

"Now, Diana, that isn't what she said," Rhone said. He patted her shoulder, then turned to grin at Lyon again.

"Rhone, will you get on with it?"

"Christina told your mother that where she came from—and God only knows where that is—an old warrior who was broken in spirit and in heart would go into the wilderness."

"What for?" Lyon asked.

"Why, to find a nice, secluded spot in which to die, of course. Needless to say, your mother didn't take kindly to being called an old warrior."

Lyon stared at the ceiling a long minute before daring to look at his friend again. He was dangerously close to laughing. "No, I don't suppose she would," he whispered.

"Well, part of it is Mama's own fault," Diana interjected. "If she hadn't agreed that her heart was broken, Christina wouldn't have insisted on taking her with her. She told Mama she'd help her find a lovely spot."

"That was good of her," Lyon said.

"Lyon, Mama hadn't had her chocolate yet. She hadn't had her maids pack any of her possessions, either. Christina told her it didn't matter. One didn't have to pack when one was going to die. Those were her very words."

"Your mother started shouting then," Rhone announced.

"Rhone wouldn't let me interfere," Diana whispered, "and Aunt Harriett was laughing."

"Not until your mother was inside the carriage," Rhone commented.

"Was she shouting James's name?" Lyon asked.

"Well . . . no, of course not," Diana muttered. "What has that got to do with anything?"

Neither Rhone nor Lyon could answer her. They were too busy laughing.

It took Lyon several minutes before he could speak again. "I guess I'd better get back to Lyonwood."

"What if Christina hides Mama somewhere in the countryside and won't tell you where?"

"Do you really believe Christina would harm your mama?" Rhone asked.

"No," Diana whispered. "But she sounded as though it was the most natural thing for . . . an old warrior to do." Diana let out a loud sigh. "Christina has some unusual notions, doesn't she?"

"She's bluffing, Diana. She's pretending to give our mother what she wants."

"Lyon, would you like me to ride along with you to Lyonwood?" Rhone asked.

Lyon could tell by the gleam in his friend's green eyes that he was up to mischief. "Why do you offer?" he asked.

"I could help you search the estate," Rhone drawled.

"Very amusing," Lyon snapped. "Now see what you've done? Diana's crying again. You deal with it, Rhone. I don't have time. Come down to Lyonwood this weekend with Aunt Harriett and Diana."

Lyon strolled over to the doorway, then called over his shoulder, "If I haven't found your mother by then, Diana, you can help search."

Rhone contained his smile. "He's only jesting, sweetheart. Now, now, let me hold you, love. You can cry on my shoulder."

Lyon closed the door on Rhone's soothing voice. He shook his head in vexation. He'd been so wrapped up in his own life, he hadn't realized Rhone was falling in love with Diana.

Rhone was a good friend . . . but a brother-in-law . . . Lyon would have to adjust to that possibility.

Christina wouldn't be surprised by the attraction. No, she'd been the one to instruct Rhone on his destiny, Lyon recalled with a smile.

Ah, destiny. He decided it was now his destiny to go home and kiss his wife.

The desire to take Christina into his arms, to make slow, sweet love to her, made the journey back to Lyonwood seem much longer than usual.

The sun was just setting when Lyon rode toward the circle drive in front of his house. He squinted against the sunlight, trying to make out the sight he thought he was seeing.

As he rode closer, he recognized the man dragging his shoes down the steps. It was Elbert. What was he doing there? And what in God's name was he doing with Lyon's boots? Lyon was close enough to see his dozens of shoes and boots lined up on the steps, the walkway.

Lyon dismounted, slapped his horse on the hindquarters as a signal to take to the stables, then called out to Christina's former butler. "Elbert? What are you doing with my shoes?"

"The madam's orders, my lord," Elbert answered. "Didn't know a man could own so many boots," he added. "Been at this task near an hour now. Up the stairs and down the stairs, then up—"

"Elbert? Give me the reason why," Lyon interrupted, his voice irritated. "And what are you doing at Lyonwood? Did Christina invite you to visit?"

"Hired me, sir," Elbert announced. "I'm to be Brown's assistant. Did you know how worried she was about me? She knew I wouldn't last with the old bat. Your misses has a good heart. I'll do my part, my lord. I won't be shirking me responsibilities to you."

Christina did have a good heart. His gentle wife knew Elbert wouldn't be able to find work with anyone else. He was simply too old, too feeble. "I'm sure you'll do fine, Elbert," Lyon said. "Glad to have you on staff."

"Thank you, my lord," Elbert returned.

Lyon noticed Brown standing in the open doorway then. His butler looked upset. "Good afternoon, my lord," Brown called out. "It is so very good to have you back," he added. His voice sounded strained to Lyon, relieved as well. "Did you see your shoes, sir?"

"I'm not blind, man. Of course I saw them. Would you care to explain what in thunderation is going on?"

"Your wife's orders," Brown announced.

"Past wife," Elbert interjected with a cackle.

Lyon took a deep breath. "What are you talking about?" He addressed his question to Brown, believing his young butler would make more sense than the old man snickering with laughter behind him.

"You're being divorced, my lord."

"I'm what?"

Brown's shoulders sagged. He knew his lord wasn't going to take the news well. "Divorced."

"Cast out, my lord, pushed aside, forgotten, dead in her heart—"

"I get your meaning, Elbert," Lyon muttered in exasperation. "I'm aware of what the word divorce means."

Lyon continued into the house. The old servant shuffled

after him. "Those were her very words. My mistress is divorcing you the way her people do. She said it was quite all right to get rid of a husband. You have to find someplace else to live."

"I what?" Lyon asked, certain he hadn't heard correctly. Brown's insistent nod indicated he had.

"You're cast out, pushed aside—"

"For God's sake, Elbert, cease your litany," Lyon demanded. He turned back to Brown. "What is the significance of the shoes?"

"They signify your departure, my lord," Brown said.

The butler tried not to stare at the incredulous look on his master's face. He was in jeopardy of losing his control. He stared at the floor instead.

"Let me get this straight in my mind," Lyon muttered. "My wife believes the house belongs to her?"

"And your mother, of course," Brown blurted out. "She's keeping her."

Brown was biting his lower lip. Lyon thought he might be trying not to laugh.

"Of course," Lyon drawled.

Elbert tried to be helpful once again. "It's the way her people do," he interjected, his voice gratingly cheerful.

"Where is my wife?" Lyon asked, ignoring Elbert's comments.

He didn't wait for his servants to answer him but took the steps two at a time to reach the bedrooms. A sudden thought made him pause. "Did she cut her hair?" he called out.

"She did," Elbert shouted before Brown could open his mouth. "It's the way of it," Elbert insisted. "Once the hair's cut—well, then you're as good as dead to her. You're set aside, cast—"

"I've gotten her message," Lyon shouted. "Brown, bring my shoes inside. Elbert, go sit somewhere."

"My lord?" Brown called out.

"Yes?"

"Do the French really follow these laws?"

Lyon contained his smile. "Did my wife say it was the law?" he asked.

"Yes, my lord."

"And she told you she was from France?" he asked his butler.

Brown nodded.

"Then it must be true," Lyon announced. "I would like a bath, Brown. Leave the shoes until later," he added before turning back to his destination.

Lyon smiled. There were times when he forgot just how young and inexperienced Brown was. Of course, he'd been lied to by someone who radiated innocence and sincerity. Christina.

His wife wasn't waiting for him in their bedroom. He really hadn't expected her to be there. The sun still gave sufficient light for her to stay outdoors. Lyon doubted she'd return to the house until darkness forced her to do so.

Lyon walked over to the windows to look out at the setting sun. It was a magnificent sight, and one he'd never taken the time to notice until he'd married Christina. She had opened his eyes to the wonders of life.

And the wonder of love. Yes, he did love her, so ferociously it almost frightened him. If anything happened to her, Lyon didn't know how he'd be able to go on.

That odious thought wouldn't have intruded on his peace of mind if he hadn't been so concerned about Christina's reunion with her father. Lyon was more than uneasy.

She believed he'd try to kill her. Richards hadn't been able to tell Lyon much about Christina's father, but the fact that Stalinsky had been involved in the Brisbane affair, with such shameful results, worried Lyon.

How simple it would be if Christina would trust him, confide in him. Lord, he felt as if he was being asked to fence with an enemy with a blindfold tied around his eyes.

Equal measure. Wasn't that what he wanted from Christina?

The truth hit him like a blow. He'd demanded from his wife what he'd been unwilling to give her. Trust. Yes, he wanted her absolute trust, yet he hadn't let her know how much he trusted her. No, he told himself with a shake of his head, his sin was worse. He hadn't opened his heart to her.

Christina had only questioned him once about his past. When they were on their way to Lyonwood, she'd asked him to tell her about his first wife, Lettie.

His answers had been abrupt. He'd let her know the subject wasn't one he would discuss.

She hadn't asked him again.

Yes, he was getting equal measure.

The door opened behind him. Lyon glanced over his shoulder and saw the servants carrying the tub and pails of steaming water into the room.

He turned back to the landscape and was in the process of drawing off his jacket when he saw Christina.

His breath caught in his throat. The sight was more magnificent than the sunset. Christina was riding bareback. The gray stallion she'd chosen was racing across the grounds with such speed his legs were a blur.

She rode like the wind. Her golden hair flew out behind her. Her back was as straight as a lance, and when she directed her mount over the hedge that separated the wilderness from the immediate grounds, Lyon started breathing again.

Christina was far more skilled than he was. That fact became obvious as he continued to watch her. He was arrogantly pleased, as if her skill somehow reflected on him. "She's my lioness," he whispered, excusing his reaction.

She was so incredibly graceful . . . and he had offered to teach her how to ride.

Another incorrect assumption, Lyon realized. As incorrect as believing he would actually gain an apology from her for yesterday's folly.

Lyon was chuckling to himself as he stripped off his clothes. He ignored his servants' worried glances. He knew they weren't used to hearing him laugh. Then he stretched out in the long tub, his shoulders propped against the back. Brown was occupied getting fresh clothing ready for him.

"I'll take care of that," Lyon told his butler. "You may leave now."

Brown started for the door, then hesitated. When he

turned around to look at his employer, his expression showed his concern.

"What is it?" Lyon asked.

"My lord, I would never presume to intrude upon your private affairs, but I was wondering if you'll be honoring your wife's decision."

Lyon had to remind himself that Brown was very young and hadn't been in his household long enough to know his lord's ways well. He'd never have asked such a ridiculous question otherwise. "Why, of course, Brown," Lyon drawled out.

"Then you'll let her divorce you?" Brown blurted out, clearly stunned.

"I believe she already did divorce me," Lyon answered with a grin.

The butler wasn't at all happy with that announcement. "I shall miss you, my lord."

"She's keeping you, too?" Lyon asked.

Brown nodded. He looked miserable. "My lady explained that we are part of her family now."

"We?"

"She's keeping the full staff, my lord."

Lyon started laughing. "I really wish you'd stay," Brown blurted out.

"Quit worrying, Brown. I'm not going anywhere," Lyon announced. "As soon as my wife walks into the house, send her to me. If she can divorce me so easily, then there must be a quick way to remarry again. This little problem will be resolved by nightfall, I promise you."

"Thank God," Brown whispered. He hurried out of the room, closing the door behind him.

Brown could hear his lord's laughter all the way down the hall.

Christina met the butler at the bottom of the steps. When he informed her that the Marquess was upstairs and wished an audience with her, she gave him a disgruntled look before giving in to his request.

When she walked into the bedroom, she came to a sudden stop.

"Close the door, sweetheart."

Christina did as he asked, but only because she wished privacy for their confrontation.

"Did you enjoy your ride?" Lyon asked.

The mildness in his tone confused her. Christina was ready for a fight. Lyon didn't seem to be in an accommodating mood. "Lyon," she began, deliberately avoiding his gaze, "I don't think you realize what I've done."

"Of course I do, my dear," Lyon answered, in such a cheerful voice that Christina was more confused than ever.

"You're going to have to start all over. You'll have to court me, though now that you are aware of my . . . unusual upbringing, I doubt you'll—"

"All right."

Christina looked at him. "All right? That is all you have to say to me?" She shook her head, let out a long sigh, and then whispered, "You don't understand."

"Yes, I do. You've just cast me aside. Elbert explained."

"You aren't upset?"

"No."

"Well, why not? You told me you loved me," Christina said. She moved a step closer to Lyon. "Your words were false, weren't they? Now that you know—"

"They weren't false," Lyon answered. He leaned back and closed his eyes. "God, this feels good. I tell you, Christina, the ride from London gets longer every time."

She couldn't believe his casual attitude. Christina felt like weeping. "You cannot humiliate me and then act as though nothing has happened. A warrior would kill another for such an offense," she told him.

"Ah, but you aren't a warrior, Christina. You're my wife."

"Was."

He didn't even open his eyes to look at her when he asked, "Exactly what did I do?"

"You don't know?" She had to take a deep breath before she could go on. "You shouted at me in front of a witness. You shamed me. You disgraced me."

"Who was the witness?" Lyon asked, in such a soft voice that she had to move a bit closer to hear him.

"Bryan," Christina announced.

"Didn't I yell at you in front of Richards, too? I seem to remember—"

"That was different."

"Why?"

"You were shouting because I fainted. You weren't angry with me. Surely you can see the difference."

"I do now," Lyon admitted. "Do you wonder why I shouted at you in front of Bryan?"

"No."

Lyon opened his eyes. His irritation was obvious. "You scared the hell out of me," he announced. Each word was clipped, hard.

"I what?"

"Don't look so surprised, Christina. When I walked inside that tavern and found you sitting so peacefully in the midst of the worse scum in England, my mind could barely take it in. Then you had the gall to smile at me, as if you were happy to see me."

He had to stop talking. The memory was making him angry again.

"I *was* happy to see you. Did you doubt that I was?" she asked.

Her hands rested on her hips. She tossed her hair over her shoulder and continued to frown at him. "Well?" she demanded.

"Did you cut your hair again?"

"I did. It is all part of the ritual of mourning," Christina announced.

"Christina, if you cut your hair every time you're unhappy with me, you'll be bald in a month's time. I promise you."

Lyon drew a long breath, then said, "Let me get this straight inside my mind. I'm never to raise my voice to you in future? Christina, it won't work. There will be times when I shout at you."

"I don't care if you raise your voice to me," Christina muttered. "I shall also let my temper show on occasion," she admitted. "But I would never, ever let an outsider see my displeasure. That was the humiliation, Lyon."

"Oh? Then I should have dragged you into the back room to shout at you in privacy?" he asked.

"Yes, you should have," Christina agreed.

"You took a foolish risk, Christina. You were in danger, whether you realized it or not. I want your apology and your promise never to take such a risk again."

"I shall have to think about it," she said. Now that she was forced to consider what he was saying to her, she realized she had been in a bit of danger. There were too many men in Bryan's tavern for her to subdue . . . if they'd all decided to challenge her at the same time. She'd thought she'd gained the upper hand, though, after the single challenger had backed down . . . and after she'd mentioned her husband was the Marquess of Lyonwood. "Yes," she repeated, "I shall have to think about these promises you want from me."

She could tell from Lyon's ferocious expression that he didn't care for her honest answer. "I warned you that it wouldn't be easy for you," she whispered.

"That's what this is really all about, isn't it?"

"I've just said—"

"You're testing me, aren't you, Christina?"

She made the mistake of getting too close to the tub, realizing her error a second too late. Lyon grabbed her and pulled her down into his lap. Water sloshed over the sides of the tub.

"You've ruined my gown," Christina gasped.

"I've ruined others," Lyon told her when she quit struggling. He cupped the sides of her face and made her look at him. "I love you."

Her eyes filled with tears. "You humiliated me."

"I love you," Lyon repeated in a harsh whisper. "I'm sorry you felt humiliated," he added.

"You're sorry?"

A single tear slid down her cheek. Lyon wiped it away with his thumb.

"I'm sorry I frightened you," she whispered. "I shall try not to do it again."

"Tell me you love me," Lyon demanded.

"I love you."

"Should I believe you?" he asked. His voice was husky, coaxing.

"Yes," Christina answered. She tried to push his hands away when she realized he was actually insulting her. "Of course you should believe me."

"But you don't believe me when I tell you I love you," Lyon said. "You have it in your head that it's only a temporary condition, don't you?" He kissed her slowly, tenderly, hoping to take the sting out of his gentle rebuke. "When you learn to trust me completely, you'll know I won't change my mind. My love is forever, Christina."

Lyon didn't give her time to argue over that fact. He kissed her again. His tongue flicked over her soft lips until they parted for him.

And then he began to ravage her mouth.

Christina tried to protest. "Lyon, I must—"

"Get your clothes off," Lyon interrupted. He was already pulling apart the fastenings on the back of her gown.

No, she hadn't meant to say that. But her thoughts got confused inside her mind. Lyon had pulled her gown down to her waist. His hands cupped her breasts, his thumbs rubbed her nipples, forced her response. His mouth had never seemed so warm, so inviting.

There was more water on the floor than in the tub. Lyon didn't seem to mind. He was determined, and he had Christina stripped out of her soggy clothes in little time.

Christina didn't want to struggle. She put her arms around his neck and let out a soft sigh. "The water isn't very hot," she whispered against his ear.

"I am."

"What?"

"Hot."

"Lyon? I want—"

"Me, inside you," Lyon whispered. His mouth feasted on the side of her neck. His warm breath sent shivers down her spine. "You want to feel me inside you," he rasped out. "Hard. Hot. I'll try to go slow, but you'll want me harder, faster, until I'm touching your womb and you're begging me for release."

Christina's head fell back so that Lyon could kiss more of her throat. His dark promise of what was to come made her throat tighten and her heartbeat quicken. "I'll stay inside you until I'm hard again, won't I, Christina? And then I'll pleasure you again."

His mouth settled on hers for another long, drugging kiss. "That's what you want, isn't it, my sweet?"

"Yes," Christina answered. She sighed against his mouth. "It's what I want."

"Then marry me. Now," Lyon demanded. He kissed her again as a precaution against any protest. "Hurry, Christina. I want to . . . Christina, don't move like that," Lyon ground out. "It's torture."

"You like it."

She whispered the truth against his shoulder, then nipped his skin with her teeth, her nails. She moved again to straddle his hips, rubbing her breasts against his chest.

Yet when she tried to take Lyon inside her, he wouldn't allow it. His hands settled on the sides of her hips, holding her away from his arousal.

"Not yet, Christina," he groaned. "Are we still divorced inside your head?"

"Lyon, please," Christina begged.

He drew her up against him until her heat rested on the flat of his stomach. His fingers found her, slowly penetrated her. "Do you want me to stop?" he asked with a growl.

"No, don't stop."

"Are we married?"

Christina gave in. "Yes, Lyon. You were supposed to court me first." She moaned when he increased the pressure. She bit his bottom lip, then opened her mouth for him again.

"Compromise," Lyon whispered as he slowly pushed her downward and began to penetrate her.

She didn't understand what he was saying to her, thought to at least try to question him, but Lyon suddenly shifted.

His movement was forceful, deliberate. Christina couldn't speak, couldn't think. Lyon was pulling her into the sun. Soon, when she could bear the scorching heat no longer, he would give her sweet release.

Christina clung to her warrior in blissful surrender.

"We should have gone downstairs for dinner. I don't want your mother to think she can hide in her bedroom. She must eat all her meals with us in future, husband."

Lyon ignored his wife's comments. He pulled her up against his side, draped the bed covers over her legs when he noticed she was trembling, then began to tickle her shoulder with his fingers.

"Christina? Didn't your father ever yell at you when you were a little girl?"

She turned and rested her chin on his chest before she answered him. "That's an odd question to put to me. Yes, Father did yell."

"But never in front of others?" Lyon asked.

"Well, there was one time when he lost his temper," she admitted. "I was too little to remember the incident, but my mother and the shaman liked to tell the story."

"Shaman?"

"Our holy man," Christina explained. "Like the one who married us. My shaman doesn't ever wear a cone on his head, though." She ended her comment with a dainty shrug.

"What was the reason for your father to lose his temper?" Lyon asked.

"You'll not laugh?"

"I won't laugh."

Christina turned her gaze to stare at his chest so that his golden eyes wouldn't break her concentration. "My brother carried home a beautiful snake. Father was very pleased."

"He was?"

"It was a fine snake, Lyon."

"I see."

She could hear the smile in his voice but didn't take exception. "Mother was also pleased. I must have watched the way my brother held his prize, and the shaman said I was envious of the attention given my brother, too, for I went out to capture a snake of my own. No one could find me for several hours. I was very little and in constant mischief."

"Ah, so that is why your father lost his temper," Lyon announced. "Your disappearance must have—"

"No, that isn't the reason," Christina interjected. "Though of course he was unhappy that I'd left the safety of the village."

"Well, then?" Lyon prodded when she didn't immediately continue with her story.

"Everyone was frantically searching for me when I strutted back into the village. Mama said I always strutted because I tried to imitate my brother's swagger. White Eagle walked like a proud warrior, you see."

The memory of the story she'd heard so many times during her growing years made her smile. "And did you have a snake with you when you strutted back into the village?" Lyon asked.

"Oh, yes," she answered. "The shaman recounted that I held it just as my brother had held his snake. Father was standing on the far side of the fires. Mother stood beside him. Neither showed any outward reaction to my prize. They didn't want to frighten me into dropping the snake, I was told later. Anyway," she added with a sigh, "Father walked over to me. He took the snake out of my hand, killed it, and then began to shout at me. Mother knew I didn't understand. Father had praised my brother, you see, yet he was yelling at me."

"Why do you think that was?" Lyon asked, already dreading her answer.

"My brother's snake wasn't poisonous."

"Oh, God."

The tremble in her husband's voice made her laugh. "Father was soon over his anger. The shaman announced that the spirits had protected me. I was their lioness, you see. Mama said Father was also sorry for making me cry. He took me riding with him that afternoon and let me sit on his lap during the evening meal."

The parallel was too good to pass up. "Your father was frightened," Lyon announced. "He loved you, Christina— so much so that when he saw the danger you were in, his discipline deserted him. Just like my discipline deserted me when I saw the danger you were in yesterday."

He dragged her up on top of him so he could look into her eyes. "It was his duty to keep my lioness safe for me."

Christina slowly nodded. "I think you would like my father. You're very like him in many ways. You're just as arrogant. Oh, don't frown, Lyon. I give you a compliment when I say you're arrogant. You're full of bluster, too."

She sounded too sincere for Lyon to take insult. "What is your father's name?" he asked.

"Black Wolf."

"Will he like me?"

"No."

He wasn't insulted by her abrupt answer. In truth, he was close to laughing. "Care to tell me why not?"

"He hates the whites. Doesn't trust them."

"That's why you have such a suspicious nature, isn't it?"

"Perhaps."

She rested the side of her face against Lyon's shoulder.

"You're still a little suspicious of me, too, aren't you?"

"I don't know," she admitted with a sigh.

"I trust you, my sweet. Completely."

She didn't show any reaction.

"Christina, I want equal measure. I will have your trust. And not just for a day or two. Those are my terms."

She slowly lifted her head to stare at Lyon. "And if I'm unable to meet your terms?" she asked.

He saw the worry in her eyes. "You tell me," he whispered.

"You'll set me aside," she whispered.

He shook his head. "No."

"No? Then what?"

He wanted to kiss her frown away. "I'll wait. I'll still love you. In your heart you really don't believe me, do you? You think you'll do something to displease me and I'll quit loving you. It won't happen, Christina."

She was humbled by his fervent words. "I worry." Her confession was whispered in a forlorn voice. "There are times when I don't think I shall ever fit in. I'm like a circle trying to squeeze into a square."

"Everyone feels like that at times," Lyon told her, smiling over her absurd analogy. "You're vulnerable. Are there times when you still want to go home?"

His hands caressed her shoulders while he waited for her answer. "I couldn't leave you," she answered. "And I couldn't take you back with me. You're my family now, Lyon." Her frown intensified. "It really isn't going to be easy for you, living with me."

"Marriage is never easy in the beginning," he answered. "We both have to learn to compromise. In time we'll understand each other's needs."

"Your family and your staff will think me odd."

"They already do."

Her frown was forced now, and a sparkle appeared in her eyes. "That was unkind of you to say," she told him.

"No, it was an honest admission. They think I'm odd, too. Do you care so much what others think of you, Christina?"

She shook her head. "Only you, Lyon. I care what you think."

He showed her how pleased he was to hear her admission by kissing her.

"I also care what you think," Lyon whispered. "Will my shoes be lining the steps outside again?"

"The old ways are familiar to me," Christina explained. "I was so angry with you. It was all I could think to do to make you realize how unhappy you'd made me."

"Thank God you didn't try to leave me."

"Try?"

"You know I'd chase you down and drag you back where you belong."

"Yes, I knew you would. You are a warrior, after all."

Lyon moved Christina to his side, determined to finish their conversation before making love to her again. Her hand moved to his thigh. It was a distraction. Lyon captured both her hands and gave her a gentle squeeze. "Christina?

Did you ever love another man? Was there someone back home who captured your heart?"

Her head was tucked under his chin. Christina smiled, knowing Lyon couldn't see her reaction. He'd tensed against her after he'd asked the question. He hadn't been able to keep the worry out of his voice.

He was letting her see his vulnerability. "When I was very young, I thought I'd grow up and marry White Eagle. Then, when I was seven summers or so, I put those silly thoughts aside. He was my brother, after all."

"Was there anyone else?"

"No. Father wouldn't let any of the warriors walk with me. He knew I had to return to the whites. My destiny had already been decided."

"Who decided your destiny?" Lyon asked.

"The dream."

Christina waited for his next question, but after a minute or two, when she realized he wasn't going to ask her to explain, she decided to tell him anyway.

She wanted him to understand.

The story of the shaman's journey to the top of the mountain to seek his vision captured Lyon's full attention.

The dream made him smile. "If your mother hadn't called you a lioness, would the shaman ever have—"

"He would have sorted it all out," Christina interrupted. "I had white-blond hair and blue eyes, just like the lion in his dream. Yes, he would have sorted it out. Do you understand now how confused I was when Sir Reynolds called you Lyon? I knew in that moment that I had found my mate."

The logical part of Lyon's mind saw all the flaws in the dream, the superstitions of the rituals. Yet he easily pushed reason aside. He didn't care if it didn't make sense. "I knew in that moment, too, that you'd belong to me."

"Both of us fought it, didn't we, Lyon?"

"That we did, love."

Christina laughed. "You never stood a fair chance, husband. Your fate had already been decided."

Lyon nodded. "Now it's your turn to ask me questions. Would you like me to tell you about Lettie?"

Christina tried to look up at Lyon, but he wouldn't let her move. "Do you want to tell me about her?" she asked, her voice hesitant.

"Yes, I do. Now ask me your questions," he commanded, his voice soft.

"Did you love her?"

"Not in the same way I love you. I was never . . . content. I was too young for marriage. I realize that now."

"What was she like?"

"The complete opposite of you," Lyon answered. "Lettie enjoyed the social whirl of the ton. She hated this house, the countryside. Lettie loved intrigue. I was working with Richards then. The war was coming, and I was away from home quite a lot. My brother, James, escorted Lettie to various events. While I was away, he took her to his bed."

Her indrawn breath told him she understood. Lyon had wanted to tell Christina about his first wife so that she would see how much he trusted her. Yet now that the telling had begun, the anger he'd held inside him for so long began to fade. That realization surprised him. His explanation wasn't hesitant now. "Lettie died in childbirth. The babe also. It wasn't my child, Christina. James was the father. I remember how I sat next to my wife, trying to give her comfort. God, she was in terrible pain. I pray you'll never have to endure it. Lettie wasn't aware that I was there. She kept screaming for her lover."

Christina felt like weeping. The pain of his brother's betrayal must have been unbearable. She didn't understand. How could a wife shame her husband in such a way?

She hugged Lyon but decided against offering him additional sympathy. He was a proud man. "Were you and your brother close to each other before his betrayal?" she asked.

"No."

Christina scooted away from Lyon so she could see his expression. His gaze showed only his puzzlement over her question. Lettie's sin no longer affected him, she decided.

"You never gave Lettie your heart," she announced. "It's your brother you've yet to forgive, isn't it, Lyon?"

He was amazed by her perception. "Were you close to James?" she asked again.

"No. We were very competitive when we were younger. I grew out of that nonsense, but my brother obviously didn't."

"I wonder if James wasn't like Lancelot," she whispered, "from the story of Camelot."

"And Lettie was my Guinevere?" he asked, his smile gentle.

"Perhaps," Christina answered. "Would it make his deception easier to bear if you believed it wasn't a deliberate sin?"

"It wouldn't be the truth. James wasn't Lancelot. My brother took what he wanted, when he wanted it, regardless of the consequences. He never really grew up," Lyon ended.

She ignored the harshness in his voice. "Perhaps your mama wouldn't let him," she said.

"Speaking of my mother," Lyon began with a sigh, "you have a plan to keep her here?"

"I do."

"Hell. How long?"

"Quit frowning. She'll stay with us until she wishes to leave. Of course, we have to make her want to stay first," she qualified. "I have a plan to help her, Lyon. Together we'll draw her back into the family. Your mama feels responsible for your brother's death."

"Why do you say that?" Lyon asked.

"She kept him tied to her skirts," Christina answered. "Diana said your mother protected both of you from your father's cruel temper."

"How could Diana know? She was only a baby when Father died."

"Aunt Harriett told her," Christina explained. "I questioned both your sister and your aunt, Lyon. I wanted to know all about your mama so that I could help her."

"How long will this take? I don't have the patience to sit through meals listening to her talk of James."

"We aren't going to let her speak of James," Christina said. "Your mama's very determined." She kissed Lyon on his chin, then said, "But I'm far more determined. Do I have your complete support in this undertaking?"

"Will you be taking her out into the wilderness to find a place for her to die?" he asked. He chuckled over the picture of Christina dragging his mother outdoors before adding, "Diana's worried you really will do just that."

Christina sighed in exasperation. "Your sister is very naive. I was only bluffing. Would you like for me to explain my plans for your mama?"

"No."

"Why not?"

"I'd rather be surprised," Lyon answered. "I just thought of another question to ask you."

"That doesn't surprise me. You're full of questions."

He ignored her rebuke and her disgruntled expression. "Do you realize you sometimes lapse into speaking French? Especially when you're upset. Is that the language your family spoke?"

Twin dimples appeared in her cheeks. Lyon thought she looked like an angel. She wasn't acting much like one, however, for her hand suddenly reached down to capture his arousal.

Lyon groaned, then pulled her hand away. "Answer me first," he commanded in a husky voice.

She let him see her disappointment before she answered him. "Father captured Mr. Deavenrue to teach me the language of the whites. If Mother had been allowed to speak to the man, she would have told him that I was going to return to England. Father didn't think that was significant. He didn't understand that there were different white languages. Deavenrue told me later, when we became friends, that he was very frightened of my father. I remember being amused by that fact," she added. "It was an unkind reaction, but I was only ten or eleven then, so I can excuse my attitude. Deavenrue was very young, too. He taught me the language of the whites . . . his whites."

Lyon's laughter interrupted her story. She waited until

he'd calmed down before continuing. "For two long years I suffered through that language. Day in and day out. Mother was never allowed near Deavenrue. He was a handsome man, for a white," she qualified. "In fact, everyone stayed away from him. He was there to complete a task, not to befriend."

"Then it was only the two of you working together?" Lyon asked.

"Of course not. I wasn't allowed to be alone with him either. There were always at least two old women with me. In time, however, I really came to like Deavenrue, and I was able to persuade my father into being a little friendlier to him."

"When did Deavenrue realize he wasn't teaching you the correct language? And how did he converse with your father?"

"Deavenrue spoke our language," Christina answered. "When my mother was finally allowed to visit Deavenrue's tipi, and she heard me reciting my lessons, she knew immediately that it wasn't the same language she'd been taught when she was a little girl."

"Was there an uproar?" Lyon asked, trying not to laugh again.

"Oh, yes. Mother caught Father alone and let him see her displeasure. If he hadn't been so stubborn in keeping her away from the missionary, two years wouldn't have been wasted. Father was just as angry. He wanted to kill Deavenrue, but Mother wouldn't let him."

Lyon laughed. "Why didn't your mother teach you?"

"Her English wasn't very good. She decided Deavenrue's English was better."

"Why do you prefer to speak French?"

"It's easier at times."

"Tell me you love me in your family's language."

"I love you."

"That's English."

"The language of my family now," Christina said. She then repeated her vow of love in the language of the Dakota.

Lyon thought the sound was lyrical.

"Now I will show you how much I love you," Christina whispered. Her hands slid down his chest. She thought to stroke him into wanting her but found that he was already throbbing with desire.

"No, I'm going to show you first," Lyon commanded.

He rolled his wife onto her back and proceeded to do just that.

A long while later husband and wife fell asleep, wrapped in each other's arms. They were both exhausted, and both thoroughly content.

Lyon awakened during the night. He immediately reached for his wife. As soon as he realized she wasn't in bed with him, he rolled to his side and looked on the floor.

Christina wasn't there either. Lyon's mind immediately cleared of sleep. He started to get out of bed to go in search of his wife when he realized the candles were burning on the bedside table. He remembered quite specifically that he'd put out all three flames.

It didn't make sense until he saw the black book in the center of the light.

The leather binding was scarred with age. When Lyon picked up the book and opened it, a musty smell permeated the air around him. The pages were brittle. He used infinite care as he slowly lifted the first pages of the gift Christina had given him.

He didn't know how long he sat there, his head bent to the light as he read Jessica's diary. An hour might have passed, perhaps two. When he finished the account of Jessica's nightmare, his hands shook.

Lyon stood up, stretched his muscles awake, then walked over to the hearth. He was chilled but didn't know if it was the temperature in the room or Jessica's diary that was the cause.

He was adding a second log to the fire he'd just started when he heard the door open behind him. Lyon finished his task before he turned around. He knelt on one knee, his arms braced on the other, and stared at his lovely wife a long minute.

She was dressed in a long white robe. Her hair was tousled, her cheeks flushed. He could tell she was nervous. Christina held a tray in her hands. The glasses were clattering.

"I thought you might be hungry. I went—"

"Come here, Christina."

His voice was whisper-soft. Christina hurried to do his bidding. She put the tray down on the bed, then rushed over to stand in front of her husband.

"Did you read it?" she asked.

Lyon stood up before he answered her. His hands settled on her shoulders. "You wanted me to, didn't you?"

"Yes."

"Tell me why you wanted me to read it."

"Equal measure, Lyon. Your words, husband. You opened your heart to me when you told me about James and Lettie. I could do no less."

"Thank you, Christina." His voice shook with emotion.

Christina's eyes widened. "Why do you thank me?"

"For trusting me," Lyon answered. He kissed the wrinkle in her brow. "When you gave me your mother's diary, you were also giving me your trust."

"I was?"

Lyon smiled. "You were," he announced. He kissed her again, tenderly, then suggested that they share their midnight meal in front of the fire.

"And we will talk?" Christina asked. "I want to tell you so many things. There's so much we must decide upon, Lyon."

"Yes, love, we'll talk," Lyon promised.

As soon as she turned to fetch the tray, Lyon grabbed one of the blankets draped over the chair and unfolded it on the floor.

Christina knelt down and placed the tray in the center of the blanket. "Do you want me to get your robe for you?" she asked.

"No," Lyon answered, grinning. "Do you want me to take yours off?"

Lyon stretched out on his side, leaned up on one elbow,

and reached for a piece of cheese. He tore off a portion and handed it to Christina.

"Do you think Jessica was crazy?" she asked.

"No."

"I don't either," Christina said. "Some of her entries are very confusing, aren't they? Could you feel her agony, Lyon, the way I did when I read her journal?"

"She was terrified," Lyon said. "And yes, I could feel her pain."

"I didn't want to read her thoughts at first. Merry made me take the book with me. She told me that in time I'd change my heart. She was right."

"She kept her promise to your mother," Lyon interjected. "She raised you, loved you as her own, and made you strong. Those were Jessica's wishes, weren't they?"

Christina nodded. "I'm not always strong, Lyon. Until tonight I was afraid of him."

"Your father?"

"I don't like to call him my father," Christina whispered. "It makes me ill to think his blood is part of mine."

"Why aren't you afraid now?" He asked.

"Because now you know. I worried you'd think Jessica's mind was . . . weak."

"Christina, when you walked into the library and I was talking to Richards, we had just finished a discussion about your father. Richards told me about an incident called the Brisbane affair. Did you hear any of it?"

"No. I would never overlisten," Christina answered.

Lyon nodded. He quickly told her the sequence of events leading up to the murders of the Brisbane family.

"Those poor children," Christina whispered. "Who would kill innocent little ones?"

"You won't like the answer," Lyon said. "I wouldn't have related this story to you if it wasn't important. Brisbane's wife and children were all killed in the same way."

"How?"

"Their throats were slashed."

"I don't want to picture it," Christina whispered.

"In Jessica's diary she talks about a couple she traveled with to the Black Hills. Do you remember?"

"Yes. Their names were Emily and Jacob. The jackal killed them."

"How?"

"Their throats . . . oh, Lyon, their throats were slashed. Do you mean to say—"

"The same method," Lyon answered. "A coincidence, perhaps, but my instincts tell me the baron murdered the Brisbane family."

"Can't you challenge him?"

"Not in the way you'd like me to," Lyon answered. "We will force his hand, Christina. I give you my word. Will you leave the method to me?"

"Yes."

"Why?"

"Why what?" she hedged.

She was deliberately staring at the floor now, avoiding his gaze. Lyon reached over and tugged a strand of her hair. "I want to hear you say the words, wife."

Christina moved over to Lyon's side. Her hand slowly reached out to his. When her fingers were entwined with his, she answered his demand.

"I trust you, Lyon, with all my heart."

Chapter Sixteen

Merry and I made a promise to each other. She gave me her pledge to take care of you if anything happened to me, and I gave my word to find a way to get White Eagle back to his family if anything happened to her.

From that moment on, my fears were gone. Her promise gave me peace. She would keep you safe. You already had her love, Christina. I could see the way she'd hold you, cuddled up tenderly against her chest until you fell asleep.

She would be a better mother to you.

*Journal entry
November 3, 1795*

Lyon was trying to keep his temper under control. He kept telling himself that breakfast would be over soon, that Richards should be arriving at any moment, and that he was pleasing his wife by being patient with his mother. The effort cost him his appetite, however, a fact everyone at the table seemed compelled to comment upon.

He was surrounded by family and considered that a most unfortunate circumstance. His Aunt Harriett had arrived the previous afternoon with Diana. The Earl of Rhone had just happened to show up an hour later.

The coincidence was forced, of course. Diana had pretended surprise when Rhone strolled into the house. His sister was as transparent as water. Lyon wasn't fooled for a minute. He had had the necessary talk with his friend last evening. Rhone had asked for Diana's hand. Lyon was happy to give him all of her. He kept that thought to himself, for Rhone was in the middle of his obviously prepared dissertation on the seriousness of his pledge to love and protect Diana. When Rhone finally slowed down, Lyon gave him his blessing. He didn't bother to advise his friend on the merits of fidelity, knowing that Rhone would honor his commitment once he'd spoken the vows.

Lyon was seated at the head of the table, with Rhone on his left and Christina on his right. His mother faced him from her position at the opposite end of the table. Aunt Harriett and Diana took turns trying to draw the elderly Marchioness into conversation. Their efforts were wasted, though. The only time Lyon's mother glanced up from her plate was when she wanted to make a comment about her James.

Lyon was soon clenching his jaw.

"For heaven's sake, Diana, unhand Rhone," Aunt Harriett blurted out. "The boy will starve to death if you don't let him at his food, child."

"James always had a very healthy appetite," Lyon's mother interjected.

"I'm certain he did, Mother," Christina said. "Do you like your room?" she asked, changing the topic.

"I do not like it at all. It's too bright. And while we're on the subject of my dislikes, please tell me why you insist that I not wear black. James preferred that color, you know."

"Mama, will you please stop talking about James?" Diana begged.

Christina shook her head at Diana. "Lyon?" she asked, turning to smile at him. "When do you think Richards will arrive? I'm eager to get started."

Lyon frowned at his wife. "You aren't going anywhere. We discussed this, Christina," he reminded her.

"James was always on the go," his mother commented.

Everyone but Christina turned to frown at the gray-haired woman.

"When are we going to discuss the marriage arrangements?" Aunt Harriett asked, trying to cover the awkward silence.

"I really don't wish to wait a long time," Diana said. She blushed before adding, "I want to be married right away, like Lyon and Christina."

"Our circumstances were different," Lyon said. He winked at Christina. "You aren't going to be as fortunate as I was. You'll wait and have a proper wedding."

"James wanted to marry. He simply couldn't find anyone worthy enough," Mama interjected.

Lyon scowled. Christina placed her hand on top of his fisted one. "You look very handsome this morning," she told him. "You must always wear blue."

Lyon looked into his wife's eyes and saw the sparkle there. He knew what she was doing. Yes, she was trying to take his mind off his mother. And even though he understood her intent, it still worked. He was suddenly smiling. "You always look beautiful," he told her. He leaned down to whisper, "I still prefer you without any clothes on, however."

Christina blushed with pleasure.

Rhone smiled at the happy couple, then turned to speak to Lyon's aunt. "Do you still believe Diana and I are mismatched? I would like your approval," he added.

Aunt Harriett picked up her fan. She waved it in front of her face while she considered her answer. "I will give you my approval, but I don't believe the two of you will be as compatible as Lyon and Christina. You can see how well they get along."

"Oh, we are also mismatched," Christina interjected. "Rhone and Diana are really much more suited to each other. They were raised in the same fashion," she explained.

Aunt Harriett gave Christina a piercing look. "Now that you're part of this family, would you mind telling me just where you were raised, child?"

"In the Black Hills," Christina answered. She turned to Lyon then. "The Countess will certainly tell, and I really should prepare your family, don't you think?"

"The Countess wouldn't say a word," Lyon answered. "As long as the money keeps pouring in, she'll keep your secrets safe until you're ready to tell them."

"Tell what secrets?" Diana asked, frowning.

"She's entitled to her privacy," Rhone interjected, winking at Christina.

Aunt Harriett let out an inelegant snort. "Nonsense. We're family. There shouldn't be any secrets, unless you've done something you're ashamed of, Christina, and I'm certain that isn't the case. You're a good-hearted child," she added. She paused to prove her point by tilting her head toward the elderly Marchioness.

"James was such a good-hearted man," she blurted out.

Everyone ignored that comment.

"Well?" Diana prodded Christina.

"I was raised by the Dakotas."

Christina really believed her statement would gain an immediate reaction. Everyone just stared at her with expectant looks on their faces. She turned to Lyon.

"I don't believe they understand, my sweet," he whispered.

"Who are the Dakotas?" Aunt Harriett asked. "I don't remember meeting anyone by that name. They must not be English," she concluded with another wave of her fan.

"No, they aren't English," Lyon said, smiling.

"A large family?" Aunt Harriett asked, trying to understand why Lyon was smiling and Christina was blushing.

"Very large," Lyon drawled.

"Well, why haven't I heard of them?" his aunt demanded.

"They're Indians." Christina made the announcement, then waited for a true reaction.

It wasn't long in coming. "No wonder I haven't heard . . . good Lord, do you mean savages?" she gasped.

Christina was about to explain that she didn't care for the word savages—the Countess had often preferred that description—and that the Dakotas were gentle, caring people, but Aunt Harriett's and Diana's bold laughter interrupted her bid to defend.

Aunt Harriett was the first to regain control. She'd noticed that Rhone, Lyon, and Christina hadn't joined in. "You aren't jesting with us, are you, Christina?" she asked. She felt lightheaded but kept her voice soft.

"No, I'm not jesting," Christina answered. "Rhone? You don't seem too surprised."

"I was better prepared for such news," Rhone explained.

"Are the Black Hills in France, then?" Diana asked, trying to sort it out in her mind.

Lyon chuckled over that question.

"James loved to go to France," the mother announced. "He had many friends there."

Aunt Harriett reached over to take hold of Christina's hand. "My dear, I'm so sorry I laughed. You must think me terribly undisciplined. It was such a surprise. I pray you do not believe I now think you inferior in any way."

Christina hadn't been upset with their reaction, but she assumed Aunt Harriett thought she had. She smiled at the dear woman, then said, "I pray you do not believe I think you are inferior in any way, Aunt Harriett. In truth, I have come to realize that my people are far more civilized than the English. It is a confession I'm very proud to make."

"James was always civil to everyone he met," the mother announced.

Aunt Harriett patted Christina's hand, then turned to glare at her relative.

"Millicent," she muttered, using the elderly Marchioness's given name, "will you let up, for God's sake? I'm trying to have a serious conversation with Christina here."

Aunt Harriett turned to smile at Christina again. "I eagerly await your stories about your childhood, Christina. Will you share them with me?"

"I would be happy to," Christina answered.

"Now, I would advise you not to tell anyone outside this

family. Outsiders wouldn't understand. The ton is a shallow group of twits," she added with a vigorous nod. "And I'll not have you subjected to malicious gossip."

"Did you have strange habits when you lived with—"

"For God's sake, Diana," Lyon roared.

"It's all right," Christina interjected. "She is only curious."

"Let's change the topic for now," Rhone advised. He frowned at Diana, then contradicted his displeasure by taking hold of her hand.

Aunt Harriett didn't like the peculiar way Diana was staring at Christina. Her mouth was hanging open. The silly girl was looking quite fascinated.

Concerned about Christina's feelings, the aunt hastened to turn Diana's attention. "Lyon? Diana insisted on bringing that ill-disciplined pup Rhone gave her. She's tied up in the back," Aunt Harriett explained. "Diana was hoping you'd keep the dog while we're in London. Isn't that right, Diana?"

Rhone had to nudge Diana before she answered. "Oh, yes. It would be cruel to keep her tied up in the townhouse. Christina, did you have a puppy when you were a little girl? Were their dogs in your . . . town?"

"It was called a village, not a town," Christina answered, wishing Diana would stop staring at her so intently.

"But were there dogs there?" Diana persisted.

"Yes, there were dogs," Christina answered. She turned to wink at her husband when she felt his hand tense under hers, then turned back to look at her sister-in-law. "They weren't considered pets, though," she lied. "And, of course, they never stayed long."

"James always loved animals. He had a beautiful speckled dog he named Faithful."

"An inappropriate name, if you ask me," Lyon commented. "Wouldn't you agree, Christina?" he asked, duplicating her wink.

Brown appeared in the doorway at that moment and announced that Sir Fenton Richards had just arrived. Both Christina and Lyon stood up to take their leave.

"I'd like to ride along with you and Richards," Rhone called out.

Lyon glanced down at Christina, received her nod, then told Rhone he'd be glad for his help.

Christina was halfway across the dining room when Diana called out to her.

"Christina? Why didn't the dogs stay long?"

She was going to ignore that question until she realized Diana was still gaping at her. Lyon's sister was looking at her as though she'd just grown another head or two. "What happened to the dogs?"

"We ate them," Christina called out, trying to tell her lie without laughing.

Aunt Harriett dropped her fan. Diana let out a gasp. Lyon never even blinked until his mother's determined voice called out, "James never ate his dog. He . . . oh, God, what have I just said?"

Everyone joined in laughing. The elderly Marchioness even cracked a smile. It was a small one, but a smile all the same.

Christina thought it was a nice beginning. Lyon's hug told her he thought so, too.

"Diana, I was only jesting with you. We didn't eat our pets. You needn't worry about your pup. I won't have her for dinner. You have my word."

"She never breaks her word," Lyon advised his sister. "Unless, of course, she gets very hungry," he added before he pulled his wife out of the room.

Richards was highly puzzled when Lyon and Christina came strolling into the library, smiling as though neither had a care in the world. Their manner was certainly at odds with the mysterious note he'd received the day before.

"Has your problem been resolved, then?" Richards asked Lyon in lieu of greeting.

"No, we still need your help," Lyon announced. He sobered quickly. "How tired are you, Richards? Feel up to taking another ride?"

"Where?"

"The Earl of Acton's former estate," Lyon answered.

"That's a good four hours' ride, isn't it?"

"From London," Lyon reminded him. "Only two from here."

"Who's living there now?"

"No one. My inquiries tell me the house is boarded up."

Richards turned to Christina. "I could use a spot of tea, my dear. I'm rather parched," he added. "I set out at dawn and didn't take time to breakfast."

"I shall see to serving you a full meal at once," Christina said. "You'll need your strength for the task ahead of you," she added before she hurried out of the library.

Richards shut the door, then turned to Lyon. "I sent your wife on a false errand so I could speak to you in private."

"I don't have any secrets from Christina," Lyon returned.

"You misunderstand," Richards said. "It isn't a secret I'm about to tell you. But your wife will become upset. You might wish to wait until our return from this mysterious journey before telling her. Baron Stalinsky is back. He arrived yesterday. He wanted to come to meet his daughter immediately. When I heard his intent, I waylaid his plan with the lie that you and Christina were off visiting distant relatives in the North. I told him you would both be returning to London day after tomorrow. I hope that was the right thing to do, Lyon. It was a spur-of-the-moment fabrication."

"It was good thinking," Lyon answered. "Where is the Baron staying?"

"With the Porters. They are hosting a party for him Wednesday evening. The Baron expects to see his daughter there."

Lyon let out a long sigh. "It can't be put off," he muttered.

"Does Christina still believe her father will try to kill her?"

"She planned to bait him into trying," Lyon said.

"When are you going to explain it all to me?" Richards demanded.

"On the way to Acton's place," Lyon promised. "Rhone's coming with us. It should be quick work with the three of us at it," he added.

"What is this mission?" Richards asked.

"We're going to dig up the roses."

Lyon, Richards, and Rhone didn't return to Lyonwood until late afternoon. Their moods were as foul as the weather.

Christina had just walked inside the back of the house when the trio of soggy men rushed inside the front door.

They met in the hallway. Lyon was drenched to the skin. When he saw Christina in the same condition, he shook his head with displeasure. Droplets of rain flew from his hair.

"You look like a drowned cat," Lyon muttered to Christina. He was struggling to get out of his sodden jacket, glaring at his wife all the while. Her burgundy-colored gown was indecently molded to her body. Clumps of hair hung over her eyes.

Richards and Rhone were being ushered up the steps by Brown. Lyon blocked their view of his wife.

When his friends had disappeared upstairs, Lyon confronted his wife. "What in God's name were you doing outside?"

"You needn't yell at me," Christina shouted. "Did you find—"

"Do you have any idea how many damn rosebushes there were? No?" he bellowed when she shook her head. "Your grandfather must have had an obsession for the things. There were hundreds of them."

"Oh, dear," Christina cried. "Then you weren't successful? I told you I should have gone with you. I could have helped."

"Christina, you're shouting at me," Lyon announced. "I found the box. You can calm down."

"I'm not shouting at you," Christina said. She lifted her wet locks and threw them over her shoulder. "I can't be very sympathetic over the difficulty you had. I've lost the damned dog."

"What?"

"I've lost the damned dog," Christina repeated. She forced herself to calm down. "It appears that both of us have had a pitiful day. Give me a kiss, Lyon. Then please put your jacket back on. You must help me look for Diana's puppy."

"Are you crazy? You're not going back outside in this downpour, and that's that."

Christina grabbed hold of Lyon's soggy shirt, kissed him on his hard mouth, then turned around and started walking toward the back of the house. "I have to find the dog. Diana's upstairs trying desperately to believe I didn't eat the stupid animal," she muttered.

Lyon's laughter stopped her. She turned around to glare at him.

"Sweetheart, she can't really believe you'd do such a thing."

"I never should have made that jest," Christina admitted. "I told her I was only teasing. I don't think she believes me, though. I was the last person seen with the pup. I heard her mention that sorry fact to Aunt Harriett several times. Lyon, I only wanted to let the puppy run for a while. The poor little thing looked miserable all tied up. Then she took off after a rabbit, and I've spent the rest of the day looking for her."

Rhone came sloshing down the stairs. His soft curses caught Christina's attention. Without pausing to speak to either Lyon or Christina, Rhone opened the front door and went outside.

They could hear him whistling for the dog through the door. "See? Rhone's helping to look for the pup," Christina stated.

"He has to," Lyon told his wife. "He wants to make Diana happy. And the only reason I'm going to give into your request is because I want to make you happy. Got that?" he muttered before slamming out the front door.

Christina didn't laugh until he'd left, knowing that if he heard her, his bluster would turn into real anger.

Her husband found the undisciplined puppy about an hour later. The dog was curled up under the overhang behind the stables.

Once Lyon was warm and dry again, his mood improved.

After a pleasant dinner he, Rhone, and Richards all retired to the library to share a bottle of brandy. Christina was thankful for the privacy. She wasn't feeling well. She'd been unable to keep down the rich meal she'd just eaten, and her stomach was still upset.

Lyon came upstairs around midnight. Christina was curled up in the center of their bed, waiting for him.

"I thought you'd be asleep," Lyon said. He began to strip out of his clothes.

Christina smiled at him. "And miss the chance to see my handsome husband disrobe? Never. Lyon, I don't think I shall ever get used to looking at you."

She could tell by his arrogant grin that he liked her praise. "I shall show you something even more handsome," Lyon teased. He walked over to the mantel, lifted a black lacquered box from the center, and carried it over to the bed. "I transferred the jewels from the old box to this one. It's more sound," he added.

Christina waited until Lyon was settled in bed beside her before she opened the box. A small square cloth covered the gems. She seemed hesitant to remove the covering and look at the jewels.

Lyon didn't understand her reticence. He took the cloth, unfolded it, and poured the assortment of precious jewels in the middle.

They were the colors of the rainbow, the sapphires and rubies and diamonds. They numbered twenty, and their value by anyone's standards would have kept a gluttonous man well fed for a very long while.

Lyon was puzzled, for Christina continued to show no outward reaction.

"Sweetheart, do you have any idea of the price these gems will bring?"

"Oh, yes, I understand, Lyon," Christina whispered. "The price was my mother's life. Please put them away now. I don't want to look at them. I think they're very ugly."

Lyon kissed her before he complied with her wish. When he got back into their bed he pulled her into his arms. He briefly considered telling her that Baron Stalinsky was in London, then decided that tomorrow would be soon enough to give her that ill news.

He knew Christina thought they had more time before setting their plan into motion. Her birthday had passed two weeks before, and she'd made up her mind that her father must have had other business to keep him away from England.

Lyon blew out the candles and closed his eyes. He couldn't remember when last he'd been this tired. He was just about to drift off to sleep when Christina nudged him.

"Lyon? Will you promise me something?"

"Anything, love."

"Never give me jewels."

He sighed over the vehemence in her voice. "I promise."

"Thank you, Lyon."

"Christina?"

"Yes?"

"Promise me you'll love me forever."

"I promise."

He caught the smile in her voice and suddenly realized he wasn't nearly as tired as he thought he was. "Tell me you love me," he commanded.

"My Lyon, I love you, and I shall continue to love you forever."

"A man can't ask for more than that," Lyon drawled as he nudged her around to face him.

He thought he'd make slow, sweet love to his wife, but in the end it was a wild, undisciplined mating, and thoroughly satisfying.

The blankets and pillows were on the floor. Christina fell asleep with Lyon as her cover. He was so content he didn't want to sleep just yet. He wanted to savor the moment, for in the back of his mind was the thought that this night could well be the calm before the storm.

Chapter Seventeen

Forgive me for not writing in this journal for such a length of time. I have been content and haven't wanted to remember the past. But we are now preparing to leave our safe haven. I shall not be able to speak to you again through this journal for long months, until we are both settled. My plan is to catch up with another wagon train. The way west is crowded with newcomers. The valley below is the only way the wagons can go to get into the mountains. Surely someone will take pity on us and offer us assistance.

Is it a fantasy for me to think that you and I might survive?

I will finish this entry with one request, Christina. I would beg a promise from you, dear child. If you do survive and one day chance upon this diary, have a kind thought for me.

And remember, Christina, always remember how very much I loved you.

Journal entry
May 20, 1796

The time had come to face the jackal.

Christina was nervous, though not nearly as nervous as her husband. Lyon's expression was grim. The ride from their London townhouse to Porter's home was silent. Yet once they'd reached their destination, Lyon seemed disinclined to let Christina out of the carriage.

"Sweetheart, you're sure you're all right?"

Christina smiled up at her husband. "I'm fine, really."

"God, I wish there had been a way to keep you out of this," he whispered. "You look pale to me."

"You should be complimenting me on my new gown, Lyon. You chose the fabric, remember?" she asked. Christina pushed open the door of the carriage.

"I've already told you how beautiful you look," Lyon murmured.

He finally got out of the carriage and turned to help his wife. He thought she looked quite beautiful. The royal blue velvet gown was modestly scoop-necked. Her hair was curled into a cluster with a thin blue velvet ribbon threaded through the silky mass.

Christina reached up to brush a speck of link off Lyon's black jacket. "You also look beautiful," she told him.

Lyon shook his head. He pulled her matched blue cloak over her shoulders. "You're doing this deliberately. Quit trying to ease my worry. It won't work."

"You like to worry, husband?" she asked.

Lyon didn't bother to answer her. "Give me your promise again," he demanded.

"I'll not leave your side." She repeated the vow she'd already given him at least a dozen times. "No matter what, I'll stand next to you."

Lyon nodded. He took her hand and started up the steps. "You really aren't frightened, are you, love?"

"A little," Christina whispered. "Richards has given me his assurance that justice in England is equal to that of the Dakotas. He'd better be right, Lyon, or we shall have to take matters into our own hands." Her voice had turned hard. "Strike the door, husband. Let's get this pretense of joyful reunion over and done with."

Richards was waiting for them in the foyer. Christina was surprised by his enthusiastic reception. Lyon had lost his grim expression, too. He acted as though he hadn't seen his friend in a long while, which was exactly what they wanted everyone to believe.

After greeting their host, a dour-faced man with a portly figure, Christina asked if Baron Stalinsky was in the receiving room.

"I can imagine how eager you must be to meet your father," Porter announced, his voice filled with excitement. "He's still upstairs, but he will certainly be joining us in a moment or two. I've kept the list of guests to a minimum, my dear, so that you may have time for a lengthy visit with your father. You must certainly have a book's worth of news to exchange."

Lyon removed Christina's wrap, handed it to the butler waiting beside them, then told Porter he'd take his wife into the drawing room to await the Baron.

Her hand was cold when he clasped it in his own. He could feel her trembling. The smile never left his face, but the urge to take Christina back home and return to face her father alone nearly overwhelmed him.

The Dakotas had the right idea, Lyon decided. According to Christina, verbal slander was all that was needed for an open challenge. What followed next was a battle to the death. Justice was swift. The system might have been a bit barbaric, yet Lyon liked its simplicity.

There were only eighteen guests in the drawing room. Lyon counted them while Christina had a long conversation with their hostess. Although his wife stood next to him, he paid little attention to what the two women were discussing. Richards had walked over to join him, and he was trying to listen to his friend advise him on the merits of the changing weather.

When their hostess left, Christina turned to Richards. "Are you aware that our host previously worked for your government in the same manner as you?"

"I am."

She waited for him to say more, then let him see her displeasure when he failed to comment further. "Lyon, Mrs. Porter surely exaggerated her mate's position, but she did mention a fact I found most enlightening."

"What was that, love?" Lyon asked. He draped his arm around her shoulders and pulled her closer to him.

"She's a gossip," Christina began. "When she saw the way Richards greeted you, she boasted that her husband held the same favor when he was a younger man. I asked her why he'd retired, and she told me she didn't know all the facts but that his last assignment had soured him. It seemed he handled a project that caused a good friend of his some discomfort. Yes, she actually used that word. Discomfort."

"Discomfort? I don't understand. Do you, Richards?" Lyon asked.

Richards was staring at Christina. "You would do well to work for us, Christina. You have ferreted out what took me hours of research to ascertain."

"Lyon, can you guess the name of Porter's good friend?"

"Stalinsky," Lyon said in answer to Christina's question.

"Porter wasn't guilty of error, Christina. His only mistake was in befriending the Baron. He trusted him—still does, for that matter. The baron is a guest in his home, remember. God's truth, I think you'll understand what an easy man the Baron is to trust when you finally meet him."

"By England's standards, perhaps," Christian replied. "Not by mine. Appearances and manners often cloak a black soul. Are you still unconvinced that Lyon and I are right about the Baron, then?"

"I'm convinced. The court might not see it our way, however, and for that reason we're bypassing our own legal system. There are those who believe Jessica had lost her mind. The argument that your mother had imagined—"

"Did she imagine the mark she gave the baron in his right eye when he tried to kill her? Did she imagine that her friends' throats were slashed? Did she imagine she stole the jewels and hid them under the roses? You've seen the gems, Richards. Did you only imagine you saw them?"

Richards smiled at Christina. "You really should work for me," he said in answer to her challenges. "Now, to refute your arguments. One, the baron could have others testify for him, telling a different story of how he came by the scar. Two, Jessica was the only one who saw the baron kill the husband and wife on that wagon train. No one else saw anyone, according to the writing in her journal. It would be next to impossible to track any of those people down to determine how the couple was killed. We have only Jessica's diary to tell us what happened. In a court of law that wouldn't be enough. Three, there wouldn't be any argument about the jewels. But," he added in a whisper, "we have only Jessica's account to say that her husband had acquired the gems by foul means. He was a king, remember, and the jewels were but a part of his treasury. The fact that he was a ruthless dictator is the last of the rebuttals I will give you. If that is dragged out in court, it will mean little. The Baron would simply retaliate by bringing witness after witness who would testify to his kindness toward his subjects."

"He will admit his sins to me," Christina whispered.

"And your husband and I will gain justice for you with or without your father's admission."

"Christina, your father has just walked into the room." Lyon made the announcement with a wide smile, but his hold on his wife tightened.

The moment had arrived. With it came a fresh surge of anger. Christina forced a smile onto her face, turned from her husband, and began to walk toward the man waiting for her just inside the entrance.

She understood his physical appeal as soon as she looked at him. Baron Stalinsky was a man who commanded attention. He'd aged well. His hair wasn't white, but silver-tipped. The years hadn't made him stoop-shouldered or pot-bellied, either. No, he was still tall, lance-thin, regal in his bearing. It was the color of his eyes that attracted attention, though. They were a piercing blue. Christina was sorry they shared so many physical attributes.

The Baron was smiling at her. His eyes were filled with unshed tears, and surely everyone in the room could see the dimple in his left cheek.

Christina concentrated on the scar beneath his right eye.

She stopped when she was just a foot away, then made a formal curtsy. And all the while she prayed her voice wouldn't betray her.

She knew she'd have to let him embrace her. The thought made her skin crawl. All the guests in the room had focused their attention on this reunion. She never took her gaze off the jackal and was sickened by the fact that everyone was probably smiling over the sweetly emotional reunion.

It seemed to Christina that they stared at each other for a long while before either spoke a word. She could feel Lyon by her side, and when he suddenly took hold of her hand, she recovered her composure.

Lyon was trying to give her his strength, she thought. "Good evening, Father. It is a pleasure to meet you at last."

Baron Stalinsky seemed to come out of his stupor then. He reached out to clasp Christina's shoulders. "I'm overjoyed to meet you, Christina. I can barely think what to say to you. All these precious years wasted," he whispered. A tear escaped from his thick lashes. Christina pulled her hand away from Lyon's grasp and reached up to brush the tear from her father's cheek. The touch was witnessed by the guests, and Christina could hear their sighs of pleasure.

She let him embrace her. "I thought you were dead, daughter," he admitted. "Do you know how happy I am to have you back, child?"

Christina kept smiling. The effort made her stomach hurt. She slowly pulled away from her father and moved next to Lyon again. "I'm a married woman now, Father," she announced. She quickly introduced Lyon, then prayed he'd take up the conversation for a minute or two. She needed to catch her breath.

"You cannot imagine our surprise to learn you were still alive, Baron," Lyon interjected. His voice was as enthusiastic as a schoolboy's. He kept up the idle chatter until the other guests, led by the Porters, rushed over to express their congratulations.

Christina played the pretense well. She smiled and laughed whenever it was appropriate.

It was bearable only because Lyon stood by her side. An hour passed and then another before Christina and her husband were given a few moments' privacy with Stalinsky.

"Father, how did you come by that scar below your eye?" Christina asked, pretending only mild interest.

"A boyhood accident," the Baron replied, smiling. "I fell from my mount."

"You were lucky," Lyon interjected. "You could have lost your eye."

The baron nodded. "I was thinking quite the same thing about your scar, Lyon. How did that happen?"

"A fight in a tavern," Lyon said. "My first outing as a man," he added with a grin.

One lie for another, Christina thought.

Lyon gave Christina's shoulder a gentle squeeze. She recognized the signal. "Father, I have so many questions to ask you, and I'm certain you have as many to ask me. Does your schedule permit you to lunch with us tomorrow?"

"I would love to, daughter," the Baron replied. "Daughter! It's a joyful word to me now."

"Will you be staying in London long, Baron?" Lyon asked.

"I have no other plans," the Baron answered.

"I'm pleased to hear that," Christina interjected. She prayed her voice sounded enthusiastic. "I've already sent word to my stepfather. When he receives my message and returns from Scotland, you must sit down with him and put his fears to rest."

"Stepfather?" the Baron asked. "The Countess didn't mention a stepfather, Christina. She led me to believe . . ." The Baron cleared his throat before continuing. "It was a bizarre story, and one look at you would certainly make a mockery out of what she actually suggested . . . tell me about this stepfather. What fears does the man harbor, and why?"

"Father, first you must appease my curiosity," Christina said. There was laughter in her voice. "Whatever did the horrid old woman tell you?"

"Yes," the Baron sighed, "she is a horrid woman." He made the remark almost absentmindedly.

"Do I detect a blush?" Christina asked.

"I fear you do, daughter. You see, I have only just realized how gullible I was. Why, I did believe her story to be true."

"You've pricked my curiosity as well," Lyon said. "The Countess is very upset with Christina. She was against our marriage because of the matter of my wife's inheritance. The Countess seemed to think she'd control the money," Lyon explained. "Now tell us what fabrication she gave you."

"I've been played for a fool," the Baron returned, shaking his head. "She told me Christina was raised by savages."

"Savages?" Christina asked, trying to look perplexed.

"Indians of the Americas," the Baron qualified.

Christina and Lyon looked at each other. They turned in unison to stare at the Baron. Then they both burst into laughter.

The Baron joined in. "I really was naive to believe her fool's story," he said between chuckles. "But I had heard from the Countess—years ago, you understand—that Jessica had left with a newborn baby girl to join a wagon train headed through the wilderness."

"She did do that," Christina acknowledged. "And it was on the way that she met Terrance MacFinley. He became her protector. Terrance," she added with a soft smile, "didn't know my mother was still married. She told him you'd died. My mother's mind wasn't very ... strong." Christina paused after making that comment, furious inside when the Baron nodded agreement. "Terrance was a good man. He told me about my mother."

"But what did you mean when you said I could put your stepfather's fears to rest?"

"Oh, it's a small matter," Christina stalled. "Jessica died when I was just a baby," she continued. "Terrance kept me with him. In one of my mother's sane moments, she made him promise to take care of me until I was old enough to be returned to England."

"How did she die?" the Baron asked. His voice was low and filled with emotion. Tears had gathered in his eyes again. "I loved your mother. I blame myself for her death. I should have recognized the signs of her condition."

"Signs?" Christina asked.

"Of her mind's deterioration," he explained. "She was frightened of everything. When she realized she was going to have a child, I think it was all that was needed to push her completely over the edge. She ran away from me."

"Did you go after her, Father?"

"Not right away," the Baron admitted. "There were business matters to attend to. I had a kingdom to run, you see. I abdicated three weeks later, then went back to England. I fully expected to find my wife with her father. Yet when I reached the Earl of Acton's home, I found out Jessica had fled again. She was headed for the colonies. I, of course, made the assumption she was going to her sister's home in Boston and posted passage on a ship to follow her."

"Mother died of the fever," Christina said.

"I hope she didn't have too much pain," the Baron commented.

"It must have been terrible for you, searching in vain for the woman you loved," Lyon stated.

"Yes, it was a bad time," the Baron acknowledged. "The past is behind us, Christina. I look forward to speaking to this Terrance. How long did he stay with your mother before she died?" he asked.

"I'm not certain of the exact length of time," Christina said. "One night, when the wagon train rested in the valley below the Black Hills, Jessica was awakened by a thief," Christina said. "The couple she was sharing her quarters with were both killed by the villain. Jessica got it into her head that it was you, Father, chasing after her."

Christina paused to shake her head. "She packed me up and ran into the hills. MacFinley saw her leave. He went after her, of course, for he loved her fiercely. I'll be completely honest with you, Father. I don't understand how Terrance could have loved my mother. From what he told me about her, I would think he should have pitied her."

"MacFinley sounds like an honorable man," the Baron said. "I'm eager to meet him to give him my thanks. At least he made Jessica's last hours more comfortable. He did, didn't he?"

Christina nodded. "Yes, but I don't think she really knew he was there with her. Terrance told me he actually spent most of his time protecting me from her. She was so crazed she didn't even remember she had a child. All she talked about was the sin she'd snatched out of some wall."

She paused again, watching for a reaction. The Baron only looked perplexed.

After a long minute he said, "That certainly doesn't make sense. A sin out of a wall?"

"It didn't make any sense to Terrance either. He told me he kept trying to get through to my mother, but all she would talk about was taking the sin and burying it. A tragic ending, wouldn't you agree?"

"Let's not talk about this any longer," Lyon interjected. "Tonight should be a happy reunion," he added.

"Yes, husband, you're right. Father, you must tell me all about the past years and what you've been—"

"Wait!" The Baron's voice had a sharp edge to it. He immediately softened his tone and gave Christina a wide smile. "My curiosity is still to be appeased," he explained. "Did your mother happen to tell Terrance where she buried this sin?"

"Under the blood roses of her father's country home," Christina answered with a deliberate shrug. "Blood roses, indeed. Poor woman. I pray for her soul every night, and I do hope she has found peace."

"I also pray for my Jessica," the Baron said.

"Terrance happened to see the man sneaking toward Jessica's wagon."

Lyon let the lie settle and waited for a reaction. It wasn't long in coming. "You mean the thief?" the Baron asked.

He hadn't blinked an eye. Christina was a little disappointed not to have rattled him. "Yes," she said. "He blames himself for thinking it was only one of the night watchmen. Terrance was late in joining the wagon and didn't know all the people yet. He vows he'll never forget the man's face." Christina quickly described the clothing the thief was wearing from the description in Jessica's diary.

And still there was no outward reaction from the Baron.

"Even though he knows my mother was crazed, there's always been a quiet fear in the back of his mind that it might have been you. And so you see what I mean when I tell you that once he has met you, his fears will be put to rest."

"Tomorrow you both can catch up on all of the past," Lyon said. He could feel Christina trembling and knew he had to get her away from the Baron soon.

Lord, he was proud of her. She had played her part well this night. She had faced the jackal without showing the least amount of fear.

"Shall we go and find some refreshments?" Lyon suggested.

"Yes," the Baron agreed.

Christina, flanked by her husband and her father, walked into the dining room. She sat between them at the long table, sipping from her glass of punch. She didn't want to eat anything, but her father was watching her closely, so she forced herself to swallow the food Lyon placed before her.

"Where did you receive your schooling, Christina? Your manners are impeccable," the Baron announced. "I cannot believe this Terrance MacFinley was responsible," he added with a teasing smile.

"Thank you for your compliment," Christina returned. She was smiling at her father, but her left hand was squeezing Lyon's thigh under the table.

"MacFinley and his close friend, Deavenrue, kept me until I was seven years of age. Then I was placed in a convent in the south of France. The sisters taught me my manners," she added.

"So there was a Deavenrue after all," the Baron said. "The Countess said he was a missionary who'd stayed with you in the village of the Indians."

"He was a missionary for a short while, and an excellent teacher as well. While I was in Boston Deavenrue came to my aunt's house quite often to see me. The Countess didn't like Deavenrue. Perhaps the rascal told my aunt I'd been with the savages just to provoke her," Christina added. She laughed. "It would be just like Deavenrue. He has the most bizarre sense of humor."

Lyon put his hand on top of Christina's. Her nails were digging into his thigh. His fingers laced with hers, and he gave her a squeeze of encouragement. He was anxious to get Christina out of Porter's house, yet he knew he had to wait until the last lie had been given.

Christina couldn't stand the pretense any longer. "Father, the excitement of the evening has exhausted me. I hope you won't be too disappointed if I go home now. Tomorrow I'll have Cook prepare a special meal just for the three of us. We'll have all afternoon to visit with each other. And, of course, MacFinley will be here in two, three days' time at the most. Then we must have another get-together."

"As soon as two days?" the Baron asked. He looked pleased with that possibility.

"Yes," Lyon answered for Christina. "Terrance lives just beyond the border," he explained. "He surely has Christina's request by now. Why, he is probably on his way to London even as we speak."

"Lyon, Terrance can't travel by night," Christina said. "Are you ready to take me home, husband? I'm terribly fatigued," she added with a flutter of her lashes.

They said their farewells moments later. Christina suffered through another embrace by the Baron.

Lyon pulled her onto his lap when they were once again inside his carriage. He was going to tell her how much he loved her, how very courageous she had been, but the carriage had barely rounded the corner when Christina bolted out of his lap and begged him to have the vehicle stopped.

Lyon didn't understand until Christina started to gag. He shouted to the driver, then got the door open just in the nick of time. He felt completely helpless as he held his wife by her shoulders. She threw up her meal, sobbing without control between her soul-wrenching heaves.

And when she had finished he wrapped her in his arms again. He held her close to him and tried to soothe her with soft words of love.

Lyon didn't speak of her father. Christina had been through enough torment for one evening.

God help her, there was still more to come.

Baron Stalinsky left the Porter residence a few minutes before dawn. Lyon was informed of his departure less than fifteen minutes later. Richards had placed a watch on Porter's house, for he was just as convinced as Lyon was that the Baron wouldn't waste any time running to the Earl of Acton's country home to dig up his treasure.

Christina had told her lies well. Lyon was proud of her, though he laced his praise with the fervent hope that once this deception was over, she'd never have to lie again.

Baron Stalinsky was very good at his deadly game. Neither Christina nor Lyon had noticed any visible change in his expression when MacFinley was mentioned. And when Christina said that MacFinley had seen the man who'd killed Jessica's friends, the Baron hadn't even blinked.

There wasn't any MacFinley, of course, but the smooth way Christina had told the story, added to the sincerity in her voice, must have convinced the Baron. He believed the story all right, to the point of rushing out at dawn to regain the jewels.

The morning after the reception Lyon had sent a note to the Baron pleading to reschedule their luncheon for three days hence, explaining that Christina was indisposed. The Baron had sent his note back with Lyon's messenger, stating that he hoped his daughter would soon recover, and that he would be pleased to honor the later date.

That evening Richards called on Lyon to tell him that the Baron had booked passage on a seafaring vessel bound for the West Indies. His departure was in two days.

He had no intention of ever seeing his daughter again. So much for fatherly love, Lyon thought.

Lyon hurriedly dressed in the dark. He waited until the last possible minute before waking Christina.

When his leaving couldn't be put off any longer, he leaned

over the side of the bed, let out a reluctant sigh, and then nudged his wife awake.

"Sweetheart, wake up and kiss me goodbye. I'm leaving now," he whispered between quick kisses on her brow.

Christina came awake with a start. "You must wait for me," she demanded, her voice husky with sleep.

She bolted up in bed, then fell back with a groan of distress. Nausea swept over her like a thick wave. She could feel the bile rising from her stomach. "Oh, God, I'm going to be sick again, Lyon."

"Roll over on your side, sweetheart. It helped last night," Lyon reminded her. His voice was filled with sympathy. "Take deep breaths," he instructed while he rubbed her shoulders.

"It's better now," Christina whispered a minute or two later.

Lyon sat down on the edge of the bed. "Exactly."

"Exactly what?" Christina asked. She didn't dare raise her voice above a whisper, fearing the effort would bring back her nausea.

"Exactly why you're staying here, Christina," Lyon announced. "Seeing your father has made you ill. You've been sick twice a day since the reception."

"It's this stupid bed that makes me sick," she lied.

Lyon stared at the ceiling in exasperation. "You told me the wooden slats made the mattress more accommodating," he reminded her. "You aren't going anywhere, my love, except back to sleep."

"You promised I could go with you," she cried.

"I lied."

"Lyon, I trusted you."

Lyon smiled over the way his wife wailed her confession. She sounded quite pitiful. "You still do trust me, wife. I'll get his confession, I promise you."

"My sore stomach is just an excuse you're using, isn't it, Lyon? You never meant for me to go along. Isn't that the truth of it?"

"Yes," he confessed. "I was never going to let you go

along." His voice turned gruff when he added, "Do you think I would ever put you in such jeopardy? Christina, if anything every happened to you, my life would be over. You're the better half of me, sweetheart."

Christina turned her head so that he could see her frown. Lyon realized then that his soft words hadn't swayed her, knew he was going to have to take another tack. "Does a Dakota warrior take his mate along to help him fight his battles? Did Black Wolf take Merry with him?"

"Yes."

"Now you're lying," Lyon stated. He frowned to let her see his displeasure.

Christina smiled. "If the injury had been done to Merry's family, Black Wolf would have taken her with him to see justice done, husband. Lyon, I made a promise to my father and my mother."

"To Black Wolf and Merry?"

Christina nodded. She slowly sat up in bed and was pleased to find that her stomach was cooperating with the movement. Ignoring Lyon's protest, she swung her legs to the side and stood up.

"Damn it, Christina, you're my mate now. Your promises became mine the moment we were wed. You do belong to me, don't you?"

The challenge in his voice couldn't be ignored. Christina nodded. "You're beginning to sound a bit too much like a warrior for my liking," she muttered. "I would like you to bring me a cup of tea before you leave. It is the least you could do for me," she added.

Lyon smiled, believing he'd won. "I shall fix it myself," he announced.

Christina waited until he'd left the room. She dressed in record time, taking deep, gulping breaths to keep her stomach controlled.

When Lyon returned to their bedroom, he found his wife dressed in a black riding outfit. He let out a soft curse, then sighed with acceptance.

"I must do this for Jessica, Lyon. Please understand."

351

Lyon nodded. His expression was grim. "Will you do exactly what I tell you to do, when I tell you to do it?" he barked.

"I will."

"Promise!"

"I promise."

"Damn!"

She ignored his muttering. "I'm taking my knife with me. It's under the pillow," she said as she walked back over to the bed.

"I know where it is," Lyon said with another drawn-out sigh. "I really wish you wouldn't insist on sleeping with it. The table's close enough."

"I'll think about your suggestion," Christina answered. "Now you must give me your word, Lyon. You won't take any chances, will you? Don't turn your back on him, not even for a second. Don't leave your fate in Richards's hands, either. I trust him, but I have far more faith in your instincts."

She would have continued her litany of demands if Lyon hadn't stopped her by pulling her into his arms and kissing her. "I love you, Christina."

"I love you, too, Lyon. Here, you carry this. It's fitting that you have it, for it was fashioned by a warrior whom I also love. My brother would want you to have it."

Lyon took the weapon and slipped it inside his right boot. Christina nodded with satisfaction, then started out the door. "Lyon?" she called over her shoulder.

"What now?" he grumbled.

"We must make him say the words."

"We will, Christina. We will."

Richards was waiting outside the front door for him. Lyon's friend was already mounted and holding the reins of Lyon's stallion. A few minutes were spent waiting for Christina's horse to be readied.

Lyon paced the walkway while he waited. "We have plenty of time," Richards announced when he took in Lyon's grim expression. "Remember, even if he took men along to help, there are still over a hundred of those prickly rose bushes to be dug up again."

Lyon forced a smile. "I don't think Stalinsky took anyone with him," he remarked as he helped Christina mount her steed. He then climbed atop his own horse with one fluid motion. "How many men do you have posted there?"

"Four of my best," Richards answered. "Benson is in charge. The Baron won't know they're there, and they won't interfere unless he tries to leave," he added. "My dear, are you sure you're up to this outing?"

"I'm sure."

Richards gave Christina a long look, then nodded. "Come along, children. Let's get this done. The captain of Percy's ship is waiting for his passengers."

"Passengers?"

"I've decided to go along. I promised your wife justice would be served. Though we're gaining it through the back door, so to speak, I'm going to be there to make certain. Do you understand my meaning?"

Lyon gave a brisk nod. "I do."

"I don't," Christina admitted.

"I'll explain it later, sweet."

They were the last words spoken until they reached their destination some four hours later. After they dismounted, Richards handed Lyon the moldy box they'd retrieved from the ground on their last visit to Acton's estate.

"I've replaced the real gems with glass replicas. Wait until I get into position before you confront him."

Lyon shook his head. He handed the box to Christina. "She's going to confront him," he told Richards.

One of Richards's men came over to lead their horses away. He spoke to his superior before pulling the mounts into the forest surrounding them. "You were right, Lyon. Stalinsky came alone."

They separated then. Richards went up the front path and turned to circle the right side of the house. Lyon and Christina moved to the left. He paused before rounding the corner, opened the box his wife held in her hands, and lifted two pieces of cut glass. At first glance they did look like the real thing. They were good enough to fool the Baron, Lyon decided, for the brief minute he wanted him fooled.

He then explained what Christina was going to do.

Baron Stalinsky was kneeling on the ground, his shoulders bent to his task. He was muttering obscenities as he struggled to pull the stem of one fat bush out of the ground. He wore black gloves to protect his hands and worked with determined speed. A narrow shovel rested on the ground beside him.

"Looking for something, Father?"

The Baron whirled around on his knees to confront Christina. Dirt streaked his sweaty forehead and angular cheeks.

He didn't look very commanding now. No, he was a jackal to be sure. The sneer on his face reminded Christina of an angry animal baring his teeth. The look sickened her, and she thought she wouldn't have been surprised if he'd started growling.

Christina faced her father alone. She stood a good twenty feet away from him. She had his full attention, of course, and when she thought he was just about to spring forward, she lifted the box and took out a handful of the fake gems. She casually tossed some of the jewels into the air. "Are these what you're looking for, Father?"

Baron Stalinsky slowly came to his feet. His eyes darted to the left and then to the right. She decided to answer his unspoken thought. "Lyon? I believe my father is looking for you."

Lyon walked over to stand next to Christina. He took the box from her, then motioned her to move away. Christina backed up several paces immediately.

"This fight is between the two of us, Baron."

"Fight? I'm an old man, Lyon. The odds wouldn't be fair. Besides, I have no quarrel with you or my daughter. Those jewels belong to me," he added with a wave of his hand toward the box. "Jessica stole them. In court I'll be able to prove they're mine."

Lyon didn't take his gaze off the Baron. "There isn't going

to be a day in an English court, Baron. In fact, as soon as you've answered a single question for Christina and a few more for me, you can be on your way. It's going to be simple for you. I won't have my wife involved in a scandal," he lied.

"Scandal? I don't know what you're talking about," the Baron replied. His voice reeked with authority.

"The murder trial would be upsetting for Christina. I won't have her humiliated." Lyon paused in his explanation to throw a bright red ruby over his shoulder. "It will take you days to find all of these. I'll toss the rest into the creek behind the bluff, Baron, if you don't agree to answer my questions. The current's swift."

"No!" the Baron shouted. "Don't you realize what they're worth? You're holding a fortune in your hands!" His voice had turned coaxing, eager.

Lyon noticed that the Baron's right hand was slowly moving to his back. Reacting with incredible speed, he drew a pistol from his waistcoat, took aim, and fired just as Stalinsky was bringing the hidden pistol around to the front.

The shot lodged in the Baron's hand. His pistol fell to the ground. Lyon threw the box on the ground, retrieved Christina's knife from his boot, and had the Baron by his throat before he'd finished his first howl of pain.

"Christina wants you to speak the truth. She knows Jessica wasn't crazy and wants to hear you say it." Lyon increased his pressure around the Baron's neck as he threatened, then suddenly threw the Baron backwards. He stood over his prey and waited for him to look up. "After you've answered my questions you can pick up your precious gems and leave. You've booked passage for the West Indies, but I've convinced the captain to leave today. He's waiting for you and the next tide, Baron."

The Baron's eyes narrowed. He stared at the box for a long minute, then turned to Lyon. The tip of his tongue ran over his lower lip. "I don't have to answer your questions. Everyone knows Jessica was out of her mind. When I go to the authorities—"

"Lyon," Christina called out. "I don't think he quite grasps the situation."

"Then let me make it simple for him," Lyon said. "Baron, if you don't tell me what I want to know, you won't be going anywhere. I'll slit your throat. A fitting end, wouldn't you agree, after all the throats you've cut?"

"What are you talking about?" the Baron asked, feigning confusion. He clasped his injured hand to his chest.

"Come now, Baron. You know what I'm talking about," Lyon answered. "You've gotten away with your murders all these years. Haven't you ever wanted to boast of your skill? You couldn't, of course, until now. Is your ego so inflated you haven't any need to admit something you know you'll never be hanged for?"

Stalinsky pretended to struggle to his feet. Lyon saw him reach into his boot and extract a small pistol of the sort a woman would carry. He lunged at Lyon as he pulled the pistol forward. Lyon kicked the weapon out of his hand, then lashed out again with the side of his boot to hit the Baron's injured hand.

The screech of pain echoed throughout the countryside. "This is your last chance, Baron. My patience has run out." He flipped the knife from one hand to the other. "Was Jessica crazy?"

"Christina," the Baron shouted. "How can you let him terrorize me this way? I'm your father, for God's sake. Have you no mercy? Do you really want him to slit my throat?"

"No, Father," Christina denied. "I don't want him to slit your throat. I'd rather he cut your heart out, but Lyon does have his preferences, and I must let him have his way."

The Baron glared at his daughter. He stood up. A gleam appeared in his eyes, and he actually started to laugh. "No, Jessica wasn't crazy." He laughed again, a grating sound that chilled Christina. "But it's too late to do anything now, Lyon."

"Terrance MacFinley would have recognized that it was you sneaking around the wagon train. Isn't that right?" Lyon challenged.

"Your deductions are most amazing," the Baron said with a chuckle. "Yes, Terrance would have noticed me."

Lyon pushed the box towards Stalinsky with the tip of his

boot. "One last question and then you may leave. Were you behind the Brisbane murders?"

The Baron's eyes widened. "How did you—"

"You outsmarted our War Department, didn't you?" Lyon asked, trying to sound impressed and not sickened. He was deliberately playing upon the Baron's vanity, hoping the bastard would feel safe enough to admit the truth.

"I did outsmart them, didn't I? I lived off the money Brisbane had received for the secrets he'd sold, too. Oh, yes, Lyon, I was smarter than all of them."

"Was Porter involved in your scheme, or did you act alone?" Lyon asked.

"Porter? He was as stupid as the rest of them. I always acted alone, Lyon. It's the reason I've survived these many years, the reason I've been such a wealthy man."

Lyon didn't think he could stand to look at the man much longer. He motioned to the box, the backed up several paces. "Pick it up and get out of here. If I ever see you again, I'll kill you."

The baron scurried over to the box. He flipped it open, barely glanced at the contents, then slammed it shut with a snort of pleasure.

"Are you finished, Lyon?"

Richards, surrounded by his men, strolled out from their hiding places.

"Did you hear?"

"All of it," Richards announced. He touched Lyon's shoulder before walking over to the Baron.

"Damn your . . ." the Baron shouted. He stopped himself, then glared at Lyon. "I'll make certain your wife's humiliation is complete. I promise I'll say things in court about her mother that will—"

"Close your mouth," Richards bellowed. "We're taking you to the harbor, Baron. In fact, Benson and I shall be your travel companions on your trip back to your homeland. I believe you'll get a nice reception. The new government will undoubtedly be happy to let you stand trial."

Lyon didn't stay to listen to the Baron's demands to be given a trial in England. He took hold of Christina's hand without saying a word and started walking toward their mounts.

Richards was right. They were using the back door to gain justice. Baron Stalinsky would be returned to his homeland, where he would be judged by his former subjects. It would mean a death sentence. And if, by some chance, the new government proved to be just as corrupt, then Richards and Benson were prepared to take care of the Baron.

By the time he and Christina returned to their London townhouse, she was looking terribly pale.

He ignored her protests and carried her up to their bedroom. "You're going back to bed now," he told her as he helped her get out of her clothes.

"I will be better now," Christina told him. "It is finished."

"Yes, love. It is finished."

"I never believed Jessica was crazy," Christina told Lyon. She put on her silk robe, then wrapped her arms around her husband's waist. "I never believed that."

The sadness in her voice pulled at his heart. "I know you didn't," Lyon soothed. "Jessica can rest in peace now."

"Yes. In peace. I like to believe that her soul lingers with the Dakotas now. Maybe she waits for Merry to come and join her."

"I don't think Black Wolf would care for that hope of yours," Lyon said.

"Oh, he would join them, too, of course," Christina replied.

She sighed into his jacket, then kissed him on the base of his throat. "It's his destiny to meet Jessica in the Afterlife," she announced.

"Yes, destiny," Lyon said. "Now it's your destiny to quit being sick every morning and night, my love. You've kept your promise to your mother. The treasure is being returned to the rightful owners. Richards is going to see to the sale of the gems and the distribution of the money. We're going home to Lyonwood, and you'll get fat and sassy. I command it."

Christina really did try to comply with her husband's commands. The sickness eventually left her. She gained

weight, too—so much, in fact, that she thought she waddled like a duck. She wasn't very sassy, however, for she spent most of her confinement trying to soothe her husband's worries.

She denied being with child until it became ludicrous. Poor Lyon was terrified of the birthing. Christina understood his fear. He'd watched Lettie go through terrible pain. She'd died a horrible death, with the babe trapped inside her.

Christina used denial and then reason. She told Lyon she was strong, that it was a very natural condition for a woman to be in, and that she was Dakota in her heart and knew exactly what to do to make the birthing easier. Dakota women rarely died in childbirth.

Lyon had a rebuttal for each of her arguments. He told her she was too small for such a mighty task, that it wasn't at all natural for such a gentle woman to have to go through such terrible agony, and that she was English, not Dakota, where it most counted—in her womb, for God's sake, not her heart.

Ironically, it was Lyon's mother who softened Lyon's fears somewhat. The elderly woman was slowly returning to her family. She reminded her son that she was just as small in stature as Christina was, and that she had given her husband three fine babies without making a single whimper.

Christina was thankful for her mother-in-law's help. She didn't have to threaten to drag her new confidante outside into the forest to choose a burial site any longer. Lyon's mother finally admitted she wasn't quite ready to die yet. The woman still liked to talk about James, but she interlaced her remarks with stories about Lyon and Diana, too.

Deavenrue came to visit Christina. He stayed a month's time, then left with six fine horses Lyon had chosen as gifts for the Dakotas. Three men eager for the adventure went along to help Deavenrue.

The missionary helped to ease Lyon's mind about Christina, but once he'd left, Lyon was back to scowling and snapping at everyone.

Baron Winters, the family's physician, moved into their

house two weeks before Christina went into labor. She had no intention of letting the physician help her, of course, yet she had the good sense to keep that determination to herself. His presence calmed Lyon, and Christina was thankful for that.

The pains began after dinner, then continued into the night. Christina didn't wake her husband until the last possible minute. Lyon had time only to wake up and do as Christina instructed. He was holding his infant son in his arms minutes later.

Christina was too exhausted to weep, so Lyon wept for both of them while their magnificent little warrior bellowed his indignation.

He wanted to name his son Alexander Daniel.

She was having none of that. She wanted to name him Screaming Black Eagle.

Lyon was having none of that.

In the end, they compromised. The future Marquess of Lyonwood was christened Dakota Alexander.